HONOUR OF THE GRAVE

THE MONSTER HOPPED up and down ecstatically as it squeezed the life from Angelika. Franziskus saw Angelika's face turning blue. He leapt up and, with the tip of his sword, speared her attacker through its right eye. Jelly popped from the eye and oozed onto the blade. The beastman turned to see Franziskus shuffling to keep his hands on the hilt of the rune-incised sword he'd liberated from Elennath. The creature hissed at the blade, and backed away from it.

Franziskus took a moment to theorise that the runes spelled some kind of elven charm inimical to Chaos. Then he shouted, shouldering all his weight into the sword hilt. He forced the blade in...

More Warhammer from the Black Library

· GOTREK & FELIX ·
TROLLSLAYER by William King
SKAVENSLAYER by William King
DAEMONSLAYER by William King
DRAGONSLAYER by William King
BEASTSLAYER by William King
VAMPIRESLAYER by William King
GIANTSLAYER by William King

· THE VAMPIRE GENEVIEVE NOVELS ·
DRACHENFELS by Jack Yeovil
GENEVIEVE UNDEAD by Jack Yeovil
BEASTS IN VELVET by Jack Yeovil
SILVER NAILS by Jack Yeovil

· THE TALES OF ORFEO ·
ZARAGOZ by Brian Craig
PLAGUE DAEMON by Brian Craig
STORM WARRIORS by Brian Craig

· THE KONRAD TRILOGY ·
KONRAD by David Ferring
SHADOWBREED by David Ferring
WARBLADE by David Ferring

· WARHAMMER NOVELS ·
RIDERS OF THE DEAD by Dan Abnett
BLOOD MONEY by C. L. Werner
THE DEAD AND THE DAMNED by Jonathan Green
STAR OF ERENGRAD by Neil McIntosh
THE CLAWS OF CHAOS by Gav Thorpe
ZAVANT by Gordon Rennie
HAMMERS OF ULRIC by Dan Abnett,
Nik Vincent & James Wallis
GILEAD'S BLOOD by Dan Abnett & Nik Vincent
THE WINE OF DREAMS by Brian Craig

A WARHAMMER NOVEL

HONOUR OF THE GRAVE

ROBIN D. LAWS

To Lou Ford and Nick Corey

A BLACK LIBRARY PUBLICATION

First published in Great Britain in 2003
by BL Publishing,
Games Workshop Ltd.,
Willow Road, Nottingham,
NG7 2WS, UK.

10 9 8 7 6 5 4 3 2 1

Cover illustration by Christopher Moeller

© Games Workshop Ltd 2003. All rights reserved.

Black Library, the Black Library logo, Black Flame, BL Publishing, Games Workshop, the Games Workshop logo and all associated marks, names, characters, illustrations and images from the Warhammer universe are either ®, TM and/or © Games Workshop Ltd 2000-2003, variably registered in the UK and other countries around the world. All rights reserved.

A CIP record for this book
is available from the British Library

ISBN 1 84416 004 1

Set in ITC Giovanni

Printed and bound in Great Britain by
Cox & Wyman Ltd, Cardiff Rd, Reading, Berkshire RG1 8EX, UK

No part of this publication may be reproduced, stored in a retrieval system, or transmitted in any form or by any means, electronic, mechanical, photocopying, recording or otherwise, without the prior permission of the publishers.

This book is sold subject to the condition that it shall not, by way of trade or otherwise, be lent, re-sold, hired out or otherwise circulated without the publisher's prior consent in any form of binding or cover other than that in which it is published and without a similar condition including this condition being imposed on the subsequent purchaser.

See the Black Library on the Internet at
www.blacklibrary.com

Find out more about Games Workshop
and the world of Warhammer at
www.games-workshop.com

This is a dark age, a bloody age, an age of daemons and of sorcery. It is an age of battle and death, and of the world's ending. Amidst all of the fire, flame and fury it is a time, too, of mighty heroes, of bold deeds and great courage.

At the heart of the Old World sprawls the Empire, the largest and most powerful of the human realms. Known for its engineers, sorcerers, traders and soldiers, it is a land of great mountains, mighty rivers, dark forests and vast cities. And from his throne in Altdorf reigns the Emperor Karl-Franz, sacred descendent of the founder of these lands, Sigmar, and wielder of his magical warhammer.

But these are far from civilised times. Across the length and breadth of the Old World, from the knightly palaces of Bretonnia to ice-bound Kislev in the far north, come rumblings of war. In the towering World's Edge Mountains, the orc tribes are gathering for another assault. Bandits and renegades harry the wild southern lands of the Border Princes. There are rumours of rat-things, the skaven, emerging from the sewers and swamps across the land. And from the northern wildernesses there is the ever-present threat of Chaos, of daemons and beastmen corrupted by the foul powers of the Dark Gods.

As the time of battle draws ever near,
the Empire needs heroes
like never before.

PROLOGUE

PILED HIGH, THE corpses formed a bloody ridge. Arms and legs, some broken, others twisted, jutted out from the heap. Thickening blood dripped down from the uppermost bodies, running down mud-spattered faces and spreading through the fabric of tunics and leggings. It was early yet, and the stench of rotting had yet to rise up and overcome that of emptied bladders and evacuated bowels. The sky was red from distant fires. Crows cawed. Flies buzzed, ready to lay eggs, which would pop forth as maggots, which would feed, which would grow into flies, which would buzz elsewhere, to find more meat for more maggots.

Angelika crept quickly but carefully forward, watching where each foot fell. It would be no good slipping in the mud, or hearing that awful, telltale slurking noise that informed you you'd just got your boot stuck. The orcs who'd fallen upon these soldiers and slaughtered them would have mostly moved on by now, having sorted through the corpses for weapons and armour pieces, the only varieties of loot they had any use for. But there could always be stragglers. Or her fellow looters. Angelika's profession was not an elevated one, and you could never trust someone you met out here not to slit your throat for the trinkets you'd mined. You did not want to fall down or get stuck or become in any way distracted.

Angelika Fleischer had blacked the pale skin of her cheeks and forehead with soot, to make herself harder to see from a distance. She was tall and her limbs were long. Raggedly cut locks of hair jutted from the top of her narrow, sharply symmetrical head. The irises of her eyes were dark, so much so that it was hard to distinguish them from the pupils. These unrevealing eyes sat high in her face, above imperious, down-sloping cheekbones. Her lips were thin and precise. A short, thin line of white scar tissue fissured from the right corner of her mouth, marring the icy perfection of her beauty. She wore neither earrings, nor necklace, nor rings on her fingers. Her tunic and leggings were of brown leather that had worn so soft it seemed at first glance like deerskin. They were stained in many places, and crisscrossed with rudely sewn patches and repairs. Both garments were immodestly tight, though she had draped a short skirt of gauzy rags around her waist. In this land, it was hard enough, and you did not want to give men in the taverns any further reason for annoying catcalls, which drew attention. The sleeves of her tunic clung tight to her arms, and ended in frayed cuffs several inches before her wrists. Gloves protected her palms, though she'd snipped away their fingers and thumbs, to leave her own bare and free to work.

Work she did. She knelt down over a stray body, one the orcs had not tossed into the pile. It was hard to make out colours, with all the gore and mud, so she couldn't guess the man's origin or regiment. But from the cuff-frills, you could tell he was an officer. The breastplate was already long gone, so it was an easy thing for her to reach down and pluck off each carved ivory, gold-rimmed button, one, then the next, then the next. Angelika tucked the resultant handful of buttons into the soft leather pouch that hung from her belt. She yanked open the tunic to see if the man had a ransom wrapped around his chest – perhaps a money belt, or thin strands of gold. But no. She scuttled backwards to grab the heel of his left boot. For some reason, if it was in the boot, it would nearly always be in the left one. She wiggled the heel and twisted and wriggled and worked it off. In the handful of years Angelika had been making her living as a looter of battlefields, she had become very good at getting boots off. There, wrapped around his ankle, she saw a necklace of pearls and silver. She snatched it up and tightened her fingers around it.

An exhalation of breath, made visible by the air's increasing chill, rose up from one of the bodies in front of her. Someone was not quite dead. Angelika halted herself in midgesture, with the stillness of a hunted animal, her face remaining expressionless. Her eyes methodically scanned the tangle of corpses ahead of her. She saw the man who was still breathing. Heard him groan: a low, weak grunt. It spoke to Angelika of fear and disappointment. His throat was slick with bright-coloured blood and, as Angelika studied him further, she saw his tunic was also soaked through with red. He gurgled and his chest jerked slightly upwards.

Angelika looked slowly around and moved towards him, gingerly finding solid footfalls in the few spaces the carpet of corpses offered. She squatted beside the man. His face was wide, his beard bushy and grey. The veins of his face lay close to the surface of his skin, mapping a lifetime of drained ale flagons. His right eye was pale blue. A black leather patch, studded with agates and with an opal in the middle, covered the left. She could easily tell he was a veteran campaigner.

His living eye registered the sight of the woman kneeling over him, and he tried to reach a fleshy arm up at her. But strength had left him, and it sank back into the muck the moment he tried to raise it. He groaned again, making a sound that seemed to Angelika fretful, almost babyish.

'Not me,' he said.

'Yes,' Angelika said, but gently, 'you.'

She put the fingers of her right hand together and moved them slowly towards his face. She lay them softly against his left cheek. She felt the wet of the blood and the soft tangle of matted beard hair. She felt the coarser stubble on the part of his cheek the dying man usually shaved.

'Not–' the veteran said, but then he deflated, and Angelika saw that his one good eye had gone blank. It wasn't so unusual to find soldiers who hadn't finished dying yet, especially against orcs. They were less than thorough with their defeated foes. After a human victory, you found most corpses stripped of obvious valuables, which was bad, but you faced less chance that the man you were searching would suddenly bolt up and clamp bloodied hands around your throat. It was a different set of complications, depending on which side won.

She broke from her stillness and reached over to snatch the jewelled eye-patch from the dead man's face. She tucked it into her purse's wide, waiting mouth. She checked his tunic for buttons but they were nothing special. He'd spent all his vanity coin on the fancy patch, clearly. She half-straightened herself, casting her eyes about for an officer type. They were always the most lucrative.

She heard another groan, behind her, and turned. A long, thin dagger was already in her hand. She saw nothing moving. Just the big ridge of piled bodies. She watched a plume of breath escape from her lips up into the air.

'Please,' a voice said. A young voice, male. Speaking the tongue of the Empire. It was not the kind of trick a brutish orc was capable of playing.

Angelika remained still, kept her blade out.

'Please,' the voice repeated. 'Over here,' it said.

Angelika's eyes went to where the voice seemed to be coming from, but her feet remained planted in place.

'Please,' the voice said. 'I am stuck under bodies. Whenever I open my mouth, it fills up with blood. Someone else's, I am pretty sure. Help me get out. Please.'

Angelika knew the Empire, and in a past existence had learned to tell one accent from another. The young man's voice came from somewhere up in the north-east. A long way from where they stood, close to the Blackfire Pass, between the southern flatlands of the Empire and the lawless reaches of the Border Princes.

She still had not moved.

'Please help me out,' the young man said. His voice was getting louder, finding strength. 'My name is Franziskus.'

'Franziskus,' she said, 'shut up. You'll bring the greenskins back.'

'I'm over here,' he said, much more quietly. 'Please. Quick. Under all this weight... My lungs – being crushed.'

'Then don't use them so much.'

Angelika had pinpointed the location of the voice and began to step towards it. Finally she saw the movement. It was midway up in the stack of corpses, pointing upwards. She saw wriggling. And shoulders. Of his features, all she could make out was a helmetless head, a mop of what was probably blond, possibly curly, hair soaked flat with congealing blood.

'Please get me out of here. See what part of me you can grab onto and then pull.'

'No.'

There was quiet for a moment, and in it Angelika could hear faraway drums.

'No?' the voice finally said.

'No. Now shut up before I open your throat, on the risk of your attracting orcs.' She'd moved closer to him, so she could speak more quietly. She could see his forehead now, and his eyes, though she did not think he could see her. He kept blinking his eyelids as more blood dripped onto his face from above.

'Please, I promise you, I'll be absolutely silent,' Franziskus said, also barely audible. 'I foxed the orcs into thinking me dead, but I'm not injured. I'll not be a burden to you. All I need is help out, then I'll be on my way. Alone, no burden to you.'

'No.'

'No?'

'Are your ears, too, filled with blood, or are you always hard of hearing?' Angelika's voice remained even, its tone flat and unenlightening.

'But why deny me mercy?'

A moving glint, high and to the left, caught Angelika's eye. It was a pendant, bearing the holy hammer symbol of Sigmar. It was gold. The pendant hung from a clutching hand, out-thrust from the ridge of bodies. Franziskus's squirming had set it to swinging, slightly.

'Why deny me mercy?' Franziskus repeated.

'Your throat remains uncut. Is that not mercy?' She rose up on her toes and plucked the pendant like it was a grape on a vine.

'Why decline me the help I need?'

Angelika began to look for other riches to pick from the corpse pile. Her eyes fixed on a cufflink, perhaps of silver.

'Have you laid eyes on me?' she asked. She reached forward to grab a dead wrist with her off-hand. In the other, her knife sawed at cuff fabric. 'What do you think I am doing here?'

'Did I hear you comforting someone, just now?'

'No.' She tore the cut fabric of the sleeve away and dropped it, with the cufflink, into her purse.

'I am sure I heard this.'

'Hope deceives you. You mistake my nature.'

Franziskus stopped to breathe and Angelika carried on as if she would hear no more of him. She found a boot sticking from the mass of the slain and began to twist and pull at it. It was stuck securely to its master's leg, and resisted her stoutly.

'Then what is your nature?' Franziskus eventually asked.

Angelika pulled some more at the boot. It would not be budged. She wrinkled up her nose at it. It was a flaw of her nature, she admitted to herself, that she was often too stubborn to give up a uselessly difficult task. If she fell into the same old trap, she could easily stand here for half an hour trying to get this one stupid boot off, even though she had no assurance that there was anything good inside it, and even though all around her there were hundreds of other boots on hundreds of other feet.

She realized that Franziskus had said something else to her, but that she had not been paying attention and could not say what it was. She wrinkled her nose again, this time at herself, and then saw a crushed-up hat lying between bodies. It might have a hatpin on it. She yanked at it and, to control the extent of distraction he posed, decided to keep talking to the young man, to answer his previous question.

'You mistake me for some kind of nurse or rescuer. I am here, Franziskus, to loot the bodies of your comrades.' She jangled her purse in his direction. 'Medals, gemstones, coins.' She freed the flattened hat, but found no jewels or pins in its band. Instead, there was a small envelope of brown and waxen paper. She slipped open the flap and looked inside. It contained a darkish powder, one she recognized from the smell. This man had brought with him a little extra surprise for the orcs, and its waxy envelope had even kept it dry. But he had not gotten a chance to use it. Angelika tucked the envelope into the breast pocket of her tunic. The hat she tossed over her shoulder, and it splatted in the muck behind her.

'Why?' he said. His voice's pleading tone was gaining in insistence.

She snorted. 'Why do you think?'

Franziskus began a greater flurry of wriggling, shifting his shoulders back and forth in the evident hope of sliding himself free. At the end of his struggle, he grunted. It seemed to Angelika that he had succeeded only in settling the bodies above him even more heavily upon his chest and limbs. He huffed whimperingly as Angelika removed a succession of boots, to find only a series of soaked and mildewy socks, each covering a set of toes half eaten by trenchfoot.

'You think I am shocked,' Franziskus struggled to say. He stopped to gulp in air. 'And shocked I am, I'll admit. I am new to war, you see. This was my first battle.'

'You should have stayed away.'

'A man of my station is obli– ' Franziskus cut off his own thought, as if suddenly aware of the futility of his line of argument. 'Please, there is no reason not to help me. Please help me.'

'Once,' said Angelika, pausing before the pile of corpses to decide where to start next, 'I came upon a battlefield, and set about doing my business, and found a man, a big barrel of a sergeant, lying with a broken arm, pinned under a big piece of cannon. It had exploded at the seams, gone flying through the air, and flattened him into the soft earth.'

'I have heard of such things,' Franziskus said.

She surveyed his reddened face and leaned back against the bodies as if they were a brick wall, to rest up a bit. 'He just needed it rolled off his arm, and he called to me, and I had not been doing this for long.' From her new vantage point, she saw a hand with a fat ring on it, and reached forward to work it down over the knuckle. The blood that slicked the hand made it easier work than it otherwise would have been. 'I was reluctant, because he was a big man, but he pleaded with me as you're doing now. And I went to him, and helped him, and rolled the cannon off his arm. And then, with his good arm, he grabbed a sabre and tried to spit me with it, cursing me as a looter and the desecrator of his comrades.'

'But I won't do that.'

'So you say.'

'I am of noble birth; my word means something.'

'Perhaps you even believe that, in your current straits.' She moved away from the stacked bodies to the scattered pile of dead opposite it, where it would be easier to systematically search each corpse.

'Do you believe in nothing?'

'Yes.'

While he mulled that over, Angelika found a headless artillerist and rolled him over on his back, for better access to buttons and belt buckle.

'You care for nothing but gold?'

'What else is there?'

'I am only a fourth son but still, my family can pay a good reward if you free me.'

'How great a reward?'

'Greater than an assemblage of medals and cufflinks.'

Her tongue darted along inside her cheek. She shook her head, moved on to another corpse. 'I believe only in gold I can place immediately in my hand.'

Franziskus began to breathe quickly in and out, in the manner of a crazed horse or dog. Angelika stood up to survey other areas of the battlefield, to see which might be safely ripe for plucking.

'Then, in general pity's name, I implore you. As one child of Sigmar to another.'

Angelika rounded on her heels, towards him, and for the first time spoke with heat in her voice. 'Your gods and heroes mean nothing to me. They are fairy stories only, tales we tell one another to persuade ourselves that we are more than just meat and bone. All is blood and corruption on this plane, and what lies beyond it is naught. And man – man is nothing more than a finer-looking orc, wrapped up in brocades and finery and books and music but a ravening savage nonetheless. I clean up after what you nobles do, with your never-ending wars of loot and conquest. It's as close as I've found to a worthwhile pursuit in this stinking charnel house of a world. So do not speak to me of pity. It is a word without meaning. It is a lie.'

Franziskus listened as Angelika paused to recover her expended breath. 'Your words are well-schooled, your accent refined. How did– '

She heard mud squishing under boots and glottal growling in the orcish tongue. She pushed her arm through the pile of cadavers and clamped a hand over Franziskus's mouth. She cursed and said, 'They're coming back.'

'I will let go of your mouth now,' she said, scanning what lay ahead of her, to the left and to the right. She did not let go of Franziskus's mouth. She had carefully surveyed the scene before approaching, but now it had all gone out of her head. 'I will let go of your mouth now, but if you so much as cough...'

It was all flat ground, with hills rising up on both sides, up towards the mountains. It was scattered bodies all around, and mud, and – there. A good hundred feet away, an upturned cart, its wheels lopped off its axle, scorch marks up and down its unfinished wood.

She slowly removed her hand from Franziskus's face, ready to clamp it back again if he made a peep. 'They're coming back. Your best hope lies in silence. Be a corpse, Franziskus, or they'll make you one.'

Then she sprinted towards the cart. During the length of her run, she heard nothing but blood rushing in her ears. Saw the battlefield and the strewn corpses floating past her, slowly, as in one of those dreams where you need to run from something, but your legs can scarcely move. Finally she hit the ground beside the cart, rolling in, skidding through mud, slamming into its singed wooden side. As soon as she stopped she could hear other things again. She heard the crows overhead, then another orcish sound, possibly laughing, though Angelika did not know for sure if orcs were capable of laughter. It was not a cheerful or encouraging sound. She wedged both hands in the tiny space between the top of the cart and the muddy ground. It hurt; the cart was heavy and her angle was all wrong. She heard snorting and throaty barking. She girded herself, got the cart up a few inches and then, on her belly, wriggled under the space she'd made. The cart fell back down onto her neck and shoulders, but she scraped along anyhow and worked herself all the way inside. She turned and there was the dead face of a soldier, burned to the quick and grinning yellow teeth at her.

She winced and wriggled away, up towards the front of the cart. A little diffuse red light was working its way under the cart, which meant that maybe there was a space to peep through. Angelika crawled until her eyes and nose sat right in front of this small space between cart and ground. She saw big boots made from scraps of fur and cloth and leather. She saw legs: some naked, green, and muscled; others greaved in mismatched bits of battered metal armour. Counting them, she decided that there were either five or six orcs. Judging their size from the legs, there wasn't a single one of them she'd ever want to fight against.

The legs were stepping their way through bodies on the scattered plain. They hadn't yet reached the big ridge of corpses but they seemed to be poking their way in that direction. Most of the orcish talk seemed to come from one big specimen, possibly the one with the most valuable armour. Angelika wished she could understand them but the orc tongue wasn't just something you could pick up by sitting about in taverns or going to study at a monastery. It was a good enough guess, though, that the well-armoured one's grunts and hisses were orders. He stood there barking, and the others, in response, picked their way through the bodies.

One bent down low enough that its head suddenly entered her field of vision. It was big, shaped like a malformed melon, with a face that was mostly jaw, from which well-chipped ochre tusks, each about the size of Angelika's dagger, jutted unevenly up and down. The orc grabbed at a corpse's wrist with its massive green hand, and stared at it long enough for a white globule of snot to gather in one of its tiny, triangular nostrils, then slide down to its lip, finally disappearing into its mouth. Then the orc, blinking its red-rimmed eyes in frustration or annoyance, let the body's wrist flop listlessly back into the mud.

Angelika could not think what it was they were looking for. Not valuables, certainly. Nor weapons – there were a few pieces lying only partially buried in the mud, and these the orcs ignored.

She turned her head slightly to see what was happening to the side, closer to the body pile. She saw another orc, this one with pus-filled buboes, each the size of a copper coin, all over the skin of its squashed and narrow head. It ducked down over the body of the old bearded soldier, the one she'd helped die. The orc sniffed the dead man like a dog would, then rubbed its purulent face over the torso. Then it shook its head and vengefully spat a wad of phlegm into the corpse's dead eye.

Angelika understood: they were looking for someone who was still alive. This one could tell somehow that the old veteran was still warm. But not warm enough, which is why he was angry. They'd keep going, she realized, until they found Franziskus. And then the boy would take his revenge on her, pointing out the cart. Angelika told herself that she should have slit his throat when she had the opportunity. But the trouble is, you almost never know whose throat you should cut until afterwards.

A round of low shrieks and gravelly gabbling rose up to the left. Angelika could no longer see any orcs and scrambled to adjust her position, to change her field of view. She hit her knee on a rock and nearly cried out. She pushed her body up flush with the front of the cart, and through the crack could now again see orc feet. Some were dancing up and down. Others were firmly planted. They were in front of the corpse pile. Angelika could not really see what was going on, but from the positions of the legs could guess: they'd found Franziskus and were hauling him out.

She turned again, in the confined space under the cart, looking for a better weapon than her dagger. She imagined them suddenly pulling the cart away and tried to think of the best defence. Probably it would be to leap towards them as soon as the cart moved, to scrabble her skinny, mud-slicked body between orcish legs, and keep on going past them. She would run to the right, past the corpse ridge, then up into the hills. Angelika was fast but had never tried to outrun orcs.

Her spindly legs might not be a match for the big pillars of muscle underneath those brutes, but that would not stop her from trying. From the sidelines, she'd watched several battles, and knew that often soldiers died because they gave up too soon. Angelika would not die from giving up.

It bothered her that she would not be given the chance to avenge herself against the boy for squealing. Still, he would meet a gruesome end, though at hands other than her own.

She saw Franziskus dangling upside down, then being dropped headfirst into the muck and blood. He rolled over onto his back and reached to his belt for a weapon, but a vast orc boot came crunching down on his wrist. Franziskus bucked and cursed. His face turned red with the effort, but they had him good. His off-hand was still free and Angelika readied herself for what would happen next. The boy would not speak orcish but he could still tell them what they needed to know.

Then the pustule-ridden orc bent down over Franziskus's legs with an oversized cabbage sack. For some reason, its burlap had been dyed a splotchy purple. It had a big drawstring on it, of muck-stained cord. The buboed orc rolled the bag up over the boy's feet and shins while two others held his legs. The bag went up over Franziskus's waist. Then to his chest. The orcs roughly jammed his seized arms down over his torso. Then the bag went up past his shoulders.

Franziskus turned his head towards her. He surely couldn't tell, Angelika knew, that he was meeting her eyes. He directed an imploring expression at her nonetheless. Moving his lips in slow exaggeration, he mouthed the words: *Please. Help. Me.*

Then the bag went up over his head and the drawstring pulled shut and one of the biggest orcs seized it by the top and hefted it over his back, so that all but the cord, dragging in the muck behind him as he walked, disappeared from Angelika's view. The other orc legs and orc boots followed, wasting no time in heading back where they'd come from.

Angelika saw something white and trembling in front of her and at length realized that it was her own hand. She thought that perhaps it would be appropriate to vomit but the physical urge to do so was not in fact upon her. Feeling the cold of the muck she lay in, she wrenched herself up to a sitting position, even though this meant painfully craning her neck.

She could not believe it. The boy hadn't given her away.

Angelika would have to wait a good long time to be sure there would be no more orcs coming.

It had been a certainty to her that the boy would point the finger. She had it all pictured in her head and everything. She was all prepared for what to do next.

She leaned her head against the wood of the cart, letting her breathing slow. She reached up to her face with dirty fingers and felt something wet coming down from her eyes. She assumed it would be blood, from some wound she hadn't noticed getting, but when she looked at her fingers there was no red liquid. So it must have only been tears.

It was sad, she supposed, that the orcs would torture and mutilate and for all she knew even eat the boy. He had turned out to be better than the norm. But there was certainly nothing she could do about it. Or should do. She understood the world better than he.

SHE STOOD ON a granite promontory, up in the hills, looking down at the massed orcs as they moved down south through the pass, back into the border reaches. The walls of mountain rock on both sides gathered up and magnified the grunting and chanting of the orcs below. It felt like they were groaning right into her ear. But she was safe from them; she would look like just a speck, up here, and they were occupied with their unruly march.

The mud was drying already. She looked at a big cake of it on her outer thigh and smacked it off. Idly she wondered which side had initiated the battle in the first place, the patrolling Imperials or the invading orcs. It did not really matter, but Max, to whom she would sell her catch, maintained an interest in military matters and liked to know these things. He said he was writing a book, which he wasn't, but Angelika could get a slightly better price on her wares by humouring him. Even so, she did not know what she was waiting for. She could glean no further information for Max by watching the orcs now. Even though they held great torches aloft – tree trunks, wrapped in looted cloth and dipped in flammable pitch, each carried by three or four straining, stumbling orcs – details were hard to make out. Maybe an expert on orcs could look down and find signs to interpret, but Angelika had no interest in becoming an expert on orcs.

She turned to go and then stopped. She turned back, to see more clearly what she had just seen, in the corner of her eye. Emerging from a blind spot behind a rock outcropping was a huge cart. Angelika had to pause and compare it with the size of the figures around it to get an accurate sense of its scale. Its wheels – she counted a dozen, then recounted and corrected the figure to ten – were greater in diameter than the height of any nearby orc. Its surface was a flat platform of long planks, somewhere between eighty and one hundred feet long. It boasted neither rails nor sides. Over a hundred sweating, bare-backed orcs, suffering under the lashes of multiple drivers, pitched forward in a series of great, uneven lurches, dragging it behind them. In the middle of the cart there towered an enormous wooden figure. The figure, depicting an orc with gaping mouth and antlered helmet, terminated at the waist, which was flush with the planks of the cart. It looked hollow, like it had been knocked together with nails and scraps of board. The eyes on its squarish face were set on different levels, and several of its large, triangular teeth had already fallen loose and were dangling from the round cave of its stupidly open mouth. Angelika could not tell if the splotches of dark on the figure's surface were paint or dung or mildew.

Her knees felt unsteady, and a voice at the back of her head told her to run, but Angelika kept looking at the thing, confident in the half mile of distance between them. The big figure had only one arm, and this was a separate, levering piece, attached with a big wooden pin to its shoulder. This moveable arm terminated in a great round hammer, its striking surface easily eight, perhaps even ten, feet in diameter. Chains held it up, in ready position. Angelika, squinting, thought she could make out a pulley contraption set into the platform of the cart, to which the chains were fixed.

Several dozen orcs, all tiny to her eyes, milled around the figure. One in particular seemed larger than the rest, and stood at the cart's forward edge, fists at hips, watching the slave orcs as they strove to yank his conveyance onward. She saw that his foot stood on something, and that the something was moving.

It was a familiar, squirming sack, dyed purple and splotchy, its drawstring now trailing down over the lip of the cart.

So they had not killed the boy yet. It did not take brilliant deduction to realize that the orcs intended to perform some kind of ceremony involving their big crude statue. It would entail placing Franziskus under the hammer's shadow, then loosing the chains, so it would fall upon him, pounding him to paste.

Angelika turned to go. Now she had an interesting fact to share with Max for his imaginary book. It would not be necessary to stay and watch the ceremony. She could imagine the results with sufficient vividness. She crept quietly along the flattish projection of rock she'd been standing on and down to a trail through the brush and bramble. The trail forked two ways, up towards a mountain switchback, or down the face of the hill to the pass. Up around the mountain lay her route to town, and Max, and her money and a hot drink and a softish bed.

She took the trail's downward leg. Angelika had never heard of a thing like the statue. Maybe she could make some more money by making a sketch of it, to sell to scholars or something. Max would know of such scholars, perhaps. They were the sorts of people he was always drinking with. Angelika had heard maybe that there was a market for information. It would be especially true, wouldn't it, when it was information on the Empire's most dangerous enemies? Yes, she was pretty sure of it. So, the reason she was getting closer was to make a sketch. For the money.

Stunted, leathery-leafed trees lined the trail, and Angelika kept low behind them. It was not hard to match the cart's slow progress. If anything, Angelika, the thumps of her heart radiating up through her chest, wanted it to go faster.

A dried, weedy branch reached out to caress her, leaving a line of burrs hanging from her leggings.

She would not do anything foolish, she told herself.

She pulled the back of her hand across her forehead, wiping sweat away.

Maybe you could say, in some sense, that the boy deserved rescuing, but she would not allow herself to be tempted towards such stupidity.

Drumming started up, somewhere in the distance, and echoed across the walls of rock.

There were hundreds of orcs around, maybe more, and any one of them could kill you with a single blow.

A rock rolled out from under Angelika's foot as she put it down on the path, and she windmilled her arms to try to keep her balance. She crashed into one of the low, bushy trees, grabbing a branch for support. Its bark felt greasy.

Especially that biggest of the orcs, up on the cart, standing over Franziskus. That one could kill you with a single dull fingernail.

Up ahead, she saw that her path dead-ended. The pass widened out, and the trail went right down to its flat bottom. She could stay put, clamber back up the incline through sharp rocks and boulders, or continue on to where the orcs were. She stayed put, cursing her folly.

She heard whip cracks and orcish shouts and looked over to see that the cart drivers were trying to get the haulers stopped. Some at the front had halted, while others behind them trudged peevishly onwards. A pileup began, and the haulers began to push and shove at each other. One particularly large specimen, pushed from behind by a humpbacked, dull-eyed orc, turned and opened his maw wide, exposing his tusks and sending a great spray of spittle back towards his tormentor. A third orc, beside the humpback, squinted as spare sputum hit him, then lurched forward to clamp thick, horny fingers over the larger orc's lower jaw. He pulled downwards, smashing his victim with his spare fist. Haulers all around these two joined in, limbs flying, jaws gnashing, as the drivers up on the cart directed their whips into the brawling mass. A small chunk of something fleshy and greenish sailed out from the tangle of brawling orcs. Angelika guessed it for a finger or possibly an ear.

Her shoulders seized up in warning as she heard something behind her. Twisting backwards, she saw a trio of orcs making their way quickly down the trail, their eyes on the fight. They intended to join it, but unless she went somewhere, they would run right into her. They blocked her route back into the hills. Her only way was forwards, towards the greater mass of orcs. At least they were distracted.

Angelika leapt. She was in mid-air, sailing over the bushes. She hit the gravelly ground at ravine bottom. The wheels of the cart, now motionless, stood in front of her. She could hear screaming and growling, but no orcs were looking her way. They'd all be up at the front of the cart, where the fight was. She sprinted in between two of the tall, spoked wheels, rocks and pebbles spraying out behind her. Once under the cart, she looked for the best way to hide. The axles were high and wide enough that she could haul herself up on them, and maybe not be seen when the commotion died down up front. She chose an axle in the middle, which would give her more choices when she had to run. Angelika hefted herself up and laid herself out on her back, across the axle. It was not comfortable, but she could balance herself and was not in immediate danger of falling off. What would happen when the cart started moving again, she could not predict.

The sounds from up ahead were trailing off to yelping and isolated snarls, so Angelika could only guess that the orc leaders had violently snuffed out the brawl. She would be stuck here for a while, until the next distraction. This would probably occur after the cart started up again, and then reached its final destination. She could creep away then. This would teach her forever, she thought. She promised herself that the next time she saw someone being carried off to an awful fate, she would act true to her beliefs, and leave him to his destiny. She made a point of feeling the hardness of the axle as it dug into her spine; she would recall this sensation when next she got an imbecilic temptation to do otherwise.

She thought about possible escape routes. Both the brushy inclines on either side of the pass would be good ways to get out, so long as they remained free of orcs.

The cart stayed stopped. Perhaps this was its final destination.

She heard something to the left, and strained to see it, through wheel-spokes. Four orcish pallbearers carried a wooden pallet past the cart's far side. Angelika could not fully see the honoured corpse they bore, but he was at least as big an orc as the one she'd seen atop the cart, lording it over Franziskus's sack.

The pallbearers halted when they reached the front of the cart, and Angelika saw the pallet being hauled up onto it. It looked for a moment as if the corpse would fall off, but then she saw it was bound to the pallet with knotted lengths of cloth.

Angelika sifted her memory for what little she knew of orcs and their ways. The big dead orc must be the previous leader, killed in the battle. The big live orc must be taking over. The ceremony in which Franziskus was about to be sacrificed was to celebrate the live one's ascendance, or to mourn the dead one's loss, or both.

There was a thumping up top, and the planks of the cart rattled and vibrated just inches from the top of Angelika's head. She could tell that all of the hopping up and down was taking place near the cart's forward edge. She heard the exultant howling of an army of gore-mad orcs. Horns blew and the throng silenced itself somewhat. A deep, bellowing voice boomed out over them.

This would be it. That would be the big orc giving its speech. Things were reaching a head. It was time to go. She dropped down from the axle and back under the cart, pointing herself towards the trail she'd come from. Then, up by the front-most wheel, she saw it: the dangling drawstring. It bobbled up and down, so she knew the boy was still inside the bag. He would be right within reach. She edged forward, towards it. She reached, stretching her fingers out, nearly brushing the drawstring with their tips. Then she pulled them back. What was she thinking? You couldn't stop at a time like this. Pulling on the drawstring would accomplish nothing anyway. She'd have to reveal herself to the orcs to get up on top, then get him out of the bag, then... There was no chance. She bolted from under the cart back towards the trail, her head swivelling to see if any orcs spotted her.

She made it to the start of the incline, then scrabbled upwards, grabbing dirt and rocks as handholds, then got up to the line of bushy trees, and dove for the ground behind them. She flattened herself to the earth and thanked the nonexistent gods for her good fortune. She poked her head up watchfully.

She saw the cart. The new leader had freed the old, dead one from his pallet and held him by the scruff of the neck. Below him, orcs capered and banged drums and shook fists and screeched on dissonant bugles. Grabbing the massive corpse by clapping both hands around its head, the new boss drew it close to him and kissed its cruel, upcurving lips. Then he turned and hurled the body into the waiting mob, which seized it and bore it aloft, passing it backwards. The orc army threw their old leader's body up into the air, then caught it, then threw it up, each time letting loose with an animal cheer. Sometimes the body would sink below the level of the crowd, to resurface moments later with a tusk or digit missing: they were taking souvenirs of their slain hero. Gradually the body turned from venerated item to punching sack, resurfacing bloodier each time before finally disappearing forever near the back of the throng. The new boss orc threw his heavy arms up into the air and screamed something that could not have been articulate even in orcish. Angelika could not help shuddering.

She looked at the bag, in which Franziskus squirmed. The big orc was shouting some more, but an orcish oration could not last long. The next step would be the boy's demise.

Angelika leapt from the bushes and ran down towards the cart again, letting the slope of the incline propel her downwards and forwards. A couple of stray orcs stepped from behind the front wheels of the cart, to intercept her. They were squat and shovel-faced, runts by the standards of the others she'd seen today. Maintaining her momentum, blade in hand, she flew towards them. She felt her knife find purchase in flesh, ducked low to evade a swiping hand, and felt wet warm blood spackle her face and arms. The closest orc lurched over, clutching its windpipe. The other, behind her, was in the midst of a backswing with a huge, well-notched battleaxe. She jumped into the air, landing on the back of the hunched-over orc, and used him as the springboard for a second leap, which took her up onto the edge of the cart. As her arms and chest impacted painfully with the cart's planks, she saw the second orc's axe come down on the other's spine, where her legs had been a moment before. The axe head sunk deep into the first orc and out through the belly side; its owner struggled to free it.

Angelika pulled her dangling legs up onto the cart. She saw Franziskus, freed of the bag, the boss orc towering over him, dragging him by the hair. The orc was pulling him towards a set of shackles under the hammer's shadow. Angelika saw the boss's head turn towards her, its red eyes fury-filled. It howled. It reached down and punched Franziskus savagely in the stomach. Franziskus curled up, gasping, hugging knees to chin. A sling stone whistled in from the crowd below; it went far wide of Angelika and plunked against the wooden statue. The boss orc looked at it and growled something at his men. He'd be telling them not to fire any missiles his way, and also that he could take care of one scrawny human woman himself. Then he advanced on her. There were other orcs on the platform, four of them near the back, all in good armour. They stepped up, but the boss waved them back, too.

He did not deign to pull a weapon, merely drawing his massive hands into claws and loudly cracking their joints. He stepped ponderously forward. He cocked his head to one side and seemed to grin, shaking big wattles of loose skin that trailed from his bony jaw.

Angelika felt the leaden weight of her feet, planted on the planks of the cart. She felt the puniness of the tiny knife in her hand. She gulped and sprinted forwards. The orc swung prematurely, and she slipped under his blow to jab her knife up at his throat. But she could not reach, and the knife hit his blackened breastplate, bending like a blade of grass. She rolled, trying to make it through his trunk-like legs, but he closed them on her, and squeezed. She felt wrenching pain as he grabbed one of her legs and twisted it. She wriggled herself forwards and somehow out of his grip. She turned and rolled and hit the planks. Air bolted from her lungs as her opponent kicked her in the side with metal-toed boots. She rolled again and up to her feet and staggered forwards. In blurred peripheral vision, she saw that Franziskus had crawled his way back, most of the way past the wooden figure. The orc lieutenants stood watch over him; one seemed ready to smash him with a hammer if he got too far away.

Vibrations of the boards she stood on warned her to turn back to see her foe. He was charging. She stood her ground. At the last moment, she ducked and kept on going, grabbing onto a hilt poking out from a scabbard at his belt. She stumbled gracelessly past him, a huge hacking sabre now in her hands. A throat-scraping cheer went up behind her. The orcs were happy for the added attraction. She was an addition to the ceremony. They wanted her to put up a colourful fight before their leader finally dispatched her.

She struggled to heft the immense weapon. She grabbed it with both hands, held it overhead, and charged the orc boss, who now stood with feet spread complacently apart, awaiting her charge. Angelika rushed towards him, then her head was ringing and she was flying backwards through the air. She landed on her behind. What echoed around her was definitely the laughter of orcs. The boss had reversed her charge merely by clipping her on the forehead with the heel of his hand, which he still held out to her in mocking display. She struggled to her feet, picked up the heavy sword again, and once more charged. This wrung another crash of laughter from the open-throated throng.

As she ran, she looked to Franziskus, still lying sprawled, and saw that she had caught his eye. She thought she saw him nod. She ran at the orc, whose grinning mouth widened. She held the sword aloft, as she had before. But at the point of impact, she swayed low, instead sticking the weapon between the orc's legs, and pushing him. Tripping on the sword, he fell backwards, landing flat and spread-eagled, near the shackles.

Franziskus kicked forward, loosing the chain. It went slack. It rang and jangled through the pulley. The hammer dropped. The figure rocked. The orc boss's eyes widened. He slid himself forward. The hammer landed. It caught only the boss's skull, squashing it flat and sending a jet of grey matter squirting down the length of the cart, to stop short of the feet of his lieutenants.

Angelika staggered back upright and felt terror's power fill her bones. She saw one of the lieutenants reach down to seize Franziskus, but then a second stopped his hand, following up with a sudden butt to the forehead.

Of course. Now they will fight to see who becomes boss, ignoring distractions. She stumbled towards the lad and grabbed him by the collar of his tunic. A tumult arose behind her and she spun to see a mass of orcs clambering up on the cart to get them. She fumbled in her breast pocket, for the envelope she'd found back on the battlefield. The flash powder. She scooped into the envelope with her fingers and threw the contents at the swarming orcs. She closed her eyes in advance of the flash, then opened them to see gobbets of thick smoke filling the air, and blinded orcs stumbling into one another.

Yanking Franziskus's collar, she half-dove from the cart. They landed badly, in a tangle together, but extricated themselves and dashed for the bushes, ignoring their pain. Angelika, in the lead, seized the lad when they reached the low trees. She pulled him down and they watched the writhing frenzy as partisans of the various battling lieutenants cheered on their candidates, or brawled viciously amongst themselves. They waited for vengeful outriders to come beating the bushes for them, but none bothered. As one tottering lieutenant seemed to win out, rivals' pulped bodies quivering at his feet, they slipped away.

THEY DID NOT start talking until they were well clear of the orcs, on a down-sloping road around on the mountain's other side. The adrenaline had left them, and now their bones ached and bruises throbbed.

'I knew I could count on you,' Franziskus said to her.

'Nonsense.'

'Despite what you said, basic human goodness won out.'

She snorted derisively.

'Your basic, human goodness.'

'You mean idiotic, suicidal foolishness.'

'You say this, but it is merely to assuage your pride.'

'Shut up.'

'I will prove my gratitude to you. You saved my life and I owe you everything.'

'You'll do whatever I ask?'

Franziskus fervently nodded.

'Then sod off,' she said.

He stopped, looking surprised.

'I mean it. Go away. And if you tell anyone of the weakness I showed today, I'll creep after you and gut you while you snore. Do you understand?' She stopped, too, looking up at the sky. Dark clouds were coming in, hiding the stars. She looked at Franziskus, who turned his gaze from her and kept going.

'I have sworn to repay you, and repay you I shall,' he said, eyes closed, nose upturned.

'Cretin,' she said.

'Basic human goodness,' he said.

'Everything I said to you was the truth, and everything I did was a lie,' she said.

The two continued down the stony roadway, disappearing from view.

CHAPTER ONE

IT SEEMED WRONG, Angelika Fleischer thought, for the sun to shine so brightly on such carnage. It was not carnage, in and of itself, that troubled her; in fact, it was from dead men that she made her livelihood. Even so, the sky could show a little decency, and darken itself with clouds.

Shading her eyes, she leaned against the trunk of a thin and contorted pine tree on a jagged, rocky hillside – one of thousands that lined the length of the Blackfire Pass. She watched as soldiers cleared the dead from the silenced battlefield below. To get a better look, she swung her long, slim body out from the tree, clinging to its rough surface with the curled fingers of her right hand. Her elbows, cheekbones, and knees were sharp. Spiked fronds dangled from her dark mop of thick hair. Angelika wore a black tunic over black leggings. It was too big for her, but she had tied it off tight at the waist, so that the remainder became not so much a skirt as a gesture acknowledging the idea of a skirt. It concealed a leather purse, and a scabbard with a five-inch knife in it. Her blade had a twin; it waited for her just below her right knee, tucked into her boot. Angelika's boots did not match the rest of her shabby attire: neither scuff marks nor a layer of mud could fully conceal their expensive leather.

The soldiers below wore uniforms of black and yellow. Silvery helms sat upon their heads; the officers had tall feathers, dyed bright green, pluming up from them. Shiny breastplates protected the chests and guts of the richer soldiers. Low or lofty, all wore tunics that were black on the right side and yellow on the left; their leggings reversed the pattern: dark left legs and lemony right ones. This get-up marked the men as soldiers of Averland, the Imperial province directly to the north. Angelika rolled her eyes every time she saw these ludicrous uniforms. They made the men look like oversized and ungainly bees.

The largest number of them swarmed near a vast trench, about two hundred feet long and fifteen feet deep. Some men were still digging, with spades of iron. Most now dragged enemy bodies to the edge of the hole, where the diggers poked at them with their shovels and then rolled them in. It was rare to find an orcish body that did not dwarf those of the victorious humans. The smallest of them had to be at least six feet tall; some reached seven or even eight feet. No matter what their size, their heavy bodies rolled into the pit like the carcasses of slaughtered cattle. They slid down on top of each other, into an ignominious heap. Thick arms draped over lolling heads. Muscular legs sprawled across broken-backed torsos. The orcs already in the pit looked white and ghostly; several soldiers worked to spade powdered lime from barrels onto them, coating them with chalky dust. The Averlanders' thoroughness impressed Angelika. It was well known that the bodies of slain orcs, if left out in the open to rot, bred a number of deadly diseases, from brown-water to blood catarrh. Yet the armies of the Empire rarely took the time to properly dispose of such corpses, especially when they polluted lands outside their own.

Angelika made her living as a looter of battlefields. In her experience, most such places were vast expanses of mud, churned up by gruelling engagements that lasted hours, if not days or weeks. Here, on the other hand, the rich grasses of spring had scarcely been disturbed. The fight must have been quick. Angelika saw how the steep mountains on either side of the valley converged to a narrow point, just to the north. Dense stands of pine lined the canyon walls. It would be easy for the Imperial troops to hide behind them, wait until the advancing orcs began to bottle up, and then pour down on them, aided both by surprise and by higher ground. Many of the slain orcs were scorched, others were cooked through so that flesh hung loosely from bone. This meant that wizards had been among the ambushers, though there was no sign of them now. Mighty witch-men had better things to do than shovel out graves for orcs.

The Averlanders had already borne their own dead over to a large wooden cart, where they were stacked, wrapped in the burlap tarpaulins the men had carried them in. A sergeant-at-arms stood by the cart, with pen and parchment, counting the swords and armour pieces of the fallen. These were expensive items of property, and in most cases would belong to the dead men's families. The army would levy only a small charge to ship them back to their inheritors.

'It is better when the orcs win,' Angelika said.

Her companion, Franziskus, turned his face toward her, to show the exact scandalised expression she had expected to provoke. He was a young man, with long curly hair and broad, open, and not entirely unhandsome features. His teeth were perfect pearls, and his eyes were blue like a summer sky. Angelika wanted him to just go away. His presence was her punishment for a terrible mistake she'd made. Nearly six weeks back, just to the south of their present position, she'd rescued him from a tribe of orcs, but how did the boy repay her for her foolish altruism? Did he go home to his family? Did he return to his unit? No, he stuck to her side like a burr to a trouser leg! Never sparing her from his reproving expression or piercing looks. Tramping after her in his fraying officer's coat and finely stitched pantaloons, mottled with faded bloodstains that – like himself – refused to go away. He'd appointed himself her protector, without admitting the irony inherent in the declaration. He would accompany her, fight by her side, repay his debt to her. Or so he kept saying. Though he had, on a couple of occasions, been somewhat useful, in fact all he did, truth be told, was tag along after her, slow her down, and natter his tiresome, naïve, nobleman's morality into her ear.

'Surely even you do not take the side of the orcs,' Franziskus said. He was not as adept as Angelika at keeping his footing on their precarious lookout spot. He hugged himself tightly to a tree as the soles of his boots slipped against a mossy plane of exposed rock. His cheeks had drained of their usual apple-skin colour; he might, it seemed, be suffering from a touch of vertigo.

'I'll admit I speak in the short term. I wouldn't like it if the orcs won the war, and smashed civilisation altogether. Who would I sell my goods to then? Individual battles, though, are a different thing. After the Empire wins, they strip a battlefield clean. Why, by the time those sergeants leave, I'll be lucky to find a glass eye or a brass nose-hair trimmer. They won't search the orc corpses, but what do they have on them, anyway? Worthless blades, bone necklaces, and little leather bags full of owl pellets! Now, if it had been the other way around, the orcs would only take the weapons and armour pieces, leaving me with plenty of purses, jewels, and lengths of gold chain to sort through at my leisure.'

'Sort through with bloodied hands.'

'No one asked you to come along.'

Franziskus gave her another characteristic frown. He returned his gaze to the battlefield, mused a while, then started up again: 'Luckily for you and for everyone, a string of orc victories is now quite unlikely. The old black and yellow are on the march again. Averland will push the accursed greenskins deep down into the pass.'

'So an optimist would say. Me, I'll wager that there will be plenty of bloodshed to go around. You've heard the same stories I have. The orcs mass in the south, their armies daily swelling.' Spotting a faint path that wound through a thicket of boulders, she let go of the tree, and dropped down. Without looking back to Franziskus, she embarked on the treacherous path, holding her arms out like wings for balance, as she carefully put one foot in front of the other. She heard scraping on the rocks behind her: the sound of Franziskus keeping up.

'These men might face setbacks,' he said, 'but all we've seen for weeks are Averlandish victories. Can't you see what must have happened?' His ankle trapped between rocks, Franziskus pitched abruptly forward, and made a quick though graceless adjustment. It left him unsteady but upright.

'No, but I sense you'll correct my ignorance.'

'The count must be well again.'

'The count?'

'Leitdorf, the Elector of Averland. He must have recovered from his latest bout of melancholy. Surely you know of him?'

'Mad Marius, you mean.'

A soldier turned toward them and Angelika froze. Franziskus did the same. The soldier was about two hundred yards off, and seemed to see little threat in them. He gave them an indifferent up-and-down, then returned to his task: refitting a wheel to a cart's axle. Angelika resumed her journey through the boulders.

'So it's Marius I have to blame for my slim pickings these past few weeks?' she said.

'It can only be so. Everyone knows that strange moods rule Marius Leitdorf, as he rules Averland. At times he burns across the field of battle on his mighty charger, sword swinging right and left to cleave his foes. Yet when he is gripped by some unquenchable gloom, he retreats to his flame-blackened castle, and locks himself inside his moldering library to brood. When last I was in Averland, wagging tongues had it that he'd cloistered himself again, that his functionaries had fallen back into corruption, and his soldiers, into laxity and drunkenness. But look upon those heaps of stinking, slaughtered orcs and the tiny tumbrel of slain Averlanders. That's not the work of a demoralised force! Only one explanation is possible: Leitdorf rides again!'

They came out of the rocks and onto a grassy incline. Gravity tugged them, and it was hard not to go rushing down the slope to the flatland below.

'This is your chance to join them, then,' Angelika said, 'and fight at your beloved Leitdorf's side.'

Franziskus turned his head away from her. 'I am from Stirland, not Averland. And I reek of failure. I am not worthy to fight under a hero as great as he.'

'Pah! Your hero is a butcher. You're too far back to see him clearly.'

'Someday,' Franziskus said, 'you'll understand.'

'I understand only too well as it is.'

They reached the battlefield's edge, where some crows tugged peevishly at the tough green flesh of a gaunt, beheaded orc. About eighty yards off, their bolder compatriots flapped around the cart loaded with human casualties. Hornet-clad soldiers kept them at bay with thrusts of their polearms. A sergeant spotted Angelika and Franziskus and waddled in their direction, waving his arms. The wind blew his way, so it took a while before Angelika could make out what he was saying.

'Away, away!' he shouted, in a town crier's cadence. 'We have no need for doxies here! Nor their panderers!'

Angelika felt her fingers wrap tight around her knife's hilt. She hated to be mistaken for a camp follower. The sergeant kept on toward them. She braced herself. Franziskus raised a hand lightly to her shoulder. She shrugged it off. 'No one calls me a whore,' she hissed.

Franziskus stepped around her. He returned the sergeant's wave. The man's square head and jowly jaw was characteristic of the southlands.

'You mistake our intentions, sir,' Franziskus said. 'We are merely travellers, passing through. We'll not disturb you, or your men.'

'Halt right there,' the sergeant said, reaching for the sabre that hung from his belt. Franziskus stopped, and the Averlander left his weapon in its scabbard. 'You there. Why do you wear the coat of a Stirlandish officer? Did you bring an honest man to grief?'

'No sir, I did not.'

Angelika noticed a tremble in Franziskus's chin. Despite herself, she felt embarrassed for him, and hoped that the sergeant wouldn't remark on it. She reminded herself that Franziskus's misfortune was none of her business, and that she should make an honest run for it if the Averlander decided to chop at him with his sabre.

'Did you perhaps lift that coat from a fallen officer? Eh, border rat? I'm told an expeditionary force from Stirland came to grief around here – and not too long ago, either.'

Franziskus tensed his jaw to end the quivering. Now his eyes began to betray him, by blinking rapidly.

'I bought it from a peddler,' Franziskus said. 'Not knowing what its braids and epaulets signified. I merely thought it would be a warm coat.'

The sergeant pulled his sabre slowly from its sheath. 'It will not warm your worthless hide, border rat. Drop that coat right here. Then be on your way.'

The Averlander's attention was fully on Franziskus, so Angelika could sidle over. Her blade was out, resting against her palm and wrist, shielded from the sergeant's view. She checked the other soldiers, marked out their positions, and estimated distances and running times. She calculated the arc of a throw that would send the point of her dagger into the side of the sergeant's neck. She edged into the best position to make the throw.

Franziskus shrugged his shoulders, letting the coat drop from them. 'You are right, sir,' he said. 'I haven't the honour to wear this coat.'

If Angelika were in his shoes, she thought, she would throw the coat over the sergeant's head. Then she would stab him hard, three or four times, before getting out of there. But Franziskus just took the garment and folded it over an extended arm for the obnoxious man to take. The sergeant slid his weapon back into the scabbard and regarded Franziskus. He didn't touch the coat draped over the young man's outstretched arm.

'You wouldn't be a deserter, now, would you?'

'No,' Franziskus said.

'Because even if he's been marked down as dead, a man still has a duty to return to his unit.'

'I wouldn't know that, sir. Like you say, I'm just a border rat.'

AS THEY WALKED toward the Castello del Dimenticato, it seemed to Angelika that Franziskus was shivering more than his sudden lack of a coat warranted. Though the wind was a little sharp, it was a sunny spring day, and she'd been perfectly comfortable without an outer garment of any kind. A piercing comment came to her tongue, but she let it sit there, rather than give voice to it.

They'd quartered themselves at the Castello for nearly a month now, and had come to know it well. It was a walled town in the middle of nowhere, populated by people for whom anything was a step up. It was located just inside the gullet of the Blackfire Pass, south of Averland.

Their destination sat at a remove from the pass proper. It was hidden in a nearby basin where a quartet of lesser mountains met. Angelika and Franziskus dawdled along a rocky trail that connected pass to basin, taking care to avoid the many fist-sized stones strewn across it. An ancient cut in the rock, about twenty feet wide and at least forty high, loomed over them, sheltering the trail. Eroded crisscrosses from an ancient excavation marked its rocky surface. Though Angelika was no expert in such matters, she knew it had to have been made by dwarfs. Perhaps there had been diamonds or gold in the rocks, thousands of years ago, giving the dwarfs good reason for their excavations. They were gone now, at any rate, as were any traces of riches in the nearby hills. The founders of the Castello, however, had reason to appreciate the old handiwork. The cut provided the town with an easy approach to the pass, hidden from the view of any orc armies that might happen to rampage their way up to the Imperial border, which lay less than a week's ride north. Several residents of the Castello – including the cackling old man who'd rented them their small hovel – had assured Angelika that orcs had never spotted the Castello, and would continue to miss it in the future. It seemed a perfect perch from which to launch her looting sorties. She regretted not settling in it sooner.

The two wanderers reached the point where the rocky course opened into the muddy basin. The town sat flush against a cliff face on the opposite side of the basin. To reach its gates, they still had to cross half a mile of wet earth, denuded except for weeds and hardy grasses.

The Castello's walls were twelve feet high and made of salvaged wood, reinforced on the inside with bands of rusted steel – also salvaged. They were grey from weathering and their planks were uneven, so that the tops of the wall reminded Angelika of an orc's jagged tusks and teeth. Large boulders had been arranged on the field to direct enemies toward the front gate. Towers stood on either side of it, so that defenders could fire bolts from crossbows and ballistae on any orcs, skaven or bandits who might try to overrun it. As far as Angelika could gather, the Castello had never been seriously threatened. It looked stronger than it really was. If she were given the task of breaking it, she would do it with fire.

The founder was a former mercenary named Davio Maurizzi; she'd seen him from a distance a couple of times. Some called him a 'border prince', which was a title anyone who lived in these lawless lands could claim for himself, especially if he occupied a defensible position and had a few men willing to pick up swords on his behalf. Maurizzi was Tilean, which explained his town's strange foreign name. Apparently it meant Fortress of the Lost, or some such thing.

Arriving at the gates, they shouted up to the guardsman. He was called Halfhead, because he had a scar that ran all the way from his crown to his jaw; it was a souvenir of when he'd been clouted full in the face by an orcish war-axe. He should have lost half his head, but didn't. The gate was open but it was the custom to shout up and pay respects anyhow. Halfhead smiled down at her, idiotically.

As they passed through, competing smells from four or five stalls reached them. The town's vendors all clustered by the gates, so no one entering or leaving could avoid them. Food sizzled on iron plates, heated by coals, or boiled in pots suspended over logs whitened by low flame. There were soups and bratwursts and schnitzels and noodles (both northern and Tilean-style) and charred medallions of meat that were supposed to be beef. Angelika's stomach churned; she'd had a bad sausage here, not long after they first arrived. Even though she knew that the fare in the tavern was not cooked under cleaner circumstances, her gut wouldn't permit her to sample any of these wares. Anyway, her appetite hadn't yet recovered from the sight of the dead and lime-caked orcs. A draught of liquor was what she needed now. She wended her way through the stalls, reaching the staggering laneway that would take them to the town's least despicable tavern.

Franziskus, who had paused to contemplate a pan-sized, crispy schnitzel, broke away to catch up with her. He did not have to ask where they were going.

The Dolorosa La Bara shuddered at the end of a laneway, its dirt-grey timbers leaning slightly to the west. It was a one-storey structure large enough to accommodate a hundred drinkers, provided that they were willing to cluster a little. A faded sign hung above its creaking double doors; on it was a painted image of a coffin, its lid closed over the vociferously protesting form of a mercenary, clad like a jester. His wailing head, clawed fingers, and shoeless feet protruded from the casket, which was pierced through by a mammoth spike. Droplets of red blood shot from the point of impact – the artist had obviously relished this gruesome detail. Later hands had touched up his work, so that the blood stayed fresh, even though the rest of the cartoon had faded. Angelika had heard various translations of its Tilean name, ranging from the Not Quite Dead Tavern to Painful the Coffin. None of them seemed exactly right to her, and the Tileans in town never deigned to provide an accurate rendition, so she stuck with the foreign name.

It was early, and only the Castello's most devout drunkards congregated in the tavern. Giacomo, the proprietor, sat on his high wooden stool behind the bar, one eye open. He was in his late sixties, an age few in these untamed parts had any great hope of reaching. He had thin bones and a large, round head, adorned by a meagre spread of silver hair. A snow-coloured moustache, kept trimmed to a strict minimum, dwelled above his narrow upper lip. When he saw Angelika, he leapt up from the stool and reached under the counter for a fat-bottomed, blackened bottle of brandy. He poured her two shots, judged by sight, into a chipped ceramic cup. She took a sip, wrinkled her face up, and carried the cup over to a corner table. Franziskus hesitated at the bar.

'What is it today, my son?' Giacomo asked him. 'Whole or half?'

Franziskus gulped and said, 'The sights I've seen today require a whole flagon. At least.'

Giacomo tutted and poured him a full tankard of ale. Franziskus carried it to the table Angelika had selected.

'If today teaches us anything,' he began, 'it is that we must seek more honourable employment. The yellow and black will continue their march, and your days of easy plunder have ended.'

'One day tells us nothing. The course of any war swings like a pendulum. And if, contrary to its entire known history, the Blackfire Pass becomes a site of sudden peace, there are still plenty of other places with battlefields in need of my attention. Though of course I wouldn't expect you to accompany me on any long journeys.'

Franziskus sighed and stopped arguing. She sipped her brandy and let it warm her. She closed her eyes and concentrated on its heat running up through her breastbone. Beads of sweat materialised on her forehead. Angelika leaned back to feel them slowly evaporate.

Heavy footfalls filled the tavern. The flooring shook under Angelika's feet. Without seeming to do so, she turned to see who was coming in. More than a half dozen men were barging in together, jostling broad shoulders as they tried to navigate through the doorway two at a time. In front of them wavered a stall keeper – the bratwurst seller. While looking the other way, he crooked his baby finger at Angelika. The men looming over him all bore the colours of Averland. Close up, with their barrel chests and boxy fists, the men in the black and yellow uniforms seemed less amusing. Each wore a gleaming breastplate, in which Angelika could see a reflection of poor Giacomo, backed up against his shelf of bottles and kegs. The first two carried helmets under their arms, like extra green-plumed heads. The other men kept their helmets on, and their hands near the hilts of their swords. Their postures, in relation to the men in front of them, told Angelika that they held no rank. Their featherless helms confirmed this assumption.

The officers presented a mismatched pair. One was a giant, six and a half feet in height, his face a bony mass of jaw and cheekbone. His neck was as big as his head; he moved it around to direct an intimidating glare at each of the bar's few patrons, Angelika and Franziskus excepted. The other paused to lean his slender frame against the back of a chair, assuming an attitude of impudence. His chestnut hair receded just a touch. The slightest of double chins formed and unformed itself under the line of his jaw. His eyes glittered intelligence; their irises were the colour of steel. He met Angelika's gaze and held it, levelly, before stepping, with exaggerated delicacy, toward her. Without looking directly at it, he seized the back of a chair and dragged it close to him, its legs bumping the uneven planking of Giacomo's floor. He set the chair down next to Franziskus's, touching it. Franziskus shifted his chair over, making room for the slim man. The officer smiled unamusedly and sat down, legs spread spider-wide, and took the liberty of a long and appraising look at Angelika.

'They call you Angelika Fleischer,' the slender man said.

She shrugged. 'What do they call you?'

'I am Benno Kopf. My half-brother here is Gelfrat Kopf.' He indicated the other officer, the big man. 'Perhaps our family name means something to you?'

'Perhaps not.' She kept her hands on the table and remained still. One of the greatest flaws of the Dolorosa La Bara was its lack of alternative exits.

Benno Kopf reached down to his waist, and, unfastening the clasp of his pouch, withdrew a piece of jewellery, which he dangled in front of her. It was a pendant, swinging on a silver chain. The back was silver too. On the front, an emblem was marked out in marcasite, diamond, and obsidian: it depicted a sabre against a black shield, on a field of white.

'This emblem means something to you,' Benno said.

'And to you, also, I gather.'

'Eight weeks ago – or is it nine? – you who sold this piece of jewellery to a travelling merchant named Max Beckman.'

'Are you asking me a question?'

Benno smiled, showing her a mouth full of small and crooked teeth. 'You're a proud person and don't like to be challenged. I bear no ill wishes towards you. I merely find myself in need of certain facts. If you choose to make this transaction difficult...' He leaned back, to give her a clear view of Gelfrat's full height and bulk, and his glowering expression. 'My half-brother and I respectfully urge you to cooperate,' he concluded.

'Yes, I sold that piece to Max Beckman. I hope he made a good profit on the sale.'

'Your associate knows how to smell the wind, and does not, I think, regret his dealings with us.' He flashed another charmless smile. 'The question Max could not answer for us is: from whom did *you* acquire this piece?' He started swinging the pendant again.

Angelika daintily scratched her face, just above her eyebrow. 'You've learnt a lot about me. I assume you know how I make my living, then.'

'You steal from slain men, fallen on the field of valour.'

'Then that is where I got your pendant.'

'We need to know exactly where. It belonged to another of our half-brothers, Claus von Kopf. You unwrapped it from his dead fingers, perhaps?'

'In fact, I found it lying in a footprint, in the mud.'

'On a battlefield?'

'Yes, but it wasn't clear which of the bodies it had come from.'

Benno leaned forward. 'You needn't be afraid of offending us. We scarcely knew him. In fact–' He turned to his brother. 'We can be frank here, can't we, Gelfrat?'

Gelfrat grunted unrevealingly.

Benno turned back to Angelika. 'Neither of us were raised alongside him. Our father has a number of sons, by a number of women. Though naturally it is tragic that Claus has died in battle, we Kopfs are born to fight, and thus to die. Claus was my father's legitimate son; he lived on cakes and honey, while Gelfrat and I have had to scrabble and scrape. In his demise, either of us may find opportunity for advancement. Our father will have to reach down into the ranks of his many bastards and choose one to legitimate. Perhaps you have heard his name – Jurgen von Kopf.'

Angelika twitched her shoulder, dismissively. 'He is a great man in Averland, I take it.'

'Great. And rich. The von Kopfs have for many generations served the electors of Averland, as statesmen and generals. It is our father who pursues this war against the orcs, and it is his victories that protect the Empire's naked underbelly.'

Honour of the Grave

Franziskus cleared his throat, as if asking permission to speak. 'I have heard your father's name. So you say it is not Count Leitdorf who presently leads the armies of Averland?'

'He has delegated the task.'

Angelika broke in. 'My assistant's interest in the intricacies of Averlandish politics exceeds mine.'

'Then I shall cut to the heart of the matter: Gelfrat and I don't care if you had to saw off Claus's arm to get the pendant. We merely need to find his effete, snuff-sniffing bones and haul them back to father for proper burial, in accordance with the family rites.' He interlaced his fingers and cracked his knuckles. 'We are eager to please our sire. As we speak, other bastards also jockey to seize the vacant position of favoured son. Thus we are hungry to execute his wishes, and will react intemperately to those who decline to assist us.'

Before replying, Angelika took a slow sip of her brandy, and let it work its way through her. 'It is always sad when sons grow up without the affection of their fathers. It makes them impolite. And grasping.'

Gelfrat balled his fist and stepped closer.

'Wait,' said Franziskus.

Benno put up his hand, showing Gelfrat the back of it. 'Please, speak,' Benno said. 'I did not catch your name.'

'My name is Franziskus.'

'You were with Fraulein Fleischer when she found our family emblem?'

'Ah, no, we met several weeks after that. Listen, you must excuse my friend's sharpness of tone.'

Angelika made a coughing noise.

Franziskus pushed his chair back, attempting to strike a more casual pose. 'I am recently of the Empire, and I am just getting used to the customs of the borderland. People here pay little heed to rank, and you must give respect to get it in return.'

'I'll show you respect!' Gelfrat spat. He lunged at Franziskus, but Benno stood, interposing himself between his brother and the smaller man.

'No, Gelfrat. This fellow is right. I have tried to secure with knife-edged words what I should be accomplishing with silver.'

Gelfrat positioned himself toe-to-toe with Benno, bumping his half-brother's breastplate with his own. Benno grinned at Gelfrat. He spoke through his teeth. 'Remember what we agreed.'

Gelfrat stormed across the tavern, to the bar. He slapped its wooden top. 'Give me ale!' he bellowed. Giacomo hastened to fill the order.

Benno retook his seat, cupped his right hand in his left, and addressed Angelika. 'We will pay you a hundred crowns to lead us to the site of Claus's demise.'

'Two hundred.'

'We are not rich men.'

'One hundred and seventy-five.'

Benno moved his head sorrowfully back and forth.

'One fifty.'

'One twenty-five.'

'Done.' Angelika proffered her hand, for shaking. Benno hesitated, apparently unused to performing the gesture with a woman. Gelfrat grunted.

Benno shook her hand. 'We have an arrangement, then.'

To THE SETTLERS of the Castello del Dimenticato, the notion of a straight road was a civilised frippery. They'd clustered their shacks, sheds, and hovels haphazardly together. If a space between buildings continued for more than fifty feet, the locals called it a road. Homes rested on poor foundations, or none at all. Roofs slumped in the middle. Doors rested uneasily on yawning hinges. Most of the houses were made of hardened mud, reinforced by scraps of timber, but a handful of larger cottages were built of stone. Angelika and Franziskus stepped lightly along the meandering, dirty path that served as one of the town's main arteries. Neither carried a lantern; they relied instead on meagre bands of light escaping from shuttered windows. They trod slowly, eyes down, alert for heaps of rotten food, spreading pools of urine, and for the turds of dogs. This caution marked them as more finicky than most of their neighbours.

Franziskus said, 'I don't trust them.'

'Good,' Angelika said. 'You shouldn't.'

'Yet you've agreed to accompany them.'

Honour of the Grave

'Their money will look better in my purse than it does in theirs.'

'They are graspers and pretenders, frank in their lust for undeserved rank!'

'All rank is undeserved, so they are no worse than their so-called betters.'

'You say such things just to shock me.'

'Seeing as my new clients disgust you, you'll naturally want to stay behind while I take them where they want to go.'

Franziskus stopped short. A woman posed in the open doorway of a stone house, lit by the firelight behind her. The edges of her flaxen hair glowed. She leaned languorously against the doorframe, cocking out an angular hipbone. She blinked her emerald eyes at him, then slipped back into the building, closing an oak door behind her. Franziskus stared at it. He shook his face from side to side, like a beagle, to wake himself from his trance. He turned. Angelika was waiting for him, in the middle of the lane, hands behind her back. A wicked smirk pulled at her lips.

'I've been boring you, I see.'

'No,' said Franziskus, too quickly and too loudly. He took several long strides to close the gap between them.

'Did one of the local rent girls catch your eye, Franziskus?' Her grin widened. 'Which of them was it? Gisela? Teapot?'

He couldn't help but turn back and look at the door of the building. 'No, none of those. She was not of their – she was–'

He started; Angelika had stuck him in the ribs with her elbow. 'Go on, Franziskus. You've been a good boy ever since you first started tagging after me. You're entitled.'

'No,' he said, eyes on the door.

She pushed him. 'I know how men are. I won't think less of you. Go on.'

Annoyed, he moved out of the range of her shoves. 'It's not that at all. I was merely... captivated by a moment of beauty.'

She uttered a throaty laugh.

'Not everything is ugly or some kind of cynical joke. I saw a woman who was beautiful. Such a person can stand in a doorway and not be a harlot. A man can look upon her and react without base and carnal lusts.' He marched past her. Without matching his increased pace, she followed. If she were lucky, his dudgeon would prove permanent, and, when she reached the hovel they'd rented, she'd find no trace of him. But Angelika had never considered herself lucky. She watched Franziskus disappear around a corner into the gloomy night.

She slowed her pace a little more, to savour this rare moment of solitude. She thought about going back to La Bara, but, for all she knew, the Kopfs would still be there. The hours she'd spent watching as the Averlanders filled their throats with ale had already been wearying enough. There were other taverns, but they would also be full of sweating, shouting, farting men. It occurred to Angelika that she should just disappear from town and never come back, leaving both Kopfs and Franziskus behind. But night was not a time to travel through the wilderness alone, and she wanted those hundred and twenty-five crowns.

She rounded a corner. A figure appeared out of the darkness to pin her against a cold stone wall. Though he barely came up to her waist, he was stout and muscular, and held her fast. A reek of ale wafted up from him. He had her right arm pinned, so she couldn't get to the knife on her belt. Neither could she reach the other one in the cuff of her boot. She grunted, trying to push off from the wall, but the bastard was strong and had a low centre of gravity. She twisted to look at his ill-lit features. She'd assumed from his belligerence and strength that he would be a dwarf, but now that she looked at him, she knew him for a halfling. He had a wide and beardless face, sunken eyes and a prominent brow, topped by curly locks. Both of his circular ears had large wedges cut out of them. The blotchy pink remains of an old burn marred his left cheek; a wide, red worm-like scar wriggled around his throat.

He pushed his shoulder into her and opened his mouth, letting his wide tongue come out to slurp up a skein of drool that had fallen onto his chin. 'So who are we, girlie?' he asked, staring wild-eyed into her face. His voice was high and boyish, lending his lechery an extra layer of obscene menace. Keeping his shoulder pressed in hard, he waggled his broad hands at her, apparently searching for her breasts.

'If those hands go any further, I'll cut them off.'

He grinned, but ceased his pawing. 'Ah, girlie talks, does she? Girlie talks mean. I like that.'

Angelika squirmed. 'Let me have my knife and I'll really give you a thrill.'

He ground his shoulder into her kidney. A groan escaped her lips.

'So girlie, I haven't seen you in town before. Tell me who you might be.'

She slid sideways along the wall until she had him off balance. Then she snaked forward to grind a thumb into his neck, digging deep into a pressure point. Grunting indignantly, he shifted his weight off her. She clamped her hands around each of his ears, held his face in position, and kneed him between the eyes. She wanted to do it again, but his skull-bone was hard and had hurt her knee. She let go of him, scudded back, and pulled out her knife.

Reeling back, he blinked tears from his eyes. Blood ran out of his nose and into his mouth. He wrenched a dagger from his own belt.

'I only asked you for simple information, girlie,' he complained, breathing tiny red bubbles, which quickly popped. 'Now I'll have to teach you a lesson.'

She thought of a retort but didn't bother. Halflings were too easy. All you had to do was remind them they were short. She extended her legs, leaned back to widen her first swing, and waited for the little lout come to her. He wiped his mouth with his free hand. The blood was still flooding down – it covered his chin. He took a half-step at her and feinted, jabbing his blade like a pig-sticker. Angelika tilted her head to the side and clucked at him, wordlessly taunting him for the feeble move.

'Oh, you're one of those ones,' he said, 'who think you're so...' He charged her; she dodged him but couldn't get a decent opening. They circled each other in the middle of the lane, dirt scraping under the toes of their boots. None of the nearby windows were lit. But few locals would risk their necks to intervene in a scrap, anyway.

'You think I don't know how to handle a knife,' the halfling said. 'I just don't know whether to cut you with my right hand, or my left.' He tossed the dagger back and forth from one hand to the other. Angelika watched the blade, not the man. She chose her moment and kicked out with her long and slender leg. Her toe caught his knife in mid-air, between right hand and left. It twirled end over end, up past the halfling's head and into the darkness behind him. He looked up, disbelieving.

Angelika kicked him in the throat. He gasped and gargled. He spat up more blood. She dropped back into a defensive crouch. Her plan was to goad him into a stupid charge, then use his own momentum to plant her knife deep into him, just below the Adam's apple. He reached to his right hip for a longer, sturdier weapon, a short sword. He copied her crouch and shifted his weight from side to side.

'All right,' he said. 'You're not just any girlie. Someone taught you how to fight. Maybe I should have heard your name before.'

'They call me Bleeder of Halflings.'

He curled his lip. 'There's a difference between talking mean and talking smart.'

'Sorry if I seem suddenly unattractive to you.'

He hefted the sword in his hand, as if testing its weight. He stuck it up into the air, screamed a strangled battlecry, then turned his arse to her and ran across the lane, scattering up gravel and dust. He darted into the mouth of an alleyway. She sprinted after him but stopped short a good ten feet before the unlit alley entrance. She'd paid him back sufficiently; she didn't need to kill him. Besides, it could be a trap: he might have any number of cronies in there waiting to leap on her.

Still, she hated to let such a thing trail off, without proper resolution. His interest in her name troubled her. She stood before the alley, panting, then decided to wait until her breath had returned to normal. She heard nothing, saw nothing, down the laneway.

'Angelika!' It was Franziskus. He'd come back for her. He seemed worried. 'Is everything all right?' he asked.

'Of course,' she answered.

CHAPTER TWO

THEY RODE THROUGH green flatlands, ice-topped mountains rising up on either side of them. The sun had just slid behind the peaks to the right of them, as they travelled south. The sky was yellow, interrupted by purple bands of cloud. Unseen birds twittered from the trees that lined the foothills. All day long, white bellflower blossoms had covered the grassy slopes; now the blooms had closed themselves up, against the fading light.

They were eight hours south of the Castello. The party would have made better progress, were it not for the typically Imperial attitudes of its leaders. They couldn't just provide horses for everyone, that would show insufficient deference to hierarchy. The officers, Benno and Gelfrat, rode sleek and muscular stallions. Angelika, as a guest (or as a woman – it wasn't clear which), had been given a pokey mule with a patchy coat and a resentful glare. The ordinary soldiers had to make it on foot. So did Franziskus, whose status lacked clarity. This situation meant that the party moved only as quickly as its slowest man – who in this case was a paunchy fellow with greying mutton-chops and a bad wheeze, named Ekbert. In a mixed group, the horses were an impediment: they prevented the group from moving up into the hills, where the going would be slower but safer. Angelika eyed the trees and remembered how the Averlandish forces had used them to ambush their orcish prey. She wanted to be up in the hills herself, on the good side of all that cover.

Angelika had offered Franziskus a turn on the mule; she hated the surly beasts, so it was no great sacrifice. Franziskus had been offended by the very suggestion. He still seemed piqued by their exchange on the street, the night before. Angelika wasn't sure why he'd got so huffy, but saw little reason to tax herself puzzling him out.

Benno and Gelfrat kept themselves close at hand, riding to keep her flanked. It seemed they were worried that she might up and bolt on them. There was little chance of that: she hadn't yet separated them from their coins.

Benno in particular had been giving her close attention. He'd slapped on some perfume that smelled like Araby spice. Angelika had given some thought to his new attitude and had not settled on an opinion about it. He was more fetching from certain angles than from others. The weak chin was a problem, but the spark in his eyes might compensate. She'd certainly bedded worse specimens. For the moment, however, there was business between them, and that would take precedence over any other stirrings.

Gelfrat's odour had not changed since their last meeting. He still smelled of the Dolorosa la Bara. He took frequent pulls on his water skin, which probably contained something more than water. He'd begun the day's travels with a blank and guarded expression, and had steadily grown more bored and petty with the death of each hour.

'You,' he grunted, interrupting Angelika's uneasy survey of the thickening trees to the left and right. He had allowed his horse to fall back and was now riding alongside Franziskus. Franziskus craned a wary head up at him.

'Yes?'

'Where are you from?'

'From nowhere, like everyone else around here.'

'You don't sound like you're from nowhere.'

Benno pulled his horse's reins and circled back toward his half-brother.

'If my accent offends you, I apologise,' Franziskus said, keeping his tone bland and even.

'I want to know where you're from.'

Benno reached Gelfrat's side. 'Maybe it is time to find a good camp for the night.'

Gelfrat kept his eyes on Franziskus. 'I want to know why he's with us.'

'Because he is with her,' Benno said, jabbing a thumb in Angelika's direction. 'Let's remain intent on our mission, shall we?'

Ignoring his brother, Gelfrat kept on, 'You sound like a Stirlander. Why aren't you in Stirland?'

Franziskus shrugged. Benno sighed and rode ahead, catching up to Angelika. She expected him to beg pardon for his comrade's poor manners, but he said nothing. He fidgeted with his helmet strap and kept his eyes straight ahead.

'I said, why aren't you in Stirland?'

Angelika saw movement up in the hills, to her right. She put up her hand.

Gelfrat was too preoccupied to see her signal. 'I *said*–'

Benno shushed him. Gelfrat's muscles bunched up; red embarrassment flushed his face.

'What do you see?' Benno asked her.

'Figures in the trees.' With a flick of the head, she showed him where. Gelfrat kicked his horse. It bolted ahead. Benno followed. Angelika jumped free of her mule and ran to follow the two brothers; Franziskus came too. The soldiers stayed stupidly put. Soon, the officers' horses were rearing up, refusing to press on through a scattering of large rocks. Gelfrat turned his horse around and rode back to their men. Benno calmed his mount, then leapt down from his back. He landed on his ankle, and exclaimed, more in surprise than pain. Angelika pointed up into the pines.

'You see them?' she asked Franziskus. He nodded.

Benno limped over. He stood behind Angelika's outstretched arm and squinted. 'I don't see.'

'They're gone,' Angelika said.

'Did you get a good look at them?'

She shook her head. They had only been dark figures moving through the trees. But two of them were much shorter than the other; they might have been halflings. Like the knave who'd accosted her the night before.

'It could be anyone up there, correct?' Benno said. 'This whole pass crawls with goblins, skaven, outlaws... and Sigmar knows what else.'

'If someone were keeping a watch on you,' Angelika asked, 'who would it most likely be?'

Benno raised his eyebrows and threw up his hands. 'No one. No one would know why we're here. Or care.'

'Because we are being followed.'

THE CLOUDS THICKENED overhead, and by the time dusk had finished its transformation into night, they had filled the sky entirely. They left the party in darkness, with not even the faint light of the stars to travel by. Angelika could hear the rattling of buckles against breastplates, and the breath of the men and horses around her, but she could see nothing. She stretched her hand out and spread its fingers. She could not see that, either.

Benno slapped reins to his horse's neck and called the party to a halt. 'A devil's choice,' he said. 'We camp here, under the noses of our watchers, or we light lanterns – making it easy for them to follow us.'

'If they follow us,' Gelfrat's voice boomed from the blackness, 'I say we make our stand here.'

'What say you?' Benno asked.

It took Angelika a moment to realise that the Averlander was addressing her. It was not the usual thing, for an Imperial officer to solicit advice from a border rat – or from a woman, for that matter. She pulled her cloak tighter. The temperature had been steadily dropping for the past hour. 'Gelfrat's right,' she said. 'This is the Blackfire Pass, so we have to assume the worst – that whoever's following us plans to attack. If we camp here, we can find a good place to defend ourselves from, and conserve our strength. Otherwise, we're just waiting to be ambushed. And if I'm wrong, and there's no one chasing us... a few more hours, here and there, will make no difference to your brother now.'

Gelfrat muttered a complaint. The foot soldiers whispered to one another, uneasily.

'I'd like to do this without lanterns,' Benno said, 'but then again, I would prefer to be abed in Grenzstadt, with a sweet-smelling harlot snoozing on either side of me.' Angelika heard him dismount; he landed with surprising lightness. 'Ekbert, Heinrich! Strike those flints of yours!'

Angelika wormed her way off the back of her mule. It twisted its neck to snap at her. She coiled her muscles as someone touched her, cupping a hand around her shoulder.

It was Benno; he spoke into her ear. His breath was warm. 'We don't want to be camping out here on the plain, do we?'

'No,' she said. 'Up in the hills. We can probably find a big rock to huddle against, that will shelter us from the wind. If we're lucky, we can find a place with few approaches, which will be easier to guard. Tell the men to pick up any dead wood they find; we can lay it out on the pathways, so anyone coming will knock into it, and make noise. Branches with dead leaves still stuck to them are the best; they give off a good rattle.'

'There's no sense in the whole lot of us tramping blindly about. You and I will go,' Benno said, 'and then come back for the others, when we've found something.'

She nodded. Her travelling companions appeared all around her, painted in a warm yellow light: the men had lit the first of the lanterns. Angelika went to Franziskus and told him the plan.

'I'll go with you,' Franziskus whispered.

'No, you stay here. If we both go with Benno, the others will suspect skullduggery. Stay here, and impress Gelfrat with your wit and scholarship.'

'I'd have better luck training a boar to dance the gavotte.'

She patted him on the cheek. The gesture was meant to be reassuring, but she got a funny look in return. So she punched him on the shoulder – hard. Franziskus blinked. 'I'll be back before you know it,' she said.

Benno approached, lantern in hand. It lit up the bones around his eyes, and the underside of his neck, giving his face a sinister aspect. 'East or west?'

'Our pursuers were over there, to the right, so let's take the leftward hills.'

With nimble strides, Benno kept up with her. They walked in silence across the pass's flat bottom, towards the east. Angelika liked a man who knew how to shut up. Behind her, she heard the whickering of horses and the low voices of their companions. A laugh erupted from the group, followed by an angry growl from Gelfrat, and then silence. Benno's lantern summoned circling bugs, which made a secondary halo around its ball of light.

They reached a slope, obscured by tall weeds and slick with dew, and battled their way up it. The brass links that clasped Benno's elaborate cuffs clicked against the steel of his breastplate.

'I should have lightened my load before setting out,' he gasped.

'If we stumble into a nest of orcs or skaven, you'll be grateful for that armour.'

As the slope gave way to rockier ground, the lantern swung wildly in Benno's hand, casting crazy shadows on the boulders and between the trunks of pines. She went ahead of him, so that it was her shadow, like a giant's, that rippled across the hillside. Angelika thought she heard Benno slip, but when she looked back, he had already recovered. He was sweating and his face was flushed with effort. She stopped to choose a path, and to let him regain his breath. He wiped his hands on his black and yellow leggings.

'It is a difficult life here,' he said, 'but you may do as you like, hah? Go to find treasure one day, and ride with soldiers the next? No one to tell you what to do, or where to be.'

She couldn't imagine what he was getting at, so she elevated an eyebrow and cocked it at him. 'The rest of you all have heavy armour, too, don't you? And if you have to leave such costly gear behind with the horses, you won't want to let it too far out of your sight, will you? So there's no point picking a spot too far into the hills...'

He shook his head, in what she took to be agreement. She pointed to a spot about fifty feet up, along a steep and narrow pathway. 'That looks promising. Hold the lantern this way.' Benno moved the light, and she saw a telltale smudge across the sheer face of a large chunk of granite. 'See that? Soot from an old campfire. You know what that means?'

Honour of the Grave 55

'I don't claim to be a woodsman.'

'It means, if that was good enough for somebody else to camp on, it's good enough for us. I'll climb up to make sure it's all right. You stay here to signal the men.'

'I hope you value it,' Benno said.

'Value what?'

'The freedom you have.'

Her only answer to this was to scamper up the trail. The rock provided a nearly perfect place for them to rest for the night. And only one path led up to it. It would give them shelter from gusts coming down off the mountain. Loose earth padded the nearby ground, so the bedding would not be too rocky. Some past camper had thoughtfully dug a firepit for them, which they could safely use, when morning came, to warm their bones. She looked for tripwires and snares, and found none. She searched the rocks for chalked signs left by goblins or beastmen; there were none of those, either. It would be a tight fit here, with all the men, and there was the danger that someone might roll off and drop down a hundred feet to the hard slope below... She decided to keep this minor drawback to herself. She would find no better spot, and was already growing weary herself. She waved to Benno, who circled his lantern in the air, alerting the men below to come and meet them. She sat, claiming the spot with the softest-looking ground, and huddled in her cloak. Her behind soon found a sharp rock, and she fought to dislodge it from the earth. It turned out to be bigger than she'd thought, so instead she moved over a little, leaving the pointy stone for whoever wanted to squeeze up next to her.

She heard the men approaching and tensed up, taking her dagger from its sheath. They were making too much noise; if there was a predator waiting for them in the hills, it would know about them now. As they combed the hill for dead branches, they made an even greater ruckus. Angelika regretted her suggestion but it couldn't be retracted now. Franziskus was still out there with the rest of them, no doubt diligently proving the superiority of his wood gathering. After a while, having heard no outbursts of sudden agony, she relaxed, and let slumber take her. Angelika had trained herself to fall asleep quickly, but to maintain a consciousness of her surroundings when dozing, and to jolt awake on the slightest sign of danger.

Someone approached. She opened her eyes. It was Franziskus, about to shake her shoulder. She leaned aside, and he pulled back. He took his place beside her. But the sharp rock jabbed his buttock, so he stood and walked to her other side, and settled in. They watched the Sabres lay down bedrolls, circling each other grimly as they vied for the best spots. They tested their choices, lying down and locating the stones that lay beneath their rancid blankets. Stones large enough to be dislodged were torn from the loose earth and tossed into the bushes or off the precipice, where they thudded loudly. Angelika cringed. These were idiots, not woodsmen. One of the men began to gather sticks for a fire.

'No fires,' Angelika called out. The soldier's head turned towards her, but then he continued piling up kindling. She sat up, called out to Benno. 'No fires. We're being pursued, remember. Cold food only.' The stick-gatherer mouthed a curse, thinking that Angelika could not see his face from where she sat. The men fumbled through their packs for cooked sausages and bits of sinister-looking cheese rind.

She put her back against the rock and shut her eyes. Loud snoring followed. She realised it was her. She adjusted her position, turning her head away from Franziskus, and managed to doze without further eruptions.

She woke up when she felt someone pressing up against her from the other side. It was musky-smelling Gelfrat. She slitted her eyes open, and them saw Benno signalling his half-brother to move away from her. Gelfrat snorted. Benno kicked his boot until he shuffled over, leaving a good two feet between himself and Angelika. She shifted back toward Franziskus, laying her head on his shoulder, and returned to her slumbers.

She was awake. It was morning. Grey light. An aching back. And something was wrong. She lifted her head from Franziskus's still-sleeping shoulder. She looked around. Gelfrat's heaving bulk shuddered to the left of her. The other men, except Ekbert, slept in a rough circle at her feet. She creaked her complaining leg muscles upward, to assume a crouch. She heard rustling. Her knife came out. She crept over to the path, rising a little. Her new viewpoint revealed a man, a few yards down the trail from her, crawling on all fours. His eyes met hers. Angelika saw a dagger's blade clenched in his mouth. The whites of his eyes stood out against grime-coated skin. He wore a green kerchief on his head, and a sheepskin vest over a filthy white shirt. Behind him came another half-dozen men, all slipping up the trail on hands and knees.

She hunched down so he could see her eyes. 'By the time you get that knife out of your mouth and into your hand,' she said, 'I'll have a nice hole cut in your neck.'

The man bobbed his head carefully up and down. He reminded Angelika of a dog with a bone clamped in its jaws. He signalled, to stop the men behind him from coming closer.

'Now I'm going to reach over,' Angelika said, 'and take the knife from your mouth. Then both of us will slowly stand up. Then we'll all have a polite conversation, with no unnecessary bleeding. Yes?'

The creeping man repeated his nod. She did as she'd said, reaching out with her off hand to delicately take hold of the dagger hilt. He opened his mouth, letting the weapon drop into her palm. She tossed it behind her. Supporting herself with the hand that had just held his blade, she rose from her crouch. The ambusher mirrored her movements. At his full height, he was still half a head shorter than her. His bare arms, however, were well developed. One of his eyelids fluttered nervously.

'Turn around,' she told him. He turned. She placed her blade just below his neck, but did not touch it to his skin; that would be rude. 'Tell me your name.'

'Isaak.'

'This is your chance to see how much your friends truly like you, Isaak.' She raised her voice to speak to the men on the trail. 'As you can see, Isaak is in some trouble here. I don't want it to get any worse, and I expect you all feel the same. So let's all stay still and silent, while I awaken my companions. I'm sure you were sneaking up with some neighbourly intention; perhaps you wanted to warn us of poor weather ahead, so I reckon we'll soon be sharing a laugh over this awkward misunderstanding.'

'Do as she says,' said Isaak.

Angelika whistled sharply, and didn't stop until the men behind her began to stir. Benno and Franziskus were the first to be fully awake; they jostled the others. They leapt up, swords ready. Angelika waved them back. Benno's men looked to him. He took a backward step, indicating that they should follow Angelika's cues.

Angelika spoke to Isaak: 'Our friend, Ekbert, who was guarding the horses down there. You haven't done anything permanent to him, have you?'

'His skull will hurt, when he comes to.'

'Well then. Nothing like a prisoner exchange first thing in the morning.'

'I've seen you before,' Isaak said. 'At the Dolorosa la Bara. You've been staying at the Castello. What are you doing with these murderous sons of dogs?'

'Murderous?'

'Watch your tongue, border rat!' shouted Gelfrat.

'They wear the black and yellow, don't they? Whose side are you on?'

'I serve my own interests. Who are you, and what is your grudge against them?'

'We are Prince Davio's men. We fight under the banner of the Legione del Dimenticato. And the men behind you are cruel slaughterers, who have slain our brothers for no good reason.'

Gelfrat charged forward to be next to Angelika. He shook his sword at Isaak. 'Treacherous mercenary scum! If your crawling lizard of a so-called prince had honoured his word, we wouldn't have had to waste our time punishing you!'

'I see,' Angelika said, handing Isaak's dagger back to him. 'This is some prior dispute, to which I am not a party.' She stepped sideways, moving well clear, so that nothing stood between Isaak and Gelfrat. Both turned dumbfounded heads in her direction. Neither moved to attack the other. Angelika leaned her back against the rock and crossed her arms. She hoped she wouldn't end up with too much soot on her clothing, but the gesture was worth some extra washing. 'Since no one wants to die today,' she said, 'perhaps we should put our weapons down.'

From her new vantage point, Angelika could better see Isaak's fellows. They seemed to have little in common, except that they were all men. The mercenary behind Isaak sported long, dark hair, and stared blankly ahead with yellow, glassy eyes. He'd wrapped himself in a long, blue coat, and had tied a strip of red cloth across his forehead. Next in line, a short, middle-aged man glowered. The white, curly hair on his head matched that on his chest, which was bared under an open linen shirt. The butts of twin pistols stuck out from his wide leather belt. Behind him was a fat man with a red nose from too much rum. He coughed and trembled in a damp knit tunic and hooded wool cloak. There was nothing about these men to identify as a unit, or even soldiers. None wore armour.

She'd keep her eyes on the pistol-carrying man. If this all went wrong, it was his guns that would pose the greatest danger.

Gelfrat and Isaak locked gazes. Isaak swallowed; Gelfrat was easily a foot taller than he, and outweighed him by at least a hundred pounds. He did not shift a muscle.

'Bah!' said Gelfrat, turning from the smaller man, 'We'll deal them a thrashing, if that's what they want! But it's not why we're here.' He strode over beside Angelika, placing his spine against the rock, as she had. She moved aside to give him room. With his free hand, he punched at the rock.

Angelika leaned forward, looking again at Isaak's men. 'You don't perchance have any halflings with you?'

'I trust my own kind only,' said Isaak.

'But it was you, spying on us from the trees, last night?'

'I don't know what you mean. We came upon your man by chance this morning, on our way back home.'

'I see.'

'I don't know what reasons you have to accompany these men.' He ventured to take a step towards her. 'But if you've agreed to work for the yellow and black, you should know you've signed on for a deadly bargain. You heard them admit it. They paid the prince so we would help them against the orcs. Yet when we failed to take as many greenskin heads as their war leader wanted, they came to slay us!'

'Liar!' Gelfrat spat. 'You stopped killing orcs entirely, when they got too much for you. You, and the border rat sellswords of the other border rat princes – you retreated inside your crapulent forts as soon as the fight grew tough! Cowards!'

Isaak shortened the distance between himself and the big man. 'My comrades were watering their horses by a stream, assuming we were safe from attack, when your men came crashing through the woods towards them. Nothing to worry about, they thought, they're our allies. Then out came the swords and pistols, and a dozen good souls were murdered, before they could even draw their blades!' Isaak's men followed him onto the small, circular ledge where Angelika had made camp. She squeezed up against the rock, thinking of the long fall, should anyone be shoved off. Franziskus had foolishly planted himself near an edge. She tried to catch his eye, to beckon him away from it, but he was too intent on the two angry men.

'I don't know what happened,' Gelfrat conceded. 'I was not at the fight you're talking about. All I know is that the border princes betrayed us, and had to be shown the cost of that.'

'You don't deny that they were basely slain, then?'

Gelfrat looked down on his adversary. 'Do you deny that your men then attacked one of our regiments, which was already taxed and wounded from fighting the greenskin? That you slew them nearly to a man? Is that what you slimy rodents call a fair fight?'

Isaak made fists. 'That was just vengeance!'

'They weakened themselves battling the orcs – who aim to destroy us all – and you took the chance to cut them down like stalks of wheat. I say our only error was in not killing more of you!'

The pistolier gripped the polished oaken handles of his weapons. His eyes parted ways: one pointed at Gelfrat, the other, at Benno. Angelika decided that her hundred and twenty-five crowns were in jeopardy.

'How long have you been out on the trail, Isaak?' she said.

'Nearly a month. We were sent south, to recruit replacements for our fallen friends.'

'These men were allowed to enter the Castello unmolested. Prince Davio could have easily taken them hostage, or worse. It could be that he's reconciled with the Averlandish commander. You know how quickly allegiances shift, hereabouts.'

He sank the back of his left hand indecisively into the palm of his right. 'All things are possible in the Blackfire...'

'Perhaps then you should know for sure where Davio stands, before you wreak any more vengeance for him. If he's settled his dispute, he won't be happy for you to stir it up again.'

He stood thinking, his tongue working around the inside his mouth. After taking a long pause, he said, 'I will remain facing you, as will my comrade Ivan, here.' He indicated the gunman. 'The rest of my band will turn their backs to you, and head down the trail. Then the two of us will follow. We will leave your man as he is now, tied up. We'll ride away, and you will not pursue us.'

'No doubt you've already stolen our horses,' said Benno. 'So it's an easy promise to make.'

Isaak employed a dark-rimmed fingernail to pick at a morsel of food lodged between his front teeth. 'We don't want to kill each other over mere horseflesh, do we?'

Benno shook his head.

'If you do cross us,' Isaak continued, 'we'll grant you no mercy. Our numbers equal yours, and we know this country better than you.'

'Be gone then,' Gelfrat said, 'before your boasts fatally bore me.'

The border men executed their retreat as Isaak had said. Following Gelfrat's example, the Averlanders affected postures of varying disinterest. Gelfrat studied his fingernails, as if contemplating their overdue annual cleaning.

As he turned to go, Isaak said, to Angelika, 'You've saved your companions from harm, but you must not trust them.'

Scornfully, Gelfrat cleared his throat. When he saw that Isaak and Ivan had reached the slope below, he stepped towards the trail. Benno held him back. 'Wait till we see them ride off.'

'What if they stick a knife in Ekbert?'

'They'll leave him for us to deal with.' A hardness had appeared on Benno's face, provoking a doubtful look from his half-brother.

'You don't mean to—'

Benno went to relieve himself against the big rock. His men took the same opportunity. As they watered the boulder, Angelika cast a revolted look up into the white-grey sky.

The faint sound of hoofbeats echoed up from the valley. Benno pulled at the drawstring of his leggings, adjusted his codpiece, and headed down the path, angrily kicking away the branches they'd laid down the night before. 'It's fortunate that Angelika was with us, to hear them coming, or our bellies would now gape open.' He spoke in a raised voice, but his nose pointed heavenward, so it wasn't clear who he was talking to. 'Sigmar knows, it would be foolish to expect an actual member of the company to execute my orders.'

'Do not take it out on poor old Ekbert,' Gelfrat said, in a pleading tone. Angelika found it comically strange, coming from him. He bounded around the soldier called Heinrich, who had been between the two brothers.

'The Black Field Sabres do not tolerate dereliction. You know that.'

'But Ekbert has been a Sabre since before we were born.'

'Discipline must be maintained,' replied Benno.

'For years, he rode at our father's side!'

'And you know what father would demand, if he were here.'

Gelfrat hung his head. Angelika noticed a couple of the other soldiers exchanging worried looks. This Ekbert had made little impression on her, and she couldn't see herself caring two hoots for his fate. Even so, she felt a certain tautness above her breastbone.

They found Ekbert lying on his side, among the weeds and wildflowers. His wrists were tied together, as were his ankles. Isaak's men had taken the mule and horses, as well as all the breastplates and helmets. Ekbert wriggled as the company drew near, wheezing and puffing, his face slick with dew. Blades of grass stuck to it. Benno stood over him, and wrinkled up his nose. The old campaigner had soiled himself.

'Heinrich, untruss this goose,' Benno ordered. The younger soldier slunk reluctantly up and sliced the thin, dirty cords that bound Ekbert's wrists and ankles. He scuttled back as soon as he was finished. Ekbert stayed down even after Heinrich had freed him. 'I'm sorry,' he burbled.

'I've never seen sorrier,' said Benno. He kicked him in the teeth. Gelfrat flinched.

'Such are my just desserts,' Ekbert moaned. The kick had split his lip; he bled onto his mutton-chops.

'You deserve far worse. We could all be dead now. *Get your fat carcass up!*'

Trembling, Ekbert heaved himself to his hands and knees. Gelfrat came to him, stretching out an arm to grasp. Benno pushed it away. Ekbert tottered up on his own.

Franziskus grabbed Angelika's elbow. She looked down and saw that she'd had her dagger an inch out of its scabbard. She shoved it back in. She nodded to Franziskus. He let her go. His eyes were moist, she saw.

'This calls for thirty lashes,' Benno said. 'If it were anyone else, it would be Ekbert who'd administer the whipping. But in this case, the honour must fall to his defender. Gelfrat?'

Gelfrat leaned back. 'Benno, don't–'

'Lieutenant, the formality of the circumstance calls for you to refer to me as lieutenant.' Benno turned to Heinrich and instructed him to retrieve the lash from Ekbert's pack.

A decision registered on Gelfrat's face. He held out his hand to receive the lash's handle. He put his other hand on Ekbert's shoulder. 'Come over to that log there,' he said, indicating the dark trunk of a fallen tree, its bark riddled with lichen and round beige shelves of fungus. Ekbert moved to it with a sleepwalker's slowness. He removed his coat and shirt, draping them over the log.

'Don't stint,' Ekbert told Gelfrat. 'Strike hard, and cleanse my debt of honour.'

Angelika turned her back, to spare herself the sight of Ekbert's punishment, but there was no escaping his cries, or the sound of wet leather crackling into his flesh.

CHAPTER THREE

WITH EVERYONE NOW on foot, Angelika argued for a route that concealed them in the hills. Benno insisted that they stick to the bottomlands, instead of tramping through rocks and brambles. But then the sky began to rumble, and the travellers could not be sure whether it was thunder, or the booming of orcish war drums. They chose the hills.

Ekbert trudged with laboured steps; his coat hid the spreading blood that glued the shirt to his back. Gelfrat kept by his side, to steady the old man if needed. Angelika protected herself from the sight of this, and what it aroused in her, by keeping to the head of the party, alongside Benno. In today's grey light, he didn't look good from any angle.

About two hours into their journey, a drizzle started up. They took a moment's shelter beneath a tall and leafy oak; Gelfrat passed his wineskin. Angelika took a sip, but it was rancid. She wished she'd thought to bring some brandy.

'It won't get any drier,' she said, watching the sky darken. They pushed on. The rain grew heavier, soaking through their cloaks and tunics. Angelika spotted a small cave, and they all squeezed into it. Soon after they had arranged themselves inside, spears of sunlight broke through the clouds, and the rain resolved itself into a mist. Angelika reached out a hand, and declared it time to move on. Benno plodded after her without comment, his soldiers trailing behind him.

When there were about three hours of light left in the day, Angelika stopped to peer up at the mountaintops. Landmarks were scarce here; one section of the pass looked pretty much like any other.

'I think I recognise that peak there, with the cleft in the middle,' she said. 'If I'm right, we've got about a league left to go.' She increased her pace, thinking of the best spot to hide her pay. She'd decided that these Averlanders were bad men – same as any men – but they would not try to cheat her. She kept an eye for a trail leading down into the valley, finding one about fifteen minutes into her search. She stopped to listen: she heard birdsong and a light wind playing on tree branches. Satisfied that it was safe to descend to open ground, she whistled a warning to the men behind her and took the path down. It was a light trail, most likely made by boars or deer. Midway along, she surprised a fat marmot, grey with a brown ruff at the back of its neck. It sat up and shrieked angrily at her, but did not think to run until she stamped her foot at it.

'We could have eaten that,' Gelfrat said.

'Are we here to dine on marmot, or recover your brother's bones?'

She reached the flat terrain of the valley floor and looked around to orient herself. For many hundreds of yards, lightly forested slopes, dotted with boulders and stones, gradually gave way to level scrubland, which extended all the way across the valley to the hills and mountains on the pass's opposite side. She saw a curtain of rock ahead. Angelika kept walking, skirting the grade, until she saw a place where the mountain rock descended to the valley, in a sheer curtain of crumbling limestone at least forty feet high. A recently fallen slab of stone lay at its feet, others teetered up on the cliff's edge. Angelika knew this spot; it was her landmark.

'How much further?' asked Gelfrat.

'We're there,' she said. She walked, hugging the cliff wall, until she stopped at the edge of a bowl-shaped depression. It was an old sinkhole filled in by soil washed down from the hills. New spruces, few of them higher than six feet tall, competed for space along its slopes. Angelika waded into them, parting the young trees.

'Wait,' yelled Benno, from the sinkhole's edge. 'This is it?'

'Yes,' said Angelika, continuing down into the thickly massed spruces.

'When you first came upon this place – how did you know where to look?' asked the Averlandish officer, placing a tentative boot over the depression's edge. 'I see only trees.'

'In the same way I find any fresh battle,' she called back. 'I followed the crows.'

She heard the sound of spruce needles brushing against cloth: Benno, Gelfrat and the others had descended and were wading through the trees. Something crunched under her boot. She lifted up the sole: she'd stepped on a finger bone, snapping it. 'We're here!'

She couldn't remember exactly where she'd picked up the emblem, except that it had been in a patch of muddy, treeless ground. As she slipped between spruces, her toe hit a skull, making it roll over. She dropped to her knees and set it respectfully next to its ribcage, which lay nearby and wore torn black-and-yellow. Angelika could hear that some of the others were close by.

'How will we recognise your brother?' she called. 'Or do you mean to haul back all your comrades?'

'Officer's cuffs have gold threading!' Benno shouted. He seemed to be over to her left. 'Failing that, we'll judge by the boots. They were buckled in gold. Their heels bear the mark of Grenzstadt's best cobbler!'

Angelika ducked down to finger the cuffs of the skeleton at her feet. They seemed ordinary enough. She thought it impolitic to mention that she'd taken the gold buckles from a pair of boots, and sold them. If she could remember where she'd found that particular haul, she'd have Claus's remains... She closed her eyes, trying to picture the moment. She'd sat on a large, bench-shaped stone while she'd pried the buckles loose from the boots, and it hadn't been too far from where she'd laid hands on them. 'Look for a boulder, flat enough to sit on!' she shouted.

'Like this?' Franziskus called. She tracked the sound of his voice, parting trees until she found him. He was by the stone, and kneeling over a tunic, which lay in the midst of a pile of scattered bones. Wolves had been at it, or wild pigs, perhaps.

She stood and waved her arms above her head. She could see the top of Gelfrat's head, poking up over the trees around him. 'Over here!' she proclaimed. Gelfrat crashed over to her. After examining her discovery from a distance, he unhooked the scabbard from his belt and used it to jab tentatively at the skull, and tunic. Benno appeared. Gelfrat used the scabbard to lift the ripped and bloodied shirt, and held it up before him. Benno took it and stretched it out. The garment was large; its wearer had been nearly as big as Gelfrat. Benno checked the cuffs.

'That's him,' he said. 'Are the boots here?'

'They're missing,' said Angelika.

Benno subjected her to a prolonged and searching look. She blinked blandly back at him.

'It's Claus, then?' Gelfrat asked.

'It's Claus,' said Benno. The two stood and regarded the bones.

'Well then,' said Angelika.

Gelfrat turned and embarked on a search of the needle-strewn ground around the flat rock.

'So this is him?' Angelika said.

Benno nodded, distractedly.

'Then my payment has now come due.'

'In a moment,' he said. 'You didn't find a... second pair of boots, also with golden buckles?'

'I don't recall saying I found any gold buckles.'

'There is a second officer. We must find his remains as well.' He glanced at Gelfrat, then headed off in the opposite direction, vanishing into the trees.

Beckoning Franziskus to come with her, Angelika slipped gracefully through the little forest. He kept up well, mimicking her stealth. The others still thrashed enthusiastically amongst the spruces, unconscious of their movements. She led Franziskus to the sinkhole's westward edge, then hefted herself up the slope, grabbing onto trunks and branches as she went. Soon her fingers were sticky with their resin.

'Where are we going?' gasped Franziskus.

'Just follow,' she said.

Shouts came from below. She craned her head to see Gelfrat bouncing up and down amid the spruces, shaking his fist. The big man was chasing, but he wasn't agile enough to thread between trees. He kept smacking into them. He ducked to hurl a stone, but it landed wide of them and tumbled back down the incline. Angelika reached the lip of the bowl and gave Franziskus a hand up. Gelfrat was now battling his way up the slope, but for every forward stride he took, he slid half a step back. Angelika yanked on Franziskus's arm and pointed to the hills.

'What are we doing?' asked Franziskus. She did not answer. She ran at full speed across a small stretch of flatland, then bounded up onto an incline of exposed, yellowish rock. Nature had arranged it into a rough set of terraced steps. She leapt from one ledge to the next.

Franziskus scrambled to match her. Blood crashed in his temples; he heard more shouting from below. He did not dare turn around to see if the Averlanders were giving chase, or how close they might be. Above him, Angelika sidestepped into a copse of scraggly pines. She was a blur between trees. He copied her leap and landed, to slide on wet needles. Franziskus pounded after her, as she hit the peak of a ridge and then dropped down past it, disappearing from view. He reached a flat bit of ground, which wound like an overgrown road, hugging a wall of mountain rock. Finally he found her, behind a tall bush with broad and waxy leaves. She was hunched over, with her hands on her knees, and out of breath. Beads of sweat fell from her face to the forest floor. He threw himself against a tree and heaved in cool lungfuls of mountain air. It took him a while to find the power to speak.

'Why – what did we just do? Why did we run?'

'They were lying to us,' she said. 'They weren't there for Claus's sake. Something else is afoot.'

'You misjudge them. They are good and fine soldiers. Better than me.'

'They've deceived us.'

'It's because of the thrashing they gave Ekbert, isn't it? It's turned you unfairly against them. You don't understand –

Honour of the Grave

Benno's commands were harsh but correct. It was Gelfrat who was in the wrong.'

'No, no, it's nothing to do with that. There's another one of them – my guess is another von Kopf – and they think he might still be alive.'

'What?'

'When we found Claus's bones, did it seem to you like they knew what to do with them? For all their talk of taking the body back for proper interment, you'd think they'd have brought a coffin or casket with them. A fine box of inlaid oak, at least. But they had nothing of the kind. And then when they asked about a second pair of buckles...' She paused to stop and breathe again, and to listen for the sounds of pursuit. 'You see, I've been holding back something from them, too.'

'I don't like the sound of this.'

'It wasn't the cawing of crows that took me to the scene of that battle. I'd been following the Averlanders for weeks. I watched them as they drove off a force of orcs three times their number.'

'That disappointed you, I'm sure.'

'They left the battlefield too clean for my tastes, if that's what you mean. I followed them north, keeping a few hours behind them. Then I heard the clanging of swords. In accordance with my usual caution, I stayed well back of the fray. I merely assumed they'd found a new party of orcs to fight. It wasn't until a troop of motley battlers came out from the trees, wiping their swords clean, that I realised they'd been fighting other men. Even then, it never occurred to me they were Prince Davio's irregulars – I'd taken them for common bandits.'

'A fact you chose not to mention to Benno and Gelfrat.'

'To avoid awkward questions. Like: were any of their men still in the midst of dying when I secured their valuables.'

'And were they?'

'The important point is this: late in the skirmish, I saw several of the Averland side get up and run for the hills. Three of them had been playing dead. And one had something glinting on his boots, as he ran.'

'The second set of gold buckles.'

'Which would make him the other officer they seek.'

'And this is why you ran?'

'If it's him they truly want, and we can find traces of his passing, then we can go back and demand a higher price for what we know.'

Franziskus sat down, flourished his cloak around him, and crossed his arms. 'Once more I've made myself a party to dishonour.'

Angelika smacked her hands together, then wiped the sweat from her hair. 'What harm have I done them? I took them to Claus's body, as I'd promised, then departed before they even had the chance to pay me. To me, that sounds like the height of generosity.'

'But you left merely in hopes of extorting greater sums in future.'

She set off to the north. 'You speak in hypotheticals. Who knows? It's unlikely, after so many weeks, but we might even find him in one piece. What would be wrong with that?'

'Now you're speaking rhetorically.'

'This is the way,' she said, eyes on the trail ahead. 'They fled as we did, running up that terraced incline, there – see? – and into these woods. And there's only one way to head from here.' Angelika proceeded slowly, scanning the forest floor, in case she might spot a button on the ground or a tuft of yellow fabric still stuck to a jabbing branch. A finch, his throat adorned in bright red feathers, landed nearby and warbled, showing them the way. After a few minutes, they spotted an upward path, which would lead them higher up into the mountains. It presented them with a choice of routes. 'So, you're a skinny young Imperial officer,' mused Angelika, 'and you've fled into the mountains alongside a couple of soldiers. Do you stay down here in the foothills, or do you keep going up?'

'If I know the men chasing me are out for blood vengeance, I'll take the toughest, most discouraging path.'

'Then up we go.'

The trail terminated at the bottom of an incline made of loose, fist-sized rocks. At the top, Angelika could see a lush stand of tall weeds. She and Franziskus crawled to it like crabs, using their arms and feet to haul themselves up. Every so often, one of them would hit a patch of looser stones, and slide down with them, losing dozens of paces each time. Angelika got to the weeds first, and reached out to grab at their roots.

A thick, stout-fingered hand reached out for her, wrapping itself around her wrist. Its owner pulled her up. Her legs dangled wildly beneath her. Her rescuer was a halfling. With his free hand, he smashed her in the face.

SUSPENDED BY ONE arm, Angelika could not move back to evade the halfling's second blow. It hit her right on the bridge of her nose, just as the first one had. Her vision blurred. She stopped flailing her legs and instead jabbed them in front of her, trying to find something solid to plant them against. A rock sailed in from behind her; Franziskus had thrown it. The halfling ducked, and Angelika wrenched herself free, dropping down onto the loose rocks. She landed on her knees and slid, skidding down the incline past Franziskus, who now had his rapier out. He charged up the slope, but his efforts just loosened more rock, so he remained in one place, showering stones out behind his skidding boots. Angelika's assailant appeared at the plateau's edge, brandishing a fat-headed cudgel of lacquered wood. It was the same halfling who'd assaulted her back at the Castello. He opened his mouth and yowled at Franziskus, who stooped to lob another stone at him. The halfling popped back, disappearing from view.

Franziskus turned to check on Angelika; who'd regained her footing. 'Do we run?'

Angelika crouched to scoop up a rock. 'We need to chat with him,' she said.

The halfling stuck his head up past the weeds. She chucked her stone. It hit with a satisfying thud. The halfling cried out. He yelled obscenities in the halfling tongue – the only words of the language Angelika could recognise – and hurled himself over the ledge onto the rocks. They sprayed out at his point of impact. He shot past Franziskus, who tagged him with his rapier tip, drawing a tiny gash along the back of his weapon-hand. Then he launched himself at Angelika. She moved aside from his bullish charge, but he reached out on the way past and seized a handful of her hair in his fist. He dived, using his momentum to pull her down. She landed on her shoulder blades and elbows. She rolled onto his back and clawed at his leather helmet, hurling it aside. It hit the rocks and bounced to the bottom of the slope. She grabbed onto his ears.

'Not that trick again, girlie,' he grunted, and pushed himself up, knocking her off. He turned to smash her with his cudgel, but she'd already twisted out of the way. He clambered up. A stone hit him in the gut: Franziskus again. The halfling ducked down to claim a rock of his own, but Franziskus got him in the temple with a second lob. He barked like an animal and ran at Franziskus, who had dropped his rapier, to pick up stones. Franziskus hurled two rocks at the halfling in the course of his charge, but both fell short. The halfling swung his cudgel wide, and Franziskus ducked to miss the blow. This left his throat exposed, so the halfling wrapped his hand around it. Franziskus's eyes bugged out.

Angelika leapt on the halfling, a six-pound rock clutched in both hands. She smashed it repeatedly onto the back of the halfling's bony head. After the third blow, the halfling's knees buckled. After the fourth, he released his grip on Franziskus's throat. Between the fifth and sixth, he sank down onto the rocks, face up. His eyes fluttered shut. Moments later, they reopened.

'You should not be conscious,' Angelika said. She raised the rock above his head, ready to crush his windpipe. The halfling weakly waved his hands. 'I give in,' he said.

'Resilient bugger, aren't you?' she said.

'Mother Goatfield didn't raise no weaklings, girlie,' the halfling croaked, spitting foamy drool.

'Your name is Goatfield?'

'Toby Goatfield, not that it matters to you. The name of interest here is Lukas von Kopf.'

'*Lukas* von Kopf?'

'Don't play like you don't know it.' He paused for a fit of choking. 'That's who the Averlanders brought you here to find. And we think you know where he is. He's alive, isn't he?'

'So you came to get your head half caved-in as part of an ingenious ploy to wheedle information from us?'

He sat up. She put a foot on his chest, pushing him back down. He looked at it like he might bite her toes. 'You can arouse me into fits of tumescence all day long, girlie, if that's what you want, but maybe you'd prefer silver instead.'

Franziskus leaned forward to grab at Goatfield's greasy jacket. 'Speak respectfully to the lady, you rancid heap of gutter trash!'

Goatfield wheezed. 'You're pretty, too, boy, though you're not my type.' A satyr's grin bloomed on his wide and battered face. Franziskus lurched up, disgust contorting his features.

'Who do you work for?' demanded Angelika.

The halfling added teeth to his smile. 'It's a secret, but if you lean in and let me smell you, I might just let it slip.'

She kicked him in the groin. He doubled up, knees to chin, and made agonised noises. She waited a while, then kicked him in the behind. 'Ow! Enough torture, girlie! I work for Davio Maurizzi!' He opened an eye, looking up to the top of the slope. Together, Angelika and Franziskus took a step back.

'Do you have confederates up there?' she asked.

'What would make you think that?'

She said to Franziskus: 'He has confederates up there.' She bent down to grab a handful of the halfling's ear and squeezed it like a rag. Tears dripped from the sides of Goatfield's eyes. 'And if we took you to this Lukas, you'd just bash his brains in, wouldn't you?'

'No, no, girlie! If I don't bring him in breathing, I don't get paid!'

'And what does Prince Davio want with him?'

'As you know, the boy's father has been holding a grudge against Maurizzi, and has been killing his mercenaries. I suppose the prince reckons a hostage might change old Jurgen's tune. Your enemy's last surviving legitimate heir – that's a fine catch on any day of the week.'

'So you know Claus is dead?'

'We sifted through his bones, hours before you arrived. That makes Lukas the prize. He's worth more to us than whatever those cheese-paring Averlanders have offered you.'

'How much?'

'If you turn him over to us, we'll double their price.'

'That would be four hundred crowns.'

'A steep figure, but I'm sure the prince is good for it.' He propped himself up on his elbows.

'Why have you persisted in attacking me, then, if you had all this money to persuade me with?'

He coughed, without covering his mouth. 'I respect no one until I've tested them in combat. A habit taught to me by my beautiful mother.'

'A reckless policy.'

'I'll not have you insulting my mother!'

Angelika sighed and let him rise. 'Take us to your friends, then we can work out the details of the exchange.'

Goatfield grinned and smacked his lips. He pointed up at the plateau. 'They're waiting up there for us. You're lucky, my little sweetmeat: for some reason, they failed to come to my aid, even while you so cruelly mishandled me.'

'Perhaps they do not respect us until we test you in combat.'

They tramped laboriously up the incline, cascading more rocks down behind them. They stopped at the top, when they reached the weedy ledge, and turned to look at each other.

'After you,' Angelika told Toby.

'No, girlie – after you.'

Neither moved.

Franziskus strained up, clutching onto the tallest and sturdiest-seeming of the weeds with both hands. He grunted and lurched; Angelika grabbed his legs and pushed on them, sliding back. The halfling stepped in to brace her. Franziskus dragged his torso through the weeds and kicked himself free of Angelika's arms. Then he kneeled to take Angelika by the elbows and haul her up. Goatfield moved to grab her legs, but she muttered and kicked at his head. With Franziskus pulling on her, she wriggled up, face-first into the maze of plants. He drew her to her feet.

They were now standing on a green, boulder-strewn alpine meadow, that seemed to be squeezed by two outcroppings of mountain rock that narrowed toward them. The flatland rose gently for about three hundred yards, terminating in a dense wood of tall pines.

Two figures, who had been sitting opposite one another on the outcroppings, strode easily towards them. On the left, nearest Angelika, came an elf. Pink, unblemished skin covered his angular face. His eyes were the colour of new grass.

Honour of the Grave   75

As he walked, his shoulder-length straw-coloured hair floated out behind him. The elf was clad in a long sheepskin coat, worn over a linen shirt. His hide trousers ended in ermine ruffs; his thin shoes were made of the same material, and laced with rawhide. He smiled at Angelika. In his left hand he held a gleaming sword, five feet long and little more than an inch wide, its blade incised with runes.

Bounding at Franziskus was a second halfling, apparently bald under a cap of iron, which was adorned with a six-inch spike on its crown, and a ring of smaller jabbers which curved up like boar's tusks along its rim. His right eyebrow was black, his left was white; they met in the middle and made war with one another. A wispy moustache, of grey and red hairs intermixed, sprawled across his upper lip, then drooped down on each side, hanging past his jaw. He'd threaded the ends through a series of metal beads, each moulded in the shape of a moaning head. His frame was even broader than Toby Goatfield's; his tight shirt of mail links highlighted the blocky muscles of his chest and arms. He wore mail on his legs, too, but his feet were bare. They had red and densely tufted hair on the top of them; the soles were hardened by least an inch of callus all around. He held a double-bladed war axe, its head more than two feet wide. He curled his lips, revealing inflamed gums in full retreat from a set of crooked, oblong teeth.

Toby, who was still stuck halfway up the ledge, interrupted his struggles to introduce his companions. 'This is Elennath,' he said, meaning the elf, 'and my boon companion, Henty Redpot. Better do as they say.'

Angelika danced back to kick Toby in the face. Screaming various blasphemies, he fell from view, accompanied by the sound of sliding rock.

The elf said something about Angelika surrendering.

Angelika pulled her knife and ran for the trees, shouting for Franziskus to do the same.

Henty lifted his axe above his head and charged at Franziskus. Franziskus dived sideways to miss Henty's blow, and landed hard on his ribs. He rolled out of the path of another. Henty pressed his woody foot down on Franziskus's ankle and brought his axe cleaving down. Franziskus twisted out of the way. The axe sunk deep into loamy soil. Henty yanked at it. Franziskus used his chance to get to his feet and run. Henty roared.

Elennath, meanwhile, pursued Angelika nimbly. He leapt over boulders, his hair flowing behind him. Clasping his hands together around the hilt of his sword, he dived at Angelika's back. His swordpoint caught only air, but he landed on Angelika's legs, bringing her down. Her chin struck a rock. Her knife hit the ground and bounced. He'd lost hold of his weapon too now, so he crawled onto her back, to reach out for her knife. She elbowed him in the eye and managed to flip over onto her back.

Franziskus ran for the pines. Henty chased him. Blindly, Angelika patted grass, searching for her knife. Elennath grabbed her wrist and twisted it. He seized her knife and drew it back to strike at her throat.

Franziskus, fleeing Henty, saw this. He changed direction, curving toward Angelika, Henty at his heels.

Angelika's weaker hand found a thick branch. She swung it, deflecting Elennath's stab. The blade grazed her hip, slicing a hole in her tunic.

Belatedly, Franziskus drew his sword. He flourished it, swiping it through the air in the classic *intimidación* pattern he'd been taught by his duelling master. Henty's eyes followed its progress until Franziskus had the manoeuvre halfway completed. Then he swiped with his axe in a backhand, bending Franziskus's rapier in half and sending it thudding into the weeds.

The weeds by the ledge shook. Toby's head and arms appeared. Angelika's eyes widened. Elennath looked back. Angelika leapt into the air, knife outstretched, and brought it down. Its tip cut left to right across the surface of Elennath's face, leaving a red diagonal line that stretched from his hairline, over the bridge of his sublime and narrow nose, all the way to his jawbone. His hand went to his face. Angelika ducked down, grabbed a rock, and lobbed it at Toby. A thud. Toby disappeared, yowling.

Henty punched Franziskus in the chest, making him reel. Henty punched him in the mouth then leaned in and recovered his axe. Franziskus ran for the trees.

Angelika saw him and broke for the trees, too.

Franziskus was the first to get there. He scrambled up the side of a pine. Angelika reached the woods. She turned to hack at Elennath, whose coat and shirt were now spackled with his blood. He easily skipped around her blows.

Henty rushed in, axe raised. Angelika skidded, filling the air with brown pine needles, and tripped the massive halfling. Henty flipped nose-first into the trunk of Franziskus's tree. Elennath sliced his curving blade in at the prone Angelika. 'My face!' he shrieked. A dazed Henty fell back onto Angelika's side. Elennath's dagger-point slammed into the mail shirt protecting Henty's ribs. Henty groaned. Angelika groaned. Elennath raised the dagger for another strike, then saw that its point had snapped off.

Franziskus jumped from the tree, kicking Elennath in the temple and knocking the elf down, before landing on him. He twisted Elennath's elven hair in his fist, then smacked its owner's face into a tree trunk until he went limp.

He turned and saw that Angelika and Henty had both disengaged, and were on their hands and knees, trembling and puffing. Henty's spiked helm had fallen off his head, revealing a sparse coating of coarse red fuzz. Angelika shot a steadying hand out to grip a tree trunk, and forced herself to her feet. Henty moaned and did the same, teetering in place. Franziskus weaved up behind him. Henty angled himself in Franziskus's direction but could only gape at him with open-mouthed resignation. Franziskus seized one of his shoulders. Stumbling, Angelika grabbed the other. She placed a hand on the back of Henty's fuzzy head. Together, they smashed his face into the nearest pine tree, twice. His eyes rolled up and his legs went slack. He had only reached his knees when all signs of consciousness abandoned him.

Franziskus put a finger to the halfling's neck; a vigorous pulse still coursed through him. Angelika checked the elf – he too was alive.

The elf had a heavy pack on his back. She hauled it off him and forced its rusty buckles open. Inside was a small crossbow. She handed it to Franziskus. 'Do you know how to work one of these?'

Absently, he slipped a bolt in place, stuck his foot in the stirrup, and cranked on the crannequin. 'Passably. My friends and I toyed with such a bow, one summer, out of childish curiosity.' The world was wavering before him still; he wiggled the furrows of his forehead.

Digging deeper into the pack, Angelika found what she really wanted: a fat loop of cord. It was rawhide, and there were many feet of it. 'Seems like they expected to catch themselves a prisoner,' she said, taking her knife to cut off a suitable length of it. She wrapped it around Henty, who was still propped against the tree.

'Is it wise to spare these blackguards?' Franziskus asked. He had finished cranking the bow and held it up in firing position, squinting. He had it pointed at a large burl in a tree, which would make an acceptable target for practice.

'Are you saying we should slay defenceless foes? I'm surprised at you.'

'They're common cutthroats, to whom the laws of mercy do not apply.'

Toby Goatfield stepped into the forest and advanced holding a dagger held above his head. Franziskus spun round and aimed from the hip. He shot the bolt through the palm of Toby's weapon-hand and into a tree, fixing him to it. Goatfield looked at the wound and fainted. As he fell the bolt popped from the bark.

'Nice shot,' Angelika said.

'Thank you,' said Franziskus.

'Leaving them alive might delay the Kopfs, if they come this way,' said Angelika. 'They'll want to untie them and ask some questions. With any luck, a further melee will ensue.' She and Franziskus leaned Toby against the tree and tied him up, then did the same with Elennath. Franziskus found Elennath's elven sword and claimed it as a replacement for his ruined rapier. Angelika retrieved her lost knife. As they readied themselves to depart, Franziskus took the crossbow and bashed it into a tree, smashing it to bits.

'What did you do that for?' she asked him.

'It is not a weapon suitable for a gentleman,' he replied.

CHAPTER FOUR

ANGELIKA HAD TO admit they lacked a plan and that their movements were essentially aimless. They tramped through the alpine wood, in search of higher elevations. They moved through tangled brush, along a narrow natural terrace between slopes. The pines crowded thickly together, as if mocking their scrappier, more tenacious cousins, who clung to the rocky slopes both above and below them. They were choosing the easiest paths, simply because they were easy. As they travelled, she occupied her mind by devising various scathing comments which she could direct at Franziskus for destroying a piece of equipment as useful and valuable as a crossbow.

'Lukas's movements would have been aimless, too,' Angelika said. 'I know this terrain a little, whereas he grew up in privilege in some estate in Averheim.'

'He had a pair of soldiers with him, though. They might know how to survive in the pass.'

She stopped. There was forest to the left of them, to the right, at the front and at the back. 'So where did they go?'

'I'd look for a cave, and search for a route higher in the peaks.'

She held her hand up. 'Wait. Can you hear that?' She paused, to let Franziskus listen.

'No, what?'

'Running water. That's where they'd stop, if they were here at all. They'd refill their waterskins, and maybe wait to catch any game that came to drink at the brook.'

They followed the sound and, about a quarter of an hour later, found a stream flowing through a shallow groove of rock. They walked west along its stony banks until they reached a sheltered spot where the water widened out into a pool. A waterfall filled the pool from above; the surrounding rock, large and flat, made an obvious spot to camp. Franziskus refilled their skins as Angelika inspected the rock, then the bush around it. She waved Franziskus over.

'Here's where they camped,' she said, pointing at the ground. Franziskus couldn't understand what he was meant to see – to him there was nothing more than pine needles. 'They covered their tracks – as you'd do if you thought you were being chased – but this is where the fire was. And here.' She kicked at a pile of leaves and dead branches, uncovering some strips of torn clothing that had deep brown stains soaked into the fibres. 'Bandages. That's what tells me it was them, and not just any group of woodsmen or foragers. At least one of them was wounded.'

'But there is nothing here that proves it was Lukas and his companions.'

'What do you expect, that he'd carve his family crest on a tree?'

'It still seems doubtful. We should return to the Castello, and seek honest labour.'

She bounded up to the hill beside the waterfall. It was scarred with vertical slashes of mud, where the underbrush had been scraped away. 'Someone made their way up this hill. Not so recently, though – you can see shoots coming up inside the marks. Those tracks could easily be eight weeks old. We've found our trail!' Using saplings and bushes as handholds, she made her way up the treacherous hill.

Franziskus took a tentative hop up onto the slope, then slid back. The coating of damp needles below his feet made this just as hard to climb as the rockslide. 'Aren't you still hurting from that fight?' he called up at her.

'Only in my shoulders, elbows, knees, chin, calves, my scalp, and my innards, and the part of my skull that joins my nose to my forehead. Let's go.'

'I got a hit a few times, too.'

She lost her footing and slid, making a fresh mark on the hillside, nearly a yard long. 'You're not saying that all it takes to break you is an elf and a couple of halflings?'

'They have two months' start on us, we can afford to stop and rest for a few hours.'

'The question is, how much of a head start do we have on Benno and Gelfrat?'

'A salient point,' said Franziskus, redoubling his efforts. By scrabbling quicker, he found it easier to keep from slipping. Hands perched on hips, Angelika waited for him on a ledge, above. Water dropped down, hitting the rocky shelf she was standing on. It splattered into a shallow depression, where it collected then overflowed into the brook. The water hammered down past a chunk of sheer rock more than twice Angelika's height. It reminded her a little of a face, with two deep-set eyes and a leering mouth. She tested it for handholds, but it was wet, and slippery with moss. They would have to skirt the streambed, and head off to the north slightly, where the going was less steep. Franziskus reached her side. She showed him where they'd have to go: a tangle of thorny briars, stunted spruce, and convoluting pines.

Franziskus frowned at the forbidding vegetation. 'Do you truly think this is the path they'd choose? Wouldn't they look for something easier?'

'They might climb down again, and stick to the lower woods,' she mused. 'But look.' She pointed to a strip of yellow fabric that was tied to a bare and crooked pine branch, about twenty yards over and thirty yards up. 'Someone passed this way.'

She jumped down from the wet rock, into a mess of dead, dry weeds. They climbed through the brambles, stopping periodically to untangle their clothing from barbs and prickles. After nearly an hour of heavy exertion, the terrain flattened out again. On this plateau, the trees were straighter, the bright new growths at the end of each branch longer and healthier. Over on the rocks was another pool; alert grasses rose tall around it, through gaps between sheets of stone. Franziskus patted the ground to see how dry it was, then stretched out on it, with his head to one side and his mouth panting open. Angelika sat with a piece of fallen timber as her backrest.

They heard a snuffling sound. Angelika straightened up. 'What was that?'

'I didn't...'

They listened – nothing.

Angelika relaxed. 'An animal, I suppose.'

A branch snapped. She jumped up. So did Franziskus. They put their backs together defensively. He drew Elennath's sword; she, her knife.

They held their breath and listened to the distant chirping of birds, and the waterfall booming into the pool below.

'Why do my guts suddenly gyrate?' asked Franziskus.

'I don't know,' she whispered. She did not admit that she shared the feeling.

Her ears popped. Her tongue tasted metallic.

'Something is wrong,' Franziskus said.

'Sssh.' The backs of her hands felt hot suddenly; they had turned red and blotchy. She checked Franziskus's hands; they were the same. 'Franziskus, in your travels, have you ever encountered Chaos?'

'No,' he said. Not long ago, they'd run into an undead thing, but he didn't think undead counted. Chaos was a force people talked about, at night, when it was time to tell scary stories. It was not a thing a good person could speak of, with any certain knowledge. It was especially not a thing you were supposed to meet up with, even when you were deep in a mountain wood. 'It might only be sorcery,' he said.

'Oh, only sorcery! That's all right, then!' Angelika's knife shook nervously. She tightened her muscles and shouted into the bush. 'If you're going to come, come!'

She heard a dry, rattling laugh. It seemed to be coming from just over her shoulder. 'Do you see anything, Franziskus?'

'No.' A gust of wind came and tossed grit in their faces, it seemed to be blowing in all directions at once.

'I spit on the gods and minions of Chaos!' called Angelika. 'A pack of pustulated cowards, that's what you are! I dare you to stand and face us!'

An object rolled from the trees. Thinking it might be a bomb, they ran from it, and hid between some trees. The object lost its momentum and bounced to a stop about fifteen feet from where they'd been. It was not a bomb.

'It's someone's head,' Franziskus said.

Though it was hard to tell without looking closely, Angelika did have experience with dead bodies, and parts of them, in various stages of decay. This one seemed human, and it had been dead for three weeks, give or take. She was in no hurry to confirm her suppositions by poking it from up close.

'We must flee,' Franziskus whispered.

Something made a snorting noise. They turned to see a grey shape dashing their way. It stood upright, like a man, and had a man's torso and arms. But its head was like a mountain ram's, with two hooked horns rising from the middle of it. From each horn, on threads of fibrous pink flesh, hung unblinking eyeballs. They bobbled erratically as the creature lurched in to swipe at Franziskus's head with a crude wooden club in its human-like fist. Franziskus ducked. The club smashed bark and green wood from the pine behind him. Franziskus dodged. It opened its mouth, and foggy breath rolled over them. It stank, making their eyes water.

'Beastman!' Angelika shouted, identifying her enemy. The beastmen were the most common, and lowliest, of all the Chaos gods' servitors. They walked like men, but wore the faces and hides of animals. They had other powers, besides. That was all she knew of the things.

The beastman swung the club downwards at Angelika. She capered out of the way, but the weapon managed to graze her ankle, sending pain shooting through her foot and up into the bones of her leg.

It feinted at her. Finally it occurred to Angelika to use the weapon in her hand. Franziskus hadn't tried a strike with his sword, either.

'Die!' Angelika screamed, and pitched forward, both hands wrapped around her knife-hilt. The creature swiped at her but missed. She lost her balance, nearly colliding with a tree.

Franziskus lunged tentatively, but it was as if he had to struggle against the wind to get at the creature. It was his fear of Chaos that was holding him back, he concluded. He clenched his teeth, shook himself, and pointed his sword-tip at the creature. Then he jerked forward, but involuntarily caught himself short. The beastman turned and bared its goaty teeth at him. Franziskus felt his mouth go dry.

Angelika ran shrieking at it, dagger held double-handed, and this time she hit it, catching it just below its sternum. She felt her dagger bite through a tough wall of hair and muscle, then plunge more readily into innards and viscera. She tore all the way down to the beastman's gut, then withdrew her knife. It was thickly coated in dripping blood, as were her hands and arms, right up to the elbows.

The beastman, gutted, wobbled before them. Crimson chunks of flesh fell out of it, like sailors leaping from a sinking ship.

'You're not so tough, are you?' said Angelika.

Like tentacles, severed intestines shot from the creature's gaping body, and wrapped themselves around her. Two of them encircled her throat, trying to strangle her. They seized both her wrists, and slurped bloodily around her waist. Franziskus recoiled, and shielded his face with his arms. Angelika summoned the last of her breath to blurt out, 'Snap out of it! Hit it!' Then she succumbed to blackness.

The monster hopped up and down ecstatically as it squeezed the life from Angelika. Franziskus saw Angelika's face turning blue. He leapt up and, with the tip of his sword, speared her attacker through its right eye. Jelly popped from the eye and oozed onto the blade. The beastman turned to see Franziskus shuffling to keep his hands on the hilt of the rune-incised sword he'd liberated from Elennath. The creature hissed at the blade, and backed away from it.

Franziskus took a moment to theorise that the runes spelled some kind of elven charm inimical to Chaos. Then he shouted, shouldering all his weight into the sword hilt. He forced the blade in. He felt resistance when the tip reached the bone at the back of the beastman's skull, but a moment later it fell forward, as it punched through. The sword now skewered the monster's head entirely. A gobbet of still-pulsing brain matter dangled briefly from the tip, before dropping to the forest floor. The intestines constricting Angelika lost their vigour. They slid limply off her, leaving gelatinous trails of gore on her skin and clothing. Franziskus pulled the sword out. The beastman staggered, its hoofed feet stamping in a jagged half-circle. It turned its antlers to fix Franziskus in the gaze of their eyeballs.

It roared and lurched at him, weakly waggling its deflated viscera. Franziskus slashed at its neck. It spun around, spraying blood on the trees.

Angelika coughed and wiped her hands on the tails of her tunic. She launched herself upwards and stumbled behind the creature, gasping and wracked with pain. She felt herself blacking out again, then realised that she was still fighting the thing; it was as if she was propelled by instinct alone. It thrashed; she held onto it. She grabbed one of its horns with both hands and let her legs fly free, so that she became a dead weight. She heard a thud and was dimly aware that she'd hit the forest floor. Her eyes blinked. She'd pulled it down with her. She willed her reluctant hand to seize her boot-knife. Then she fell forward, and stabbed her weapon deep into the Chaos thing's neck. Its body went slack; she stepped aside to let it fall prone. It had stopped moving, but she hacked its head off anyway, just to be safe, then pitched it far from the body.

She floundered off, away from Franziskus, to double over and retch. But even though she felt sick, nothing would come up. Finally, leaning against one another, they took fear-drunk steps to the stream, which proved easy to reach from this elevation. They splashed chill water on their faces and sat on the cold damp rock.

Franziskus was the first to find words. 'We've got to leave here, at once.'

'We didn't go through *that*, just to turn tail and slink off.'

'If Chaos is here, it is certain that Lukas has long since been devoured. We must also assume that there are more here, and that they'll soon be upon us, to exact revenge for the one we've slain. We must go, at speed!'

'We need to check if the head it tossed at us matches what we know of Lukas. If so, we'll go.'

'No, we must flee, regardless. These are not Averlandish soldiers, or halfling mercenaries. This is Chaos!'

'We killed that one, didn't we? It didn't seem to like your elven sword.'

'We're lucky to be breathing!'

She ducked her head into the pool, then shook it, sending drops of water in all directions. 'To save a noble's son from Chaos creatures – can you imagine the reward for a deed like that?'

'Your brain is still addled, from the strangulation.' He cast a nervous glance at the woods.

'He might still be alive.'

Franziskus twisted around to face her. 'By the gods, I think I understand. That rescue instinct of yours – it has come upon you again, hasn't it?'

Her shoulders indignantly straightened. 'Now that's a load of rot!'

'Why else would you, of all people, be so intent on confronting Chaos? Suddenly, for no good reason, you intend to risk your skin for some fellow you don't even know. As you did with me!'

'You're the one who's addled,' she said, marching toward the severed head. 'Which side of my supposedly contradictory personality are you arguing with, anyway?'

'In this instance, not even the most stringent code of valour would command a pair of ill-armed persons with no experience in these dark affairs, to get themselves in a fight against Chaos.'

'I agree that proving one's valour is foolish. Fortunately, that is not my aim.'

THEY STOOD AT the foot of a trail that wound circuitously up to what looked like a cave, two-thirds of the way up one of the range's lower peaks. For much of its length, the trail was a groove through the rock – currently dry, but cut by the rushing waters of a million spring melts. At other points, it became a ledge that wound precariously around the mountain. The higher it got, the more gaps appeared in it. A persistent, screaming wind dusted the path with snow from the surrounding summits.

'I did not mean to suggest that you were wrong,' Franziskus said. 'I merely express regret that you are right.'

'You saw it, too,' Angelika said. 'That spoor over there, it could only have been the steaming dung of a Chaos beast.'

'Indeed.'

'And if I were a Chaos beast, and wanted to keep a captive to torment, and eventually eat, that cave up there would be my lair.'

'Which of us do you seek to convince?'

'You can stay here, if you want.'

'This is still the very peak of folly,' Franziskus replied, 'but I won't wait down here while you get yourself killed or captured.'

She leapt into the empty streambed. Only a thin layer of sand, interspersed with sharp pebbles, covered its naked rock. Embedded in the stone beside her, Angelika saw the shell of an ancient scallop, turned to stone by unknown magic. The trail was far from straight. It zigzagged, as the spring floodwaters did each year, following the route of least resistance, and seeking out the weakest veins of rock to slowly buff. It was steep at first, but then it evened out, as it curved around to the other side of the peak. Angelika and Franziskus had lost sight of both their original vantage point, and their destination.

'Are you sure this is all part of the same trail?' he asked her.

'How would I be sure of that?'

Clopping sounds emanated from above. They froze. It was just a quartet of mountain goats – real ones this time, not Chaos hybrids. The animals, which Angelika knew were called chamois, gazed curiously down at them from a small ledge that bore the only decent patch of grass. The three adults went back to their grazing, but there was a kid, too, and its dark, wet eyes followed their progress until they wended out of its sight.

When the upper reach of the path doubled past them, they stopped to breathe and rest. Angelika checked for likely handholds as she considered the possibility of scaling the vertical rock that separated the bends in the trail. At the very least, they'd be in for twenty-five feet of clambering. The time they would gain wasn't worth the risk of a fall. Though she felt ready to take on a dozen Chaos creatures, her sense of exuberance had not made her stupid, or hungry for unnecessary danger.

Half an hour later, they reached a point of heavy going, where the steep groove gave way to a narrow ledge that curled around the mountainside. There were several places, she could see, where they would have to press their backs to the rock and inch along sideways. But first they would have to leap a five-foot gap, and there was no space to get a run at it. Without alerting Franziskus, she took her standing jump. She landed a bit too close to the edge. She tottered, but regained her balance. Her heart thumped. She tried to compose herself as she slid along the ledge to give Franziskus room for his own jump. He took a deep breath, closed his eyes briefly in prayer. When he opened them, he made the leap perfectly. She suppressed the urge to mock his superstitious devotion to gods. Though she doubted his pious murmurings would do them any good, she found herself, at her present elevation, readier than usual to believe in the benevolence of gods. On the off-chance that they did pay kind attention to the laughable doings of the ant-like mortals they surveyed from above, it would serve no purpose to antagonise them.

The two of them made slow progress along the ledge. With each step, Angelika's elation ebbed away from her. By the time they had embarked on the final circuit around the peak, she found her senses returning to her. Franziskus was right. This was madness. They would find nothing of Lukas von Kopf except bones, cracked open and stripped of marrow. And if they did succeed in finding him and getting him down, there was no guarantee of securing a reward commensurate with the hazards of the task. What had possessed her? Perhaps the Chaos minions had burrowed their way into her mind, luring her onwards to become their snack. Or maybe she had only wanted to play the contrarian, to do whatever would most shock Franziskus. He was clearly a dangerous person to have around. She swore she would lose him for good, as soon as they got down off this damnable mountain.

But...

To admit she was wrong and reverse course – that she couldn't do.

She pressed on.

Rock gave way under her front foot. It crashed down the mountainside. Franziskus had her, his arms wrapped around her ribcage. He pulled her up. Her legs swung in mid-air. He staggered back. The foot closest to the ledge was edging off it, but he corrected himself. He backed up enough to set her down. She planted her feet, and recaptured her balance.

He still had his arms around her. His hands crossed at her breastbone.

'So this is what you've been waiting for all this time,' she said.

'What?'

'An opportunity to grasp me by the bosom.'

Now he let go, twitching his hands as if to shake off any residue of lustful thinking. 'I got hold of you below the – below the – area in question. I was most careful of that.'

She tried to get eye contact, but he wouldn't cooperate. 'Are you telling me,' she asked, 'that you paused, in that crucial moment – where the smallest slice of a second could make the difference between my survival or my falling hundreds of feet to find myself squashed flatter than a griddlecake – that you frittered away a precious instant to make sure your hands did not graze on an inch of teat?'

'Stop it!' he said.

'Stop what?'

'Your unseemly teasing.' He put a hand up before her face. 'If we are to succeed together as soldiers of fortune, I must put aside any notion that you belong to the fairer sex.'

'Ah, I see,' she said, leaping the gap made by the collapsing ledge. She landed, and reminded herself to breathe again. 'You are saying that I am no woman at all.'

He leapt the gap abruptly, recklessly. Rocks fell under his heels. Angelika grabbed his forearms and yanked him in her direction. He found his footing. Through no design of hers, his face was pressed into her chest.

'Such a statement would be insupportable,' his muffled voice said, 'in the face of contrary evidence.'

She pushed him off her. Another good reason to get rid of him: he was beginning to get the last word in.

They inched their way up the narrow pathway. Over the course of two slow and anxious hours, they circumnavigated the peak one final time. As they made the final turn, back to the face where the cave would be found, Angelika noticed that Franziskus's teeth chattered. She composed a jibe on the subject, but abandoned it when she realised that hers were doing the same.

The final stretch of trail was the least forgiving of all. Angelika and Franziskus had long since left the stream system behind. Now they faced thirty feet of downward-sloping ledge that ended in front of the cave. Its mouth hung about fifteen feet lower than where they were now. The incline would make it easier to stumble and slip off into nothingness. They studied the narrow ledge for a long time. Angelika steeled herself and wiped sweat from her palms.

A rumble erupted from the cave. To Angelika's ears, it sounded like a rockfall at first, but as it went on, growing loud enough to vibrate in her chest, it took on an animal quality that reminded her of disturbed bowels. Any creature that could make a noise like that would have to be very large.

Intertwined with this sound was another: higher in pitch, and more intermittent. It was a human sound, one of distress. There was someone still alive in there.

'Just kill me and be done with it!' the voice cried. Despite its airy pitch, the voice was definitely a man's. Even in its anguish, the precision of its consonants and the lofty lilt of its vowels were unmistakable. It screamed in the accent of an Imperial noble.

Angelika edged ahead. The ledge groaned under her feet, threatening to give way. The sound of cracking rock would have been loud enough to hear inside the cave, if it had not been drowned out by the guttural yammering. There seemed to be words in the jibbering. Angelika could not make out what the creature was saying, but supposed it must be replying to its prisoner's complaints. She thought she detected amusement, or even laughter, in the noise, but did not feel qualified to make judgments where Chaos minions were concerned. Who knew if they had emotions as the mortal races understood them?

She halted her advance. A tripwire of thin, cured animal gut had been strung across the cave mouth. It was stretched taut between two iron pegs, which had been pounded into the stone itself. The line of gut ran from the peg furthest from her into the depths of the cave. Angelika inched close enough to peer inside. She felt Franziskus signalling her to stay back, but she had no time to bother with his objections.

It was dark, unsurprisingly, but she could make out a large object that hung from the ceiling in some kind of net. Angelika saw the creature, but it took her a while to understand what she was seeing. The creature was big – perhaps ten feet tall – and round, with an enormous, scaly belly. The beast stood on stubby legs and waved long, ropy arms that were covered with coarse, dung-matted hair. Its back was also covered in the same hair. Long, black, curving claws extended from each of its foreshortened fingers. Luckily for Angelika, the creature's face pointed away from her. Its shadow fell on the cave wall, in profile; she made out a pronounced forehead ridge and a bearish snout. Long, pointy fangs protruded from the snout – or perhaps it was just a trick of the light. At any rate, the thing held a large section of pine trunk that had its limbs gnawed off and was bleeding resin. The creature was using it to poke roughly at the hanging bundle. Another cry arose, and Angelika realised that it came from the net. The creature had its prisoner suspended from the cave roof and was jabbing at him with the uprooted tree. Based on the size of the arm – and now she saw a stunted foot, with warty yellow skin, like a rooster's, but belonging to some far-off branch of the animal kingdom – based on what she saw, she figured that the creature might well be fifteen feet tall, and weigh what? A ton? Two tons? Three?

By comparison, the goat-thing had been an opponent for novices.

She turned to Franziskus. They were in no position to plan; the creature would hear them.

And they couldn't just rush in and attack it. All she had was a knife. If she survived this, she would learn to use a weapon with a longer reach.

She became conscious of a need to empty her bladder.

Dots of snow dusted down from further up the peak; they did nothing to cool her blazing forehead.

She reached out and grabbed the tripwire, twanging it like the string of a lute. Then she held it taut. As she'd suspected, there was the sound of a squeaky pulley spinning. This was followed by a crash. The cave mouth billowed dust and sand, as the creature came lunging out of it. It was as large as she'd figured. Its head was halfway between that of a bear and a pike or other toothy fish, with a huge and gaping mouth. Angelika, gut cord still in hand, jerked it outward. It pulled against one of the behemoth's rooster-skinned legs, knocking it off balance. The creature, expecting foes to be in front of its snapping jaws but not to its side, turned, wrapping the cord around its ankle. Angelika gave it a final tug, increasing her leverage by letting herself fall backwards, trusting Franziskus to catch her. The creature rolled from the ledge.

It bounced like an enormous ball down the side of the mountain. It hit an out-jutting rock, and exploded in a shower of slime and dark blood. As it smashed into a lower level of the trail, it broke a new gap in it, and splashed ichor down the mountainside. The ball of gore, fur and hide continued to roll until it was out of sight.

Franziskus held Angelika under the arms. He had caught her without hesitation. 'I will remark wittily on this at a later time,' he said.

She muttered and freed herself from his grip, though not so carelessly as to follow the monster off the side of the mountain. She moved to the edge of the cave. 'You in there! Are there any more beastmen?'

'Who calls me?'

'Answer my question!'

'Is this a trick?'

'Are there more beastmen in there?'

'Did my father send you?'

She looked back to address Franziskus. 'How do they manage to raise you all to be so stupid?'

CHAPTER FIVE

ANGELIKA DROPPED DOWN into the cave. She kept her knife out, ready to receive an attacker. Her eyes adjusted. The cave was smaller than she'd anticipated. Looking for other ways in, she saw only a narrow fissure at the back of the cave, through which she was not sure if it was possible to squeeze. Nothing else moved, except for the individual bundled up and gently swinging in the net above her head. She squinted to see how he was fastened there. The creature had used more gut string to create an elaborate lattice between several iron pegs that were spiked into the chamber's flattish ceiling. The net hung from the centre of this web of gut. On tiptoes, Angelika contemplated how exactly it could be cut down. She called Franziskus in. He entered the cave preceded by his drawn sword.

'Are there any more of them?' he asked her.

'Good question,' Angelika said. 'Are there more Chaos spawn?' she asked the prisoner in the net, in a low, hissing voice. The presumed Lukas von Kopf did not answer. 'Hey!' she said. Still no reply. She squinted at him. 'I can see you're awake. I saw you blink, just now.' She jumped up to paw at the net, sending it gently swinging. It was a difficult thing to do; the lowest part of Lukas dangled about nine feet from the stone floor of the small cavern. 'Don't make me find a rock to pitch at you,' she whispered.

'Do not presume to touch me!' said Lukas, paying no special heed to the volume of his voice. 'I have been poked and prodded quite enough!'

'Then answer my questions! There's no one else in here, is there?'

'I have not seen anyone but the beast for weeks – unless you count Thomas, there.'

'Thomas?' Franziskus peered into the shadows. His foot bumped against something. He knelt to feel what it was. He scudded back into the sunlight, his face wrinkled in revulsion.

'I take it you've found Thomas,' Angelika said.

'What remains of him.'

Angelika spoke up at Lukas: 'Was Thomas one of the men you fled with?'

'He disappointed me bitterly. He was supposed to be an experienced soldier. Yet he couldn't protect me from the beast, could he?'

'He's addled,' Angelika said to Franziskus.

'I heard that!' An inappropriate giggle worked its way through the prisoner's tone of outrage.

Franziskus looked up and spoke in a low and soothing voice. 'If you could hear yourself, Lukas, you would agree that reason has abandoned you. This Thomas person had no chance of protecting you from a thing such as that. In addition, you direct misplaced umbrage at us, we are your rescuers.'

Angelika moved Franziskus aside. 'This is foolish. We'll sweet-talk him back to sanity later. Lukas, we're getting you down from there.'

The prisoner pitched around in the net, increasing the violence of its swings back and forth. 'Not until you identify yourselves!'

'We don't need your permission; all we need to do is cut that rope.' Angelika moved back for a better look at the lattice of cords. She inspected the cavern for something to stand on. As part of her search, she kicked aside Thomas's meatless ribs. She found nothing, save for the tree trunk the creature had used as a poker. She thought for a moment that they might stick a blade on the end of it, but when she tried to lift it, she realised that it was much too heavy for that. 'I suppose I shouldn't be surprised,' she said, 'that a monster fifteen-feet tall would keep a lair without stepladders. Well then,' she called up at Lukas, 'you're just going to have to get yourself down. I'm going to pass you a knife. Use it to hack that main cord. We'll make sure we catch you. Here.' She held the knife up as far as she could reach. But it still wasn't close enough. 'Franziskus, boost me.' He stuck his knee out for her to stand on, like a man pledging his troth. She stepped up onto the proffered leg, balancing herself by placing her empty hand on top of Franziskus's blond-tressed head. She poked the hilt of the dagger up through the net, where Lukas's pink hand was curled. Lukas did not respond. 'Take the knife!' she shouted, losing her balance. She leapt down from Franziskus's knee, then got back up on it again. She stuck the knife up. 'Have your muscles atrophied, Lukas?'

'As I said, I'll not assist you until you tell me who you are,' he said, his conviction noticeably faltering. He lapsed into a frantic pant, then spoke from the side of his mouth. 'It's all a trick, isn't it? You haven't really fallen off the mountain, have you?' He seemed to be addressing the beast. 'It's another of your illusions!'

Angelika jumped off Franziskus's leg; he got up. 'I assure you,' she said, 'neither of us is remotely illusionary.'

Lukas swung silently.

'And what do you think will happen to you if we leave?' yelled Angelika. 'The creature must have fed you, or you'd have starved by now.'

'He nourished me on a hideous mush of berries, goat fat, and fermented leaves.'

'Fattening you up like a liver-goose, I reckon.'

'I wanted to die! Yet I could not resist even that damnable food!'

'How long do you think he can dangle there, Franziskus, without food or water?'

'To speculate precisely would be gruesome,' Franziskus said. 'But it's a fate I wouldn't envy.'

'Even if I faced the blackest of villains, I would want down from that net. I'd think I'd have a better chance out of it than in it.'

Lukas breathed for a while. 'This isn't a trick?'

'No, it is not.'

'Then I suppose it's safe to pass me the knife.'

She hoisted herself up on Franziskus's knee once again, and this time Lukas poked his fingers out through the netting to take the knife. Angelika fought a smirk off her face, as Lukas bounced around like a ham in a sack, struggling to stand inside the net.

'Perhaps you should steady him,' Franziskus said, offering his knee once more. She balanced awkwardly on him, grabbing Lukas's feet with her outstretched hand. Now we all look equally foolish, she thought. Her muscles ached by the time Lukas had the tough cord even halfway sawed through, and Franziskus was shaking from the strain. So she hoisted herself up, grabbing onto Lukas's foot with her other hand. Then she stepped away from Franziskus and into thin air. With her weight added to Lukas's, the half-sawn cord snapped, sending the net and young nobleman plummeting to the ground. She tried to roll, but he landed on her stomach anyway. She grunted in pain and doubled over. Lukas attempted to stand, but his feet were still on the net. He had the knife in his hand, as if poised for attack. Franziskus moved behind him, to help free him from the mesh, but he spun, jabbing the knife point out. The net twisted around his ankles and he fell. Franziskus moved to let him fall face-first. The knife skidded across the cave floor. Franziskus retrieved it and sat on Lukas's netted back, as if he were a bench.

'Listen, my friend,' he said. 'This is most undignified. I am Franziskus, late of Stirland. This is Angelika, who saved my life from orcs. We have come to save *your* life, which we can only do if you catch immediate hold of your senses. So end your silly wriggling, stop treating us like we plan to skin you, and let us get you free of this thing.'

'You are mercenaries?'

'Do I need to sit on you any longer?'

'No,' he said, in a meek and childish way. Franziskus got off him. Angelika, who was leaning against the cavern wall, gave her companion a nod of approval. She came forward, and the two of them untangled the netting from Lukas.

He was revealed to be a pale, bone-thin boy of no more than fifteen. His upper lip was thin and white; the lower, fat and pink. Dried food was caked on his chin and the corners of his mouth. His thin nose turned up at the end to reveal a pair of flaring nostrils. Jet-black hair cascaded greasily onto his forehead and shoulders. A long strand trailed across his face, like a scar; he flicked it away nervously, but it fell back to where it was. He wore the yellow-and-black of an Averlandish regiment, but both tunic and leggings were torn and spattered with dirt, gruel, blood and dung. His dark eyes darted from Angelika to Franziskus, then back again.

'It must be a terrifying thing, to be held in a beastman's clutches, for so long,' Franziskus said. Angelika could tell he wanted to give the younger boy a reassuring pat on the shoulder, but knew better than to startle him. 'A lesser fellow would have lost his mind utterly, by now.'

The boy nodded, warily.

'It's no wonder you can't tell friend from foe. But you must rely on us, to get you down from here. It's a tortuous trek down, so you must gather all your wits for it.'

'How did the monster get you here in the first place?' Angelika enquired.

'We were attacked down in the hills, near a stream. It seemed like there were dozens of them – some like mountain goats, others like wolves – and then came the biggest of them all, that made the ground shake when he walked. Thomas and Erik – another companion – fought off some of them, but they did not prevail. Erik was carried off.'

Only briefly did Angelika consider mentioning their encounter with Erik's head. 'This was right after you fled that battle?'

He sniffed, dragging the back of his hand under his nose. 'We camped, down below, for a number weeks. I had to decide what to– ' He coughed. He squinted at her, appraisingly. He cleared his throat. 'As I was saying. When we fell, all went black, and I thought I was breathing my last. But I did awake. I found myself in this net, along with Thomas. We were strung over the monster's back, as he climbed up the mountain face with his terrible claws...' Lukas scuttled to a dark corner, where he sat and covered his face. He began wailing. 'I am sorry I said Thomas was of no great use. It was his duty to protect me, and he failed me completely, but – the crunching of his bones in its jaws – slowly, it ate him slowly.'

'What happened to the other beastmen you mentioned?'

'I never saw them after I woke up here.' Lukas shrank back, huddling against the cave wall, peering doubtfully out of the opening. 'I imagine they're still around, somewhere.'

'How did the big monster get up and down from the cave? The path's too narrow for something its size.'

Lukas shrugged. 'I never got a good look. It had big claws. Maybe it used them to climb straight up. What do I know of the ways of Chaos beasts?'

'Then I don't suppose you can say why it kept you alive?'

The boy grew quiet. 'I think it liked the way I screamed.'

Franziskus sat beside him. 'I can't imagine what you've suffered, Lukas. But for the moment, you must dismiss these things from your mind. We must go.'

The boy lurched forward, balling up the fabric of his tunic in his small, alabaster fist, and punched ineffectually at Franziskus's chest. 'No! You don't see! I should die here! My capture, the Chaos beasts – all were divine punishment, for my cowardice in battle. I should not have fled! Sigmar has deserted me!'

Franziskus cradled Lukas's head, pressing it to his own shoulder. 'Sigmar deserts no one, so long as you are prepared to fight again.'

'Others may get second chances, but my family's pact with Sigmar is ancient and severe! For me, there will be no redemption!'

Angelika had gathered the net up in her arms. She made a fist of her own and pointed the knuckle of its middle finger meaningfully in his direction. 'I don't know about Franziskus here, but I intend to collect the reward for you, no matter what condition your soul is in. Shall I dash you brainless, put you back in this net, and haul you down the side of the mountain? Or do you mean to pull yourself together?'

'Angelika!' Franziskus protested.

'You shut up. What will it be, Lukas?'

Shakily, he rose. 'I don't want to die here. I wish I did, but I don't. I'll do as you say.'

'Then stop talking in riddles and let's get going.'

Lukas stood, then swooned, sinking against the cavern wall. His rescuers moved quickly to steady him. They let him down gently. Then they fed him cheese and wine, and let him rest. He fell asleep. Weapons ready, they crouched on bound bedrolls, letting day turn to night and night to morning.

EVEN WITH A night's sleep in him, Angelika expected the boy to be useless on the trip back down. Yet fear seemed to propel him, winning out over weakness and poor nourishment. When a gap approached, he leapt with a resigned and casual air, as if half hoping he'd miss. Yet he landed well each time. Once he even helped Franziskus regain his balance, when a sheet of rock hived off from the ledge he walked on. She decided she probably wouldn't need to wrap him back up in the net after all, but she carried it still, despite its rancid stink, because it could come in handy. The gut was strong stuff, and there were a hundred uses for it on a wilderness journey.

Lukas's attitude seemed to darken again when they reached the streambed, with the threat of falling behind them. He dragged his feet and tucked his round chin to his neck. She picked up a handful of pebbles, and tossed them at him to stop him from straggling. When one of her missiles hit him at the base of the skull – a better shot than she'd intended – he jogged ahead to walk beside Franziskus.

'It's obvious you're well-bred,' Lukas said.

'My background is not a suitable matter for discussion,' Franziskus told him.

'All I mean to say is, you and I, we have much in common.'

Franziskus shrugged.

'You haven't yet come out and said it.'

'Said what?'

'That you mean to return me to my father.'

'In fact, it's to your brothers that we'll convey you.'

'My brothers?'

'Benno and Gelfrat.'

'I do not know them. More of my father's scattered seedlings, no doubt. If they weren't so numerous, he might not consider his true sons so disposable.'

'I don't see what you mean.'

'Less talking, more walking!' cried Angelika, from behind them. She was closing fast. Franziskus lengthened his strides.

'I confess this only because it could weigh on your conscience, and it seems from your manner that you don't know what fate you'll be consigning me to.'

'Please, Lukas, speak more plainly.'

'My father seeks me not to clasp me to his bosom, but to place me on the chopping block. I have broken the honour code of the Black Sabres, and so must die.'

'I heard Benno and Gelfrat speak of the Black Sabres, but did not know what they referred to.'

'It is the family military company, founded nearly three hundred years ago, by the first to bear the name of my father, Jurgen von Kopf. You have not heard of them?'

'Forgive my ignorance. In Stirland, it is said that a knowledge of other provinces is a sure sign of vanity, ambition and sexual decadence.'

'All the enemies of Averland know the Black Field Sabres. Their very name strikes fear into the hearts of foes, and timidity into would-be rebels. It was they who turned the Battle of Midden Bell, when the regular black and yellows had turned and fled. It was they who crushed the mutiny against old Count Boris, at Rotermann Field. It was their support that restored the province to just rule when the cruelties of Bloody Count Giannis finally became too great to bear.'

'The emblem that Angelika found – the sabre against the field of black – that would be your regimental ensign, then.'

Lukas reached down into his shirt and withdrew an identical jewelled pendant. 'Yes. So Claus is dead, then. Ah! Our father will be proud.'

'Surely you mean to say your father will mourn his demise?'

'He will celebrate Claus's death, for he fell upholding the vow undertaken by every Sabre, when he is inducted into the company – never to survive a losing battle.'

'A harsh requirement.'

'It is on this vow that the fearsome reputation of the Sabres depends. Without it, the mere sight of our battle banner would not send foes from the field. For as long as I can remember, I have been told how vital the vow is to the prestige and power of my bloodline. Since the halcyon days of Moritz the Swift, every Averlandish elector has had a von Kopf standing at his side, as his advisor – and more.

'I barely know my father. When I was young, he was in the field, bloodying his sword as commander of the company, while my grandfather, who I did know, served at court. Some day, my grandfather said, the day will come when you will take the field yourself. You will stand beside your older brother, Claus, and Sigmar will grant you the chance to cover yourself in battle's glory. You must also prepare yourself, he said, should terrible calamity befall our house, and Claus die beside me. In that event, I must ready myself to clutch his sabre, hold it high, and charge the foe. No matter what, grandpapa said, I must never shame the company. I must uphold the vow. Yet, when the chance came, and I finally saw battle, what did I do? I ran! I spat upon the honour of my family!' He turned and pulled at his tunic, baring his hollow chest. 'I begged the beastman to kill me, as I should have been killed in that hollow, against those bandits! Yet he laughed and refused! He took pleasure in my torment!'

'So that's why he didn't eat you,' Angelika said, coming closer to the two young nobles. 'You made yourself too entertaining.'

Lukas wheeled on her, tears burning in his eyes. 'Do not mock my agony, you knife-wielding harlot!'

Angelika crossed her arms. 'I'd gut you for that, except it's what you want.'

He dropped to his knees. Angelika saw him shudder with pain as they hit the stony trail. That will bruise, she thought. 'Do it! I give you my throat!'

Instead she took him by the shirt and hauled him up. He was limp, like a rag, so it took her no great effort. 'I need your throat intact, you self-pitying little blueblood. So stop whining and start moving!' She slapped him. 'Your tale of woe may inspire bitter tears in my companion here, but all I want is the silver you're worth. I don't care two figs what your brothers do with you when I turn you over to them.'

'No, no, you mustn't do that! You must slay me now – I beg of you!'

She bared her teeth and pulled his face closer to hers. The boy's stink made her eyes water. She resolved to plunge him into a stream and see to it that he got a good washing. 'How much can you pay me to kill you now?'

He pulled at his belt, to show that his purse was missing. 'I have nothing!'

She let him fall. 'Then your fate is not yours to decide.'

He hugged her ankles and burbled. 'I was never meant to be a soldier. I never mastered the rapier, much less the sabre. When those men came to kill us, my body rebelled against me. All I could do was turn and run. You mistake me if you think I'm of any worth.'

'You're worth two hundred crowns if you're worth a penny.' She went to kick at him, but ended up just pushing on his shoulder with her foot. 'Get up,' she said. 'Get up!' Even without looking at him, she could tell that Franziskus was making sad puppy eyes at her. She stamped down the trail, and let him attend to the boy, coaxing him up to his feet, and leading him onwards.

THEY MADE CAMP for the night in the foothills overlooking the pass. This put a good distance between them and the beastmen. Angelika had made the boy scrub up in the stream. He'd performed his ablutions sullenly, and since that indignity had found little to say for himself. Silence suited him, Angelika decided; it was only when he spoke that she wanted to split open his puckered lips.

She sat on a rock and got to work, teasing one of the gut strands from the beastman's net. When she was finished, she approached Lukas, who was on top of a knoll, kicking at a patch of small blue flowers. Stealing a sidelong glimpse at Franziskus, she noted that he was still sitting cross-legged before a pile of sticks and dried plants, attempting to spark his tinderbox on it. Light was disappearing from the sky.

'It's time we rested,' she said. She looped the cord around her hand. 'Come with me.' She led Lukas to the base of a tall spruce and told him to sit. 'Hands behind your back.'

Franziskus saw this and abandoned his fire making. 'What is this, Angelika?'

Lukas's hands stayed in his lap.

'I won't have my three hundred crowns creeping away in the night.' She tied one end of the cord around the tree's trunk. She gave it a mighty yank, making certain that the knot was sturdy.

'Wait a moment. Have we rescued him, or made him our prisoner?'

'Prisoner,' said Angelika. She took hold of Lukas's left hand and tugged it until he moved it behind his back.

'You cannot do that to him,' Franziskus said. 'He is of noble birth.'

'Precisely. Never trust a blueblood, that's my credo.' She tugged on Lukas's right hand; he moved it back, too, more reluctantly, then crossed wrists with the left.

Franziskus knelt beside them and clasped his fingers around the boy's wrists in an attempt to stop Angelika from wrapping the cord around them. 'Scandalous jokes are all well and good, but this goes too far. I won't let you humiliate him.'

'Don't trouble yourself, good Franziskus,' the boy said. 'My cowardice has erased all claim to noble privilege. She may do with me as she likes.'

Franziskus left his hand in place. 'But it is uncalled for. You will not attempt to part company with us, will you, Lukas?'

'No.'

'And, when you say that, you give us your word of honour?'

Lukas nodded gravely. 'Yes.'

'Please, Angelika,' Franziskus said. 'Why would he run? He couldn't survive for a day alone in these hills. If my friendship means anything to you, let the poor fellow be.'

'We must talk,' she said, pulling Franziskus out of earshot. They both regarded him, as he stayed in place, forlornly plucking up grass shoots. 'You've got to stop sympathising with him.'

'How could I not? He's spent the last weeks as a Chaos beast's plaything. It's a tribute to his good breeding that he has any wit left in him at all. I can hardly blame him for being less than charming. Besides, the two of us have much in common.'

'That's your bad fortune. I need to know where your loyalties lie.'

'I've sworn to serve you. Not that you've accepted that.'

'Does that mean I can rely on you, when the time comes to turn him over?'

'You can rely on me in all things, Angelika.'

'Because I don't want you coming down with a case of last-moment lily-liver.'

'Do not fear. My duty to you, and to my class, are both in accord. He must be given over to his family, as honour demands.'

'But you like him.'

'I feel for his plight. He did, however, swear an oath on pain of death... I wish him no ill, but our responsibility to turn him over is clear.'

'Even though they'll make him fall on his sword?'

'I can't believe it will come to that. This von Kopf fellow will find some other way to justly absolve Lukas of his misdeeds. He's a boy of fifteen, and the man's own son. The Empire is fuelled by the honour of its nobles, but not to the point that we applaud blind and unyielding savagery.'

'I hate to correct you, but it's avarice and the lust for power that drives the Empire, not – Damn it!' She sprinted off.

The boy was gone.

She saw his head bobbing up and down, along the side of a hill. She slid down through high grass and closed the distance between them, barely conscious of her footfalls as her long legs carried her toward him. He reached the valley floor, sliding on a patch of mud, then recovered his footing. He kept running. She grabbed her knife. He stupidly stopped to look north, then south, to pick a course. He glanced back at her, then ran straight ahead. She pushed herself harder. He turned his head again, running. She flew into him, hitting his legs, and bowling him over. He somersaulted backwards. She wrenched herself around and dived on his chest. She'd reversed her grip on her dagger, and thumped him instead on the forehead with the pommel. He cried out. She thumped him again, and then stuck the bone of her forearm against his throat and pushed, until his breathing became strained.

'Franziskus is going to be very disappointed in you.'

He worked his lips as if to speak; she relaxed the pressure on his throat, giving him air. Instead of speaking though he pushed up with his shoulder, trying to roll her off him. She kneed him in the groin. His eyes widened. He fell slack, choking. Spittle drooled from his lips. Angelika got off him. He doubled up.

'So that's what your word of honour is worth?'

'My honour is lost to me,' he groaned, 'so it means nothing for me to swear on it.'

She kicked him, placing real force behind the blow this time, and again. Franziskus reached them. She expected him to pull her off, but he didn't, so she kept on kicking, moving from his ribs to his legs.

'I beg you stop!' Lukas wailed.

She stopped, and moved a couple of yards away, leaving Franziskus to help the boy up and lead him back to camp. When next she looked at them, when they were halfway up the hill, she saw that Lukas's face was red, his teeth clenched, and his cheeks stained with tears. This made her want to knock him down for another round of pummelling. Instead, she waited until they got back to Franziskus's unlit fire. Then she trussed Lukas to a tree, as tightly as she'd done the two halflings and the elf. He would have to sleep standing up. If that left him weaker tomorrow, so be it: he wouldn't be so ready to escape then.

Franziskus got a flame going. They sat on their cloaks and warmed themselves.

When the silence got too loud, Franziskus spoke up. 'He will be very sore tomorrow.'

'Pain reminds you you're alive.'

'He lied to me, and so I am angry with him. You expected him to run. Why are you angry?'

'You damn bluebloods are all the same.' She slid forty-five degrees away from the fire, so he could no longer see her face.

'What injustice have I done you?'

'I mean the whole lot of you. Your rules elevate you and permit you to tread on everyone below you. But the minute it looks like you'll have to follow those rules yourselves... That's when the truth comes out. He gave us his word, as a gentleman. Then it transpires he's not a gentleman any more, which gives him permission to lie.'

'He's still only a frightened boy, just as he was an hour ago.'

'I'm only sorry I won't personally witness him receiving the axe.'

Franziskus went quiet. 'If we aristos are as you say, then he will not get the axe. An accommodation will be made.'

'You're right.' She had difficulty getting even those words out of her mouth.

'Angelika, you seem... not yourself.'

'I preferred it when we were just sitting here, thinking our own thoughts.'

'I merely wonder if you need a reassuring word.'

'Not from you, or your kind.'

'Is there something you wish to speak of?'

'Shut up,' she said, 'before I start kicking you, too.'

'GOBLINS,' ANGELIKA SAID, bending down to point at a bare spot in the trail, where many markings could be seen in the dirt. They'd found the spot where she'd left Toby and his cronies, the day before. The cords she'd used to bind them lay tangled in the branches of a thorny bush.

'I can see marks on the ground,' Franziskus said, 'but how can you tell goblins made them?'

'It's easy when you know what to look for. Have you ever seen a pack of goblins? No? Well, the nasty things can't stand still for even a moment. They're always skittering back and forth. And when they move, they move in a sort of sideways manner. See how they slide their feet when they go?'

'I still see only disturbed dirt.'

'No one scuffs up a trail like goblins do.'

'Do you think they came upon Goatfield and the rest, and brought them to grief?'

She squinted at the trees where they'd been bound. 'I see no blood. If they found them still tied up, goblins would certainly attack them. But they don't usually have the inclination to take prisoners – they're too cowardly and dull-witted for that. I'd guess our friends got free – either on their own, or with help from Benno and Gelfrat – and then the goblins came sniffing around later, sensing something amiss.'

'Goblins!' Lukas exclaimed. For appearance's sake, Angelika had tied his wrists, out in front of him. She'd left his ankles free, though, there was no telling when they might have to suddenly run from something. 'I hate this place! Bandits, beastmen, now goblins – is there any creature or villain that does not lurk in these godforsaken mountains?'

'Nearly all the places on this earth are godforsaken,' Angelika said. 'The estate where you were brought up, with its nurses and its polished floors and its all-day games of *paille-maille* – that was the exception.' She spoke without looking at him; purple bruises covered his face, throat, and wrists. There would be worse marks under his clothing, and she was responsible for most of them. She'd woken up ashamed of her violence against him – at least, of the kicks she'd dealt him after his surrender. Several times already this morning, she had found herself on the brink of an apology. But each time she took a look at him – his haughty posture, and the childish way he rolled his eyes at her when he thought she wasn't looking – the impulse went away.

'I never got to play *paille-maille*,' said Lukas, using the back of a restrained hand to rub the damp off his nostrils.

Before her retort had fully gelled, Franziskus stepped up. 'So how do we propose to catch up with his brothers again?'

'I expected to see signs of them by now. Benno had no great love of mountain travel; maybe he decided to stay in the lowlands to await our return. For that matter, they might have gone back already, with some suitable set of bones that they could pass off as Lukas's. The only way to know for certain is to return to the hollow and track their movements from there.'

They crossed the nearby alpine meadow, where the fight against the mercenaries had begun, and jumped down onto the slope of rocks. Lukas made small complaining noises as the stones gave way beneath him. They paused at the bottom to dump pebbles from their shoes, then Angelika led them into the pine wood, heading south. After a few minutes, she gestured for silence.

'Do you hear it?' she asked Franziskus.

'No.'

'Horses.' She crept to the edge of the trees. Franziskus made to follow, but Angelika told him to wait with Lukas. He nodded gravely; she did not need to specify that waiting with Lukas meant making sure he did not run.

Angelika looked down onto the plain and saw the Averlanders. Most, including Benno, milled about a fire, where a cooking pot hung, steam escaping from around its lid. They had four ill-fed horses with them, one brown, the others grey and dull. Angelika wondered whether they'd been purchased or commandeered. Travelling horse peddlers were not a common feature of the Blackfire Pass.

One of the greys had slipped its reins and was cantering in circles around the soldiers. Heinrich and Gelfrat loped after the nag, trying to flank it. It did not seem like it was trying very hard to escape from them; it was only testing them. The nag was far from Angelika, but she thought she could detect a churlish grin on its yellow teeth.

The hill, like so many others they'd seen, was thick with pines and spruces, with no clear path down to the valley floor. She found the slope steep at first, but it became less severe as the trees gave way to weeds and ground-hugging vines. She called out to the soldiers, waving her arms: this was not a situation where it would be good to surprise them. One of the men nudged Benno, who swivelled first his head, then the rest of his body, in her direction. He stood and half-ran, several of the men puffing to keep up with his rapid pace toward her. He shouted to Gelfrat, who broke off from chasing the horse, leaving it to Heinrich. They were at the foot of the hill by the time she reached it.

'So you return to us,' Benno said, crossing his arms.

'At first I was disheartened by the way you threw rocks at me, as I left. But gradually I came to realise how much I missed your company.'

'Your companion is not with you.'

'Franziskus is back in the forest, his watchful eye fixed on a person who may be of interest to you.' She walked past Benno, toward the fire and the cooking pot.

He took her arm and seized it, preventing her from moving further – as she'd predicted he would. 'There are limits to my tolerance,' he said, releasing her arm.

Having made her point, she stood, gazing past him, up into the hills. 'You should have told me you were looking for *two* von Kopfs. It would have made the search much easier.'

Gelfrat joined the group. He was winded. 'He lives? The little maggot!'

'I see you've met him before.'

The muscles of Benno's face twitched with annoyance. He looked haggard, as if sleep had been eluding him. 'We know him by reputation. Father feared he would turn out to be a runner.'

'Old Jurgen will be pleased to get his son back in one piece, I'm sure.' She looked into his eyes, to study his response.

He was examining her expression, too. It was obvious to her that he was trying to work out how much the boy had revealed. 'Few things please my father, save victory. How did you find him?'

'Let's call it a hunch.'

Gelfrat scowled at her, and muttered; Angelika thought she caught the words *tiresome bitch*. She turned to smile sweetly at him. 'Now,' she said, 'the question of my revised fee.'

Benno closed his eyes and turned away in disgust.

'You mean to bleed more from us?' Gelfrat blustered.

'Naturally. The fee we negotiated was for me to take you to Claus's bones. Lukas's rescue from beastmen surely goes beyond the bounds of that agreement.'

When she spoke the word 'beastmen', the soldiers clustered around. Benno paled and gazed fearfully into the mountains. A couple made the sign of Sigmar.

'You met Chaos things?' Gelfrat asked. There was a quiver in his voice – perfectly justifiable, given the topic at hand.

Angelika remained outwardly nonchalant, though the mere mention of the creatures constricted her chest. 'Several waves of them, in fact. And, oh yes, we also had to fight some of Davio's men, who also sought him. Your half-brother seems quite popular in these parts.'

'It was that treacherous swine, Isaak?' said Gelfrat.

'No, a smaller, better-informed group. An elf and two halflings. Elennath, Toby Goatfield and Henty Redpot. Do those names strike any chords with you?'

Benno puffed out his lips blankly. 'No. They served Davio, you say?'

'He seems to want your Lukas for some nefarious scheme or other. Once you pay me for him, I advise you to protect him well.'

'You slew these rogues?'

'We left them hog-tied for you, up in the woods. I guess you didn't find them. The halflings are extremely formidable for their kind. I suggest you let Gelfrat handle the big one with the war-axe.'

The brothers exchanged fretful glances.

'To return the subject to my reward,' said Angelika. 'In addition to the hundred and twenty-five you owe me for Claus's bones–'

'That was never the true aim of–'

'But you are officers and would-be gentlemen, so let's pretend you were being honest. That's one twenty-five for Claus. And a live brother should be worth at least three times as much as a dead one. So that'll be five hundred: an agreeably round figure. I won't charge you extra for the fights we fought, or the mountain we had to climb.'

Failing to contain his anger, Benno shook. 'We told you: we are not wealthy men.'

'But your father, I now learn, is not just a warrior but also an illustrious politician. Meaning that the pillows he sleeps on are no doubt feathered in gold. You'll get the remainder from him, and send a courier down to the Castello to deliver it.'

Gelfrat grinned. 'Of course; I'll agree to that.'

Angelika grinned back at him. 'And – of course – you'll swear to it, on your honour as officers of the Black Field Sabres.'

The smile fell from Gelfrat's face.

'Generally,' Angelika continued, 'I feel a man's promise isn't worth the rag he wipes his sweat with. But in this case, seeing that you're both hoping to curry your father's favour, and knowing how much stock he places in the upholding of vows–'

Benno waved his hands at her. 'Enough! You've made your point.'

'Then you, Benno Kopf, swear on your honour as an officer of the Black Field Sabres that, in exchange for my delivering Lukas von Kopf to you, you will make haste to send a courier to deliver to me the sum of three hundred and seventy-five crowns?'

He placed his palm on his heart. 'I so swear.'

She repeated the vow for Gelfrat. 'Yes, I swear to it,' he grumped.

'Then I'll go retrieve him for you.'

SHE FOUND FRANZISKUS and Lukas – with his hands untied – crouching near a log. They were engaged in earnest discussion, about their upbringings, or some such nonsense. When they heard her approaching, they shut up. They seemed embarrassed. She slapped her hands together, as if she was brushing the dust off some old business, now completed.

'Time to go,' she said.

Franziskus laid a comforting hand on Lukas's back and whispered something too softly for Angelika to hear. Lukas stood and thrust his hands out for Angelika to bind them. She did so, ignoring one of Franziskus's more effective looks of disapproval.

On her return to them, she'd found a more navigable trail to the valley floor, so now she led Lukas along it. As they passed through the tree line, and could see the soldiers camped below, the boy began sniffling.

'Stop that,' she said.

'I can't.' With bound wrists he tried to hide the tears that dampened his cheeks.

'Have courage,' Franziskus said.

'I don't.' He stopped. Angelika tugged on his sleeve. He started up again.

'Remember what we talked about,' said Franziskus. 'It is your duty.'

'I don't see you doing *your* duty!'

'My duty is to discharge my debt to the one who–'

'Both of you shut up!' snapped Angelika. She grabbed Lukas by the crook of the arm and urged him onward. He pulled his elbow away from her, but she kept hold of it.

'Please don't,' he said to her.

She pulled harder.

'I beg you.'

They reached the flatland. The Sabres, led by Benno and Gelfrat, came at them as a group. They spread out, ready to block him if he ran.

Lukas dropped to his knees. 'They'll kill me!' he wailed. Angelika pulled him, to drag him up, but he was making himself dead weight. He flopped prone in the grass. She kicked him in the gut. He moaned. Having knocked the fight out of him, Angelika was able to drag him upright, though he still refused to support himself. She put her knife to his throat.

'I have no mercy for you, Lukas. Stop snivelling and pretend you're a man.'

Gelfrat surged forward and clamped Lukas by the shoulders, pulling him away from Angelika. She happily withdrew and put her knife away. Lukas kicked at Gelfrat, who lifted him off the ground, leaving his legs to flail like a stick insect's. Impassively, he held Lukas aloft until the boy had worn himself out.

'My brother, please, you must take pity on me!' Lukas cried, trying fruitlessly to turn himself in the big man's arms, and look him in the eyes.

'Sure, my brother,' Gelfrat said, baring his incisors and canines. Applying pressure with experienced precision, he embraced Lukas in a chokehold, watching carefully until the boy passed out. Disengaging immediately, he then released him, letting him drop to the ground.

Benno observed from a remove. Angelika went to his side and thrust her palm out. Still regarding the boy, he pulled a purse from his belt and let it fall into her hand. She hefted it, listening for the clink of coin on coin. She resisted the urge to open it and look at the gold inside. As much as she yearned to count it, she knew the purse would contain the correct amount. She'd already pushed the Averlanders hard, and there was no good reason to offend Benno any further.

'All right!' Benno cried, to his men. 'Time to move out!'

Angelika tucked the purse into her belt and walked over to Franziskus. She watched him watch Lukas, as Gelfrat draped his unconscious body across the back of the largest of the new horses – the grey that had earlier escaped him. He called for rope, and a soldier stepped up with a length. Gelfrat tied Lukas to the back of the horse, carefully checking each knot.

'Shall we go?' she asked Franziskus.

No response.

The men broke camp quickly, and had their packs on their backs in less than half an hour. They gathered into ranks and waited for Benno's word.

'Damn me,' said Angelika, to herself. 'Damn me, damn me. No, I won't.'

'Pardon?' asked Franziskus.

'You said they won't kill him.'

'Yes.'

'An accommodation will be made, you said.'

'Indeed.'

'And you're sure of that?'

'I am sure of it,' Franziskus said. He did not sound sure of it.

'Damn me,' said Angelika. Abruptly leaving Franziskus's side, she dashed at Gelfrat's horse. Helmeted heads pivoted, following her movement. Franziskus ran with her, toward the mounts. She leapt onto Gelfrat's nag, pivoting around to grab Lukas's tunic, just in case he wasn't tied on as well as he seemed to be. Shouts, angry and surprised, echoed around her. She kicked the horse's sides. It looked back at her with a lunatic and conspiratorial expression and bolted, jerking her onto its neck. It pounded along the valley floor; she struggled to stay mounted. She could make out shouted curses, behind her. Another horse rode up towards her; she glanced back to see if she needed to throw a knife, but saw that it was Franziskus.

'I'm going to regret this,' she yelled. Behind her, she heard the clopping of the other two horses, in pursuit. She could only assume it would be Benno and Gelfrat giving chase. Franziskus's horse was smaller than hers, but he was a better rider, and he drew up beside her. They slapped reins and sped their mounts.

'Damn me,' she said, and jerked the purse from her belt. She tossed it over her shoulder. It flew wide of Gelfrat, bouncing in the grass.

Amid the pounding of hooves, her ears picked up another sound, up ahead. She looked to the right, into the trees. It was hard to tell, with the world blurring past her, but she thought she'd caught a glint of sun on polished metal. She urged her horse in its direction. Franziskus stayed close by her. Gelfrat's voice screamed at them.

As she got closer to the origin of the glint, she became surer. Again she encouraged the horse; it was eager to run. It leapt over a depression; she nearly fell from the saddle. She hoped all the jostling wouldn't strangle Lukas or break his neck; she wouldn't put it past the forces of destiny to render this merciful gesture all the more futile.

Now she was near enough to know for sure: the hillside to the right boiled with the stunted, hunching forms of goblins, streaming down with outstretched swords and jabbing spears. They were moving too fast to count but Angelika reckoned there were about two dozen of them. Their skins were as green as the grass they slid on; their faces were narrow and their chins sharp. Angelika was too far away to see their pinprick eyes or jagged teeth, but knew they'd have them, all the same. Their conical hats flopped after them as advanced; they wore loose robes in a cacophony of colours, trimmed with stripes and chequerboard patterns. Some fired arrows from small bows, which landed far short of their targets. Two rode on the backs of gigantic, shaggy wolves that were half as high as horses. Goblins in the rear blew bleatingly on sheep-horn trumpets. The nearer ones sang a screeching song that made Angelika shudder.

Franziskus urged his horse away from the goblins, but she pointed herself right at them. The wolf riders wheeled and came at her. Angelika knew her knife was too short to do any good, but readied it regardless. Her nag whinnied maniacally, as if it was looking forward to the collision. One wolf skidded sideways as Angelika barrelled down on them, throwing its rider, who curved through empty air with booted feet pointed heavenwards. The other returned the grey horse's charge, its toothy snout wide open and a long tongue lolling out past its neck. The horse slammed right over it, and wolf and rider rolled beneath its pounding hooves. The crazy steed angled for another pass at the goblins, but Angelika tightened the reins and kicked frantically at its ribs. It straightened its course. She looked to see if Franziskus had made it through the developing gauntlet of goblins – and he had.

Benno and Gelfrat were not so blessed. She saw them rearing their mounts as they fought to turn them around. The yammering goblins had gathered themselves into a rough formation to chase them. She checked to see that Lukas was still securely strapped to the horse's hindquarters, then fixed her eyes on the route ahead.

CHAPTER SIX

ANGELIKA STOOD BEFORE the horse, resting a hand on either side of its long face. Touching the animal gave her a tranquil feeling, which she knew was only temporary. It waggled its head back and forth; she could not be sure whether it was conveying pleasure or annoyance.

'I will call you Swordhoof,' she said to it.

It rolled down its upper lip and sneezed, blowing a thick coating of equine mucus onto her face and neck. She used her fingers to wipe the muck off. By the time she'd got enough of it away from her eyelids to open them, Swordhoof had turned around and was trotting over to Franziskus's horse, which was grazing in the tall grasses beneath a rock shelf, tethered to a fallen log. The horses were damp with sweat; Angelika and Franziskus had used them to get several leagues away from Benno and company. They had just stopped to rest both the animals and themselves. To aid the beasts' recovery, Franziskus had relieved them of the saddles and packs they'd carried.

Swordhoof nosed at the other animal's tether, trying to untie the loop from the log. Angelika saw this and ran at the nag. It chortled at her, in a way she found too intelligent, and then reared up, flashing its hooves at Angelika. She backed off from it, watching in disgust as its companion jolted onward, slipping the tether the rest of the way off the log. The crazy grey drank in one last mocking look at Angelika and then galloped off at top speed, heading back down south. After a moment's hesitation, and a questioning look at Franziskus, the second horse followed, straining to keep up.

'I think your nag was a daemon in a former life,' said Franziskus. 'Or perhaps a Marienburg barrister.'

Angelika watched the horses grow smaller in the distance. 'Well, they would have been a hindrance anyway,' she said.

Lukas sat cross-legged in the grass, close to where the horse had grazed. He had his head down. He'd said little since they hauled him off Swordhoof's back.

Franziskus emerged from a patch of low vegetation, where he'd been foraging. 'What do you know of mushrooms?' he asked Angelika.

'I know that some of them are toadstools, and can kill you.'

Disappointment played across his face. 'I grow tired of field salami and raw turnip.'

'If the horses hadn't already had Benno's saddlebags on them, we wouldn't even have the salami.' They'd also acquired several blankets, a compass, and a lantern, with some oil to burn.

Franziskus raised his voice, addressing Lukas: 'Are you hungry?'

Lukas said nothing.

'Not much day left,' Angelika said, checking the sky for the sun's position.

'You don't think the goblins killed them?' Franziskus asked, referring to the Averlanders. Several hours had passed since their escape; they'd been resting for twenty minutes now, at most. The rest of the time had been spent riding north.

'No, I don't think so. They were only goblins. They might kill a few of the more aggressive ones, and the rest would run for the hills. The best we can hope is that the Sabres took some nasty hits and have stopped to tend their wounded. I wouldn't wager any money on it, though. We'd better get moving.'

'To where, precisely?'

'That I haven't figured out, yet.'

'They'll know to look for us at the Castello.'

'True.' She strode over to the boy. 'I was foolish to rescue you, wasn't I, Lukas?'

He tore fistfuls of grass from the ground and threw them into the air. The wind blew them back into his face.

'I don't have anywhere to take you where you'll be safe,' Angelika said. 'I should have left you to your brothers' cruel mercies.'

'I don't want to be killed,' Lukas said.

'I'm glad to see you're recovering your senses. Franziskus, you think I did the wrong thing, don't you?'

The blond-haired man reached into his pack, which was on the ground near Lukas, and unscrewed the pewter cap on his waterskin. 'Certitude deserts me. You may be right: he may not have had a fair chance with them.'

'How many times do I have to tell you before you believe me?' Lukas exclaimed, leaping up. 'If they get me home, I'll be strangled, or made to fall on my sword!' He wrenched the vessel from Franziskus's hands and took a long swig on it; his Adam's apple bobbed as he drank.

'Franziskus,' Angelika asked, 'you didn't see anything other than mushrooms in that brush, did you?'

'There was a pair of squirrels, but I didn't feel like chasing them.'

Knife in hand, she bounded into the bushes, looking conspicuously around her. She shrugged. She returned to the two young nobles, then shrugged again, making the gesture large. 'I thought I saw something,' she said, her voice elevated, 'but I guess it was nothing.' She moved to face the opposite way and said, *sotto voce*, 'Elennath's in there.'

'The elf?' Franziskus said, barely audibly.

'He's lying flush against a log.'

'I didn't see him.'

'He's good, but his elbow was sticking up.'

'Do we take him?'

'No. I don't know where the others are, but they must be around. Let's get our things, head for open ground, and stay on guard.'

They did as she said, stealing frequent glances at the hills to their right. When Lukas's pace lagged, she barked at him to keep up. When he asked who they were looking for, she silenced him. They walked until the sun fell behind the mountains. Then she took them up into the hills, where they backtracked south. Whenever Lukas tried to speak, or let loose a cough, or if he stepped on a dry leaf, she looked angrily at him. They heard a stream and searched it out, halting to refill their waterskins; Angelika kept anxious watch. She herded them on as the twilight thickened.

Finally they came upon a familiar cave: it was where Angelika and Franziskus, along with the Averlanders, had taken shelter against the rain. Angelika told Lukas to wait inside. She took the beastman's net from her pack and tossed it into Franziskus's arms. He made a face; the net still reeked of blood and filth. She walked to a nearby stand of leafy trees, their bark white and papery. She found a young one, and began to bend its tall trunk down.

LUKAS EMERGED FROM the cave. 'Where are you?' he called, executing a confused full circle, looking for his guardians.

'Go back in,' she hissed. She and Franziskus crouched behind a bush.

Lukas nudged out further. 'It's dark in there!'

'We left you a lantern, didn't we? Light it.'

'I don't know how to use the tinder.'

'Figure it out!'

'I already tried.'

She tapped Franziskus's arm. Crouching, he ducked into the cave. She watched as it filled with light. He ran back to her side.

About a minute later, Lukas started up again. This time, he did not venture into their line of sight. 'Why are you out there, while I'm in here?'

'Be quiet!' Franziskus ordered.

Angelika amended his order: 'Shout all you want, but pretend we're in there with you!'

'You're using me as bait!'

'Shout any complaint you want, other than that!'

Instead, he resumed his silence. Angelika and Franziskus waited without exchanging words. The sky changed from inky blue to deepest black. Night birds swooped above, catching insects.

'No, I won't be silent and go to sleep!' shouted Lukas, from the cave. He left a pause and then said, 'I don't need to thank you for it! I *deserved* to be rescued!' After another interval, he added: 'I deserve better! I have always deserved better!' Then apparently he grew tired of the effort to please them, and his comments ceased.

Toby crept up first, along the trail from the north: the direction they'd come from. He edged over to the cave mouth, and peered in. The lantern lit up his greedy smile. He stepped back. With fingers on his lips, he made a bird call, perfectly imitating the trill of the insect eaters flapping overhead. He repeated this call three times, with short, even intervals between them.

Elennath skulked through the trees, up the hillside, where there was no trail. Neither twig nor needle snapped beneath his soft-shod feet. Toby stepped back to stand beside him. Now that the light shone on Elennath, Angelika could see a long, white bandage tied across his face, bisecting it diagonally. It followed the route of the slash she'd carved in him. The elf and halfling nodded to one another; Toby made his bird call again.

They waited.

Nothing happened.

Toby repeated the bird call a little louder.

Finally, Henty tramped in from the south. He used the trail, but even so, his scraping, heavy footfalls were easily heard. Elennath twisted around to make a face at him, but he took no notice of it, trudging up to his two companions. Elennath nudged him with one elbow, and Toby with the other. Knife in fist, he nodded out a countdown – one – two–

Just before he reached *three*, Angelika and Franziskus pulled hard on the cords they held. The beastman's net lay beneath the mercenaries' feet. It flew up to envelop them, and then flung them up into the air as the tree Angelika had bent unfurled itself, returning to its full height. The mercenaries, crushed into a tight ball of arms and legs and torsos, cursed and grunted. They were bouncing up and down on the main umbilical that connected the net to the tree. Angelika and Franziskus held their weapons tight until it became clear that the cord would hold, and the suspended mercenaries were securely trapped.

'You bitch!' the elf called out. Even in fury, his voice was rich and mellifluous. 'I'll skin you for this, and wear your hide as a cloak!'

She sheathed her blade and stepped out from behind the bush. 'If you're looking for reasons for me to let you free, that would not be one of them.'

Henty spoke, scratching out his vowels and slurring his consonants. 'The elf won't kill you. I'll kill you. I'll kill you with my axe!'

'And I thought Toby was a poor negotiator,' Angelika said, ostensibly to Franziskus. 'Now I know why they let him do the talking.'

'Enough of the wit, girlie,' Toby murmured. His words were muffled: his face was pressed tight against the net, impeding the movement of his lips. 'Tell us what you want with us. Unless you plan to gut us, in which case: go ahead and try.'

'If we wanted you dead, you'd be rotting already.'

'Before, you were lucky!' Henty shouted. 'I'll kill you with my axe!'

'Your companion has a single-mindedness about him,' Franziskus remarked.

Henty snarled indignantly, as if Toby had just elbowed him.

Lukas jutted his head out of the cave. Ignoring Angelika's jabbing and forbidding finger, he came out to see the dangling captives. 'These are the ones you spoke of, who want to kidnap me?'

'Listen to the whining dandy, girlie, with his mincing tones.'

'You can't talk to me like that!' Lukas said.

'Soon as I cut myself out of here, I'll kick my boot halfway down your porcelain backside!'

'You – you...' At a loss for expletives, Lukas hopped in place.

Toby made the net bounce. 'This is the one you're risking your life for, girlie? He wouldn't do the same for you, would he? He wouldn't risk his life for anyone, the mewling coward.'

'You seem to know a great deal about him,' Angelika observed.

'He was well described to us,' said Toby.

'Your employer realized as soon as they arrived in town that he should send you after the Kopf brothers. It was only a few hours after I'd agreed to help them that you were rubbing up against me, trying to figure out who I was.'

'No, it's merely that I have a taste for bony wenches.'

'The prince is well informed about the Kopfs and their doings,' said Angelika. 'He must have a spy in their midst.'

With his tongue and teeth, Toby made a slurping noise that was vaguely contemptuous. 'All I know is to bring the whelp back, as hostage.'

'But this one is marked for death; he has betrayed his ancestral creed. If his family wants him dead, he's not much use as a hostage, is he?'

'The doings of generals and princes don't interest me one jot. I just collect my pay.'

'The prince wants him, all right, but not to ransom him off. He'll use him as a living trophy, to embarrass his enemy. The shame of the von Kopfs, on permanent display.'

'No amount of bafflegab's going to confuse me, girlie,' said Toby.

'I'm not trying to confuse you, you drooling halfwit. I want you to confirm that he'll be safer with your employer than with his father. He will, won't he?'

'Wait a moment!' said Lukas. 'What do you mean to–'

She clamped her hand over Lukas's mouth. He tried to bite her, but she was too experienced at the manoeuvre to let him do it. 'Isn't that right, Toby? Despite your cruelty and general loathsomeness, you can be trusted to get him to safety. Meaning: I can sell him to you with a clear conscience.'

'Sell him?' blurted Franziskus.

'We have no coin to buy him with, girlie. And I still don't see the point of your ramblings. Get us down from here!'

'I'll kill you with my axe!' Henty roared.

'Close your mouths, both of you!' cried Elennath. 'I'll confirm it,' he said, after his companions quieted their protests. He let loose a sigh of weary vexation. 'Yes, the prince does want the boy as his caged monkey, and he'll be guarded scrupulously. And I have a purse of coin I've been given, to cover eventualities like this. Release us, hand the snot-nose over, and it's yours.'

'How much?'

'Eighty crowns.'

A thrashing arose inside the net. It jounced on its tether. Elennath squealed in pain.

'Eighty crowns?' Henty cried. 'You've been holding out on us, elf scum!'

'You expect us to believe they trusted you and not us?' demanded Toby. The violence of the net's jerking and jarring increased. Angelika's body readied itself for quick action, in case they bounced themselves loose and came crashing onto the trail.

Elennath gave out another agonised cry, then Toby did the same.

'Not there! Not there!' he whimpered.

'Of course they trusted me! Am I not the issue of Athel Loren? Heir to the Council Sylvan?'

'Spare us your elfy hogwash!'

'And are you not a pair of drunken, vicious louts who couldn't be relied on to find their own hairy feet at the ends of their stunted little bowlegs? *Get us down from here!*'

'You're sure eighty crowns is all you've got?' called Angelika.

'*Get us down!*'

She shrugged. 'Better than nothing, I suppose. Throw down the purse!'

'I can't reach it!'

'Work at it until you can!'

'How do I know you won't just take it, and leave us up here?'

'I am going to leave you up there, to get free by yourselves. Otherwise I have no assurance that Henty won't pick up that axe of his and start swinging it about as soon as the net comes down.'

'Harlot!' Henty shouted.

'You'll notice the branch that holds you is already groaning under your weight. Another half hour or so of vigorous bouncing, and I'm sure it'll give. In the meantime, this is what I'll do for you. Lukas, come here.'

Lukas moved back. 'What?'

She bent to retrieve the cord they'd used to trigger the trap. 'Sadly, this is another of those times where you have to be tied up.'

'What?'

Franziskus got between them. 'Angelika, you can't be serious.'

'You heard them. The Castello is the safest place for him. The safest place we can get him to, at any rate. And this way, we still get eighty crowns.'

The mercenaries began to bounce themselves. The branch creaked.

'I want no part of their filthy money!' Franziskus said.

'That's generous. Now move aside.'

Lukas's knees hit the dirt. He clasped his hands together and shook them at Angelika. 'Please, you can't mean to leave me in the hands of these murderers!'

'It's me and Franziskus they want to kill, not you.' She seized his outstretched hands and looped the cord around his wrists. 'So you'll excuse me if we give ourselves the head start we need.' She cupped a hand to her mouth, to shout at Elennath. 'Be still, and toss down the purse, or I'll untie him and take him with us!'

The three stopped moving. The net gently swung.

'Now lie down,' she told Lukas.

'Please don't leave me.'

'You despise me, remember? Now lie down!'

He stretched supinely in the dirt. As she was trussing his ankles, she heard a metallic clink. She sprang over to the spot beneath the net, seized up a small leather bag, and opened it. It contained Imperial crowns. A brief look confirmed that there were probably eighty of them. She pulled the drawstring tight without investigating further, and shoved it into her belt.

Franziskus was at Lukas's side, murmuring; Angelika knelt beside him, too, and told him that he had no reason to worry. Later, she assured him, he would look back on this and conclude that she'd done him the greatest of favours. Before he could reply, she was up and had gathered the contents of her pack. She ran along the trail, towards the north. Close behind her, she heard Franziskus's footsteps.

THEY DUCKED OFF the trail after a short run, into a gully obscured by foliage. They took their bedrolls from their packs, laid them out and rested on them. They could hear the sound of crickets and, in the distance, chirruping frogs. Above them came the momentary flutter of bat wings. Perhaps an hour later, there was a commotion on the trail: the piercing, nasal tones of Lukas's voice, mixed in with Henty's grunts, as well as various leers and snorts from Toby. The trail was too far off to make out words, but the boy was still clearly alive – they could hear him complaining.

Franziskus waited until they'd passed to say: 'You did not grab your knife and charge after them.'

Angelika settled down into her bedroll. She'd found a particularly lush patch of vine leaves to spread it out on, and she meant to enjoy it. 'Why, in the name of sanity and reason, would I do that?

'I thought you might have another sudden change of heart.'

'That was a once-only mistake. This time it's on my terms.'

'Just when I think I understand you at last, you spin my head again, Angelika.'

'Beware predictable people; they're either stupid or fanatically dangerous.'

'Now you find fault in consistency of character? Is there no virtue you don't decry?'

'I'm too tired to argue. All I know is he's better off in Prince Davio's dungeon than the von Kopf family crypt. Now I hope you don't find my desire for sleep somehow unusual.'

SHE WOKE IN the morning to a grey sky and a softly snoring Franziskus. He'd dozed off without shaking her awake for her watch. She decided to let him sleep, and not to scold him for his lapse. Nothing had come in the night to carry them off or chew on their limbs, and that was all that mattered. She slunk into the bushes to relieve herself. When she got back, Franziskus had clearly been looking around for her. She sat down next to him, and worked the tension from her cramped shoulders. Then she opened her pack to hunt for the last of the field salami. She cut it in two and handed the noticeably smaller half to Franziskus. He drank from his waterskin.

Angelika remembered the money. She took out the purse and clanked it in her palm. It wasn't four hundred crowns, or even a hundred and twenty-five, but it was still her biggest haul in a long time. Certainly since Franziskus had attached himself to her.

'So what will you do with your reward?' he asked, slathering the final word of his sentence with a thick layer of irony.

'Hmp,' Angelika replied.

'That's enough to buy yourself a cottage, in some small town up north. A good one, sealed from drips and drafts. Moreover, with a touch of frugality, you could live off it the rest of your days.'

'Pah!' she said.

'Many a peasant makes do with less.'

'I'm impressed by your knowledge of the rustic life.'

'Just think: no more sorting through rotting corpses for buttons and beads. No need to cross blades with cutthroats, or wander through this awful wilderness, with its orcs and Chaos beasts. Now you can retire to an existence more properly fitting to your sex.'

'Franziskus, no one is more obnoxious than a person who enjoys giving advice.'

'But ever since we met, nearly all I've heard from you is your craving for gold. Now that you have it, I'm merely curious to see what comes next.'

'Your curiosity will have to go unsatisfied, my friend. Or whatever you are.' She rose, to get her bearings.

'I've offended you.'

'Of course you have. You should be able to get back to the Castello before nightfall. I'll meet you there in a day or two.'

'But where are you going?'

'For reasons that currently escape me, I've trusted you with my life. But I won't trust you to know where my gold is.'

'I care not a whit for gold.'

'Exactly – you value it too lightly. You don't understand what it means.' She hefted her pack onto her back. 'If I turn back and see you following me, I'll treat you as I would any other enemy. Understand?'

She could not read the look on Franziskus's face as she tramped off.

MILES AWAY, AND many hours later, she stood over a patch of sod, surveying it for hints of disturbance, and differences from the neighbouring ground. For the hundredth time, she looked all around her to make sure that no one observed her. Her mouth was dry; she'd used up nearly all her water. She was tired and wanted to rest, but would not do it here, in case someone noted her presence in this spot. Angelika walked until she came to a stream, where she'd sat before, on similar occasions. There was a flat rock she liked, and she kept going until she found it. She sat down, pulled her boots off, and dangled her throbbing feet in the chill, clear water. She closed her eyes and concentrated on the sensation of rushing water on her legs.

She was glad that Franziskus hadn't followed her. It would have been unpleasant to have had to insert a knife between his ribs. She had no doubt that she could do it – easily, if the truth be told. She'd seen enough of his fighting to know his weaknesses well. His swordsmanship was all training and no instinct. He repeated the same moves with clockwork regularity. In particular, there was a moment during his forward feint, when it would take just a single sidestep for a person to shove a dagger into him all the way to the hilt. On occasion, she'd been tempted to point this out to him, but had decided to keep the fact in reserve, in case she needed it later.

A cottage! Frugal living for the rest of her life! Pursuits proper to a woman! What rot! But if there were a way she could use her money to ensure that she could spend the rest of her life here, with her feet in this water, with warm sunlight on her face, knowing that she would never grow hungry or get bored – or suffer attacks from enemies, or have to listen to the stupid prattling of other people – well, then, that would be a retirement worth considering! Barring that, she would just have to keep all her crowns safely buried until she found a good reason to do otherwise.

She could be free of Franziskus now. She'd promised to meet up with him again, but that meant nothing. All she had to do was go further south, perhaps to some other settlement run by a different border prince. It was more dangerous down there, but it was also where all the good battles were. He might try to find her – no, he would without question try to find her – but it could be years before he caught up with her. And surely even he was capable of coming to his senses eventually?

She threw her head back and closed her eyes tighter.

In her mind's eye, she saw Lukas. His eyes were pleading to her.

Her guts rolled over. Her skin grew cold. She shuddered. She jerked her feet from the icy water.

What she had done had been wrong. Oh, he'd certainly proved himself to be a cossetted, bleating, feckless twit. But no matter who he was, she had no right to steal his freedom from him. All the others around him, from his father to his brothers to the prince of the Castello, had been ready to do it without a qualm. Angelika considered herself different from such men. She stood apart from the world, with its manifold lies and villainies. Or so she'd always told herself. Yet, because she'd allowed the boy to annoy her, she'd sold him, like she would a dog or a mule. Even though she knew he didn't know better.

She could only admit it. She'd made herself a hypocrite. No better than Gelfrat, or Toby.

Mournfully, she let the last drops of water dry on her feet, and then she put her boots back on. She refilled her waterskin and returned to the patch of ground where the gold lay buried. Standing above it, she considered whether she ought to dig it up, and refund Elennath his blood money. It would be consistent; she'd left Benno's purse behind, when she'd decided to reclaim Lukas the first time.

She left the coins in their place of hibernation. Righteousness, she decided, was a thing best doled out in small doses.

CHAPTER SEVEN

As ANGELIKA WALKED north through the pass toward the Castello, a hubbub of shouting voices and anxious cries arose. Rounding the foot of a hill, she saw a throng of men, women and children issuing from the rock cut that led to the Castello. Their distressed and dirty clothing identified them as townspeople. Wives sobbed in the arms of husbands; men pushed and elbowed at one another, as if to discharge their anger. Angelika noted that no one seemed to carry a pack on his back, or to lead a horse or mule.

She ran to reach the fringes of the mob. She seized the sleeve of the nearest man, a plump old fellow with a sandy-coloured, triangular beard, to ask what had happened.

'Siege!' he cried, widening reddened eyes. 'They marched in through the hills!' He spoke these words peevishly, as if all of the armies of the Old World had signed agreements not to march in through the hills. He made to stagger off; Angelika yanked again on the cuff of his ratty coat.

'Who? Who besieges you?' she demanded.

'The black and yellows!' he said, pulling himself free of her and melting into the crowd.

Arms crooked outward, she threw herself into the mob, surging against it, pushing her way toward the rock cut and the Castello. The cut was choked with people. A boy fell onto the rocky trail; a flabby arm pulled him up before he could be trampled. Angelika clambered up on the rocks surrounding the cut and began to climb from one outcropping to the next. Beside the pounding of blood in her ears, she could hear the sounds of a besieging regiment: the rolling cracks of drumsticks on kettledrums; the groaning of wagon wheels against their axles; whips cracking as auxiliary crews urged their lowing oxen onward, creaking artillery pieces after them. Above it all there was the low, flat buzz of excited male voices, readying themselves for the kill, and praying not to die.

After several minutes of sweat and strain, she reached a lookout point above the basin, from which she could see the Castello and its besiegers. The Castello itself had not yet been affected; its main gate was open just enough for a stream of people to squeeze out of the town. Its weathered, uneven plank walls still stood; the heads of guardsmen bobbed in its towers and on its rickety battlements.

As for the besiegers, they hadn't yet assumed formation: soldiers either ran about like heedless insects, or milled about at ease, waiting for their orders to ring out above the uproar. They were indeed Averlanders: black and yellow banners, their colours matching the soldier's uniforms, snapped in the wind, held aloft on poles of filigreed brass.

Angelika saw halberdiers, leaning against the long hafts of their huge weapons with elaborate blades. Legs spread staunchly apart, they struck haughty poses for the benefit of their minions – the common foot soldiers. Their helmets gleamed; their green plumes trembled fiercely in the wind. Plumeless, their inferiors skulked around them, pretending to take no notice, as they polished swords and fumbled with the buckles of their breastplates. Handgunners stood at a remove from both classes of fellow soldier, checking their flintlocks for defects.

Old men and young boys, wearing the green armbands of the auxiliary, helped artillerists unload mortars from a great wagon of oak planks which was held together by a frame of riveted steel. The gunners shouted and waved their arms as the knees of young and old alike buckled under the weight of cast-iron mortar barrels. Angelika watched others unload the brass-shod wooden bases from which the mortars would fire their deadly shells.

She counted three cannons, each with its own complement of oxen and anxious, milling drovers. The weapons rested on carriages of copper-bound oak, and were cast in iron. If Angelika remembered her artillery correctly, the barrels would each bear the insignia of Mad Count Marius: a sun wearing a bored expression, surrounded by flaring solar petals, alternating between large and small.

Angelika reckoned there were perhaps five or six hundred Averlandish soldiers and officers present in the basin's confines. That was not counting auxiliaries and other noncombatants. She did not place absolute store in her estimations, because she was better at counting the dead. Though it was not the smallest force she'd ever seen fielded by an Imperial state, it wasn't particularly large either. And she saw no sign of battle wizards. But this regiment could certainly do the trick, if it were massed here for the reason she surmised.

Angelika's attention returned to the fleeing townsfolk. A procession of civilians streamed out and around the small army, in carts, on the backs of mules, and on foot. Teams of foot soldiers manned checkpoints to interrupt the exodus. They searched the refugees and their belongings, confiscating swords, bows and even scythes. Angelika watched the soldiers extract departure taxes from the fleeing residents: they removed rings and necklaces, and laid claim to wheels of cheese and links of sausage. Horses and mules were taken from the refugees and led to a makeshift corral. Angelika saw a fat sergeant seize a chicken, wring its neck, and drop it to his feet – no doubt for later roasting.

The line of refugees collided with an opposing mass of civilians, some with carts, who circled around in search of favourable positions. Where these two groups met, an ever expanding, barely moving knot of the annoyed and frightened was created. The new arrivals were camp followers of various sorts, come down from Averland in hopes of wringing profit from a lengthy siege. They must have arrived before the exodus began; there would be no getting carts in now. Butchers had brought sheep and cattle to slaughter and skewer; some had already staked out places for firepits, and were spading them out, as sacks of charcoal waited to fill them. A family of entertainers, stringy as yellow beans and wearing belled, floppy caps, pounded nails into a stage. Peddlers erected canvas stalls to exchange looted goods for coin – some of the checkpoint men had lined up already, to pawn the items they'd stolen from the departing border rats. In front of one such stall, Angelika detected the threat of a brawl, as fist-shaking refugees gathered to reclaim the goods they'd just been stripped of.

Her eyes lighted on a high-walled cart, painted violet and flying a windsock in the shape of a toothy pike fish. She moved toward it, entering the crush of soldiers, evacuees and opportunists, and elbowed her way through. It took nearly half an hour to get to the cart, her toes ached from being trodden on, and her legs were splattered with mud and the dung of livestock.

The purple cart's doors were shuttered tight; its owner was too cautious to open for business until the refugees had gone, and the possibility of a riot. Angelika banged on it with her sharp, knuckled fist.

'We're not open yet!' came a voice from inside.

Angelika identified herself and backed up for the door to open. A fat and familiar face beamed at her; it was her best customer, Max Beckman. Ringlets of dark hair laid flat against his large, round skull, cemented by a grease of Max's own formulation that was scented with lilacs. He wore a sheepskin coat, dyed deep blue and embroidered with diamonds and moons. Gold rings encircled each of his stubby fingers; they were inlaid with gems which, to Angelika's experienced eye, were obviously made of glass. He reached his hand out for her and helped her up into the cart.

Franziskus was perched inside on a leather bench. Shelves and drawers cramped the interior of Max's cart; its roof was not high, and they were forced to stoop.

'I was going to ask if he'd seen you,' Angelika said, to Franziskus.

'I recognised the cart and thought it as likely a meeting place as any,' he said. He'd met Max twice before. Angelika knew he disapproved of the merchant and his business, but was mannerly enough to keep this opinion to himself.

'You'll have many competitors, I'm afraid, when it comes to plucking this battlefield,' Max said, tossing small blocks of wood into a tiny iron stove. 'Care for a toddy? Chill has gripped my bones all morning.'

She sat beside Franziskus. He squeezed over, but there was little room on the bench, so her right leg pressed tightly against his left. He cleared his throat and patted his chest.

She asked him what he'd learned.

'Did you see the Black Sabres' banner flying out there?'

'I saw banners, but not that one.'

'Benno commands this disorder, with Gelfrat as his number two.'

'All of this, just to retrieve Lukas? Their father is as mad as the count he serves.'

'What are you talking about?' Max asked, wrapping his hand in a towel, to insulate it from the heat of the stove. 'Jurgen dispatched these detachments to make an example of Davio. They intend to show the other border princes the price of defiance.' He shut the oven door and held his hands out, smiling as the warmth entered his muscles. 'When this is over, they'll fear the Empire more than they fear the orcs. Or so the theory goes.'

Angelika told Max who Lukas was, and briefly told of their exploits of the last few days. Max knew the brothers; it was he who'd sold them Claus's pendant, and pointed them to Angelika. 'You aren't ever going to do that again, are you, Max?' she said. 'Send armed men my way?'

Max perspired. 'They assured me they meant to hire you! I thought I was doing you a favour!'

She unclenched her fist and shook her head slowly. 'Never again.'

Max nodded. 'No, never, of course.'

She turned to Franziskus. 'So do the brothers know that Lukas is inside?'

'I haven't been able to establish it myself, though I assume so. I believe they passed by, found one of their father's regiments, and asserted rights of command.'

'Of course.' Realising she was too cramped on the bench, she shifted to the floor, which was covered by a worn rug from far-off Araby. 'After failing to secure Lukas, they need to make good.'

'Perhaps Davio can trade him, if they agree to attack some other border prince instead,' mused Max, placing a tin pot on top of his stove.

Angelika screwed up her face. 'I am not proud to say this...'

'What?' said Franziskus.

She couldn't look at him. 'We can't let that happen. Can we?'

'I knew you would see right eventually, Angelika.'

'Remove that grin from your face. Even if it was right to hand him to Davio, which I now doubt, the entire idea was to protect him from his family. Now they're about to snatch him anyway.'

'Unless we do something about it?'

'You stay here. I made the mistake; I can't ask you to risk your neck correcting it.'

Franziskus rose from the bench, careful not to smash his head on the roof. 'Keep those toddies warm for us, Max,' he said.

They jumped from the cart. The noise of the throng had sharpened. Franziskus put his hands to his face.

'I've never seen anything like this.'

'Orcs don't hole up in fortresses or towns, so sieges are rare these days,' Angelika said, pushing past a toothy, furtive soldier with a live goat kid slung over his shoulder. The frightened animal gave her an imploring look. 'When one does come along, everyone wants to get in on it.'

They stepped through a group of a dozen women, with faces crudely rouged, who bent to tap tent pegs into the ground. Franziskus's mouth fell open. One of the tent builders, a heavy-bosomed, curly-haired specimen who could have been his mother's older sister, parted her painted lips to leer at him. 'Fancy a tumble?' she asked.

Franziskus shivered and waved his hand in front of his face. They made their way through the tents.

'Perhaps I'm naïve...' he began.

'You are,' Angelika affirmed.

'But these people – they are acting as if this is some kind of carnival.'

'Better than a carnival, if you're a woman of trade. A man's ardour is never greater than when he thinks he might die – or after he has killed.'

'It's ghastly.'

'If their presence keeps a few soldiers from taking their urges out on the unwilling, I say we pin medals on them. Though I doubt this Jurgen will be so inclined.'

Sticking to the outskirts of the throng, thereby avoiding the soldiers in the middle, Angelika and Franziskus wended past a crew of soldiers erecting a makeshift shrine to steely Sigmar, made of scrap pine and topped with a pewter-headed hammer; a hawker toting a basket of puckered, wormy apples; and a sneaky-eyed girl intently studying the purses of passersby. They smelled cooked meat, flatulence, urine, straw, perfume, wood smoke and the stink of gangrene. They heard laughs, shouts, sobs, curses, the twanging of a lute, the banging of drums and a choking noise the origin of which they could not identify.

They skirted a checkpoint, moving upstream through the oncoming column of escapees. A shout rang out after them. They kept going; the voice grew louder and more insistent. It was a soldier, his breastplate smeared with dried mud, the creases of his face accentuated by caked-in grime. His narrow eyes huddled close to the bridge of his long nose; his open mouth revealed a conspicuous pair of buck teeth, like the chewers on a rat. 'Halt, you!' he called, waving a short staff with steel-shod tip. 'Come here!'

Angelika let him come to them. When he reached them, she said, 'What?'

'Where do you think you're going?'

'Into the Castello. Why?'

'Did you not see our checkpoint?' He slapped his staff into the curled fingers of his hand.

'You're checking people coming out. We're going in.'

'This whole area is under Imperial aegis.' His tongue clicked against the backs of his rat-teeth. 'You can't just come and go – in either direction.'

Twin fabric epaulets, flared and feather-shaped, hugged the shoulders of his tunic. Franziskus seized them, jerking

Rat-Teeth's face into his own. 'You idiot!' Franziskus hissed, through bared teeth. 'Do you not know who I am?'

The soldier's eyes darted fearfully across Franziskus's face in search of an answer. His lips worked silently up and down.

Franziskus pulled the man closer. 'I asked you a question, you useless chunk of dung!'

'I– I–'

'Tell me, soldier, who I am!'

'Ah, you are – you must be – you are one of them, aren't you, ah – sir!'

'One of them?' Franziskus thundered. 'One of them *who*?'

'Oh – ah – oh – ah – oh sir, you know. Please don't make me say. I'm sorry sir – oh, so sorry. It's all so confusing here, this press of people.' He altered his tone, dropping the officious clipping of his consonants in favour of a porridgey peasant accent. 'I'm just a poor lowly muck-tramper, please, I don't deserve no flogging! Besides, you want us to challenge everyone, yes? This is a test, yes? You don't want any people who aren't supposed to be getting through, getting through, do you?'

'You presume to tell *me* what I want from *you*?'

'Oh, ah – no, no, oh sir, no. No. Please don't...'

Franziskus pushed him away. The soldier's boots skidded backwards and squished into the cold muck. 'Then go about your business,' Franziskus growled, 'and consider yourself lucky I'm in a merciful mood!'

'Yes, sir. Yes, sir. Yes, sir,' he said, still backing away. He returned to his station, deliberately looking anywhere but at them as they continued through the crowd.

'Well,' said Angelika, as they dodged a pair of short, stubble-faced men in knit caps, carrying a rolled-up carpet. 'I see you have quite the talent for the cowing of underlings.'

'Mrm,' Franziskus replied.

'Your breeding comes to the fore, hmm?'

Franziskus said nothing.

When they got to the town gates, they saw that they were propped wide open. The bottlenecked crowd groaned with collective complaint as some of its members squeezed through, laden with property. Once free of the crush, Angelika spotted the guardsman, old Halfhead, leaning against a wall, an upturned bottle of rotgut glugging down into his mouth. She waved, and Halfhead rubbed the dribble from his lips. He held the bottle out to her. Smelling his breath, she declined.

Angelika watched the crowd struggle its way past the gates and said, 'I had no idea there were so many people in this louse-ridden town.'

'Me neither,' Halfhead answered. He offered a swig to Franziskus, who held up a hand of polite refusal.

'You're staying to fight?' Angelika asked the gatekeeper.

'I got nowhere better to go. And nobody I'd sooner stick my sword into than the type of swine who'd swear themselves loyal to von Kopfs' ilk.'

'Well, I know a thing or two about the Kopfs the prince ought to hear. Can you take me to him?'

Carefully he set the bottle down on the ground, propped against the wall. He made sure it was steady before turning to leave. 'I'm not supposed to leave my post, but right now, what does it matter?'

Halfhead threaded them through the winding lanes of the town. Finally they approached a large structure, jutting out from the rock face that formed the Castello's only impenetrable wall. The manor of Prince Davio Maurizzi teetered three storeys high; it was built of black and weathered timber. Wooden steps led up to a large porch, decorated with railings of thick and crudely worked iron. Plaster gargoyles, their once-hissing faces chipped and flattened, sat together in peevish disarray, piled in a far corner of the porch. A roughly stitched ensign hung from an awning; it depicted the walls of a fortress silhouetted by a setting sun. Wrought-iron gates separated the prince's manor from the rest of his town; they encircled a dismal expanse of dead grass inhabited by a broken fountain, and by a quartet of old statues, which depicted naked ancients, seated on plinths, bereft of heads, arms and privates.

Two men in mismatched armour of hardened leather paced the length of the porch. Halfhead gestured for Angelika and Franziskus to remain at the gate, and went up to confer with them. The taller of the two guards shrugged fatalistically, and Halfhead beckoned for Angelika and Franziskus to approach. The tall guard disappeared through the oversized front door, hammered out of iron, with stylised lion faces marked out with nails and studs. Soon the door popped open again, and they were ushered into a tiny foyer that smelled of old leather and damp socks. From there they entered a large chamber dominated by a long oaken table and a dozen chairs, all splendid, but each of a different design.

'Sit down,' said the guard, leaving the room to trudge up a creaking staircase of unfinished planking. Halfhead, it seemed, had already departed.

Angelika took a seat, next to the table's head. Franziskus surveyed the contents of the room. Its walls were decorated in brocaded fabric, most crimson or burgundy in colour. It hung from the ceiling mouldings on short lengths of wire. Burning wood glowed white and orange in a fireplace, framed by a mantle of iron. Franziskus approached a towering cabinet of pale polished elfwood, and toyed with the handles of its cupboards, wondering whether to open them.

'So – you have news for me,' came a smoke-soft voice from the foot of the raw and splintering staircase. 'Of the von Kopfs, was it?' His Tilean accent was subtle, and could be heard mostly as a drifting lilt behind his words.

Angelika had never seen the prince before, but from his bearing, she could tell that this was he. His elbows stuck out, adding majesty to his narrow frame. Downy hair, the colour and length of a mouse's, covered his wide-crowned head. Round ears angled out and forward from his skull; they should have seemed humorous, but instead suggested a pinprick alertness. Well-earned lines had etched themselves around the corners of his mouth and nose. Despite the weary semi-circles beneath them, his grey eyes shone piercingly at Angelika. For Franziskus, he spared only the briefest of glances.

He wore a fox-trimmed coat that draped down to his ankles, over a long shirt covering him to mid-thigh. It was wrinkled, and Angelika surmised that he'd just been sleeping in it. Velvet slippers, in royal purple, swaddled his feet, which were big and shaped like the paddles of oars. He stepped further toward the room but stopped at its threshold, leaning against its doorless archway. He bobbed his narrow chin at Angelika, bidding her to speak.

'I've spent the past few days,' she said, 'on and off, in the company of two Kopfs, who were undertaking a mission for their father. But maybe you know of this, already.'

He blinked and shook his head. Angelika admired his skill as a liar; most men made too great a show of their denials, but Davio's was both bland and plausible. 'Perhaps you can begin by telling me who you are.'

'I am Angelika Fleischer. This is my assistant, Franziskus.'

'Please feel free to continue.'

'When I agreed to help the Kopfs, I was unaware of their hostility toward you. Over these past few weeks, this place has been a good and congenial home to me. I've no wish for Jurgen's sons to turn it into a pile of tindersticks.'

He seemed to make a decision, and entered the room, moving to the cabinet. 'Brandy? I have a bottle from Angoumelle, just north of Chalons Forest. It is very fine.'

'Yes, please,' Angelika said.

'And you?'

Franziskus refused, pulling out a chair from the foot of the table and sitting in it. The prince curled his lip mournfully. He pried off the cork and poured generous portions into two clay cups. He handed the first to Angelika and watched solicitously as she tasted. Her eyes widened in appreciation. Then Davio sat, downed his entire cup, rose, refilled it, and sat down again.

She leaned in toward him. It was as if he exerted gravity on her.

'I am glad for your concern,' he said, 'but I assure you the Castello is in no danger whatever.'

'The hundreds of people fleeing your town seem to disagree.'

'It is mere politics. The Averlanders, they wish to squeeze us, and they will – a little. They must be seen to act. It is all a show, for the other princes. Prow-faced Jurgen will pursue his siege for a season, at the most. When he finds our shells harder to crack than he expected, he'll declare his objectives met and he'll withdraw. Sooner or later, the bright light of reason will crack through even his sturdy Imperial skull.

'We have stores in abundance. Those who now flee, to be fleeced by the black and yellows, they will learn that they were fools. Even the Kopfs aren't mad enough to waste men and munitions, with the orcs about to come steaming up from the south. It is surely a bluff.'

'Though endearing, your faith in your opponent's good sense is perhaps misguided.'

'Mere alarmism,' he mumbled, laying his arms out on the table and slumping his head sleepily onto them. A strong urge overcame Angelika to pet the fur of Davio's collar, and to run her hands along his muscular back.

'We've interrupted your slumber?' she asked him.

'Pay me no heed,' he said, straightening himself back up. 'Ever since this foolishness began, I have drifted unpredictably between sleep and waking. But you have taken the trouble to come and see me. Please unburden yourself of your tidings.'

Angelika started as he suddenly jolted to his feet. He refilled his cup and topped off hers. 'It is about Lukas von Kopf,' she said.

'Lukas?' He sipped his Angoumelle. 'There are so many of them, it is hard to keep track.'

'You know – the one you ordered to be kidnapped.'

She had never seen anyone raise an eyebrow as slowly as Davio did then. 'I had some person abducted? No one informed me of this.'

'Your hirelings say otherwise.'

'Which hirelings would these be?'

'The elf and the two halflings.'

'I have neither elves nor halflings in my employ. You've been led astray.' He inhaled imperiously.

'You don't need to deny it to me. The last thing I intend is to give him over to the Kopfs. All I want is to get him out of here and far away from them. As you know, they'll kill him, if they get him.'

He peered into her face. 'You are a lovely creature but you baffle me, utterly.'

'And you are handsome, but there's no time for your denials. Take me to him, and you have my word I'll never tell anyone of your part in this.'

Prince Davio twisted in his chair, to appraise Franziskus. 'We have much to puzzle out. Is there a reason why your assistant should be here for the rest of this conversation?'

'He's more trustworthy than I am, if that's what worries you.'

'No offence, my friend,' he said to Franziskus, 'but I find your presence inhibiting.' He turned to Angelika. 'An even rarer vintage of Angoumelle waits for us in my chambers, upstairs. Perhaps you would like to sample it?'

Franziskus scraped his chair angrily across the clay tile flooring. The sound made Angelika wince.

She rose. 'I believe I will,' she said.

She moved to the doorway. Franziskus pulled her back into the room. She removed his hand from her arm. Assuming a sheepish expression, he stepped back.

'What are you doing?' he asked.

'What it looks like I'm doing.'

'Is anything wrong?' Davio asked, with extreme mildness.

'My dogsbody has forgotten his place,' Angelika said, brushing past Franziskus. 'But it's nothing to concern ourselves with.' Head high, she ascended the stairs. Davio sneaked a glance at Franziskus before following her.

Candles of various heights appointed the princely bedchamber. They stood on tall sticks of brass or terracotta, on nearly every surface: on a bedside table, a desk, a squat liquor cabinet inlaid in the old Nulnish style. Brocade curtains hung around Davio's bed, from a frame of copper piping. The room smelled of burnt wax and perspiration.

Fire burned in a small iron stove; Davio used it to light a taper. He lit the candles. When he had finished, Angelika came up from behind him and pulled his coat from his shoulders, letting it drop into a pile at his feet. She wrapped her arms around him and ran the tips of her fingers along the tight muscles of his chest. He caught her right hand by the wrist and pulled it to his mouth. He kissed the wrist, her palm, the back of her hand. He gently bit her fingers.

She turned him around and pulled the shirt over his head.

FRANZISKUS PACED. HE looked up at the ceiling. He heard the creaking of floorboards. He tried to guess where the bed might be. He decided he did not want to hear any more. He stormed out onto the porch.

The guards were laughing, rudely gesturing: clearly, they were speculating about what precisely was happening upstairs. Franziskus summoned up all of his aristocratic authority and disdain, and his throat. They stopped, looking suitably abashed.

'Tell Angelika, when she asks for me, that I have gone to the Painful Coffin.'

They nodded. He proceeded down the porch and over the garden stones until he reached the gate. He disengaged it from its latch and stepped through it. Behind him, he heard blunted, throaty laughter.

His ears burned. He wanted to bite through his lip. He stuck his elbows out and marched to the tavern. He did not know the exact way from here, but the general direction was enough. There would be dead ends and wrong turns, but that was good. It suited his mood, to be frustrated.

The streets were deserted. And quiet. The noise from outside the walls was nothing more than a muted, distant roar from here. Every so often, a shutter would edge open, and someone inside a hovel would peer at Franziskus, from the darkness. He took no notice of any of this.

He practised what he might say to her.

Why did you do that?, he would ask.

Then she would say, *Do I answer to you?*

And he would say, *No, but–*

And she would cut him off and say, *No 'buts' about it. If anything, you answer to me. If your oath to follow me is worth a jot.*

And he would be at a loss for words.

So he would not say that. Instead he would take a different tack. He would say, *Are you refreshed, after your romp with the prince?* No, he would not say *'romp'*. He would say *'gambol'*. Gambol sounded even more carefree than romp. Something said between comrades. A backslapping sort of jape, as if he and she were not of different sexes. *I trust you had a good roister,* he would say to her, as he used to say to his male friends, when he was still part of the regiment.

Except that he had not had friends in the regiment, not per se. At least, none with whom he could have off-handedly discussed romps or gambols or roisters. He had never been able to laugh about things like that, to treat them as if they did not matter. As if love were a flippant thing, to crumble up and use as the kindling of idle conversation.

He would not say anything to her. He would act as if nothing had happened. As if he had not humiliated herself by tugging so openly on her arm. By treating her as if he had some claim on her. By once again showing her that he was a thick-witted prig who knew nothing of her world and had no hope of ever understanding or pleasing her.

He found himself in a cul-de-sac. He faced an empty barn, its door swinging on its hinges. He turned to retrace his steps, but he did not remember where he'd been. He hadn't been paying attention. He might have come from straight ahead, or from a curving laneway to the left, or he could even have squeezed in from a muddy patch on the right.

A woman stepped toward him. 'Good sir!' she called. She had flaxen hair and wore a gown of green velvet. Her low bodice afforded him a generous view of fine, firm flesh. It took him a moment to remember that he'd seen this woman before. She'd framed herself in a doorway for him, the last time he was in town, on the night they met the Kopfs.

'Good sir!' she repeated.

'My name is Franziskus.'

'And your family name would be? From your strong posture and the refined way that you speak, I know you must be of a noble pedigree.' She spoke in the charming accent of a Bretonnian, turning any hint of an indecorous 'th' or 'ch' sound into a pliant 's' or yielding 'z'.

Franziskus could not decide what to do with his hands. He was tempted to find a wall to lean against, to seem less awkward. 'I no longer make use of my family name,' he said.

She parted her lips in mournful sympathy. She seemed to be ready to say something, but did not.

'Have we been introduced before, milady?' Franziskus cringed at the stupidity of his own words. Of course they had not been introduced.

She shuffled over to him and extended her hand midair, fingers curved earthward. 'My name is Petrine Guillame.'

He bowed to take her hand and kiss it, but she retracted it as he was halfway through the gesture. Her cheeks coloured. 'Beg pardon. I am presumptuous. I have no right to expect niceties from you, Franziskus. You do not know it, but I have wronged you terribly.'

'I don't see how you could possibly have–' The wind picked up, bringing the tang of the barnyard from the crumbling stable behind him. 'Perhaps we could go somewhere more amenable to discussion–'

She surged ahead, clasping her hands together. 'No, I am afraid that there is no time.' She now stood close enough to him that he could smell the scent she wore on her neck. He could not place it, but it reminded him both of spices and of fruit. A thin skein of hair loosened itself from her pearly headpiece and fell over her forehead. 'It is I who paid your enemies, Toby Goatfield and the others, to abduct poor young Lukas.'

He gasped, a little. 'You? Why?'

Petrine looked down. 'Not all women are creatures of resourcefulness and means, like your friend Angelika. The rest of us, when fate abandons us, must favour the possible over the virtuous. To survive, we must seek the protection of powerful patrons. Yet when a woman without means attaches herself to a man of power, she is compromised. She is expected to do things. Sometimes these things are not right, but we have little choice, except to perform, as asked.'

'Who is this man, who oppresses you?'

'You have just come from his manor.'

'You followed me?'

She moved to a crumbling wall and heaved her shoulders against it. 'Yet another sin I have visited upon you. But this time I transgress in fervent hope of redemption. If the town walls fall, Davio will order poor Lukas slain. As a Tilean, vengeance is his foremost thought.'

'He does not seem to think the Castello is in much danger.'

'It is bravado only. Trust me, I know no man as I know Davio Maurizzi. The town will die, and then, so will Lukas. That is why I have been so impudent as to approach you, fine sir.'

'Please, I am not – there's no need to...'

With nimble fingers, she opened a calfskin pouch that dangled from her belt. She withdrew a roll of vellum, tied with a piece of hairy twine. 'This is a map. It will take you to the location where Lukas is being held.'

'He is not here, in the town?'

'No, the prince would not risk it. To the east, up in the hills, there is a secret encampment, a bolt-hole where Toby and his associates hide, with others of his halfling gang. I have marked how to find it. You must find Angelika, wherever she is, and go with her to this place, and take Lukas from them. Otherwise, they have orders to break his neck, if the Castello falls.' She pressed the map into his fingers, crumpling it.

He held onto her hands. 'But what of you? Will the prince not know you've betrayed his scheme?'

She pulled back and closed her eyes. 'Perhaps. But, for once, I must not think of myself.'

'Come with us, so I can protect you.'

She turned and hurried down the twisting lane. 'No, I cannot put you in further peril.'

He grabbed her, spun her around. She fell into him. His breath caught in his throat. 'But it is not necessary for you to trade your life for Lukas's. Come with us, and we'll all find safety together.'

Petrine pushed him away, but he could tell she didn't want to. 'I have not mastered the manly arts, the way your Angelika has. In woods or mountains, I would be but a hindrance to you. Worry not about me. I will find a way. I always have.' With her forefinger, she touched him on the tip of his nose. 'It is the nature of existence, that circumstances are never what we wish them to be. Were you and I in another place, with different histories... Your Angelika, she is lucky to have you.' She stepped back, her eyes staring at the ground in front of Franziskus's feet. It was as if she was drawing a line there, forbidding him to cross. Then, in a twirl of her gown, she had her back to him again, and was fleeing down the street.

'But she's not my Angelika!' Franziskus said, watching her go. He'd meant to shout it to her, but it had come out as a whisper, so, in truth, he talked only to himself.

CHAPTER EIGHT

DESPITE THE BLANKET of quiet that smothered the town, the Dolorosa La Bara bulged with shouting, laughing, coughing patrons. Items of gold, from brooches to chalices, sat heaped on a table, where drinkers frantically threw dice, sweat pouring down their faces. They'd decided, evidently, to at least feel the ecstatic mortification of losing their possessions in a game of chance, instead of giving them up to the soldiers outside the gates. Franziskus, ensconced at the bar on a well-padded stool, wondered what the eventual winner was supposed to do with his haul. Bury it, perhaps, and hope to come back later?

The young Stirlander had forgone his usual ale, electing instead to knock down cups of watered-down rum. It was diluted but burned his tongue and gullet all the same. He twitched his hand at Giacomo, the barman, who refilled him and slid his pennies from the damp wooden counter. Behind him, a hawk-nosed young man in torn mendicant's robes screamed something about the apocalypse. He'd renounced forever his vows of temperance, though Franziskus suspected that tomorrow morning's hangover might provoke their abrupt renewal.

Angelika slid onto the stool next to him. 'Evening, Franziskus,' she'd said.

He hadn't seen her come in. But, then again, it had been hours since he'd stopped looking at the doorway. 'Did you learn anything?'

'About Lukas? No.'

Giacomo needed no prompting to set a cup before her, and fill it with brandy.

She sipped, and stuck out her tongue. 'This is hard to take, after that Angoumelle.'

'Did you enjoy his finer vintage, the one he had upstairs?' Franziskus regretted the words as soon as they passed his lips. Or rather, their tone gave him away; he'd meant to sound offhand and comradely, but sarcasm had crept in anyway.

'We didn't get to it,' Angelika said. She set her brandy down and peered into it.

'So he continued to deny any knowledge of the boy?'

She nodded.

'You didn't believe him, I hope.'

'You think me the sort of person to lose all reason over a glittering pair of grey eyes and a lovely wolf's grin? Please!'

'Then why did you–' He caught himself short. He thought everyone in the bar would be looking at him, after this outburst, but the volume of his voice was nothing compared to the hysterical bellowing around them, so not a single head turned their way. He finished his drink and slammed the cup on the bar. Angelika looked at him with obvious disgust. 'Pardon my indiscretion,' he said.

She did not give him the relief of a reply.

He tried to catch Giacomo's eye, but the barkeep was occupied with the unintelligible shouts of a fat-cheeked dwarf across the way. 'It merely seems inadvisable to... to render yourself... vulnerable to the very person we suspect of being our adversary. Not just suspect – we have good reason to believe–'

'I'll be my own judge of what's safe,' she said. 'Besides, one thing has nothing to do with the other.'

'Don't think that I think I have any sort of claim on you,' Franziskus said. The rum made him feel apart from himself, like it was some other fellow he could hear talking to her. He wondered why someone didn't make this fellow shut up before he dug his grave any deeper. 'Because far from it. I don't and I wouldn't want to. The man's a villain, and I don't understand. But, as you'll remind me, what right have I to understanding? You just want me to go away, don't you?'

'We should get you home to bed, Franziskus.'

'That's what this was about, wasn't it? Your reminding me of how unwanted I am here.' He stood up, weaved, and slumped over, leaning on the counter for support. 'You didn't want him at all. He was just to hand, that's all. To teach me a lesson. A lesson I deserve.'

She clapped him on the arm. 'Stop talking, Franziskus.'

He slumped back onto his stool. 'See, that's what I keep telling myself, that I should stop talking. But there's something I keep meaning to get to, except that we haven't got to it yet. The point is, I have this.' He slapped the map, its neat roll now crushed flat, onto the counter. 'While you were – off doing what you were doing – I was on Lukas's trail.'

SHE PROPPED HIM up on the way home to their rented hovel. In the morning, she fed him a greasy meal of sausage and egg, and asked him if he remembered, perchance, who had given him the map that supposedly led to Lukas.

'That I clearly recall,' he said, massaging his temples, 'it's what happened later, after I started to drink, that eludes me.'

'Which is for the best, believe me.'

'The woman's name is Petrine Guillame.' He recounted his meeting with her.

'She hired Goatfield?'

'She serves Davio, as his executor of dirty dealings.'

'And you think she was honestly remorseful? That it wasn't a trick of some kind?'

His eyebrows hurt. He wiggled them around. 'I believed her at the time. But who knows?'

'Davio acquainted me with several of his good qualities, but, still, he styles himself a prince, so he can't be taken at his word.'

'Who do we believe, then? Should we flip a coin?'

'Either of them might be lying. But this woman of yours, she at least has given us a direction to go in.'

'But you're saying it might be a trap.'

'Was she as beautiful up close as when you saw her in the doorway?'

'Yes.'

'And she seemed willing to fall into your embrace?'

He shrugged. It hurt to shrug. 'I wanted to think so.'

'You should have pressed your case, and found out for sure.' She picked up her pack and took out its contents, laying them out on a rough-edged pine table. 'You're one to freely dispense advice, Franziskus. Would you like to hear some, in return?'

'Not really, but proceed, anyway.'

'Pleasure is rare enough in this world, Franziskus, and we all end up in our graves sooner than we think. To hell with what the priests say: few joys are more intense than that of skin against skin. If you get a chance with one who quickens your heart, take it.'

'She was in distress.'

'A little upset can heighten the sharpness of it.' She opened the larder door in search of dried meat. An under-nourished rat scurried deeper into the cupboard; tiny bits of salami lay scattered across the shelf. She closed the door. 'We'll have to get provisions from the stalls, outside.'

'There has to be more to it than that, Angelika. More than the physical.'

'So say the poets. But I say, to hell with them.'

THEY HEADED TO the gate, which was still open to allow the last few refugees to exit. Not wanting to give up their property to the Averlanders, they scaled the Castello wall to angle past the checkpoint. Even so, a stray soldier challenged them, and they had to buy his silence with silver shillings. They stopped to purchase field rations from one of the vendors and then vacated the siege camp. They hiked across the valley floor and up into the hills, as Petrine's map indicated. Initially, Franziskus worried he might collapse on the trail, but the exertion did him good. By mid-afternoon, they neared the site of the bolt hole. According to the map, they had another half-mile or so to go, up the overgrown road they'd been travelling. Like the rock cut back at the Castello, this old road was a remnant of ancient dwarf engineering.

'Smoke,' she said, pointing to the sky. A thin white stream snaked thirty feet above the treetops before dispersing.

Franziskus looked at the map again, wishing there were something on it to suggest exactly what form Toby's hideout took. Petrine's 'X' lay off to one side in what looked like a small clearing. They left the road, avoiding a patch of rashweed, and walked through tall pines. They followed the smoke to find the clearing.

The smoke rose from a hole in the earth, its sides dense with bushes and large, leafy plants. It looked like it might have been an old sinkhole, now overgrown. A fence of poles and wires surrounded it. They looked around them to see if they were being watched. Side by side, they edged out from the woods. Angelika pointed to a squarish patch of ground ahead of them, where the weeds and grasses stood out from those immediately around them. They skirted it, but got close enough to see that it was a pit trap.

Chimes and bells, mostly of brass, that were dangling from the wire fence, rang out gently. If they touched any of the wires, the chimes would clang violently, alerting the bolt hole's inhabitants.

Angelika bid Franziskus to go first. She had the better chance of success, but there was no point in her carefully making her way past if he was going to set it off anyway. He gave the wires a serious look, clasped his hands briefly together, then slowly contorted himself, lifting one leg, then the other, insinuating his way through the fence. Angelika gestured her approval and slipped between the wires after him.

They drew weapons and crept to the hole's edge. They peered in. A roof of planks sealed the hole off, about ten feet down its sides. Around the back, they could see a set of metal stairs, obscured by foliage. It led to a trap door in the planking.

'How quietly can you step?' she whispered. Angelica was now at the bottom of the stairs. She reached out with her boot and tested the planking as if it were a pool of water. She shifted her weight onto the platform. It creaked. She stopped. She let her other foot lightly down on the wood. It cracked. She heard banging below. She stopped. The banging ended. Then there were voices. Her weight was too far forward for her to keep her balance. She shifted. The boards made a complaining noise. She held her breath, and waited.

When some time had passed, and no sound had come up from below, she took another daring step toward the trap door. The board beneath her feet stayed solid and silent. She took another step. And another. And another.

When she stole a third step onto a new plank, it groaned like a banshee. She hesitated, alert for sounds. When none came she sprinted the remaining distance to the trap door. Angelika placed her fingers on the rope handle and tugged. A distinct metallic click sounded. The door was latched from the inside.

A muffled voice emanated from the depths. Angelika couldn't make it out, but it was a male voice, and could have belonged to either Toby or Henty. She held the handle tight, to keep it from rattling. The shout from below was repeated; Angelika thought he said, 'Who goes there?' or something like that.

With steady caution, she released the handle and let the door sink back into its frame. She studied its metal hinges. The metalwork was primitive, and twisted wire took the place of pins. If the hinges were better made, they'd be easier to circumvent; she could simply take her knife and slowly pry the pins loose. But she couldn't do that to these ones – she'd need to think of another way in.

She rose and made her way steadily way back to the stairs, where Franziskus anxiously waited. On her return trip, the boards let out only a pair of bad creaks, and each time, more shouts echoed from inside Toby's lair.

'They know we're here,' Franziskus said, voice hushed.

'They know someone's here,' Angelika corrected. She sat on a step. 'But will they come out to investigate?

Franziskus sat beside her. 'What is the purpose of a well-defended lair, if you obligingly poke your head out every time someone knocks at the door?'

'No, they're not stupid. Well, Henty is stupid. But the others aren't.'

They watched the door. It remained stubbornly still.

Angelika turned and walked up the steps. She headed out of the clearing into the surrounding woods, and stooped to gather armfuls of brown, dead weeds.

Franziskus stuck by her side. 'Ah – you mean to smoke them out.'

'That's the drawback of a wooden fortress, isn't it?'

He ducked to help her collect the kindling. 'If we set their redoubt on fire, they'll flee, sure enough. But will they bring Lukas out with them?'

'Probably not. So we'll have to finish them off fast, then go in to pull him from the flames.' She'd found as much tinder as she could carry, so she walked back to the hole to pile it up.

Franziskus dumped his armful of weeds and wrinkled his nose at the closed trap door. 'I don't fancy our odds, taking on those three again. We only beat them the last time by a narrow margin – and that was only because they failed to coordinate their attacks.'

'I'm not claiming this is a good plan,' she said, 'but it is the only one I can think of.' She ventured back into the woods for more dry brush.

They accumulated two more armfuls. They twisted the weeds together, to make them easier to throw, and tossed them out onto the platform. Most landed near the trap door, though some fell wide of the mark. Franziskus set to work with his tinder box. They'd kept a few bundles in reserve; he set one alight. He lobbed it at the pile of weeds. It hit, but bounced, rolling to a stop several feet away. It burned out, without igniting the wood around it, leaving only a black smudge on the planking. He lit another and handed it to Angelika. She threw it right onto the kindling. A gust blew, that fed the fire. The flame made an appreciative *whoomp* noise and consumed the weeds. Under his breath, Franziskus egged it on, begging it to spread to the wood. It did. Grey smoke curled around the weeds and charring planks. It seeped down through the cracks between boards. A chorus of angry yells bubbled up.

Angelika and Franziskus dashed up the steps and stood on the edge. The trap door flipped open, banging on the deck behind it. A halfling leapt out. It was neither Toby nor Henty.

It was a woman, her complexion darker than any halfling Angelika had seen. Her heart-shaped face was wrenched up into a snarl. Long, twisted curls of glossy dark hair flew out behind her as she bounded across the platform, shrieking a war cry and swinging a hatchet. Rows of copper rings pierced her ears and lower lip. She wore a shirt of mail, and she had to adjust the sleeve so that it would not droop over her free hand. A bronze buckle, so old that it had taken on a brilliant green patina, clung to her elbow, a rusty spike jutting from its centre.

Next to emerge from the trap door, now wreathed in a ball of smoke, was a long-faced halfling with a steel helmet poised crookedly on top of his rectangular head. He wore no other armour, just a woollen tunic and hide leggings; his naked toes splayed wide across the burning boards as he charged toward the steps. In each fist, he carried a long, curved blade; he scraped them together to produce a sound that set Angelika's teeth on edge.

Then a third halfling came from the smoke. He'd left his head unprotected; grey hair feathered at his temples, beneath a thicker mop of reddish locks. His features were lined and bulldoggish. He wore only leggings; the muscles of his chest sagged, his gut jiggled above his waistline, but his arms bulged tight and ropy. In his right hand, he carried a kite shield, nearly two-thirds his height. On his left he wore a long, leather glove, which extended past his forearm; small spikes ran along his knuckles and from wrist to elbow.

Then a fourth halfling pulled herself up through the doorway, lithe and fair-haired, her porcelain skin ruined by smallpox scars. She held a rapier and a dagger. A fifth appeared at her heels: bald, old, unshaven, with a wily, eager look about him and a club of burly oak in his gnarled right fist.

That was the last of them. No Toby, no Henty, no Elennath. No Lukas, borne forth as a hostage, a knife's-edge at his jugular. Angelika and Franziskus stepped back, and checked each other's faces for signs of surprise. She said something to the halflings about this all being a mistake, but they kept coming.

The halfling with the long black curls reached the stone stairway first. Angelika kicked her in the throat, knocking her onto her backside. As she fell, the rim of her buckle caught Angelika's leg, and pulled her forward. Angelika fought for balance on the lip of the sinkhole, then tumbled onto the smoke-shrouded platform. The scimitar-wielder dived in at her, but she hopped up like a frog to evade his twin blows. She bounced into Spike-Glove, who smashed her in the face with his shield and then followed up with a punch to the head with his reinforced fist. Franziskus pushed off from the sinkhole rim to land on him, and tear him off Angelika. Franziskus pressed the flat of his elven sword to the man's gullet, choking him. The Poxy One jabbed at him with her own slim sword, poking a hole through the fabric of his tunic. He rolled, and her next blow speared in at Spike-Glove, who deflected it with his shield.

'Hand over Lukas!' Franziskus shouted, at both of them. This halted them for a moment, and they exchanged puzzled looks. Then, in tandem, they feinted at Franziskus.

Curly-Locks swooped her hatchet at Angelika, who scooted backwards. Hatchet hit flooring. Wood splinters flew. Curly-Locks lunged, punching forward with her buckle-spike. Angelika danced back and around, seizing her shield-shoulder and spinning her. Curly-Locks tripped, falling into the smoke, but regained her feet before Angelika could find advantage. They crouched, each waiting for an opening.

'You're on fire,' Angelika told her.

'No I'm not,' she said.

'Suit yourself.'

Curly-Locks looked down to see orange fire eating at the fabric of her leggings. Her eyes bulged. She rolled to a part of the platform untouched by flames.

Poxy and Spike-Glove flanked Franziskus. Spike-Glove punched him in the stomach. He doubled over, shambling into the smoke. He choked, unable to breathe. Spike-Glove came through the cloud at him, squinting, mouth clamped shut. With his elf-sword's razor tip, Franziskus speared the halfling's upper arm, so that he was forced to drop his kite shield. Franziskus stooped to grab it and brought its sharp bottom edge down on his opponent's neck. The gloved halfling hit the platform, face first, and lay there moaning.

Angelika ran to the foot of the stairs. Scimitar and Baldy jostled shoulders, each vying to be the first to engage her. Baldy grinned savagely and let Scimitar step up. Scimitar grated his curved blades together. Angelika backed off. She tried to angle around him.

'I've fought some crazy-stupid people in my day,' he drawled, 'but you takes the prize. Only the two of you, and you attacks a stronghold not knowing who you'll shake loose to fight you.'

The poxy one, waving her sword-hand to dispel the smoke before her face, stepped through the cloud, saw Franziskus, and slashed at him. He skipped out of the arc of her blow, then used his height advantage to tear open the front of her tunic. He grimaced when the flap of cloth fell open; he'd cut her more deeply than he'd intended: from cleavage to clavicle.

He backed up. 'We've no desire to wound you,' he told the poxy halfling. 'Just let us get Lukas, and all will be–'

Her rapier cut at his legs. He jumped away. Their crossed blades rang. From the corner of his eye, Franziskus saw that Spike-Glove had passed out, and that high flames were about to roast him. Half crouching, Franziskus forked a path to his fallen foe. He grabbed hold of the halfling's legs and pulled him free of the fire. He felt a push on his hips, and then he toppled on his side: Poxy had kicked him over. He scrambled on the boards. She brought another blow raining down on him, and as he parried it, sparks flew from his elven blade.

'Why did you save him?' she demanded. She sliced at him; he rolled.

He crawled over to her. 'No one need die here. You've fought well; Toby cannot blame you.'

Angelika seized Scimitar's dropped weapon and swooped it at him. With a sideways blow of his remaining blade, he knocked it from her hand. Pain radiated through her fingers and up into her arm. He brought the curved sword bearing down on her.

A crash came from behind him. He pivoted his head to see what it was. The boards at the centre of the platform had been claimed by fire, and were collapsing into the hideout.

She punched him in the ear. He sank to the boards.

'Toby?' the poxy halfling shrieked at Franziskus. 'You serve Toby? Wretches! We'll fry your gizzards!' She lurched at Franziskus, then slumped, her features twisted in agony. Her face wound up in his lap. Blood soaked her tunic down to the waist.

Angelika heard footfalls behind her and dropped down. Curly-Locks tripped over her and sailed, sprawling onto the boards. The spike of her buckle became stuck between two planks. She fought to jerk it free, but gave up, and hurled a third hatchet at Angelika. Angelika ducked, but the handle of the spinning weapon still hit her on the temple. She blacked out.

Baldy bounded down the steps to run at Franziskus, dodging to skirt the yawning, growing hole in the middle of the planking. About ten feet from Franziskus, he slowed himself. Opening his mouth, he revealed nearly toothless gums. Strands of saliva ran from the top layer to the bottom.

Poxy's eyes fluttered open. She called to Baldy: 'Toby sent them!

'Goatfield?' Baldy's knuckles tightened around the grip of his club. 'Tell us where the back-stabbing pig is, and just maybe you'll earn yourself the mercy of a quick death!'

'We don't know where he is! We came here–' Franziskus thought fast, 'to kill him!'

Baldy stretched his left arm out and up to bunch Franziskus's collar into a wad and shake him. Franziskus chose not to resist, allowing the halfling to pull him down to his eye level.

'You lie!' Baldy shouted.

'You misunderstand! We came here looking for him!'

Curly-Locks dragged Angelika's unconscious body over, and roughly tossed her onto the platform, beside Franziskus. It bounced slightly as she landed. Another plank had burned up and teetered into a hole. Franziskus gave it a long and meaningful look, hoping that one of them, at least, would realise how little time they had before the whole thing collapsed entirely. Baldy, however, was only interested in shaking him.

'You make no sense!' he said, sprinkling the young Stirlander's face with rancid spittle.

'Toby's our sworn enemy! He holds a friend of ours prisoner!' Franziskus aimed yet another look at the flaming boards. 'We came to get our friend, and deal Goatfield the swift justice he deserves!'

Baldy butted Franziskus in the gut. Franziskus doubled over, glad that the hard-skulled halfling wasn't tall enough to head-butt him. Black smoke wreathed them. He felt a pinching grip on his elbow, and followed it. The halflings led him off the platform and stumbling up the steps.

He coughed and fell on the meadow floor, rolling onto his side and bringing his knees up to his chin. The prickly stalk of a yellow wildflower spiked his cheek. He heard a body fall beside him, and opened his eyes to see that it was Angelika. She breathed shallowly. Someone yanked his hands behind his back and tightly tied them. He watched as Curly-Locks bound Angelika, too.

Then the halflings left them alone for a while. Franziskus reckoned it was about ten or fifteen minutes. He heard them muttering but they were too far away to pick out any words. He wriggled over to see that they stood on the lip of their hole, watching the rest of their home burn up. Quietly, Franziskus took Sigmar's name in vain.

The halflings strode back over. The terrible slash he'd given Poxy had been crudely bound, with fabric torn from her trouser-legs. Any clean bandages they might have had would now be smouldering in the wreckage below. Baldy reached over and wrenched Franziskus up by the hair, into a sitting position. Franziskus made an effort not to cry out. Curly-Locks pulled Angelika up, too.

'Tell us your names,' she demanded.

Angelika still couldn't focus. Franziskus answered for her: 'I am Franziskus of Stirland. This is Angelika Fleischer. As I was saying–'

Baldy clamped stubby fingers around the front of Franziskus's windpipe. 'Speak only when spoken to, Ladder-Legs.'

Curly-Locks nodded and Baldy let go of him. When he'd finished gasping, Franziskus turned to face the dark-haired woman, who was clearly the one in charge.

'I am Lela Mossrock, unfairly exiled from the Moot – as were each and every one of us.' She swept her hand to indicate her fellows. 'You say you came here for Toby Goatfield?' She spat the name as if it were the filthiest of obscenities.

'We were told we could find him here. Have you seen him?'

Now it was her turn to grab his throat. She barely had to stoop. 'If I had, he'd be lying beside you, my hatchet sunk deep in his brain!'

Franziskus jerked his mouth, to show her he couldn't speak with the fingers jammed into his windpipe. She let go. He coughed. 'Evidently we've been deceived, no doubt by common foes. Have you done anything to offend the so-called Prince Davio, of the Castello del Dimenticato?'

She stepped back from him, cocking her head. 'I have heard of him; that is all.' She looked at the others. 'Do any of this fool's babblings make sense to you?'

They served up a variety of blank looks. Scimitar shrugged. 'Arthie and me went down there for rotgut, last autumn, but we didn't do nothing to cause no one to send no murderers our way.'

'But Goatfield knows of this place,' Franziskus said.

'Knows of it?' Curly-Locks's eyes were liquid hate. 'He tricked us into building it for him, doing nary a lick of work himself! It was here he stole my virtue, which I had carefully hoarded as the most precious of things – meant only for he who would wed me, fair and true!' One of her hatchets had reappeared in her hand; it quivered beside her head.

'And Henty Redpot? You know of him, too?'

'Henty?' Scimitar exclaimed. 'When I sees him, I'll thumb his eyes from their sockets – grind them to paste!'

'Only if you're the first to get to 'im,' growled Baldy.

Franziskus could not imagine them successfully overcoming the crazed and muscle-bound Henty, even if they worked in tandem. He decided, however, that this was an insight best left unshared. Instead he said: 'So from what you know of this Toby, he sounds like quite the master of treachery?'

'He's not half as smart as he thinks,' Curly-Locks said.

'But let's say he wanted to throw someone off his trail. He knows exactly where this place is, well enough to give directions to another party, yes?'

'Of course. Didn't you hear me?'

'This is what happened. We fell victim to his trickery. He had someone come to us, someone who made herself seem friendly to our cause; she sent us here, thinking it was him and Henty down in that fort, holding captive a young fellow we're honour-bound to rescue.'

'Honour? It's honour made you destroy our home?'

'No, it was treachery – Toby's treachery. He did this to you. We were but his pawns.'

'His dupes, more like.'

Franziskus paused for another little cough. 'I wish I could argue with you, but you are right. It was my fault. I am the one who believed this person, who turned out to be in league with your enemy.'

Angelika now seemed ready to speak.

Franziskus kept going, to cut her off: 'It was I who convinced my friend to come here, and I who dealt the worst wound to any of you.' Poxy responded to this observation with a nod of grievance. 'If you wish to avenge the wrongs done to you,' Franziskus continued, 'take me, but let my friend go. The fault is mine, and I must bear the punishment alone.'

'Or better yet,' Angelika broke in, 'come with us, and help us hunt the rat down once and for all! He's the one you really want.'

Curly-Locks took another look at the greying plume of smoke rising from their fortress. 'You speak glibly and smooth-tongued.'

'You don't have much reason to trust us, I'll grant you that,' Angelika said. 'But picture it: the look on his face when all of us show up together, to exact our reckoning on him. All of his worst enemies, gathered together by his own too-clever plan. Wouldn't that look be worth almost anything to you?'

Curly-Locks pursed her lips thoughtfully. 'It's a tempting picture you paint.'

'They lie!' Poxy cried. 'He paid them to come here. He swore he'd get us, didn't he, when we threw him and Henty out? He swore he'd bring our hard work crashing down around our ears, and look there, he's done it – just as he said!'

Curly-Locks folded her arms. 'What Reecie says makes sense.'

'I agree, it's the sort of thing Goatfield might try,' Angelika said. 'But in this case, it happens he didn't. If you believe one thing I say, believe this: I wouldn't let him pour water on me if I were on fire.'

'It's a trick Toby taught them.' The poxy one winced and clutched at her chest wound. 'First they're supposed to burn us out, then lead us into an ambush. That's why Toby and Henty ain't here themselves. They're waiting for us in the trees along the road, maybe even with that pervert elf of theirs.'

'So you know Elennath, too?' said Franziskus.

By way of reply, the scarred halfling made an obscene gesture.

'Look at the sword I had with me,' said Franziskus. 'Do you recognise it?'

The halflings searched the grass for the dropped elven blade. Scimitar picked it up and handed it to Poxy. She studied the runes on its blade.

'You've seen that before,' Franziskus said.

'So what if I have?'

'If you knew that haughty fey-man at all, you'd know he wouldn't give that sword to anyone, under any circumstances. Am I right? Especially if he needed it to ambush you down the road.'

'He was overweening proud of it, Reecie,' said Curly-Locks. 'Always saying it was forged by Elfy Such-and-Such by the Elfy smiths of So-and-So.'

'I took it from him the last time we fought them,' Franziskus said. 'My possession of it proves we're no friend of his, nor of Toby's.'

'You beat them in combat?' Curly-Locks asked. 'Why did you let them live, then?'

'At the time, we didn't know them that well.'

Curly-Locks stowed her hatchet in one of the belts on her back. She interwove the fingers of her tiny hands. 'I must ponder this,' she said.

'I say, never mind what they say about Toby,' said Poxy, or Recie, as her name seemed to be. 'They burned our place, and that's a good enough reason to skin them alive.'

'We'll confer on it,' said Curly-Locks, waving the others to follow her out of earshot.

Attempting to hear what they said was once again fruitless. Angelika tested her bonds. 'They tied these tight,' she said.

'Are you hurt?' Franziskus worked his own wrists, but they were too tightly knotted together. He tried his ankles; the rope seemed to have a little more give in it there.

'I'm sore. My head has started ringing again.' She tried to read the direction of the halflings' deliberations from the postures they'd adopted. Poxy alternately waved her fist and pointed her fingers: that was bad. None of the others provided any signs, one way or the other.

Tired, she sank to rest with the back of her head in the grass. The smoke from the fire had thinned; it blew gently across her field of vision as she gazed up into the sky. It was a summery blue now, strewn with fleecy clouds. One cloud looked like a haunch of mutton. Angelika wondered what kind of omen that would be.

Franziskus cleared his throat. Angelika pulled herself up until she was sitting. The halflings approached them deliberately, in formation, Curly-Locks at the head. Their faces said nothing of their decision.

Curly-Locks stepped in front of Franziskus. 'Here it is,' she said. 'You saved Arthie's life, so we won't beat you beyond recovery. But all the same, we'll have to beat you.' She withdrew the hatchet from her back, flipping it so that its head pointed to the ground. She swung its haft up past her shoulder and then brought it down on the back of Franziskus's head. He dropped down sideways, onto the ground. Hands seized him from behind – they belonged to the one with the scimitar, the one whose life he'd saved. They forced him back up, to receive another blow from Curly-Locks's hatchet handle. Franziskus tried to twist himself free of the restraining hands, but they had him in too strong a grip. Curly-Locks skipped back and swung the haft across the right side of his jaw. She brought it raining down on the bone above his right eye, then on his left. She cracked him in the upper lip, making his teeth cut into it. He tasted his blood; it filled his mouth. Scimitar hauled him up to his feet. Curly-Locks used the haft like a battering ram and jammed it into his sternum. She cracked it along his ribs, first down the right side, and then up the left. She smacked him on the knees. He heard a squeaky, burbling sound; through watery eyes, he saw that it was Poxy, laughing. It was the same laugh he'd heard his playmates make, when he was a child; they taught themselves about flies and beetles by pulling their legs off.

He felt his right eye close up on him. The other fluttered shut.

'His hand. The right,' he heard Curly-Locks say. He tried to open his eyes but they refused him. He heard himself scream, and then connected that sound with the sudden pain that now curled through the fingers of his right hand, which Scimitar was holding by the wrist. He was screaming, and feeling more blows land on his hand. Then it stopped, momentarily, only to switch to the left. He spat, so as not to choke on the blood welling in his throat.

'Oh, so you want to spit on us?' he heard. He felt more hits land on his legs, and in his gut. He knew he was falling, and that the halfling behind him kept yanking him back up for more.

Time ended. He was still being hit.

'Open your eyes,' he heard.

'Open your eyes,' he heard again.

'Open your eyes, I say!' The blows had stopped.

He strained his left eye open. Swirling in front of him was Curly-Locks's face, so large, so close to him, that it blotted out the sky and everything else. 'There you are,' her monstrous teeth somehow moving at a slower speed than the words coming out of them. 'I have a message for you to take to Toby, when you see him.'

He tried to say that she should take her own messages to Toby, but his tongue wouldn't work and he had no air.

'When you see him, tell him he's a father – and that Lela Mossrock has sworn his doom!'

He was then finally allowed to fall. His eyes closed themselves. He could still hear, though there was a buzzing sound, distant yet at the same time loud, overlaying everything else. Even through this, he could tell: they had moved on to Angelika, and were giving her the same treatment.

CHAPTER NINE

THE BLOODY WELTS on Angelika's face glistened in the bright moonlight, as she loomed over Franziskus. Starry pinpoints surrounded her in the dark sky. He was flat on his back. His image of her blinked in and out as his eyelids trembled shut, then open, then shut. Everything hurt.

He could barely recognise her. Gummy, drying blood matted her hair. Her left eye was puffy, protruded, sealed shut, and purple. The skin of her cheekbones had parted to reveal tributaries of exposed red flesh. Her lips were split. She brought a hand to his forehead, to move aside his long, blond locks; its fingers had curled into a crooked ball.

'Franziskus,' she choked.

'Unh,' he said.

'Franziskus,' she gasped.

'Unh,' he said again.

'Franziskus.'

'Unh,' was all he could manage.

'It's *nuh*-night. We – we–' She stopped to breathe. 'Have to find shelter. Wolves.'

He listened for wolves. He didn't hear any.

'I can't move,' he said.

'Wolves,' she said.

'Unh.'

SUN SHONE IN his eyes. He dragged himself into the shade. It hurt to move. He put his head against something and hoped sleep would take him. The angle strained his neck. He leaned up. Only one of his eyes could open: the left one. He was down in the pit, propped against a charred beam. Angelika lay across from him, her eyes open. As he wakened, pain crept up on him. At first, he felt the agony in undifferentiated form: each part of him was just as wracked as any other. Gradually, his awareness gained exactitude: his hands throbbed worst, then his shoulders, then his legs, then his gut. The head floated above this, buzzing, drunk and detached. Franziskus was no medic, but he knew enough to reckon that this was probably the worst sign of all.

'Oh, gods – please, in Shallya's name...' he said, invoking the mercy goddess. It even hurt to talk. In order to speak, he had to move the muscles of his chest and neck, and this sent ripples of ache through his back and torso, and he shuddered and groaned.

He surveyed Angelika's injuries. Her face was swollen, unrecognisable. She showed barely an inch of skin that wasn't either purple with bruises, or etched red with cuts. She lay awkwardly against the same blackened beam that propped him up. Her right thigh was folded under her leg; her torso jutted up from her waist at an angle of forty-five degrees. 'Your back,' he said. 'Did they break it?'

'No. I don't think so.' She spoke so quietly, Franziskus could barely hear her, above the rushing in his ears. 'Just moved. Like this.' A jolt ran through her. Franziskus felt a jarring twinge, in sympathy. 'Because it hurts less. This way.'

Franziskus thought about nodding.

For a long time, neither spoke. Franziskus closed his one good eye, hoping to persuade his body to go back into unconsciousness. It would not go. Now that he was awake, the pain was too strong to release him.

He examined his new surroundings. The pit was about thirty feet deep. Its sides were lined with timber that had suffered nothing worse than superficial scorching. The rest of the place, though, was now just a mound of ash, black mixed in with grey. He saw the remains of dresser drawers, of bedposts, of chests. There were bits of burned fabric and blobs of melted glass, already hardened and intermixed with ash. Long copper rods, bent by the heat into the shapes of snakes, lay scattered throughout. Franziskus surmised that the halflings had made rooms in their fortress with a system of curtain rod frames, and that the thin copper tubes were their remains.

He looked up: another hot, bright day. The position of the sun told him that it was inching up on noon.

He checked Angelika to see if she was awake. Though her eyes were shut, the pattern of her breathing indicated she wasn't asleep.

'How did we get down here?' he said. The utterance cost him a little less pain than his last attempt to speak. He was learning the limit of exertion; how much he could move before his torn and pummelled muscles would punish him.

'Don't know.' She kept her eyes closed.

'We couldn't have got down here on our own.'

'Don't remember.'

'I'll be quiet.'

'No. Talk. Distract me.'

'Were there wolves?'

'Remember something about *wuh* – wolves.'

'Were there truly wolves, or did we just think it?'

'We came down here – to – get away from wolves.'

'Were there truly wolves?'

'Not sure.'

'Would wolves not have finished us off?'

'I suppose they would have.'

'Then there were no wolves.'

'Don't remember.'

'But we couldn't have got down here by ourselves.'

'Don't know.'

'The half-folk couldn't have come back, could they? And taken mercy on us, by carrying us down here, so the beasts of the woods wouldn't finish us off?'

'Them?' She loosed a derisive snort, then paid the toll for sudden movement. She tried to settle herself back on the beam, in the least uncomfortable position she'd found for herself. She winced. Wincing hurt, too.

'You're right. They wouldn't help us.'

She agreed with him, without moving, using only her eyes.

'Maybe we fell in.'

They looked at the drop.

'We must have done it ourselves. Somehow.'

It all seemed very doubtful.

'We'll probably never know,' Franziskus surmised.

ABRUPTLY, THE SUN was on its way to setting. Franziskus realised he'd been unconscious, again. Shallya had heard his prayers, and granted them. Angelika had moved closer to him and was now lying flat on her back, hands behind her head.

'Is that more comfortable?' he asked her.

'For the moment. Every so often I stiffen, and have to shift again.'

'That hurts, I suppose.'

'Yes.' The whites of both her eyes were no longer white, but red, with blood. The swelling on her face had gone down; he could once again make out the natural shape of her cheekbones beneath her facial muscles.

'Have you slept?'

'On and off.'

'I'm going to have to move soon.'

'That so?'

'My bladder demands it.'

'Hrm,' she said.

'But I don't want to.'

She turned her head from him.

'When I move, it'll hurt.'

'If you wet your trousers here, I'll finish you off myself.'

'Do you think any of your bones are broken?'

'They're all intact, I think.'

'The same is true for me. I believe.'

'They did as they said. They hurt us just badly enough. Took us right to the threshold of permanent harm, but no further.'

'Excuse me if I fail to admire their skill.'

A noise came out of her. Eventually, Franziskus identified it as laughter.

'Get up,' she said. 'It'll do you good.'

He stayed put.

'You'll have to sooner or later. The quicker you get the muscles working, the better.'

'I wish I was dead.'

'Get up and do your business.'

He got up. He screamed. He fell.

She stood. She held out a hand for him. He rose.

IT WAS MORNING. They were black all over now. Not from bruising, but from all the ash they'd kicked up as they'd dragged themselves around. Soot coated them, so they could not tell how well they were healing. Franziskus sat against the timber walls now, knees up. Angelika lay face down a few feet from him, in a bed of dead embers.

Franziskus was reasonably sure that this was the second morning, but he had gone in and out of consciousness so many times that he had lost track. He did not want to ask and make himself sound like he was dazed from concussion, though he imagined he probably was. At his foot, he suddenly spotted a small barrel of ale. 'Where did this come from?' He clucked his tongue against the roof of his mouth. It tasted like stale beer. So he must have been drinking from the cask, he deduced blurrily.

Angelika pointed feebly to a corner piled high with half-burned boards. 'Behind there. Some provisions escaped the fire. There's even some dried meat, for when you're feeling up to it.'

She rolled over, so he figured there was no harm in talking again. 'When I was a child,' Franziskus said, 'my maiden aunt, Trine, used to read to me from storybooks. About the Moot, where the halflings dwell.'

Angelika grunted an unintelligible reply.

'I loved those stories,' he went on. 'They were my favourites. In the stories, the Moot was always a green and tender place, with rolling hills, and meadows dappled in white hissock and blue fire grass. And the halflings lived in shingled cottages, with fresh-painted walls, and they ate red-berry pasties and soft cheese. During the day, they would shade themselves from the sun, and at night they would gather to play the pipes and dance jigs. Yet, lazy and charming as they were, somehow the work would always get done. And they didn't like to fight, fighting was not in their nature. Though they would sometimes make war for the Emperor when they were needed, in truth all they wanted was to return to their quiet, rolling land to eat scones with honey and sit telling jokes, with sprigs of straw between their teeth. There was this one character in the books, my favourite, Jarmo Appleday, and he would always outsmart himself but in the end all would...'

Franziskus trailed off.

'I liked those stories,' he eventually concluded.

'I've never been to the Moot,' said Angelika.

'Neither have I.'

'It could be just like you say. The halflings we've met, they could be the exceptions.'

'It goes against what I have learned, since leaving home.'

'And what is that?'

'That to treasure any beautiful thought is to hold fast to an illusion.'

'It isn't necessarily an illusion.'

'You're usually eager to part me from all my false and foolish beliefs. Don't spare me now, just because I'm hurt.'

'Remember what that Lela Mossrock said – the whole lot of them, they were exiles. The Moot can still be like the one in your storybooks. Those peaceful, law-abiding types, they'd be quick to rid themselves of halflings like her – and Toby too – for being too savage and different.'

Franziskus craned his neck abruptly upwards. He patted at his waist. His belt was gone, and the scabbard, too. 'Those miscreants!' he protested. 'They stole my elven sword!'

DROPS OF LIQUID hit his face, waking him. The sky had greyed and light rain was leaking down into the pit. Franziskus blinked. The raindrops hurt when they hit, but they were also refreshing, so he turned his face up to meet them.

'This is as close to a bath as we'll get for a while,' he said.

'You're up,' she said.

He felt the droplets as they gathered, pooled, and ran down his neck and into the fabric of his tunic. They were cold, and he shuddered, but it was a good feeling anyway. He realised that it was no longer so painful to move his neck.

'I'm sorry,' she said. 'This is all because of my own accursed foolishness.'

'No,' Franziskus said. He tried moving his hands. That hurt, but not as bad as before.

'What do you mean, *no?*'

'Please relent.'

'I'm telling you that I am sorry, and you bid me to–'

He retreated from her, dragging his legs through the ash. 'I can't think. Let me enjoy this rain.'

'You can't think? I was the one who couldn't think, when I stormed out here, and said set the place on fire. Without checking. Without stopping to make a plan or learn the facts. I was the one who got us into this state. Beaten like dogs. It was my damnably stupid conscience eating away at me. Whenever that happens – I should know by now – it's prompting me to do something idiotic. I broke every one of my own rules. And all the precepts of common sense, besides.'

'You thought he might be in immediate danger.'

'I shouldn't have thought any such thing. Why would he be in more danger then, than the day before, or the day after? No, it was all my desire to make good, and to do it quickly and get it done with, so I could stop feeling – I let my head cloud up with virtue, and this is the result. It's right that I should suffer, but to you I apologise.'

'No need to–'

'Shut up. And memorise this moment in great detail, because I promise you it won't be repeated.'

Now he stirred in the opposite direction, pulling himself toward her, and kicking up billows of ash. 'But the blame is not yours to shoulder. The idiocy is mine. I should never have trusted that woman, Petrine Guillame. She batted those fine eyelashes my way, and I lost all suspicion. The poets say a beautiful woman must by nature have a soul to match, but now I know that's wrong.'

'I thought there was only an eighth of a chance she was leading us in the right direction, but still I went along, because I wanted to take action. That makes me a much bigger fool than you.'

'No, I am the bigger fool!'
'Horse manure!'
'That's a fine and eloquent retort.'
'Close your hole!'

THE NEXT DAY, for a few minutes at a time, they both were able to stand on their own, without their legs giving way. They counted the casks of ale: they had enough for three more days, if they drank sparingly. The dried meat would last for ages; neither Angelika nor Franziskus had recovered their appetites. Rain, colder and harder than the day before, pelted them for hours. They staggered to a dry corner, under a piece of platform that remained intact. They shivered in their shelter.

'Do I look better now?' Franziskus asked.

'Better than when?'

'My face. Is it less swollen and bruised?'

She appraised him at some length. 'Less swollen, more bruised.'

Franziskus sighed in disappointment.

'In all honesty, you look like a crushed grape,' Angelika said.

'I'm grateful for the encouragement.'

She shrugged. 'You asked.'

She looked like she was on the mend. Purple ringed her eyes, and scabs crisscrossed her face. But underneath, hints of her usual skin tone were returning.

She pulled some dried meat from her belt, bit off a piece, chewed it unhappily, then spat it back out. She stared at the leathery morsel as it lay in the wet ash. 'I did not mean to abuse you, yesterday.'

'I understand.'

'But this is what you'll suffer, if you keep on in this way, dogging my heels. I'm not a person out of a storybook, either. Not like those heroes you read about. Though sometimes I forget myself and act as if I am, by plunging into fights that are too big for me. And every so often – like now – I am forcibly reminded of my own fragility. I've asked you this many times, Franziskus.'

'I don't want to hear it.'

'But this time, you can see where it will lead you. Wretchedness and misery. You want to protect me. You can't.

All you'll earn is a share of my fate. Promise me. When we get ourselves out of this hole, you'll go back home.'

'I'm not going back.'

'Then go somewhere else. I don't care where, just get away from me before I get you murdered.'

'It doesn't matter how many times you say it, but I'm not budging, so you might as well stop.'

'You wish to kill yourself, is that it?'

'A share of your fate is exactly what I desire. Your foolishness will be my foolishness. I've thrown my lot in with you. Your knife, my sword.'

'Whether I like it or not?'

'I'm sorry if I was churlish with you, and did not accept the apologies you wished to make. I'm yours to command. I'll endeavour to please you better from now on.'

'Then swear you'll leave me.'

'I'll follow every order but that one.'

'But I'll get you killed.'

'Then I promise not to die.'

SHE KNEW SHE was getting better when night came and her sleeplessness came not from pain, but from bottled-up energy. The moon was bright and shone down on them. She stood and stretched her arms behind her, as far as they could go. They did not hurt until they were almost fully extended. She walked to the side of the pit, placed her hands together against the timbered wall, and pushed off from it, testing the muscles of her legs. She cried out and fell, landing on her knee. Franziskus woke and leapt to her side. She sat up, kneading her calf muscles. He tried to take over the massaging duties, but she fended him off.

'I feel a return of vitality and purpose,' she said. 'I feel ready again. Except that my legs disagree. You're not ready, though, are you?'

'For what?'

'We'll go together to the Castello. I'll leave you there at the cottage, then I'll—'

'You're forgetting: the Castello's under siege.'

She groaned as her fingers found an especially sore spot. 'That will be lifted by now; I guarantee it.'

'You've recovered your certitude, I see.'

'The Kopfs will have made their point and gone home. They won't waste resources with an orc army on the way. I'll drop you there and continue on.'

'To where?'

'I don't yet know, but there's got to be some way to pick up the trail again.'

'Lukas's trail?'

'Who did you think I meant?'

'How will we find him now? We've been here for days. Toby's had time to well and truly hide him.'

'If you want to help me, stop reminding me of things I already know.'

'And if you do find him – you're no match for Goatfield now. He'll turn you to pulp.'

'There will be no more frontal assaults, believe me.'

'But – you said it was folly. You said you'd learned your lesson.'

'It is, and I have. But, still, I can't have a little worm like him staining my conscience for the rest of my stinking days. I'll find him, turn him loose, and that will be the end of it, for once and all.'

'You can't.'

'I've got to.'

THE NEXT DAY, they sorted through the ash for planks that had not burned too badly, and they leaned them up against the pit wall, to make a ramp. Angelika walked halfway up before growing light-headed. She lay flat against the boards and slid down.

THE DAY AFTER, they were strong enough to get out of the pit. But then they collapsed on the edge, panting and gasping. They lay there for a while, then stood up, and tottered out of the clearing and into the woods. Franziskus had to stop and sit on a rock. Wolves howled.

They went back into the pit again to sleep away the night.

THE DAY AFTER that, they got out, and kept going.

CHAPTER TEN

CROW CALLS ECHOED through the pass.

'Don't say it,' Angelika told him.

'I had no intention of saying it,' said Franziskus.

They cleared the sides of the now-abandoned rock cut leading to the Castello, and stepped into the basin, where the besiegers had been. Curls of fog hugged close to the muddy basin floor; it lay trampled and scored with the crisscrossed paths of a hundred carts. There were no more Averlandish soldiers, or their auxiliaries. Absent, too, were the vendors, looters, spectators, whores and flagellants. Trash heaps smouldered, the smoke conjoining with the fog. Wild dogs, of mottled brown, grey, and black, fought over sheep bones and the entrails of chickens. The wheel of an upturned, broken cart squeaked on its axle; it was turning slowly, lazily propelled by a hot breeze from the south. An old, plump woman, her hair a white and unkempt mop, sat in the cart's meagre shade. She wore a dirty lace shift that had fallen down around her waist, and was banging a chunk of wood against the side of her head as she muttered and sang. One of the smaller wild dogs, which had been losing his battles anyway, trotted over to her, and regarded her quizzically. She snarled and it yelped away.

Up in the rocks bordering the basin, lonely figures prowled furtively. Whether they were refugees staring down at the ruins of their homes, or timid looters waiting for more smoke to clear, Angelika could not say. Whenever she squinted to make them out, they hid behind trees or dropped low into the grass.

They looked to the Castello. It looked like the bottom of the pit they'd just crawled from. Its walls were down; collapsed into a jumble of scorched timber and severed planks. One of the wooden towers that once flanked the gate was now a broken skeleton of bare and blackened supports. The other had disappeared entirely. Inside the walls, the jumble of hovels and shacks Franziskus and Angelika had so often threaded through was now only half recognisable. Many of the small flimsy structures seemed to be missing altogether; others stood half-smashed – missing walls or roofs. The occasional cottage of stone or brick stood as before, but with its outer surfaces blackened, or its doors and shutters torn away.

'Where did all the people go?' Franziskus asked.

Angelika shrugged. 'North would be the only sensible direction. I wonder if the Averlanders planned on sending several thousand refugees to swell through their own border.'

The two of them made their way swiftly across the field, giving a wide berth to the dogs and madwoman alike. When she reached a point two-thirds of the way across, Angelika halted. She strode to a low mound of earth that was dry and recently turned. Its shape was rectangular; it was about eighty feet long and forty feet wide. Lime dust had been sprinkled on top.

'Graves,' Franziskus said. Angelika nodded. Then the young Stirlander saw a small hand, twisted and broken, in the middle of the mound; it had been exposed by the wind. The hand was a woman's, entwined by a bracelet of copper discs.

Angelika and Franziskus looked at one another, sharing a silent understanding: this was a battlefield she had no interest in plundering, and there would be no need for the usual debate on the ethics of scavengery.

'How many?' he asked.

'Many,' she said.

They kept on, toward the broken town.

'It is madness,' Franziskus said. 'How can man slay man, when inhuman enemies wait to slaughter us all?'

'Absolutely – who needs orcs, when we have each other?'

They reached the boulder-lined road that led up to the front gate. It was littered with cannon balls, the broken hafts from various pole weapons, and countless arrows, most with burned tips. Angelika bent to pick one up, and show it to Franziskus.

'They used archers to set the walls alight.'

She looked at the high rock wall that served as the fortress's backdrop. Soot coated it. 'And there's no back way out.' The cliff was supposed to provide protection, but it had trapped the defenders inside. They approached the collapsed, blackened walls, skirting a corpse clad only in a leather jerkin. Dogs had already been at it: the leg bones were exposed. The travellers' still-healing muscles rebelled as they clambered over fallen planks and into the ruined town. They saw that it was true: many cottages and hovels past the Castello walls had indeed been flattened by cannon fire.

'What was the point?' Franziskus asked, looking at a scatter of broken timber that used to be a cramped and tiny hovel. Though he'd never spoken to the people who lived in it, he remembered them as a large clan beset by unruly, howling children.

Angelika kicked idly at a board, flipping it over so that its many nails pointed dirtward. She shrugged. 'Practice for the artillery? The joy of finding an ideal target for cannon fire? Sheer malice?'

'The latter, I'd say.'

She cupped her hands around her mouth and called out: 'Anyone here? Anyone here?'

A crow alighted atop a mud-daub wall, where a thatched roof had been burned away. It squawked a congenial hello at them and commenced to calmly groom its wing-feathers.

They walked to their cottage, which was far from the walls, and found it still standing, but stripped of rugs and furnishings. They'd lost nothing they'd miss; its worn floor coverings, uncomfortable bedding and lopsided chairs had come with the place when they'd rented it.

They made their way to the tavern. They found its sign, the one with the wretch screaming in his coffin, broken in two and strapped to a dead man's back.

'He must have thought it a valuable souvenir,' Franziskus mused.

They turned the man over; they recognised him as a regular occupant of Giacomo's benches but did not recall his name. Franziskus couldn't find any wounds on him.

'It was apoplexy, not a weapon, that killed this one,' Angelika said. 'Probably one of the Sabres came at him and he died on the spot, of fear. You can tell by the way he's all purple and splotchy.'

'As usual, you brim with charming information.'

To their surprise, Giacomo's bar was largely unscathed, save for its missing sign and a pile of broken glass beside its front steps. 'Anyone in there?' Angelika called. She moved up onto the steps, kicking aside the severed neck of a brandy bottle. It landed in the heap of glass and shattered.

She stepped inside the tavern, Franziskus behind her. Someone had chopped huge wedges from the top of the bar with an axe or hatchet. The tables were overturned; the benches, missing. The shelves, naturally, had been stripped entirely; the victorious soldiers would have greedily drained every drop of alcohol they could find.

Angelika walked behind the bar. Flies buzzed around a bucket. She peered into it. Giacomo's head lay inside it, his face upturned and imploring. She frowned and held up a palm, warning Franziskus to stay away, but he came to take a look regardless. It made him blanch, but he succeeded in suppressing the urge to rush outside and vomit.

'We should give him a proper burial, at least,' he said, when he was sure of himself.

'I'm not sure it counts as proper, with only this much of him to put below ground,' she said. 'But he kept a decent brandy, and we should show respects to someone, I suppose.'

They investigated Giacomo's closet, where they knew he kept a spade, but it had been ransacked. They used the end of a board to dig a suitable divot in the resistant, sandy earth behind his place. Blocking her nose and breathing through her mouth, Angelika went inside to claim the bucket. Returning with it, she settled it gently in the hole. She shooed the flies away and laid a bar rag over the top of the head. Though its use as a burial shroud could be seen as a desecration, she felt reasonably sure that Giacomo's soul would understand the gesture's great sincerity.

Franziskus mumbled the words of Shallya's blessing, which he'd been taught by his nursemaid, and used the board to paddle the dirt back around the bucket.

They headed in silence to the prince's palazzo. Even from a distance, it was plain to see that it had been gutted. Its roof was gone, along with much of its front wall. The metal fence around the grounds had been uprooted – concrete moorings and all – and carted off, leaving behind a trench of moist earth. Angelika and Franziskus were about to pass it by when they saw a familiar figure sprawled face-down in this new ditch. His right boot rested about fifteen feet away from him, his lower leg still inside it. In a mocking gesture, someone had repositioned the boot, so that the stump pointed up.

'Halfhead!' Angelika cried. She ran to him. When he stirred, she jolted.

'Accursed bastard dogs,' the gateman growled.

'We were about to pass you by. You're lucky the back of your head is distinctive.'

'Angelika?'

'And Franziskus is here, too. Do you want to roll over?'

'They're the unholy farts of daemons, they are. My right leg. I can't feel it. How bad does it look?'

'I'm going to help you roll over.' She frowned meaningfully at Franziskus. It took him a moment to figure out exactly what she wanted from him. Then he hopped to it. He pinched the boot cuff gingerly and picked up the severed portion of Halfhead's leg. Then he set it respectfully behind a bush, where its owner couldn't see it. The absurd thought popped into his head that the poor fellow might now have to rename himself Halfleg.

Angelika took Halfhead by the shoulder and turned him over in the ditch. His face was pale. The tip of his tongue eked its tentative way out onto dry, chapped lips. 'Water?' he asked.

Angelika reached into her pack and withdrew her waterskin. She unscrewed its pewter cap and poured some water onto the tail of her tunic, before dabbing it onto his lips. Only when they were well moistened did she pour any liquid into the wounded man's mouth. She dribbled it in slowly.

Halfhead tried to lift his head for a look at his leg. Angelika leaned in, blocking his view. He laid his head back down. 'I said, how bad is it?'

'Don't take this the wrong way, but I'm surprised you haven't bled to death.'

'My family, none of us is big bleeders. It's an ancestral trait. We seal right back up.'

'How long has it been?'

Franziskus spotted a pile of old sacks; presumably left behind by a disappointed looter. He bundled them up and placed them under the gatekeeper's head.

'They attacked at dawn. Yesterday,' Halfhead said. 'I think. I ain't been conscious the whole time, I don't believe.'

'We have to get you somewhere out of the elements.'

'I took a smash on the head when the walls came down. Woke up later, with the looting in full swing. They took everything, the ungodly swine. Stupid me, I charged out of my hidey-hole, sword a-swinging, when I saw them working to bring down the fence. Sigmar's privates, what possessed me?'

'Men act rashly at times like this,' Angelika said. These words were not especially consoling, she knew, but they were the best that came to mind.

'I suppose I was thinking I'd failed to protect the main walls, and I'd be damned if they took Davio's fence, too. So I came at them and of course it was a dozen to one and they cut me down. I think I got a couple of them, though. Made them pay for the stinking fence. They'll melt it down for scrap, I know they will. Accursed godforsaken fence.' He peeked around Angelika, at his leg.

'What of Davio? Did they get him, too?'

'I didn't see it happen, but you can bet crowns to crayfish he got himself away. If there ever was a man who knew how to regroup, it's old Davio. I guess I don't have to call him prince no more, if the thing he was prince of is now a pile of smoking rubble. My leg's clean off, ain't it?'

'From the knee down.'

'Good, because in that case I can get myself better and stick a peg on it. And then I'll find all of them swine who was tearing down that fence, and if it takes me till the last of my days, I'll gut them systematically. I memorised all their faces, and if I get them all, I can be sure I killed the one who chopped my leg.'

'Did Davio take others with him? Will he still have a force?'

Halfhead asked for more water; she let him take the skin and gurgle down as much as he wanted. He raised himself up on his elbows. He looked at his leg and made a face, like another man would at a cup of sour milk. 'Davio's finished as a mercenary chief, at least for the time being. It would take him, what, five years to rebuild what he had. Maybe more, when word of this trouncing gets about. Dogs of war, they ain't anxious to sign on with a man if they think he'll get them killed. But if Davio still breathes, you can be sure he's working some way of extracting revenge from Jurgen and his boys.'

Angelika knelt in close. 'Listen very carefully. Now that none of this matters, tell me if Davio had a boy with him. Scrawny, skin like porcelain, hair long and scraggly?'

'The prince was not that way.'

'Not that kind of boy. A hostage. A von Kopf hostage.'

Halfhead wrinkled his nose. 'Not that I know of, and I would have known. Not anywhere in the Castello, that's for certain.'

Franziskus squatted beside him. 'And was there a Bretonnian woman in his employ?'

Halfhead chewed thoughtfully at his lips. 'There was a Bretonnian he had a dally with, not long back. She was vocally enthusiastic, one might say. Or so said the boys on palace duty.'

'Petrine Guillame?'

'That might have been her name. Flaxen haired, you could say?'

'That's her.'

'Yes, I seen that one. Last time was a little less than a week ago, I think. I saw her pass through the gate, heading away.'

Franziskus caught Angelika's gaze. 'That could be just after she sent us on our wild goose chase.'

'Was she with anyone?' Angelika asked Halfhead.

'I wasn't paying any great attention,' said the gateman, lying back down. 'Though she was pretty to look at.'

'Did she have a boy with her, like the one I just described?'

Halfhead closed his eyes. 'Could have, I suppose, but it wouldn't have been him I was looking at.'

'How about a couple of demented halflings and an elf with a bandage on his face?'

'You mean Goatfield and his cronies? Swinish ne'er-do-wells! I never saw them with that Bretonny woman, though. Nor with a boy. Nor recently.'

'The woman, then. When she left, did you happen to see which direction she headed?'

'Why, the only sane direction anyone would go.'

'Which would be...?'

'With a greenskin horde on the march? The only safe way: towards the Empire. North. She went north.'

'We'll get you cared for, Halfhead.'

'Call me Werther. I hate that name, Halfhead.'

'Very well, Werther.'

She and Franziskus ducked down so Halfhead could wrap an arm around each of their shoulders. They stood to support his weight. They hobbled him out of the prince's ruined garden and – pausing periodically to huff and puff – through the maze of shattered buildings to their empty cottage. They sat him on the floor, propped against a wall. Angelika contemplated him for a moment. At no point in the journey had he made a complaint or allowed a cry of pain to escape his lips. She contrasted this with her own extravagant suffering in the pit, and felt a little ashamed.

'We'll get you taken care of,' she said. 'You're hungry, I'll wager.'

'Good luck finding anything edible in this smoking trash pile. The Averlanders cleaned this place bare. They did everything but lick the streets.'

Without further comment, Angelika departed. Franziskus cleared his throat nervously and sat on the floor beside the injured man.

'Where do you hail from, Werther?'

'Up north. In Ostland, east of Wolfenburg.' Though the place Halfhead named was part of the Empire, it was distant; Franziskus was not sure he'd ever met another Ostlander.

'Do you ever consider going back there?'

Halfhead shrugged. 'What for? It was so long ago I can't even say my memories of the place are accurate. What few people I'd care to revisit are no doubt already in their graves. Give me some more water, please.'

Franziskus handed him the waterskin. He slurped lustily.

'Why did you leave in the first place?' Franziskus asked.

'Because I hated everyone there and wanted to kill them,' he said, flatly. 'But I didn't want to hang for it, so I thought I'd find places where a man would get himself rewarded for all the killing he wanted to do.' With stubby fingers he screwed the skin's cap back on. 'Though once I got a true taste of it, I found it wasn't all I'd made it out to be.' He regarded his leg. 'Though eviscerating the ones who did this, that might feel right.'

'You've travelled all about, then?'

'More than most.'

'Have you ever been to the Moot?'

'Hah?'

'Where the halflings dwell.'

'Why would anyone want to go there? Hey, boy, tell me – you and the woman. You ever–?' He made the universal sign of sexual congress.

Franziskus shook his head. 'You'd have to ask your prince, Davio, about that.'

'Ah, the lucky son of a whore. Tileans, they get all the–'

The sound of creaking boot leather stopped him short. Angelika entered the one-room cottage, her arms piled high. Franziskus tried to look innocent. He could feel the burn of a blush on his cheeks. She gave him a questioning look. He leapt up to help unburden her arms.

She'd found a pair of sausages, a bag of apples, some potatoes, a fistful of radishes, a wedge of Middenheimer cheese, and a clay jug full of watery rum. Halfhead's eyes widened as she and Franziskus laid it out on the floor in front of him.

'Sigmar's wounds!' Halfhead swore. 'I see a miracle before me!'

'This is what I do,' Angelika said. She divided up her spoils, and, without speaking, the three of them ate. They were still hungry after the food was all gone. She took a white shirt she'd found and tore it into strips. She poured the rest of the rum on Halfhead's stump and bandaged it. Though it seemed to bother him less than it should have, the wound was a terrible one, and privately she doubted whether he'd make it alone. Neither could they take him with them, and she couldn't remain in the Castello to forage his food.

She stood. 'We must be on our way, Werther.'

He waved her off. 'Don't let me keep you. You've already done more than others would.'

As they left, Franziskus cast a guilty glance back at him; Angelika kept her eyes ahead. They saw that there was a stretch of still-extant town wall directly to the east, and, beside it, a breach that had been cleared of debris and would be easy to walk through. They meandered toward it, circumventing heaps of wreckage.

'Where are we headed?' he asked her.

'You heard him – north.'

'Back to the Empire?'

'If need be.'

'But I have sworn never to return there.'

'Then stay with Halfhead.'

They cleared the breach. Something caught Franziskus's eye and he turned to look at the wall. Pasted on its outer side was a handbill. It had their names on it, and crude drawings of their faces. It named them as Angelika Fleischer and Franziskus Stirlandzner – Franziskus of Stirland. It offered a hundred crowns for their capture, not specifying how much the reader would get if he only caught one of them. Neither did it say what they'd done to have a reward hung on them. The poster did, however, tell the reader that the amount would be payable by Jurgen von Kopf, and that the prisoners should be taken to the barracks in Grenzstadt.

'This is not good,' observed Franziskus.

Suddenly some men rushed out from behind an upturned cart, spearheads out-thrust.

* * *

SHE STOOD SHACKLED before Benno and Gelfrat. Franziskus was beside her, also chained. The ruins of the Castello were visible; they were slightly further north, and sheltered by a scattering of youngish trees. The Kopfs had about three-dozen men with them, and horses and carts, to boot.

Gelfrat raised his hand to strike her face.

'I knew you'd come here, sooner or later,' Benno said, a smile making its subtle way across his mouth. 'I even risked the wrath of our father, by staying behind.'

'Your astounding bravery has me weak-kneed,' she said. She saw Gelfrat suppress a chortle at his half-brother's expense. The big man lowered his threatening hand, turned, and walked a few paces away.

'I won't ask you again,' said Benno. 'Tell us where you've stashed him.'

'I spoke the truth the first time,' she said.

Benno moved in, standing nose-to-nose with her. 'You mean for me to believe that you sold him to two halflings and an elf, but you had second thoughts, and you now search for them, because you know not where they are?'

'I don't control what you believe, Benno. I've told you the truth, because I see no reason not to. You can take or leave it, as you see fit.'

He lunged to the side, directing a vicious underhand blow to Franziskus's stomach. The Stirlander grunted in surprise and agony, doubling over.

'Striking my companion will change nothing, Benno. We don't have him; Davio's people do. You've razed his town, but he has a last laugh still in store.'

Benno hovered the heel of his boot over the toes of Franziskus's right foot, silently threatening to grind it into him. Franziskus bit his lip.

'Where did they say they were headed?'

'Oddly enough, they chose to withhold that intelligence from me. But if you return to your father's mansion, I'm sure he'll receive a ransom message soon enough.'

He seized her by the back of her neck, pulling her face toward his. 'That is precisely what must not happen, you deceitful harlot. I – we – must be the ones to deliver him.'

She smiled sweetly and blew into his eye, forcing him to blink. Taken aback, he let go of her. 'Then I suggest you scour the hills for the mercenaries I named, or for Davio himself,' she said. 'And a Bretonnian woman, called Petrine. Franziskus can describe her to you.'

He broke away from her, kicking at the dirt. He took Gelfrat aside for a conference, away from the ears of his men. She sidestepped to Franziskus; the slight movement prompting the Black Sabre guards to lower spear-points at them.

'Without wishing to complain,' he softly groaned, 'this is perhaps not the best time to antagonise them.'

'I'm sorry, Franziskus.'

The half-brothers had finished their conference. Gelfrat wore an expression of mild disgust. Benno ground a fist into his palm. He gave orders for the soldiers to break camp. A thin young soldier with a beakish nose and a stunned, wide-eyed look approached the two prisoners and knelt to unshackle Angelika's legs. With his comrades standing guard, spears ready, she briefly entertained the thought of kicking him in the face and making a run for it.

He bent to turn the key in Franziskus's shackles. Still cuffed at the wrists, Franziskus bent down to rub his ankles. One of the guards reversed his spear to poke the Stirlander in the ribs with its butt. Franziskus straightened. The beak-nosed fellow ordered the prisoners over to a pair of waiting horses, then commanded them to mount. These were sleek and healthy steeds, tall and muscular. Franziskus calmed his horse as he slung himself awkwardly into the stirrups. Two soldiers boosted him, compensating for his inability to use his hands by pushing on his backside. The mount turned its long head back to Franziskus and let loose a welcoming equine noise.

The guardsmen turned to Angelika and grinned. She stepped peevishly to her horse. It glowered at her and flared its nostrils threateningly. The soldiers seized her; she struggled to get her a foothold in the stirrup. Groping her roughly, the men hoisted her up onto the horse's back, with such enthusiasm that she was almost pitched over the opposite side. The horse made its displeasure known with a stamp of its front foot. The guardsmen also mounted and hemmed in the prisoners' mounts with their own. They waited until their comrades were ready, and Benno gave the order to move out. In tight ranks, the Sabres rode north.

The soldier with the beakish nose kept to his position on Franziskus's left. 'Ho there,' Franziskus said to him.

The fellow, no older than he was, sniffed the air.

'What's your name, friend?' Franziskus asked.

'We've been warned about you,' said the young Sabre. 'Deserter,' he added.

'How long a ride do we expect?' Franziskus persisted.

Beaky looked away.

'Is it to Grenzstadt we're going? That would be, I'd say, a day and a half ride, with one night's camp. Yes?'

One of the older soldiers laughed gutturally; it was the closest to an answer they'd give him.

The day was warm and hazy. The men rode with practiced boredom, rarely speaking. Franziskus glanced at Angelika, but read her inky mood and could tell she was in no frame of mind for conversation, either. The terrain around the pass, with its wide and muddied lowland and the jagged, tree-strewn rock walls, remained relentlessly predictable and uninteresting. Even the animals joined in a conspiracy to increase the journey's tedium: Franziskus spotted no deer, no rabbits, not even any wild dogs; occasionally he saw small teams of swallows flit overhead, but the caws and chirps he'd come to associate with the Blackfire had all fallen silent. He brought this fact to Angelika's attention.

'Maybe it's nothing,' she said, scanning the hills to left and right. The men around them overheard, and joined her in nervous scouting.

Angelika looked up. Diffuse wisps of dark smoke snaked overhead, a slow wind carrying them from the south. She craned her head backwards, as if hoping to see the fire that went with the smoke. The guards couldn't help but do the same.

'What is it?' Franziskus asked.

'Burning trees,' she said.

He sneezed. And not wanting to beg his captors for a handkerchief, he let clear mucus spill down from his nose and onto the sparse moustache that had grown on his lip over the last week.

'Orcs,' Angelika explained, to no one in particular.

'Where?' the beaky one asked. His comrades tensed, hands drifted to weapons.

'Tell my friend here your name,' Angelika commanded. 'Engage in a few pleasantries.'

Beaky met Franziskus's eyes. 'I am Renald. Renald Wechsler.'

Franziskus nodded a greeting at him.

'Well, Renald Wechsler,' Angelika finally said, 'you can see that the smoke blows from the south. So the orcs are in the south, I'd venture to say.'

'How far south?'

'No way of telling.'

'How do you know they are orcs?'

'This happens when they mass for war. They set fire to the forests as they wait in the hills.'

'What do they mean to accomplish?'

'It's hard to say if they have any aim at all. It may just be that they're stupid, lazy despoilers, and they burn down their own staging places through idiotic carelessness. Some might say, on the other hand, that they do it purposefully, to stoke themselves before a fight. Or maybe it's a sacrifice to their gods of destruction.' She shrugged. 'All I can tell you is, it's orcs, and probably a great deal of them. Getting ready.'

Renald's complexion turned to ash; he rode up next to the unit's banner-bearers, and spoke to Benno and Gelfrat. Soon after, the column speeded its pace.

Angelika saw that their guardians were all either looking up at the smoke, or behind them, searching the hills for orcs. With Renald still on his way back, there were spaces in what had been a tight formation. She scissored her legs into her horse's side, ready to bolt through the distracted men.

The horse reared a little, and whinnied in annoyance. It stayed put. Again she kicked at it. It waggled its muzzle into the air. Her guardians took notice of her efforts and ringed her tightly.

She sat silently cursing: every time she had dealings with a horse, it gave her renewed reason to hate all of its kind.

The column picked up speed, barely stopping to rest its horses as it continued on to Grenzstadt.

* * *

BLACK TOWERS AND gabled manses jutted up past Grenzstadt's high stone walls like halberds on a rack of arms. The large town squatted at the mouth of the Blackfire Pass, interposing itself between the green pastures of the Empire and anyone who would enter it from the southern wildlands. Sun and weather had given its granite walls a tan coloration; clinging lichens added touches of green. Well-engineered and exactingly mortared, the walls rose to a uniform height. Angelika, still shackled on her truculent horse, reckoned that they had to be twenty feet high, at least. They bore no resemblance to the makeshift fortifications that had done so little to protect the Castello del Dimenticato. Atop the walls were walkways, and these were railed in oak and sheltered by shingled roofs. Averlandish soldiers, sporting the yellow and black, patrolled them, vigilantly toting crossbows.

A multitude of banners flew from the town's tallest pinnacles: the yellow and black of Averland, Sigmar's hammer, the insignia of the Black Field Sabres, and, here and there, Count Marius's solar ensign. Among these other flags were scattered, too, the meanings of which Angelika could not decode. They might be anything from the symbols of private militias to mercantile crests. Known or unknown, they all snapped in a high wind. The sky had grown dark, presaging a violent storm. The temperature had been dropping rapidly for about half an hour, and Angelika shuddered. At some point, probably back in the pit, she'd lost her cloak. Franziskus shivered, too. Benno's men hemmed them in more tightly as they approached the town; there would be no confusion, no escapes. Whirling gusts gathered up tiny pebbles and handfuls of sand, throwing the mixture in the riders' faces.

The town lay on flat land, and from Angelika's vantage point, it was hard to judge just how big it was. It had to be seven or eight times the size of the Castello, at the very least.

Paired towers flanked the south gate, topped with shingled, pyramidal roofs; soldiers stood watch beneath them, and peered through spyglasses. At the bottom of the walls, a miserable assortment of refugees, undoubtedly from the Castello, huddled, shivering against the wind. When they saw the column approach, a few ran out, shouting unintelligible pleas. They held out clawed hands in supplication. A grimy-haired woman held up a wailing baby, crying mercy in Shallya's name. But when they saw the black and yellow uniforms, the displaced shrank back, averting their wretched faces. Above, a trio of callow bravos in brocade doublets gathered, laughing; they rained the contents of a chamber pot down on the refugees and leapt about in delight and mutual congratulation.

At the procession's head, a soldier bugled out a few discordant notes on a battered brass horn, and another held aloft the Black Sabre banner. The gate's massive oaken doors immediately began a deliberate, drowsy swing inwards. By the time the formation had reached the entrance, it was able to pass through without slowing. A pair of fleet-footed evacuees made a dash for the gate and slipped in, disappearing into the city.

The gate opened onto a square, paved with stone that matched the walls. The stones had been quarried skillfully, and were clearly well maintained; none were uneven or missing, and the horses clopped easily over them. Vendors had arranged their carts and colourful canvas stalls along the inner walls, but now, in anticipation of the coming storm, they were scurrying to stow their wares. A stone statue stood on a bronze plinth in the middle of the square, depicting one of Count Leitdorf's recent ancestors. He held a sword and shield out before him. A bronze nameplate on the plinth identified the stony warrior as Parzival Leitdorf. Weathering had already softened the statue's features, and pigeons had been at it, making it look as if it were crying chalk-white tears.

Though she'd skirted Grenzstadt's walls a few times, Angelika had never ventured inside them. The town looked grander than she'd thought it would. She'd expected gloom and decay; her image of the place had been all teetering structures and peeling paint. Instead, she beheld carefully tended buildings that stood with impeccable posture. It made sense, now that she saw it; she knew that the town's coffers bulged with coin. Everyone knew that Grenzstadt was the bulwark between the Empire and the borderlands, and that it served as way-station for all troops mustering for southward campaigns. It supplied quartermasters with bread and sausage.

The people here repaired breastplates, sharpened swords, and filled gun barrels with shot and powder. Here, soldiers who were waiting to fight and die spent their meagre pay on rum, dice games, and the momentary company of painted women.

Angelika knew that the town had money because most of the things she found on dead soldiers made their way here, to be resold. Her prime customer, Max, kept a shop somewhere in the town. Many of the people who bought from him were soldiers themselves. Sometimes she wondered, when plucking a gold chain or jewelled ring from a slain gunner or halberdier, whether she hadn't already liberated the exact same piece from a previous dead man.

She savoured this reassuring cynicism, then moved on to consider the greater importance of the town. It would be very inconvenient indeed if the orcs took Grenzstadt, seeing as it stood as the Empire's final line of defence against the green-skinned marauders. Angelika knew her history: more than once, the orcs had made their howling way all the way up the pass, butchering their way through one Imperial regiment after another, only to fall before the town's stout walls, and the cannons bristling from its ramparts. Without Grenzstadt, the whole of the Blackfire would become orcish territory, and the battle lines would move far to the north. She might find herself plying her trade near the scorched ruins of Averheim, or even Nuln itself. On second thoughts, this was not unlike the situation now. It would just be a matter of plying her trade in another location – so long as she wasn't in the town when it fell. She tested her manacles, only to find them as secure as ever.

The procession of Sabres continued out of the square into a wide lane, past a succession of barracks and garrisons, sprawling and low-slung. Lanterns marked out the edges of their shuttered windows. Narrower lanes, lined by tall, gabled structures, intersected the wider road they travelled on. Some of the buildings would be shops, with cramped living quarters on the floors above them. Others would be the manses of wealthy burghers and minor nobles. The townsfolk had deserted the streets, and for good reason: cold, hard drops of rain had begun to pelt down, like a scouting party for the deluge to come.

A shout rang out from the head of the column, as it turned into a cobbled courtyard, through an open, iron gate in a waist-height slate wall. A towering manse of black oak and stucco loomed up from its centre; a pair of stone barracks stood on either side of it. At the back of these buildings, Angelika noted, was a stable complex and a collection of sheds, all made from planks that still bore the colour of fresh pine.

A duo of servants with stooping shoulders, in black velvet livery, scuttled quickly to clang the gates shut as the last of the horsemen passed through. Their cuffs and collars, which would be laced and frilly in most households, were made from coarse animal fur, perhaps a bear's.

The Sabres at the front and rear broke formation and dismounted, but those around Angelika and Franziskus remained in place. Benno and Gelfrat approached; the first held himself at a remove while his bigger sibling strode up beside Renald's horse. With an attitude of bored impatience, Gelfrat wiggled the fingers of his gloved right hand at the men. In response to this, the soldier closest to Angelika seized her by the collar of her tunic and yanked her sideways, off the horse. Arms out and feet spread wide, Gelfrat caught her without apparent effort and set her roughly on her feet. Renald, who had unsaddled himself, knelt before her to shackle her ankles once more. Franziskus received the same treatment – shoved, caught, and chained – and then the two of them were prodded toward the manse with the butts of spears. One of the soldiers took particular relish in jabbing Angelika between the shoulder blades, even when she moved as quickly as her shackles would allow. She memorised his doughy features, for future reference.

They shuffled across the cobblestones around the manse, until they reached a servants' entrance on the other side, where a trio of unpainted wooden steps led up to an unornamented steel door. Benno tugged sharply on a bell-pull. After a minute or so, the door opened. Impelled onward by sharp prods to their backs, Angelika and Franziskus stumbled inside and, hindered by the shackles, had to fight their way up a set of shallow, well-worn wooden stairs. From there, they were nudged into a great hall, with vaulted ceilings braced in rare black elfwood, that were at least twenty feet high. The walls of the rectangular chamber were done in the timelessly fashionable beam-and-stucco style, and were decorated with oversized, ornamental silver serving trays. The cavernous hall extended for a hundred feet or more, and Angelika counted more than two score of these expensive plates. She sometimes found smaller display plates on the corpses she looted, and had learned a thing or two about them: even a cursory glance told her that many of these pieces were relics of the ancient civilisations, and would command high prices. All told, the collection would be worth many thousands of crowns.

A polished oaken table, perhaps eighty feet long, stood right at the centre of the chamber, confidently asserting its owner's affluence. Two dozen chairs, their backs intricately carved with scenes of aristocratic hunters spearing boars from horseback, sat to attention along each of the table's sides. Furnishings were beyond Angelika's expertise, but it did not take a sage to know that these were also pieces of great value.

She looked at Benno and Gelfrat, and saw that they beheld the high ceilings and silver plates and intimidating dining set with a slack-jawed awe that dwarfed even hers. This was not the kind of place, it was plain to see, where they were normally made welcome. The only jaded eye in the room belonged to Franziskus; he sniffed, taking in the display of wealth with a look of mild distaste.

With delicate care, Benno took one of the chairs and moved it out for Angelika to sit on. After a moment's hesitation, she obeyed. He then did the same for Franziskus, who slid his chair up to the table just as a tall, confident figure appeared on a landing, at the head of a staircase on the room's far side.

He held his shoulders regally aloft, and swept down the steps, a plain black half-cape flowing behind him. He stood six-foot-three, with a wide chest, narrow hips, and long, sinewy legs. He wore a black shirt beneath a black, collared coat, chased with silver braid and buttons. His trousers were black, his boots were black, and his buckles silver. With his deep, wide jaw and pockmarked skin, his face reminded Angelika of a ship's prow, pitted by generations of barnacles.

Slitted eyes hid behind suspicious ridges of bone. Deep creases ran up his cheeks from just above his jaw. His hands were large – the size of paddles; he took a prolonged moment to ostentatiously crack his blocky knuckles. Spine erect, movements graceful, he stepped down the precise centre of the staircase. No announcement was required: this was Jurgen von Kopf.

He stood at the bottom of the stairs, examining Angelika and Franziskus. His large hands floated to his belt, where, without breaking stride or taking his eyes from his prisoners, he located a pair of black gloves and rolled them on. Boot heels clicked on the clay tile floor as he theatrically traversed the length of his great hall, to seat himself across from Angelika.

'You know where my son is,' he said. His voice was low, and rumbly; it was flecked with steel. He clipped the ends of his words, as if any other manner of speaking would be profligate.

'As I told your other sons, I don't,' Angelika replied. 'Though I enjoyed your grand entrance. Very dramatic; were you an actor at one time?'

He curled his upper lip, showing sharp white teeth. He nodded to Gelfrat, who placed his palm on the back of Angelika's head and pushed it down until her face was pressed hard against the polished surface of the table. Despite herself, she gasped in pain.

'Tell me where my son is,' Jurgen said.

'Flattening my face won't give me miraculous oracular powers.'

Gelfrat pushed harder.

She made choking noises until he eased off. 'I'm no fool. I don't want to be tortured. If I knew, I'd say.'

'I know some of what has transpired. Benno had a message relayed to me.' He pronounced his bastard son's name with a notably chilly tone. Angelika regretted that she couldn't see Benno's reaction. 'You claim that one of those so-called princes of the borderland has him.'

'The one whose town you had flattened – Davio Maurizzi.'

'On another occasion,' Jurgen said, 'I might meditate upon the irony of a guttersnipe such as yourself daring to reproach the actions of a Jurgen von Kopf. However, at present, I am permitted no such luxury. You will fully recount the extent of your interactions with the boy, and then tell me how we might go about laying our hands upon him.' He tapped the tops of his fingers into the palm of his left hand. When Gelfrat failed to interpret the meaning of his gesture, Jurgen cleared his throat.

Gelfrat removed his hand from her head and stepped back.

Angelika sat up, rubbing her face. Her chair creaked. She could think of no good reason to deceive von Kopf, aside from the good feeling it would give her, so she told the truth. She began with her discovery of Claus's body, and concluded with her capture by Benno's men. Her best touch, she thought, was the light and offhanded manner in which she described the battle with the Chaos creatures. Even Jurgen had to raise an eyebrow at that.

When it was clear that she'd finished, he asked, 'So you persist in your contention that you have no idea of his present whereabouts?'

'No. But if you let me and Franziskus go, we have a better chance of finding him than you and yours. I'll consider doing it, for a fee of six hundred crowns, and a pledge that no harm comes to him.'

Jurgen's laugh sounded like crinkling paper.

'Five hundred crowns, then.'

'You give a curious account of yourself,' Jurgen said. 'A looter with a conscience. Or part of one, at least.' He stood, placing the tips of his fingers on the rich wood of his tabletop. 'The contradictions and hesitations with which you salt your tale lend it the odour of truth. Though I am inclined to believe you, I must be certain. I cannot help noticing that an array of scars and contusions mars your rude beauty. Perhaps, then, you already know what it is like to be tortured.' His smile called only on the muscles closest to his mouth; the rest of his face remained stonily immobile. 'Before I have my experts proceed with you–'

A commotion arose behind a set of tall, carved doors at the end of the room. Remembering the mansion's layout, Angelika knew that they would lead into the foyer. Jurgen turned toward the sound, flushed with annoyance. The sounds stopped, and he turned back to her, opening his mouth to speak. Then the doors swung open.

A servant, balding, a snowy ruff of hair around his ears, slipped through the doors and then closed them again. With downcast eyes, he snivelled into the room, trembling. Before he was more than ten feet across the long chamber, Jurgen barked at him, and he halted.

'You have been warned that this meeting was not to be interrupted,' Jurgen said.

'I assure you I utterly understand sir, but there is an arrival of an urgent – he would not be deterred, and he asserted, asserted considerable–'

'Who dares?' Jurgen demanded.

The doors opened. A short, potbellied man stood behind them. He watched them move as if surprised that putting pressure on hinged doors causes them to swing open.

A light dusting of powder whitened the man's face; rouge, judiciously applied, brightened his cheeks. Most of his eyebrows had been plucked away, and replaced with thin, elegantly curving lines drawn with a grease pencil. The same pencil emphasized a beauty mark northwest of the intruder's straight and unobtrusive nose. In contrast to his round, generous torso, his face was gaunt; his chin receded and his cheeks, beneath the make-up, were sunken. His hair had achieved a purity of blackness possible only through prolonged dyeing; a trio of ringlets, curled like the tails of baby pigs, lay against his forehead. A velvet chapeau, in blue and gold, angled itself across his head; it was like a pill hat, but with an upturned brim, trimmed in lace. He wore a jacket of sky-blue silk, intricately embroidered with golden thread, over a golden vest with trim that matched the jacket. His trousers, which terminated just below the knee, matched his vest; even his stockings were adorned with twin ribbons of blue and gold. Angelika could not help but compute the resale value of the dozen carved-ivory buttons that decorated his coat, or the diamond-inlaid silver buckles on his thick-heeled leather shoes.

'Brucke,' Jurgen said, by way of greeting. He'd drained the anger from his voice, but Angelika saw that his left fist, which was held behind his back, stayed taut inside its leather glove.

This Brucke, whoever he was, cast a bored but questioning look in the direction of Angelika and Franziskus. 'Ah,' he said.

'My man here will escort you to the drawing room,' said Jurgen, 'where, when I have disposed with some business here, we may discuss whatever it is you wish to—'

Brucke threw up manicured hands. 'I refuse to inconvenience you.' He drew a chair from the table's corner and sat himself in it. He plunked his meagre chin into his hand and gazed vacuously at one of Jurgen's display plates. 'Please, continue.'

Jurgen glared at him.

After holding von Kopf's attention for what felt to Angelika like a full minute, Brucke dryly smacked his lips and said, 'It's just that I heard that a procession had come into town. I thought I might be the first to congratulate you on the safe return of your dear son, Lukas.'

'He is not here.'

'Oh,' Brucke said, but not in a surprised tone.

'Let us not discuss this in the presence of inferiors.'

Brucke waggled dismissive fingers at this notion. Jurgen's jaw stiffened. Brucke stood up and approached the two prisoners. 'These are witnesses, then? Perhaps they can help you find him? Oh, but I see they are shackled.' He gazed deeply into Franziskus's eyes. 'You did not bring the boy to harm, I hope.'

Franziskus, looking past the interloper's shoulder, read Jurgen's ever-stiffening expression, and declined to reply to the powdered man.

'Brucke,' Jurgen said, 'if you've come to hear a report on the progress of my efforts, I'll of course tell you all that you wish to know. Any fact pertaining to my absent son is, however, strictly within my private purview – it is a household matter.'

Brucke moved, lowering himself into the chair Jurgen had just vacated. He folded his wrinkled hands together. He faced Angelika, but looked through her rather than at her. 'But while the count is indisposed, and you prosecute the war for him, your reputation and that of Averland are inseparable,' he said.

Von Kopf coughed. 'Here is your war report, dear Anton. By example, the border princes have been taught the folly of their double-dealing. Now they will assuredly do their best to impede the orcs when they make their main push north. In the meantime, our own forces are regrouping after the victory at the Castello del Dimenticato. Though it is only half likely that the orcs will come close to us, I'll soon deploy a triple regiment a hundred leagues into the mouth of the pass, ready to repel their weakened onslaught with ease.'

Anton Brucke sniffed, and removed a lacy handkerchief from the breast pocket of his vest. He dabbed at the area beneath his nose. 'You'll agree, naturally, that your present role requires you to maintain popularity with the troops, as well as the citizenry in general.'

'Please let my servant escort you to the drawing room, where we may parley at length.'

'All I mean to say, dear Jurgen, is that you may overestimate the degree to which the common soldier cares for the upholding of the von Kopf honour. The count, in his wisdom, has always supported your family, and your company of Sabres. You are exemplars of Averlandish determination and vigilance. But we are the sort of people who understand these sorts of things. The common fellow, the groundling, the gutter-grubber, may not appreciate the reasons for rigidly sticking to the letter of dusty ancestral rules. He might perceive them as – well – *over-harsh*.'

'If you insist on making your point in front of the prisoners, perhaps you could at least get to it.'

He rose to pat an unappreciative Jurgen on the shoulder. 'Pardon my prolixity. I know you are a military man, and accustomed to short, barked orders. All I am saying is that you may wish to suspend judgment when and if you do recover custody of poor, callow Lukas. A literal application of your family oath could prove distracting at an otherwise crucial moment.'

'And tell me, Anton – does this advice come from the count, or from you?'

Brucke emitted a droll chuckle. 'You know as well as I do that the count is...' He looked at the prisoners. 'You know how the count is.'

Jurgen put his hand on Brucke's silk-coated shoulder, and squeezed hard. The courtier winced. 'In that case, I will entertain these suggestions with all respect due to the person making them.'

CHAPTER ELEVEN

'You know nobles and their ways: what did you make of that strange display, Franziskus?'

They were still shackled, but now they were bound back to back around a timber support beam. At Jurgen's command, Gelfrat and a complement of Sabres had roughly led them out of Jurgen's manor, through his courtyard, and along the streets until they reached one of the town's south towers. They'd been dragged up narrow, curving stone steps and deposited in their present location: a small room that might normally have been used to store weapons or provisions. Their ceiling was the floor on which the tower sentries walked. From a narrow window, hardly big enough to stick an arm through, Angelika and Franziskus heard the voices of the watchmen, and the occasional bout of raucous laughter. The storm had been in full cry as they were led through the streets, and now, though their clothing had dried somewhat, they were chilled and damp.

'I am no expert in high politics, Angelika. My father always avoided the court and courtiers, as much as he could. He said they were asps, the lot of them.'

'A novice in a nunnery could tell you that much.'

Franziskus clucked his agreement.

'But from what the way that Brucke fellow spoke, he would be an adviser to the count, yes?' Angelika continued.

'So I gathered.'

'And he wanted Lukas left alone.'

'That's what he said.'

'Which means there is a safe harbour for the boy, when we find him: we'll take him to the count, who'll protect him.'

Franziskus moaned. '*When* we find him?' He rattled his restraints. 'Unless he's in a secret compartment somewhere in this cell, I don't imagine we'll be doing that in the near future. Remember Jurgen's threat – at this very moment he's securing the services of a first-class torturer.'

'Naturally, we have to get out of here before we can do anything.' Pushing her back against the support beam, Angelika wiggled into a standing position. 'I was hoping he'd put us in a brig or stockade somewhere on his own estate, with the activity of servants and dogsbodies to cover our escape.'

'That thought probably entered into his calculations.'

'Or he just didn't want us dirtying up his estate with our stench of dishonour. Let's think. First we need these shackles off. Then: how many guards do you figure they have outside?'

Franziskus, who faced the stout wooden door, framed in an archway of granite, squinted doubtfully at it. 'How does that even matter? The door is firmly locked!'

'My wager is, there's one guard only; you saw how narrow the staircase is, when they hauled us up here. This is not normally a prison cell, so there's no proper place for anyone to stand guard outside that door. Maybe there's no guard at all.'

They heard coughing on the other side.

'I wish you were right, and I was wrong,' said Franziskus. 'But I don't think we can make any travel plans yet.'

'Enough gloom. I can't do all the escaping by myself.' She studied her leg-irons for weak links, then released them in frustration.

They heard muffled conversation by the door. Angelika picked out two separate deep voices. There was a third, which took her a while to pick out: it was a woman's soft cooing.

'Someone selling something?' Franziskus asked.

'Shh!' said Angelika. She strained to hear but individual words were impossible to make out. From the tone of it, her guess was that the woman was trying to overcome the reluctance of the two men. The conversation ceased. She sighed.

The door opened. Petrine Guillame, still clad in her tight, green-flocked gown, with its generous neckline, rushed through the archway, brushing past both guardsmen, who grinned like fools. Full purses hung at their belts. Franziskus kept one eye on them; and with the other, he watched Petrine throw herself to her knees before him.

Angelika, who faced the opposite way, could not see her. 'Who is it?' she asked.

Petrine clasped Franziskus's shackled hands in hers. 'I am so, so, sorry for what I have done to you, dear good Franziskus,' she breathed.

'Who is that?' Angelika called, louder.

'It was entirely unforgivable, and I beg your forgiveness for it, Franziskus,' said Petrine. 'I hope you came to no harm, against those halflings.'

'Halfl – is it that woman?' Angelika demanded. 'Guillame? Petrine Guillame?'

The guards found this amusing, and chortled and jabbed one another in the ribs.

The woman went on, ignoring Angelika: 'Tell me no harm came to you, sweet Franziskus.'

'As a matter of fact...'

'Oh no! They hurt you! I swear, I thought from Toby's description of them that they'd be no match for you, or that you'd realise you'd been led on a goose hunt before things ever came to blows! My guilt is terribly, terribly compounded!'

'Is that her?' Angelika cried.

'Yes,' said Franziskus, weakly.

Angelika shook her chains furiously. 'Count yourself lucky I'm shackled!'

'You,' Petrine said. 'You are the one.' She stood, stepped over to face Angelika, and looked down at her grimly. 'You are the one.'

'The one what?'

'You.' Hard, downward-sloping lines appeared on her brow. 'You made yourself a... *friend* to...' She cast her eyes over to the guards, to show why she didn't refer to Davio by name. 'It is because of you that I am sent here, through hardships and dangers. He wishes you to know that he meant for no injury to come to you. It was a most terrible error.'

'I hear you are also a friend to the one we speak of.'

'And it is said of you that you antagonise every one of the persons you meet, because that is the way you are. But that is not why I am here. He wants you to know it was me, not he, who had you misdirected. He is responsible for none of your pain. I thought it would be best to prevent you from recovering a certain important hostage you sought. But it was not.'

'And this is what you came here to tell us?'

'When he heard you were in trouble, he found it most imperative to prevent you from thinking ill of him.'

'How very thoughtful of him. Especially since it's only your neck he's risking to say it.'

'You are not fit to judge him. I do his bidding with the utmost willingness.'

'He is still well, I take it? Well and safe?'

She ignored Angelika's question, returning instead to Franziskus's side. She squeezed the muscle of his upper arm.

'I never dreamed you would end up here, bound to die in Grenzstadt,' she said to him, eyes sparkling with tears. 'It was never the intention. Never did we think you would be so persistent. I beg of you, Franziskus, absolve me of blame. Do not go to your grave with hate for me lodged in your heart. Go with an unfettered soul, so that you may not be blocked on your road to heaven.'

Franziskus drew back from her. 'You play false with me, I know it.'

'Yes, yes, I have, curses be on me, but I am here hoping you will absolve me.' Her slim fingers wandered along back and down to his belt. 'Promise me, as you die, that you'll blame neither me, nor Davio.' Too late, she realised her blunder. Franziskus saw the guards take mental note of the name. 'Do not blame us,' she whispered. The tip of her nose brushed the lobe of his ear. 'Do not send your ghost to haunt us from beyond.'

'It's nice of you to offer him one final roll in the hay,' said Angelika, 'but you're turning my stomach.'

Petrine stood up, huffed, and swept from the room. The guards banged the door shut; the loud clicks reverberated off the stone walls as one of them turned the lock's tumbler with his key.

'It's none of my business, Franziskus, but your taste in women is appalling.'

'When we met back at the Castello, it was not her shape, or the softness of her skin, that fooled me. It was the sincerity of her plea.'

'Sincerity?' Angelika asked.

'She was different this time. More like an actress, treading the boards.'

'That was a performance, to be sure – but to what end?'

Franziskus answered her with a metallic clicking sound. Then a louder clank. Another click, another clank. He stepped quickly over to Angelika, dropping both sets of his shackles at her feet. He held up a pair of iron keys on a ring. 'We are the beneficiaries of a classic diversion. She slipped this into the folds of my tunic as she pretended to weep and wheedle.' He squatted to insert the key's end into Angelika's wrist cuffs.

'When she brushed past the guards...' Angelika said.

He unlocked her leg-irons. 'I didn't see it, and they didn't feel it. Most impressive technique, wouldn't you say?'

'I'll say I like her better when her deceptions work in our favour.'

'She slipped me this, too.' He handed her a knife, its blade a little shorter than the daggers she favoured. She weighed it in her hand. They gathered up the chains and crept over to the door. Alert, they waited, starting each time they heard noise from the corridor.

About an hour later, the lock clicked as a jailer turned a key from the outside. Franziskus flattened himself by the door frame. Angelika stood poised with the knife ready for an inward swing; scratches on the stone floor left a mark for her to aim for. The door opened. Franziskus lunged. He looped chains around the jailer's throat. He drew the man into the cell. Angelika showed him the knife, sticking its tip to his throat. Checking to make sure he was alone, Franziskus eased the door shut and impelled him further into the room. Sweat bubbled from the jailer's face.

'There are several in Grenzstadt I'd like to stick this knife into,' Angelika told him, 'but if you stay quiet you won't be one of them.'

Franziskus led him to the beam and clapped him in his own shackles, tying them tight so he couldn't rattle them. Angelika used the knife to cut a swatch of fabric from the tail of his tunic, and stuffed it in his mouth. He whimpered and nodded, to show them he would cooperate.

Angelika stepped to the door, then backtracked to the chained jailer. She reached into his belt and snatched his purse. He dropped his head in resignation.

'This is for your own good,' she told him, opening it to find four half-crowns. 'If Jurgen caught you with a bribe dangling from your belt, he'd have you hanged for sure.' The guard seemed unconvinced of her altruism.

Then they slipped into the corridor and ran quickly down the tower stairs.

EMERGING FROM THE tower and onto the curving stone steps that led from the top of the wall to the courtyard at street level, they held their heads high and moved unhurriedly downward. The square was mercifully empty of uniformed men. Angelika listened intently, waiting for a shouted alarm. She looked for places to hide: there was the statue of Parzival Leitdorf, but that would not grant much cover. She noted a stack of barrels, piled on their sides, against the town walls, but, to get to it, they'd have to dash right across the length of the courtyard.

About thirty feet from the foot of the stairs, a four-wheeled wooden cart waited. High-backed chairs sat at attention inside it, tethered in place with cords. They were wooden and stained black; red leather pads covered their backs and arms. The disassembled parts of a matching table lay among them. A spindly-legged man in a dark frock coat emerged from a shop to peer inside the cart and then sniff up into the darkening sky. He held up a palm to feel for raindrops.

Angelika flattened herself against the stone wall that abutted the steps.

The dark-coated man took no notice of the escapees. Pointing his sharp nose in the direction of his open shop door, he snorted out a command, then strode inside. He soon emerged with three stooped, unshaven men in shirts of grimy linen. As he clucked imperiously at them, they battled a tarpaulin of waxy, blackened canvas clumsily over the back of the cart. They threw cords over it, and hastily tied them down. Their master patted his coat pockets, grimaced with annoyance, and bustled on clicking heels back into his shop.

Franziskus glanced nervously up at the tower.

The workmen finished their task and ambled back inside. Angelika sprang out from the wall, and rushed sideways to the cart. Franziskus took long strides to match her. With her dagger, she severed a couple of the cords, then held up a flap of canvas for Franziskus to crawl into. He crawled awkwardly beneath it, scraping a shin on the cart's side. Angelika ducked in behind him, and pushed Franziskus deeper into the cart. She crouched between a pair of chairs; he found a place opposite her. They heard the clicking heels of the sharp-nosed furniture merchant approaching the cart, then felt it spring on its axles as he climbed up onto the seat in front. The sound of reins smacked against horseflesh, and the cart lurched onward.

As it made a wide, slow turn, Angelika lifted the canvas to peer over the side of the cart. Franziskus looked, too, and saw Jurgen's estate up ahead. They did not breathe until the horses had clopped right past it. The von Kopf manor was neighboured by fat, blocky armoury buildings, each ostentatiously displaying the seal of a different province or city above its big bronze doors. It made sense that various electors had taken permanent measures to store armaments here – so many wars were launched from here.

The cart slowed as the armouries were replaced by opulent manors, each surrounded by a garden or courtyard. Angelika did not find these interesting, so she let the tarpaulin settle back down over her head. But then she heard a coach approaching in the opposite direction, and she looked out. The approaching carriage was blue and gold, with Count Leitdorf's sun emblem emblazoned on its side door. As it drew nearer, its driver whipped his team to a halt. Their cart stopped, too. Angelika moved the curtains carefully back into place and held her breath.

She heard a voice, addressing the furniture dealer. It was the rouge-faced courtier, Anton Brucke, inquiring after the state of the merchant's inventory. Angelika rolled her eyes and clutched her knife.

'Several classic and antique sets have recently come into my possession,' said the merchant, his voice cuttingly nasal.

Anton said something about wanting a new formal dining set, in a style the name of which she could not make out.

'We have no Nulnish carvers in town, good sir, but I can offer you a set just like–' He reached back to lift up a corner of canvas.

The two stowaways shrank back.

'No, no,' came Anton's muffled voice. 'It must be the new style.'

The merchant let the canvas drop back down. 'I have a set in the *tragische neuausgabe* manner, which inspired the style you speak of–'

'No,' said the courtier, smacking his horses with his reins, 'it must be the other.' If he said anything more, the clopping hooves of his team obscured it. Angelika watched as Brucke's coach pulled into the grounds of a modest manor, past topiary trees and eroded old statues. The merchant sniffed his disappointment loudly and then spurred his own horses on.

The carriage continued on; the estates it passed grew progressively smaller and shabbier. Finally it stopped outside a shabby manor, with a garden overgrown with weeds. Storm-damaged shutters hung precariously from its window-frames. The furniture seller rang a hand-bell, to alert the servants within. No one seemed to stir, so he rang it again. Angelika took advantage of the distraction to flap the canvas over the cart's sides and slip out. She leapt over a hedge, and landed in a garden opposite the dead woman's estate. Franziskus rolled after her. They waited, crouching, until servants came out and occupied themselves with unloading the cart's contents. When none faced their way, they returned to the lane, walking along it as if they belonged there. The road narrowed and snaked back into the heart of Grenzstadt. Shabby estates gave way to derelict ones, and then to shops and taverns.

Dusk had settled on the town. With feigned confidence, Angelika and Franziskus walked along a narrow, curving street, looking past shopkeepers as they locked up for the night. Angelika saw empty expanses of stucco wall and imagined them with bounty posters on them, like the ones Benno had plastered to the walls of the burned Castello.

A boy lit a candle in a ball lamp outside a tall, thin tavern with a plain brick façade. On a cushion beside the door, a troubadour sat, legs tucked beneath him. He pumped away on a squeeze-box, bawling out a triumphant ballad in which a hero named Konrad dispatched a succession of skaven and goblins, each in a different, gore-spattered way. A pair of soldiers, already staggering drunk, stumbled past him, and threw pennies at his head. He ducked and gave thanks as if they'd meant to reward him.

Angelika's stomach reminded her that it was empty; she headed into the tavern. She and Franziskus took seats in the darkest of several available alcoves. They ordered ale and sausages from a toothy barmaid and sat together without speaking.

'What I say is this,' a loud voice proclaimed, from the table behind them, 'the longer he stays in his black-shingled tower of his, the better.'

'You say that because you don't remember the Battle of Nebelhöhle,' came an equally deafening, slurry reply.

'You don't remember Nebelhöhle neither, no matter what you say. You was drunk the whole time.'

Raucous laughter drowned out the inebriated soldier's spluttering reply.

'They don't call him Mad Count Marius just because he's out of sorts, you know.'

'I survived Nebelhöhle because of that madness, thank you very much. Watch him go into one of them rages on the battlefield, I say, and then tell me you'd rather have that stick-up-the-backside Jurgen von sourface Kopf.'

'You ask any soldier in this place, they'd say von Kopf's a hundred times the general Leitdorf ever was.'

'You ain't never seen Marius go all red in the face, and swing that sword of his – that Runefang – so's you can feel its chill bite on the skin of your face, as it slices through the air. You ain't never seen him hack his way through a dozen bull greenskins, each three times his size. I would personally have been beheaded by one, one of the biggest, tuskiest I've ever seen, if he hadn't have cut it in two, just as it was fixing to charge me.'

A third voice cut in: 'You may still be alive, but what about all them that got themselves killed on the days when he was screaming and wouldn't come out of his tent? Give me sane, steady Jurgen any day.'

'Sane? Having us lay siege to mercenaries when we should be–'

'You're one to complain, having hauled back all them silver candlesticks–'

'That ain't the point.'

Another soldier, battle-scarred and grey at the temples, swaggered over from a far table to join the debate. 'If you think we'd be better off with Marius than with Jurgen, you're as cracked as he is.'

'That's right!' said another. 'Let him stay locked up in his attic, writing his poems and tinkering with his supposed inventions. A leader is a leader every day of the year, not just when it suits him. And there's no man more born to lead than von Kopf; he has it in his bones and in every word he speaks.'

'Counts like Marius, they owe their power to the divine blessings of Sigmar the Hammer, just like the Emperor does. To question them is to question Sigmar's wisdom.'

'Or so they want you to think.'

'That's sedition and blasphemy both.'

'At least, unlike some I could name, I don't get no dreamy look in my eyes whenever I see a pasture full of sheep.'

'What's that got to do with anything?'

The men roared with laughter and called for more ale. Franziskus, who had been assiduously eavesdropping on the soldiers, shifted his gaze to Angelika, and saw that she stared distantly past him. He was about to speak her name, to snap her from her reverie, but something about her expression gave him pause. Her eyes moved from side to side, as if she were lost in a memory, reviewing some distant event. Franziskus thought he saw fear in her eyes. He'd seen her afraid – while fighting the Chaos creatures – but this was different, in a way he could not place.

The barmaid arrived to plunk plates of sausage and overflowing flagons in front of Angelika and Franziskus. Angelika shook herself like a dog emerging from a pond, and all hint of her odd disquiet was gone. 'So,' she said, as if they had been talking all along, 'what do you think the odds are that Petrine and Davio have Lukas secreted away somewhere here, in Grenzstadt?'

'Davio? Here? I doubt it very much.'

'And why risk her life to free us?'

'Maybe it is as we said: that he wanted to make amends.'

She laughed derisively.

'Even if they did it for selfish reasons, I'm still grateful.'

'What does it accomplish, to have us free?'

'Jurgen's not the sort to just let us go,' mused Franziskus. 'He'll have his men looking for us under every flagstone.'

'So at the very least, we become a diversion, while they hatch their plan.' She gnawed appreciatively on her sausage, its clear juices running down her chin. 'The first step is to find Petrine again – this time on our terms.'

'Easier said than done, with Sabres after us. I don't see how we have any choice but to creep out of the gates, as soon as we can. I suggest the north gates: the guards might be less vigilant on the other side of town.'

A hunting horn blew; a new voice bellowed. 'All right, you stinking rabble!' The noise in the tavern subsided, but did not die. 'Shut yourselves!' the voice screamed. 'Word just came! You'll want to be at least half sober on the morrow! The call to assemble has gone out – Jurgen will address us all, two hours past sunrise, and you know how he is if he catches a man dozing! Finish up and crawl back to barracks, if you value your hides!' The soldiers groaned and bombarded the crier with rinds of pumpernickel. But then they quietened, drained their flagons and muttered resentful goodbyes.

Angelika wiped ale froth from her lips with the back of her hand. 'Say you're Davio. You have Lukas, and aim to use him for your revenge. When would be the best time to do that?'

'When the greatest number of eyes is fixed on my enemy.'

'We can't leave,' Angelika said. 'Lukas is somewhere here, in Grenzstadt.'

CHAPTER TWELVE

FRANZISKUS WOKE WITH the sun on his face. His tunic was off and bundled under his head. He reached his hands out to feel the surface he'd been sleeping on: it was a flat stone roof, cool and dusted with glittering sand. Brushing away the dirt and tiny pebbles that had embedded themselves into the skin of his chest and forearms, he sat up. He remembered where he was, and how he and Angelika had arrived there.

Already awake, Angelika had stationed herself, crouching, behind a crenellated battlement. They were on top of an armoury, across the street from Jurgen's estate. They could have chosen one of its neighbours, but they had picked the one belonging to the city of Nuln because it seemed the easiest to climb. Its rough stones provided good handholds for a rope-free climb, and Angelika had clambered up them with a scuttling prowess that reminded Franziskus of a peddler's monkey. She'd unfurled a rope down to him, and then he'd had to groan his aching way up twenty feet of wall. All the time his heart had been hammering at him, as he imagined Nulnish guards appearing and blasting away at him with their flintlocks. He'd concluded his dismal performance by collapsing, gasping, on the armoury roof. He'd made a resolution to strengthen his arms, and to practise climbing, so that he would never humiliate himself in this way again.

Fierce cramping in his arms, neck, shoulders and chest gave him a vivid reminder of this promise. It occurred to him that he ought to check the roof for points of entry. Now that it was morning, there might be people in the building. A wooden trap door, just a few feet away from them, provided the only way to get from the interior to the roof. Angelika had, it seemed, already dealt with it: she had shoved an old straw broom through the handle, to block it shut. Franziskus wondered just how often the Nulners checked this door; roof inspections would not be a frequent thing, he anxiously concluded.

Squatting to stay behind the low crenellations, he stretched his cramped muscles, then waddled to Angelika. He asked her how she thought they might have to wait.

'Sun's been up for an hour or so,' she told him. That left another hour until the start of Jurgen's address. A hubbub of mingling conversations arose from his manor grounds: a few hundred soldiers, all uniformed in yellow and black, had already gathered below.

'We didn't think to bring any breakfast, did we?' Franziskus asked.

'Stop complaining. We had sausage last night.'

A flock of vendors appeared with their carts, once again competing for prime locations. Soups bubbled in pots; thick strips of bacon sent up clouds of delicious, fatty smoke from small iron griddles. Franziskus blinked desolately down at them. 'The great epic heroes, they always eat heartily,' he said.

'That's because they're written by court poets, whose bellies are typically full. And put your shirt back on. With your ribs sticking out like that, you're making me hungry, too.'

He complied.

'You need more regular meals, Franziskus. For your own good, find yourself a different kind of life than this.'

Offended, he stiffened. But instead of a retort, he opted for a change of subject. 'What were you thinking of, last night, in the tavern?'

'Hmm?'

'Before the food came. You wore a strange expression.'

'Did I?'

'You seemed a world away.'

'I don't like towns,' she said.

He waited for her to explain, but she went back to watching the courtyard. Franziskus gave up and leaned against the battlement. He knew her well enough by now; there'd be no point in trying to extract an explanation from her. Still drowsy, he drifted back to sleep.

She peered down as more soldiers arrived, shouting jocular greetings to their fellows. There was much clapping of shoulders, some pounding of backs, and even the occasional bear hug. The troops were still buoyant from their victory at the Castello, Angelika concluded. Among them, though, were men hobbling on crutches, and others with bandaged hands or heads. A column of wounded men paraded in, perceptibly darkening the mood of their still-healthy comrades. The battle, it seemed, had not been quite as one-sided as Angelika had thought.

A wooden platform had been assembled for the occasion. Servants rushed to smooth folds on the yellow and black cloth banners that draped over it, obscuring its construction from the crowd. Two designs repeated themselves along the bunting's length: the Black Sabres' ensign, and the von Kopf family crest, which was nearly the same, except that it was framed by a bear and an eagle. Angelika noted the absence of Count Marius's sun emblem.

Sergeants arrived, accompanied by drummers and buglers. Angelika kicked the toe of her boot against Franziskus, jarring him awake. He stirred, spat the taste of sleep from his mouth, and positioned himself to watch the action below. As one, the sergeants bellowed and waved. The meaning of their various cries remained a mystery to Franziskus, who had been a junior officer, and had merely watched as the sergeants of his regiment herded the soldiers about. Somehow, the soldiers all knew what the yells meant, even with a half-dozen sergeants bawling at once. The uniformed men left the street and entered the courtyard, where they gathered themselves into ranks and columns with impressive speed. With stiff legs, the sergeants inspected their ranks. Every tenth man or so would attract his sergeant's attention for some infraction, and would be forcibly shoved to one side, or would be made stand in place to receive a full-throated tongue-lashing. The display reminded Franziskus why he felt so little nostalgia for military service, even though his rank had exempted him from the worst humiliations.

'You think it will be Toby and his cronies who deliver Lukas?' he asked.

'Who else? The only question is, where will they come from?'

Franziskus was about to ask what they were supposed to do when Lukas appeared. He stopped short. It went without saying that they couldn't fight their way through four regiments of soldiers. They could not hope to rescue the boy here. At best, they'd get an idea where he was headed next, after von Kopf took possession of him. Two places would be most likely, Franziskus reasoned. The first, somewhere in Jurgen's manor. The second, the very cell he and Angelika had briefly stayed in.

Several officers, their helmets bearing floating plumes of green or sapphire, paraded in a square formation. Angelika counted two dozen of them. They grouped into a double row at the left of the platform, angled out to face the men. Franziskus pointed out Gelfrat, in the second row, his bulk almost obscured by the men in front of him.

Heralds bearing long trumpets filed out in front of the platform. They raised their instruments, from which pennants flaunting the von Kopf crest hung. Unlike Jurgen's run-of-the-mill servants, these fellows were resplendent with shining brocades. They even had tiny bells on the ends of their pointed slippers. The musicians blasted out a shrill, stirring fanfare. Snare drums were hit, their rattling sound echoed off the armoury buildings and back into the courtyard. Soldiers straightened their spines. Drummers appeared from behind Jurgen's manor, in a formation built around the man himself. Jurgen rode a tall white stallion, its muzzle pointed skywards, mimicking his. He proceeded with exacting slowness, shoulders level, his jet half-cape flowing behind him. He steered his tall steed to the front of the platform and dismounted, his tall boots landing directly on the stage. He held his arms out to form a V, with his palms out to his men. Sergeants growled deep in their throats, giving the men permission to cheer. This they did, loosing a low roar that began thunderously, but petered out unevenly, as the soldiers ran out of breath. It was not the most spontaneous cheer Angelika could imagine, but it filled the street regardless.

Jurgen lowered his arms slightly, then repeated his V gesture, prompting a hoarser chorus of hurrahs. His platform was bare: there was no lectern, and no row of seated underlings to back him. He strode along the front lip, so close to the edge that a lesser man would worry about toppling over. He shaded his eyes theatrically, and regarded his men.

'My Sabres,' he said. 'My Averlanders.' He projected his cutting voice easily across the square; Angelika and Franziskus could hear him just as if he were standing next to them.

'I speak to you today,' Jurgen declaimed, 'so that you may revel in your present glory, and anticipate victories yet to come. You have taught those who would betray us that it is better to suffer the stern expectations of our friendship than the fatal lash of our swords.

'To show strength can be a costly thing. As I look out upon you, my loyal men, I see bruises. I behold burns and scars. And last night I read from the roll of the dead. I honoured those among your number who made the final sacrifice, in the pursuit of our power. Do not mistake me, my brave and determined war-makers: in this world, power means survival. To strike swiftly, to aim without error: to do these things is to do work of mighty Sigmar, our divine god. Those of you with blooded hands are holy men, baptised in our foes' defeat.

'Those of you who have not yet slain the foe shall soon have the chance to join their blessed ranks. An even greater enemy – the cursed greenskin – gathers to make brutal war, as he has done since his kind first walked this earth.

'Does he think us weak? Or is thinking beyond his nature? Such ponderings are immaterial! We must simply face him on the field of honour, as we always have, and give no quarter. And face him you soon will.

'Among you there may be some whose hearts girlishly quake at the thought of battle. Do not be led astray by this shameful, sinful impulse! It is better to die in glory than to live in shame. As you wait to charge like battering rams into the greenskins' discordant ranks, remember that a coward's shame stains not only his own memory, but the hopes and reputations of his family, for a dozen generations! Would you vilely spit upon your mother's breast? Would you dig up your father's carcass and play idly with his bones? No, you would not, and will not! You will stand against the foe, and prove yourself Averland's bulwark! You will—'

The banners edging Jurgen's platform rippled. They flapped. Soon it became obvious that this was more than just wind playing with the cloth; someone prowled beneath von Kopf's stage. Sniggers briefly coursed through the ranks and the files, to be abruptly squelched when sergeants coughed in warning.

Jurgen stopped mid-sentence, seeing that he no longer possessed the sole attention of his men. He paced quickly to the lip of his stage, as the bunting redoubled its flapping.

Pushing it aside, as nimbly as a *dell'Arte* player through a stage-curtain, came Toby Goatfield. He was followed by Elennath and Henty Redpot. They had Lukas with them, he was cowering with stooping shoulders. As he pulled Lukas from the bunting, Elennath swiftly removed a gag from the boy's mouth and stuffed it in his belt. Angelika doubted that many of the soldiers had caught this; Jurgen would certainly have missed it from the platform.

The sergeant at the head of the column nearest to Toby reached for his baton and came forward; Jurgen signalled for him to pause.

Toby directed a wide grin at his would-be assailant, and then at the assembled soldiers as a whole. Finally he pivoted to acknowledge Jurgen.

Angelika squinted: distance made it hard to tell whether the dark marks on Lukas's face were bruises, or dirt. The boy carried himself listlessly. He hung his head; his long, greasy locks fell over his face, obscuring it. Angelika realised that she'd poked her head out past the parapets, and could easily be seen if anyone happened to look up to the armoury roof. She uncoiled herself and crouched back down.

'Please pardon our disgraceful interruption,' Elennath cried, his elven accent ringing. 'But my master thought this moment of gathering and celebration would be most suited to a joyous occasion. By the largesse of my lord, Prince Davio Maurizzi–'

A rustling of angry murmurs went up among the crowd. Elennath gave them time to settle. 'Prince Davio Maurizzi wishes to make amends for his terrible misjudgments and misalliances, by providing to you – the great warrior Jurgen von Kopf...' The elf trailed off, as if he'd momentarily lost the thread of his rhetoric. 'Here is your son, who we have discovered alive and well, a survivor of an engagement against bandits, and of imprisonment by the forces of Chaos itself!' He waited for the soldiers to gasp at the mention of Chaos, and they obliged him. 'O joyous event! By fate's miraculous intervention, the border princes have a chance to gain your forgiveness!'

Lukas swivelled his head, looking for a place to run. A smiling Toby clamped a tight, stubby paw on his right arm; Henty did the same on his left. Angelika saw Toby's lips move, no doubt muttering some vivid threat into the boy's ear.

'It is nonsensical,' Franziskus said to her. Realising that he was whispering for no good reason, he tried to speak in a normal manner. 'They know Jurgen wants him dead, don't they?'

Toby shoved Lukas up to the edge of the platform. The boy resisted for a moment, going slack and flopping back. His bobbing head turned to take in the audience of soldiers, and he changed tack, allowing the halfling to boost him up. Lukas slapped his arms up on the platform and windmilled his legs, as the two halfling mercenaries boosted him up. Jurgen who was standing, fixedly, shook himself to step over and lend his son a hand.

'I don't understand,' Franziskus said.

'Look at him,' Angelika said, as Jurgen stepped back from the spindly form of his lost son, eyeing the men assembled before him. 'You can see the calculation he's making, can't you?'

Franziskus watched as Jurgen faltered. 'He's asking himself if he can dash the boy's skull open in front of his men – and has decided that he can't.'

'Exactly right. You're becoming a skilled judge of character, after all.'

'Thanks to your former and remorseful foe,' Elennath called, addressing the crowd, 'the future leader of the Black Field Sabres is saved!'

Toby raised a gnarled and jubilant fist. 'Three cheers for Jurgen von Kopf!'

The cheers sang out. Soldiers shook their fists as Toby had done, yelping out a trio of hoorays. These contained more ardour than the cheers before.

'It is an omen of victory!' Elennath proclaimed. 'Our lord, Prince Davio, commends you all to your task, as you ready yourselves to face the greenskin hordes!'

'Victory!' Toby echoed. The soldiers joined him in thrusting their fists skyward, stamping feet or clattering sabre hilts against their breastplates. A growing crowd of civilians, who had gathered on the street, added their own voices to the cheering. Overcome by enthusiasm, a vendor of griddlecakes expressed his pleasure by tossing his wares up into the air. The passersby were only fleetingly perturbed by the shower of hot batter; they returned quickly to their own giddy shouts and bellows. Among the civilians, a new chorus of 'Victory!' went up, and soon the soldiers themselves had taken it up.

Jurgen had moved to the centre of his platform, and posed in an attitude a sculptor might choose for a memorial statue. He held his right hand behind his back, Angelika noted. She recalled the gesture from their interrogation: the hand would be coiled into a fist, tight with contained fury.

Lukas looked from side to side and covered his loins with his hands, as if he were naked. He inched to the back of the platform, behind his father.

Gelfrat broke from the officer's formation to steam toward the mercenaries. Henty spotted him first, licked his lips, and braced to receive a charge. Jurgen followed Gelfrat's progress. He took an affected step up and raised his arms for quiet. Gelfrat saw this and froze for an instant, then backtracked behind the platform.

'Indeed!' Jurgen said. He repeated the word several times, until the crowd quieted itself. 'Prince Davio has capitulated himself to us – as we knew he would!' He paused, to invite further cheers. As the crowd's roar washed over him, he feigned a smile, pulling the muscles of his stony face away from his teeth. 'As these emissaries say, it is indeed an omen of victory.' Jurgen faltered, furrowing his brow.

Angelika followed his line of vision: the three mercenaries were now on the move, backing toward the courtyard gate, between the columns of fighting men. They were making a slow, sly exit. Toby and Elennath bowed low as they backtracked; the halfling seemed to sweep an imaginary hat out before him.

Jurgen snapped his gaze forcibly from them. 'Yea, even our old enemies proclaim the inevitability of our triumph!' he resumed.

Toby hooted his approval for Jurgen, rousing the soldiers around him to join in.

'Brilliantly and brazenly played,' Franziskus said.

Angelika nodded. 'If I could bring myself to admire anything about them, it would be their gall.'

Jurgen called to Gelfrat. The big man heaved himself up on stage. Jurgen spoke instructions into his ear; Gelfrat took frozen, goggle-eyed Lukas by the forearm and tugged. Head down, Lukas meekly followed him as he jumped from the back of the platform. A complement of fellow officers moved from their formation with dignified speed, hemming the boy in. They led him into the manor.

Angelika gathered up the rope. 'That's our first question answered – we know where he is. For the moment.' She crossed to the armoury's far battlement and looped the rope around one of its merlons, knotting it tight. 'I don't suppose you have a plan less stupid than mine?'

'What's yours?'

'We sneak into the manor, find him, and whisk him out without being caught.'

'That is a stupid plan. But I have no better.'

She told Franziskus to climb down first. He tugged on the rope to show that he was down. She rubbed her hands, grabbed the rope, and began her descent. At the halfway mark, she saw a man standing behind Franziskus, a friendly arm draped around his chest. From their respective postures, she could tell he had a knife to Franziskus's back. It was

Honour of the Grave 217

Benno. He beckoned her to continue down. She took an instant to consider her choices, then did as his gesture demanded. She touched down on the dirt floor of the alleyway, in front of Franziskus.

'I should have been looking,' Franziskus said to her.

'Don't reproach yourself,' said Benno, wearing a cat's smile. 'I had myself cleverly hidden.'

'Let me go,' said Franziskus. 'We must rescue poor Lukas from your father's custody.'

In an almost playful gesture, Benno shoved him forward, out of the range of his knife. He sheathed his weapon. 'Franziskus,' he said, 'I couldn't agree more.'

BENNO ENTERED THE small back room and threw a sheet of folded paper down on an uncomfortably low table, where Angelika and Franziskus were sitting. Angelika picked it up; it was a broadside, offering a bounty for their capture. The drawn likenesses were much the same as the posters they'd seen before, but this sheet was printed on a press, and the reward for their hides had doubled.

'Your father wastes no time,' she said to Benno. She tossed the broadside into Franziskus's lap. He unfolded it and stared at his image in mournful revulsion.

'As you've probably gathered, he's never one to let a slight slip by.' Benno sat and tucked into the meal spread before them: there were apples, coarse-skinned pears, round loaves of sour bread with sage; wedges of pale cheese; fat, peppery sausages, curled in the Kislevian manner, and a pot overflowing with sauerkraut. A clay jug of sharp cider sat in a ring of condensation next to a pitcher of lukewarm, yeasty ale.

The three of them sat among high, teetering wooden shelves laden with bolts of cloth. All the colours of the Empire's uniforms were represented, but bolts of yellow and black were the most common by far.

Benno had taken Angelika and Franziskus directly to this hiding place, a few lanes away. It was the back room of a fabric shop, owned by a friend of his. The friend had not been introduced by name: he was well into his sixth decade, enjoyed the blessing of an imperious mane of flowing white hair, and bore himself with full military rectitude. He had no left arm, so it required no genius of deduction to mark him as a veteran of the wars. It was he who'd supplied their food, while Benno had been out gathering his intelligence.

The cloth merchant had also taken their clothes from them. Benno had remarked that they could be smelled a mile away, which would be a drawback when they went to get Lukas free. They now sat wrapped in robes of coarse muslin. The robes were laced securely at the front, sparing Franziskus a crisis of modesty. Their drying garments hung on a cord suspended over their heads.

'It's as you suggested,' Benno now said, cutting free a thick disc of sausage and popping it into his mouth. 'They've stored him in the same cell we put you.'

'And, naturally,' Angelika said, 'they'll be doubly watchful now.'

'Could be. But my father knows better than anyone what a spineless dishrag Lukas is, and I can say for certain he's not expecting you to break the boy out. I stole a few moments with him, and he reckons you've long since fled to the borderlands. He'll wait till the war's over to send bounty hunters after you in earnest.'

'He's also not expecting you to suffer a sudden spasm of brotherly love,' said Angelika.

'Love?' Benno laughed. 'I promise you, I'm motivated by my own narrow interests.'

Though she did not trust him, Angelika felt a pang of new affection for the Averlander. She liked a man who spoke without hypocrisy. There would be no falling into his arms, or any other such nonsense, given all that had passed between them. That didn't mean she couldn't briefly enjoy the way the lines of his face crinkled, or take pleasure in his wolfish way of devouring food.

'I don't understand,' Franziskus said to Benno, as he carefully chose an apple.

'What happens to me if my father falls into Davio's trap?' Benno asked, rhetorically. 'There's no advantage in being his son if he gets himself disgraced. Which–' he paused for a vigorous round of chewing, 'is exactly what will happen to him if he disposes of Lukas, as I'm sure he intends to do.'

'Why go to all the risk of helping us free him?' Angelika asked. 'Why not just warn him to leave the boy alone, and be done with it?'

'Warn him?' Benno laughed again. The one-armed shopkeeper was hovering at the doorway, and chortling knowingly. 'Jurgen von Kopf doesn't listen to my warnings. Not where the family honour is concerned. Remember, I'm just one member of his vast society of bastards.'

'But the soldiers on that parade ground seemed to think the sun shines out of your father's backside,' Angelika said. 'What makes you so sure they won't forgive a little murder in the family?'

'My father's a clever man with tactics and troop deployments, but when it comes to the feelings of the unwashed, he's thicker than a fencepost. I, in contrast, am a common man. Or was, before I learned of my parentage and pressed for a commission.

'He thinks the people love him because of the legend of the Black Sabres: family honour, and the selfless pursuit of deadly purpose. And our swagger and reputation, they're part of it, I'll grant. But the true reason people here stomp and cheer for him is that he isn't Mad Count Marius. He doesn't suddenly turn around and kill his own men, and later explain himself by saying they were possessed by his dead mother's daemonic spirit. He doesn't fight like a whirlwind one day, then ride off to mope in his castle the next. Now, with Jurgen at the helm, we can count on winning battles without having to pray that our commander won't be too deranged to lead the charge today.'

'So if they find out that Jurgen's killed his son, to satisfy some mouldy old family ritual...'

'...then they decide he's as mad as Marius, and that's the end of everything. They will only fight half-heartedly when the orcs come. So he loses his post, or we get slaughtered by greenskins, or both. Me, I'd sooner just let Lukas slink into exile, like the cowardly little snot he is. And the two of you,' he said, pointing his cheese-blade at them, 'you're the ones who are going to slink him off.'

Angelika leaned away and crossed her arms. 'What makes you think we wish to do that?'

'You explain it to me. For some unaccountable reason, you've appointed yourselves his mother hens, haven't you? So it happens that our interests intersect. We both want the boy where my father can't get him.'

'And why should we trust you?'

He refilled her cup. 'It's you who's been playing crooked with me, Angelika. Oh, I admit we didn't tell you about Lukas, from the beginning. A mistake, it seems, now that I look back on it. But compared to what you did to us... running off without warning, reneging on the deal to turn our brother over... Not to mention selling him to halfling mercenaries.'

She stood and stretched, feeling his hungry look on her as she arched her back. 'And I suppose you want us to do this for nothing, as usual.'

He held out empty palms. 'I've told you a dozen times: I'm a poor man. Perhaps one day, when I lead the count's armies, I will toss you a golden cup or a string of pearls.'

She took a final swig of ale. 'Let's get this over and done with, then, before your largesse makes me swoon.'

THEY CLEARED A space in the cloth merchant's back room; he laid out bedrolls for them and left them to sleep.

'So – can we trust him?' Franziskus asked.

'We can never trust anyone,' she answered, closing her eyes. She hadn't slept much, on the armoury roof, and found it easy to slip into slumber. Soon she was faintly snoring, leaving Franziskus to struggle for comfort on his bedroll. Their plan called for night action, and he knew he should get as much rest as he could. Knowing this just made it harder. He lay on his right side, then on his left. He rested a bolt of cloth under his head. He pulled off his tunic and covered his face. He thought about the heat. The dustiness of the room began to concern him. He became sure that his throat was coated with the stuff. He sat up to cough and sputter.

He looked at Angelika. He told himself he was checking to see how her cuts and bruises had healed. Sometimes she was beautiful to him, sometimes not. Now, with the muscles of her face entirely relaxed, and her lids of her eyes closed and fluttering with dream, she was as lovely as he'd ever seen her.

He imagined himself reaching over to brush her soft cheeks with the backs of his fingers. Then a thorny realism took over his daydream, and he pictured what would happen if he did such a thing: her danger-sharpened reflexes would jolt her immediately into action. She would burst up, produce a dagger from nowhere, and probably plunge it deep into his eye. If he was lucky, she would stop short, merely threatening him with blindness, disfigurement, and mortification.

He lay back down on the bedroll. He tried to picture a life for the two of them, different from the one they now had. Franziskus envisaged a cottage. In his mind's eye, he thatched its roof, covered it in stucco – no – he would shape it from blocks of shale, mortared together. Its stone floor would make it cool in the summer, he decided, as sweat beaded his forehead and soaked the hair at the back of his neck. In the winter, they would need to keep the fire roaring, but that would not be such a hard thing, because this cottage of theirs would be far from everywhere, in the depths of a forest, with no shortage of firewood. But it would not be the prickly woods of the Blackfire's mountains, nor one populated by goblins, beastmen and mercenaries. Maybe somewhere in an elven glen, he thought, quickly stipulating that they would be on good terms with the elves, who would would not be like Elennath in any way.

He revised his vision again. The home he would truly like for their cottage would be the Moot. Not the wretched place he now imagined, having met so many awful halflings, but the storybook one. He pictured Angelika, rocking in a chair, a blanket on her lap, surrounded by halfling children eager to hear stories. There would be a touch of grey in her hair, and wrinkles at the sides of her mouth, softening them. She would smile at the little halflings, and then she would tell them of her adventures, from way back. She would tell them about...

About robbing corpses, and about fathers who wanted to murder their sons, and brothers wanting to betray their fathers and...

Franziskus sat back up again. Angelika moaned softly and turned over. He imagined himself drawing a knife of his own, and putting it to her milky-white throat, and demanding that she beg for his mercy. Voice barely cracking, she would tell him how sorry she was, for opening his eyes to this filthy world. She would admit that she should have left him with the orcs that were about to kill him. He would get her to admit the truth – that, like Lukas, he'd be better off mourned and dead than as a rootless survivor with no home to return to.

He considered slipping away, and going back to his father's estate, to bow his head and admit to his shame. He would not leave a note; he would just go. Angelika would not weep to see him gone. She kept telling him this was what she wanted. She was not lying to herself; she truly did wish to be rid of him. No matter what he told himself, he was just a millstone, dragging her down.

He would leave.

He stood.

But then he was back on his bedroll. First on his right side, then his left. He turned on his belly, and then on his back. He covered his face with his tunic. He dozed, readying himself for the action to come.

HE WOKE FEELING that he'd slept for hours. His eyes were dry and his mouth like glue. The room was empty, except for their clean clothing that was still hanging on the length of twine. The strange feelings he'd had when he couldn't sleep – the crazy lusts and unforgivable bitterness – had evaporated. He wondered how he could have thought them at all, and put them neatly out of mind.

He heard voices on the other side of the door. He walked into the shop, where Angelika and the proprietor were idly talking. She was disinterestedly asking him about the present state of his business. He, fastidiously clipping his single set of fingernails with neat, straight front teeth, murmured that trade could either get worse, or better; it depended on how things went. Franziskus hailed them and asked where he might find a chamberpot. He relieved himself and returned. A shrug from the proprietor told him that Angelika had returned to the back room, and that the man was glad for this. Franziskus checked the shop's small, circular windows, noting the orange light of late afternoon. Rubbing his eyes, he shuffled back into the store.

Benno reappeared not long after. He was empty-handed, so they finished off the remains of breakfast. None of them was very hungry, anyway.

Benno unveiled the plan. It was simple: he'd take them in as if they were his prisoners.

Angelika said, 'I hope this isn't merely a ruse to get us to march happily into jail.'

'What an amusing comment that is,' said Benno.

He would banter with the guards, keeping them at ease. If they asked why they were to go in the same cell as Lukas, he would shrug and tell them his father wanted it that way. His tone would carry the suggestion that Jurgen was not to be questioned. This would sound more authentic than an elaborately detailed explanation.

'Won't they already have contrary instructions? Not to let anyone in, under any circumstances?'

'No doubt,' said Benno, 'but I've checked the roster, and I know these men. Olli Unruh grew up on the same streets as me, he is just a little bit younger. I've cultivated him a long time. He thinks if he sticks by me he'll have a fine career. Maybe even end up as adjutant, when I command the Sabres, which would be quite a step up for a man such as him. Then there's young Renald; he's a nervous one, and not prone to asking questions.'

'Renald Wechsler,' Franziskus said. 'He was among those who kept watch, as you rode us north.'

'Ah,' said Benno.

'If he's nervous, though, he might be a stickler, afraid to contradict his orders?'

Benno twitched his shoulder; it would have been a shrug, if he'd put more effort into it.

Angelika examined the daggers Benno had scrounged for her. He hadn't been able to lay his hands on the ones his men had taken from her. 'So we get them to open the cell door, then what?'

'Then we kill them.'

'Kill them?' Franziskus said.

Benno responded with a second shrug; this one had slightly more energy behind it. 'There's no other way. They'll catch on when we start to unshackle the boy, won't they?

We'll have to make quick work of it, too. Make our first blows count.'

'Isn't it enough just to overpower them?' Franziskus asked.

'That's fine for you, maybe, but I can't have witnesses.'

'Couldn't you somehow coax them into silence?'

'Can't risk it.'

Franziskus looked to Angelika, for support in his argument. She was jiggling her wrist, testing the weight of her knives.

'If it's any consolation, Franziskus, they're both bad men. Olli would happily cut your head off, if I told him to. Your friend, Renald, I've heard, gets all sweaty whenever he spots a scrawny little boy. He follows street urchins into dark alleys, that sort of thing.'

'It's convenient you can say so.'

'If they were truly righteous men, I'd wait until the roster changed. Lukas's life for Unruh and Wechsler's – it's a fair trade, I promise.'

'Franziskus,' Angelika said, 'let him tell us the whole thing from the start, without interruption.'

Benno shifted on his stool. 'I go in. You're my prisoners. I put Olli and Renald at ease. They open the door. We kill them. We unshackle the boy, hustle him down the steps, get him into a cart. The three of you drive away in the cart, never to breathe Grenzstadt's air again. *Voila!*'

'Where do we take him?' Franziskus asked.

'That's your choice. Just keep him away from me and my father.'

'The count's man – Brucke. He told Jurgen not to harm Lukas. We were thinking, maybe the count might protect him?'

Benno tongued at his teeth, clearing out errant food morsels. 'I wouldn't recommend it. Fancy courtiers like him will betray you just for the pleasure of running in circles.' His tongue found a large chunk of something; he reached in with his fingers to extract it from his gums. He balled his prize between thumb and forefinger and flicked it away. 'And the count himself – Sigmar knows what he would do with a boy like Lukas. Imprison him? Make him his catamite? Blow him up, in one of his experiments? If it were me, I'd stay clear. Go south again.'

'Where the orcs are massing.'

'Then go to Wissenland. Go to the forgotten isle of the peg-legged dwarfs, for all I care. Just get him free of here.'

To WHILE AWAY the time until night settled in, they played cards. The shopkeeper joined them, rattling his tin cash box. He changed Angelika's half-crowns into smaller coins. Benno regarded this transaction with apparent curiosity but did not ask where she'd got the money. Angelika gave Franziskus half of her coins, which he promptly lost to her. To keep him in the game, she gave them back. She won money from Benno and the storekeeper, too. Sometimes she lost part of her stake, to one or the other of them, but always won it back on the next hand. Franziskus never won. As the game wore on, his hands began trembling. He dropped his cards, and they always landed face up. The storekeeper glowered at him like he was an idiot. Benno seemed to feel sorry for him, which was worse. The third time his cards slipped from his damp fingers and onto the table, Benno asked Angelika: 'I hope your friend here is ready, for tonight.'

'He's ready,' Angelika said, exposing a winning hand, and sliding more of Benno's coins across the table and into her lap.

FINALLY THEY LEFT the shop. The unnamed merchant had a small cart prepared for them. A mule was already hitched to it. The animal sniffed the air, pointed its snout at Angelika, and hissed. Angelika hissed back. The cart was covered in canvas, dyed yellow and rusty red. Angelika and Franziskus clambered inside, from the back. Benno took a seat up front; his friend handed him the reins. Without further discussion, Benno urged the mule on. It clopped through Grenzstadt's streets. Angelika sat beside Franziskus, but he could tell she was studying him for signs of lost nerves. He stuck his nose out and chin up. He promised himself he wouldn't fail her. He'd served her well so far, he thought. When it was time to act, he'd done what was needed. It was the anticipation he couldn't stand.

* * *

THE CART STOPPED. They heard the faint jingling of buckles as Benno hitched the reins to a post. He came around to the back. Without lifting the canvas flap, he said, 'We're here.'

Angelika emerged from the cart. In a low voice, she said to Benno, 'You stay here. The two of us will go.'

'What?' he mouthed, as Franziskus climbed out.

'We'll go. We'll get the door open without killing anyone. You stay here and watch the cart.'

'We can't change the attack now. You should have–'

'I only decided it just now.'

'Two against two lessens the odds.'

'We'll take the risk. You underestimate us.'

She set off. He seized her arm, pulled her back. 'You think you can save the guards this way?'

'No good has ever been done in this world by murder.'

He anxiously surveyed the darkened square for observers. 'You know the world better than that! If Lukas goes missing, they're dead anyway! What do you think happened to the two guards who let you escape yesterday?' Benno gave Angelika a brief chance to admit she didn't know, then went on. 'They were executed this morning. Gross dereliction, my father called it. In military punishment, he favours a modern approach: death by gunshot. Now they lie in beggar's graves. If *we* kill Olli and Renald, their families still get pensions, at least. They die as heroes, felled by bandits. Would you deprive them of both lives and honour?'

Angelika glanced up at the tower. 'In that case...' She shook her head violently. 'All three of us go. But we pull blades on them and give them the choice. Stand and fight and die, or run away and live.'

'Better to strike without warning.'

'You need our help. We'll do it my way.'

Benno let loose a stream of murmured profanities, nodded his clenched jaw at her, and led the way to the foot of the curving stone stairs that led to the tower. They ran up. Franziskus drew his new rapier, then remembered he was supposed to be a prisoner. He stuck it back into its scabbard without breaking stride. Once inside the tower, and no longer exposed to passersby, they slowed their pace. Hands on the backs of their heads, Angelika and Franziskus took up their roles as resentful captives, edging reluctantly up the stairs. Angelika even stopped for a moment, making Benno prod her with the flat of his outstretched sabre. They looked from side to side, as if alert for opportunities to make a break for it. The performance went to waste; they saw the guardsmen only when the front of the door came within sight.

'Found some more work for you, boys!' Benno called out, in his most jovial manner.

'Commandant Benno?'

Benno's nose twitched. The voice did not belong to either Olli or Renald. Finally as he cleared the curving wall, he got a good view of them. Renald was there, but the other guardsman was a new recruit, one whose name he could not recall. The new fellow was short and dark-eyed, with a complexion that suggested some Tilean or even Araby blood in him. Both regarded Benno and his prisoners with undisguised bafflement. They wore breastplates, carried sabres, and had burnished steel helmets on their heads.

'Renald,' he said, 'where's Olli?'

'He's come down with the croup, sir.'

'That so? Well, I've found you some more guarding to do. I personally caught these two lurking around my father's manor. Guess the reward stays in the family, hah?'

'Good for you, sir.'

'Unlock the door,' Benno said. 'I want to get these two shackled, quick.'

The unfamiliar guard hesitated. 'Commandant, sir, we was clearly told...'

'Told what? What's your name?'

The guard took a deep breath and tapped the heels of his boots together. 'Gottfried, sir. Nino Gottfried.'

'Speak up, Nino. What were you told?'

'Your father's orders, sir – we was strictly instructed, there was no, no condition at all where we could even – If we even think of unlocking this door, sir...' He made the throat-slitting gesture across his throat. 'You understand, sir.'

'My father will be pleased you spoke up for his orders. I'll commend you to him. But the situation–'

Angelika winked at Franziskus. Renald saw this and came down the steps at them, pointing his sabre at her. Nino loosed his sword, too, and held it out before him, unsure who to aim it at.

'They were planning a move, sir,' Renald said to Benno. 'I saw this one give the sign to the other.'

'Treacherous sow!' Benno cried, smacking the back of Angelika's head with his free hand. She exclaimed in genuine pain. Benno refixed his gaze on Nino. 'You think my father wants them to escape a second time? Open the cursed door!'

Nino's sword clattered to the floor as he fumbled in his belt for the key ring. Benno wrinkled his face in annoyed impatience. He tapped his foot. Nino's fingers shook, jangling the keys. He stuck the key in the door but it wouldn't turn. Benno skipped up the steps to swipe it from his hand. Renald jabbed his swordpoint in Angelika's direction, and then in Franziskus's. Benno opened the door. He swept inside. Nino bent to scoop up his sabre and point it at Franziskus's throat. Renald prodded Angelika, pushing his hilt-guard into her side. He ordered her up to the door. Angelika regarded him with slow contempt. She and Franziskus moved slowly up the stairs. Renald and Nino stood aside to make room for them. They shuffled resentfully into the cell.

Lukas hung shackled from the wooden beam in the centre of the room. A long spike had been driven into the beam, about seven feet from the floor. His wrist shackles were fastened to it, forcing him to stand with arms above his head. His hair had been shaved off, leaving a dense, black stubble on his scalp. Red lines marked the razor cuts of a careless barber. The boy had a freshly fattened lip, purple and swollen. His eyes fluttered and widened. 'Franziskus!' he cried.

Benno, already at his side, worked a key into the wrist cuffs. 'Come here!' he barked, to Nino. 'It's stuck!'

Nino hopped to it. Renald saw that Angelika's belt still had a pair of daggers in it. 'Their weapons!' he exclaimed, warning Nino, who halted mid-stride.

'But why–' he choked, as Benno snatched his sabre from his hand. Angelika seized Renald's sword-arm. Franziskus punched him in the gut. He bent over, gasping. Franziskus gaped guiltily at him. Angelika twisted Renald's arm until he groaned and opened his hand, dropping the sabre to the floor. Benno stuck a foot behind Nino's leg, pushed him over on his back, and crouched over him, a knife to his throat.

Franziskus shook his head and stepped to the door, swinging it shut. He picked up the keys, which Benno had dropped, and freed Lukas. Limp, the boy fell into Franziskus's arms, nearly knocking him over. Franziskus lowered him to the floor. 'I knew you would come,' he said.

Benno used the point of his sabre to herd Renald and Nino into a corner. Angelika bent over Lukas; he flinched when he saw her. 'You're hurt?' she asked. He nodded. 'Injured,' she asked, 'or just fatigue, from the way they hung you?'

'Fatigue,' he breathed.

'You'd better find the strength to run, and find it fast!' she told him.

'Commandant, sir,' Renald said, 'why are you doing this?'

Benno picked up a metal lamp, which burned on the floor, and held it up, gazing intently into the guards' faces. His right hand kept a sword steady at their chests. 'My accomplices want to spare your lives. I think it's safer not to. Convince me that if I tell you both to flee town and never come back, you'll do it, and you'll do it now, without getting yourselves caught.'

'Please, commandant, sir...' said Renald.

Benno moved the sword to him. 'Unconvincing,' he said.

'Sir,' said Nino, 'if you stop now, if you let us reshackle the boy, I swear to you we'll never–'

Benno lifted the lantern until it was next to Nino's cheek; both men could feel the heat of its flame. 'A poor line of argument.' He set the lamp down. 'I'll repeat myself, one last time. Can you run from here, now, and never be seen again? Or must we slay you?'

'We'll run,' gulped Nino.

'Is the boy ready?' Benno asked Angelika.

'Can you stand?' she asked Lukas.

With difficulty, young von Kopf made it up to his knees; Franziskus extended an arm to him.

'No.' Angelika curtly shook her head. 'He must do it on his own power.'

Lukas strained, grunted, stood, wavered, and then was steady.

'The boy is ready,' Angelika told Benno.

'Here is how we will proceed,' Benno instructed the men. 'We will all walk quickly down the steps together. When we hit the courtyard, you will silently walk to the city gates and–' He turned to Angelika. 'It won't work. The men on the gates may know they're supposed to be on duty.' He took a step back. 'I'm sorry, fellows.' He levelled his sabre. Angelika braced herself to leap at him and pull him away from the guards.

Boot soles scraped outside the closed door. A voice boomed: 'What in the fiery halls of Hell is this?'

Gelfrat.

Benno swore. He dived for the door. So did Angelika. They pushed their weight against it. Gelfrat was pushing from the other side.

Renald and Nino rushed Franziskus. He drew his rapier and stepped in front of Lukas, swiping it through the air to keep the guards at bay. Lukas stumbled to retrieve Nino's dropped sabre.

'Explain yourselves, you manky swine!' Gelfrat shouted, as Benno and Angelika's feet slid on stone. He'd shoved them back a couple of inches, opening the door a crack.

'Help us!' Angelika shouted to Franziskus.

'We're occupied over here!' he replied.

'You two! I knew it!' Gelfrat bellowed.

'And Commandant Benno, too!' called Renald.

'You're a dead man, Renald!' Benno said, his lips sideways.

The door was six inches open. Angelika shifted her posture for better leverage but it was no use.

'Benno?' Gelfrat howled. 'What goes on here?'

'Gelfrat, my brother, listen to me...'

'Half-brother!'

The door was nine inches open.

'We must get the boy far from here, before our father ruins himself!'

'We? We, you say?'

The gap was a foot wide.

Nino picked up the lamp and threw it at Lukas's head. The boy ducked. The oil sprayed wide. A small puddle of it burned in a far corner. Franziskus craned his head to see if there was anything the flames might catch on. There didn't seem to be. Just stone and more stone. Nino charged him. He slashed Nino's cheek. Nino stepped back, hand on face, blood drizzling through his fingers. Renald ceded space to Franziskus.

Gelfrat shoved the door open another three inches and then squeezed into the gap, jamming his wide, thick body between door and frame. Benno reared back and slammed his weight into the door. Gelfrat grunted; his face turning red. Angelika pushed harder.

Gelfrat shoved again. 'The witch has entrapped you in her honey snare, has she?'

'This is for the family good, Gelfrat. The good of all the von Kopfs.'

Gelfrat clenched his teeth. Veins danced on his neck and forehead. 'I am so glad to catch you in treachery, Benno. There's no set of guts I hate worse than yours.' He got his arms up and his palms flat against the door. Using the wall to brace himself, he won another couple of inches.

Lukas edged toward the door. Renald moved to block him.

'People call me a brute,' panted Gelfrat. 'But you – I may strike hard, I may shed the blood of men. But I strike in honest warfare, or when drunk, or angry. You, Benno. You – You're worse than a brute. Cold. Calculation. Narrowing your eyes, deciding pain or mercy like you're writing in a ledger book. Cruel, heartless. And now–'

Grunting like a hog on the slaughter table, he forced the door another foot, squeezing his way into the room, clear of the door. With no resistance to counter their weight, Benno and Angelika fell onto the door as it slammed back shut.

Gelfrat wrapped his paw around the back of Benno's neck. Benno swung a fist into Gelfrat's side; the big man took no notice of the blow. He put his thumbs in the middle of Benno's throat. 'Even if you weren't competition,' he said, as Benno's eyes bugged, 'I have dreamt of this for nearly a year now.'

His head turned on its beefy neck as Gelfrat felt the tickle of Angelika's dagger tip on it. He threw Benno to the floor. He turned to her and laughed, moving away. 'You can try it, strumpet. But I say for certain, there's no chance of your getting that all the way in. Not on the first try, which is all you'd get.'

'How about a deal?' Angelika proposed. 'Let the three of us leave, and you can have your brother all to yourself.'

'Half-brother.'

'What say you?'

'I say I'll kill all four of you.'

She cut open his leg, above the knee. She skirted back. He drew an oversized sabre and hacked down at Benno, who rolled out of the way and onto his feet.

Renald pulled a knife and rushed at Lukas. Franziskus stepped into his path and the two went sprawling onto the floor, where the oil burned.

Gelfrat clanged his sword into Benno's, knocking him into Nino. Nino moved his hand from his bloody cheek to punch Benno in the kidney. Benno elbowed him in the face, enlarging his wound. Blood spattered the wall.

Lukas took his chance and ran with uncertain balance for the open doorway. Nino navigated wide of Benno to pursue the prisoner. He slammed himself into his quarry, pinning Lukas against the wall of the curving stairwell.

Angelika ran for the doorway. Gelfrat, widening his stance, obstructed her. She crouched with her knife. He feinted at her, then turned to parry an incoming blow from Benno's sabre. The two Kopfs grunted and pushed their swords together. Angelika couldn't get past them.

Lukas butted his forehead into Nino's cheek. Nino shoved him back, but twisted his ankle on the steps. Lukas ran up the stairs.

'You idiot!' Angelika groaned. 'Don't run *up*!' Then Lukas was gone.

Renald rolled on top of Franziskus. His helmet teetered off and clunked onto the floor. Franziskus butted him in the head, stunning him long enough to flip him onto his side.

Benno manoeuvred Gelfrat into turning his back on Angelika. She cut across Gelfrat's shoulder, tearing a gash below his neck and notching the leather strap that held his breastplate in place. He roared and swung at her with his sword. The blow went wide. While he was off-stride, she dashed around him and out onto the steps. He turned to deflect a blow from Benno's sabre. She had a good opportunity to strike at the back of his neck, but declined to take it. She ran.

Nino came at her, grabbing at her ankles. She turned to kick him. He pulled her off her feet. She went down, shuddering as her tailbone landed on a stair edge. She ground her heel in Nino's eye. He whimpered and let himself slide away from her. She hopped to her feet and resumed her upstairs run.

Franziskus had lost track of his rapier. Renald was lying on it, as well as his own. Franziskus got up and seized him by the armour straps. Renald dug fingers into his leg. Franziskus kneed him in the temple. The guard rolled off the weapons and tottered up. Franziskus kicked his knife out of reach, then ducked to grab the hilt. Renald kicked at his throat, scoring only a glancing blow, but which prevented Franziskus from rearming. Franziskus launched himself at Renald, grabbing his wrists and pinning him against the wall.

Benno and Gelfrat traded swooshing sabre swings; none came sufficiently close to so much as *ting* against the other sword. Gelfrat backed Benno against a wall. He lunged in, sabre slashing. Benno tripped him. He fell into the wall. His sabre-blade landed on Renald's left hand – Franziskus still held it by the wrist – chopping through his middle, ring and little fingers. Severed digits hit the floor at Franziskus's feet. Renald only realised what had happened when he saw Franziskus's horror and followed his eye-line. He saw his shattered hand just as the gore began to spurt from it. He sank to his knees and, cradling his hand in his good one, crawled on his knees into the corner, to scream hideously.

Franziskus's first thought was to go to the poor fellow's side, but he cleared his head of this ridiculousness and rushed for the door. Gelfrat stepped free of his duel with Benno long enough to smash Franziskus in the throat with his forearm. An airless gasp issued from Franziskus's gaping mouth. He staggered back, hitting the support beam.

Gelfrat glanced back at Franziskus for the merest moment, checking the results of his handiwork. This gave Benno an opening. Benno brought his sabre ringing down on Gelfrat's steel helmet, pounding a pronounced dent into it, and knocking it off-kilter. The force of his strike sent him reeling off balance, erasing the chance for a follow-up blow.

Franziskus dashed at Gelfrat, spearing the back of his calf with his rapier's sharp tip. He saw his hit draw blood but Gelfrat paid it no heed. Instead, the big man prepared for a heaving swing at his half-brother's legs. Benno leapt over the blow, then fell far short with an ill-timed overhead chop with his own sabre. Gelfrat bashed his weapon into the side of Benno's breastplate. Franziskus saw Benno's eyes widen from the impact, then dashed for the open doorway. He pelted up the stairs.

LUKAS HIT THE top of the stone stairs. They terminated in a small stone room, scarcely bigger than his cell. A set of rough wooden steps led up into open air. Through this opening, he saw starlight. He hesitated. Battle sounds clattered up from below. He eked his way up the steps.

He'd clambered his way to the top of the watchtower. The observation deck was square: about twenty feet on each side. Crenellated battlements surmounted its walls, embrasures alternating with merlons. Four men stood watch there, manning a ballista. There was a cannon, too, but none of them attended it. They wore Averlandish uniforms, though not the Black Field crest. Several glass lanterns, mounted on metal poles, spread orange light on their startled faces. Three of them reached to their belts for long swords, thicker than Franziskus's rapier, but lighter than von Kopf sabres. The fourth pulled a matchlock pistol from his sack, and knelt to load it. The others scolded him as they charged the escaped prisoner.

The first to reach him was Thomas Steinhauer, who was tall and lanky and, at the age of sixty, was considered ancient by his fellow soldiers. He was far too old, they persisted in telling him, to be breaking his back lugging his weapons and armour about, or to be wearing out his feet marching from one battle to the next, or even to be straining his eyes peering out from his watch post here on top of the south wall. Secretly, he agreed with them, but his pride did not let him make any such admission. He had served in Averland's army when both Jurgen and Count Marius were mere infants. Now, after the failure of his masonry firm, he was back in it again, cursing fortune's fickle gods. He threw himself at Lukas and clouted the spindly lad across the side of the head with the guard of his sword-hilt, sending him crashing to the stone floor. His mouth leaking spittle, he kicked at Lukas's throat, until the boy rolled over to protect it. Then Thomas kicked at his ribs.

The gunner, whose name was Werther Weiss, who had yet to do anything of interest to anyone, including himself, fumbled in his pack, looking for his tinderbox. He had never had a chance to fire his pistol, except at targets, and he was determined not to lose this opportunity, even though his mates were yelling at him.

The second to reach Lukas was Sebastian Arzt, who was short, with cheeks like a forest rodent puffed up with nuts. Sebastian was young and wished to become a field medic, and from there, when he had completely his military duties, a real physician. This would enable him, he reckoned, to quickly enrich himself, so that he could marry into a family with a good name. He kicked at Lukas's hands, which the boy had put out to protect his face.

Werther Weiss found his tinderbox. He teased the fuse from his matchlock between its steel and flint.

Theophilus Ruprecht, bow-legged and irritable, was the third to reach Lukas. When he was annoyed, which was frequently, he showed it by hunching his shoulders back and forth, in a curious lateral motion that any of his comrades could distinguish from up to half a mile away. He was about thirty years old, or so his mother told him. He wanted to die a soldier, though he did not care who he fought for. By his reckoning, he'd killed four orcs, sixteen goblins, two elves, and three people, over the course of his career. Two of those goblins, he'd killed with the same blow. He was proud of that. He took his sword, reversed it, clasped mail-gloved hands around the blade, and used the hilt as a bat, to smash down on Lukas's vertebrae.

Werther Weiss struck his flint.

A knife flew into Theophilus Ruprecht's eye. He fell to his hands and knees and bellowed out his pain and fear.

Angelika had appeared at the top of the wooden stairs.

Weiss's flint failed to light his fuse.

Arzt and Steinhauer looked at each other as they each kicked at Lukas. Both hoped the other would run to engage the lithe, black-clad woman who now sprinted at them. Steinhauer turned to meet her charge, gripping his longsword tightly. She ran at him headlong. Ruprecht briefly stopped his moaning, and for a prolonged moment the only sound came from her soles scuffing lightly on the stone flooring. Arzt paused his kicking and watched her. Abruptly she altered her trajectory and curved toward him, leaving Steinhauer stupidly braced for a nonexistent impact.

Lukas crawled away from him. He put his foot on the back of the boy's neck.

Arzt swung his sword at Angelika. She dived at his legs.

Weiss had finally got an ember going on the end of his fuse.

Angelika landed on Arzt, slashing with her knife, cutting a hole in his trousers, and injuring his leg. He caught her in the face with the flat of his sword.

Weiss's fuse sparked into life.

'Not now you stinking fool!' Steinhauer shouted at him. 'You'll hit Sebastian!' Lukas was motionless under Steinhauer's boot.

Weiss smiled. He did not like Sebastian Arzt well enough to give up such an excellently good chance to try his gun. He took aim at the two figures wrestling on the floor. He was reasonably sure he could hit the woman in the head.

Arzt knocked the knife from Angelika's hand. It skidded into the middle of the deck.

Cutting it close, Weiss watched his fuse burn down.

Angelika seized Arzt's wrist and twisted; the sword slid from his hand. She rose up, straddling him. She balled twin fists and pummelled his face with them.

Weiss followed her movement with the barrel of his gun. By sticking her head up, she'd removed any chance of his hitting Arzt. He pulled the trigger.

The burning fuse slammed down onto the firing pan. It extinguished itself. No bullet flew.

Weiss had forgotten to load his pistol.

He cursed and leapt for his pack, for his box of shot and powder.

Blood, cascading from Angelika's nose, mingled with Arzt's own, and dripped into his eyes. He punched out; she weaved so he only hit her shoulder. The blow was powerful, though, and knocked her off him and to the side.

Steinhauer left Lukas to lie on the stone floor. He stepped to Angelika and stood over her with sword upraised. He couldn't bring it down without the risk of hitting Arzt if he missed her. He dropped the sword at his side.

Weiss found his tin box and fumbled with its lid.

Steinhauer grabbed Angelika from behind, wrapping both hands around her neck. He dug his fingers into her windpipe; she flailed her arms. Arzt punched her in the stomach. Steinhauer tightened his grip on her throat, making her sputter.

Ruprecht, the knife still buried in his eye, collapsed. He rolled over on his back. He resumed his pitiful groaning.

Franziskus made it to the top of the steps. Without breaking stride, he pounded toward Arzt and Steinhauer. Ruprecht's cries masked the sound of his approach.

From his box, Weiss took a paper cartridge of gunpowder.

Franziskus wheeled his sword at Steinhauer. He laid a crimson slash across the side of the old man's face and neck. Franziskus tried to reprise his move, but his opponent got his forearms up and in the way. Franziskus's rapier cut open a yellow sleeve and a black sleeve, as well as a little bit of flesh beneath.

Lukas struggled to his feet, looked about for a weapon. His mouth dropped open in horror as he watched the fight.

Angelika, released from Steinhauer's grip, jammed the heel of her hand into Arzt's codpiece. He huffed and cursed but recovered and trapped her between his legs.

Ruprecht flopped himself over on his back, chest heaving. Blood bubbled from his mouth.

Steinhauer looked at his sword, lying on the floor. 'You'd run through an unarmed man?' he demanded of Franziskus.

Franziskus stepped back and gestured to the sword. Steinhauer stooped to sweep up his blade. He grinned. 'Stupid sack of dung,' he said.

Weiss stuffed his cartridge down the muzzle of his pistol.

Ruprecht died.

Arzt squeezed Angelika between his legs and rolled, smashing her into the floor.

Steinhauer came in hard and fast to hack at Franziskus. Franziskus parried, his wrist twisting from the blow. Steinhauer followed up with a surprise underhand; Franziskus danced back. He hit the battlement and ducked fast to miss a third blow.

Angelika wrapped her fingers around the hilt of the dagger that jutted out of Ruprecht's dead eye.

Franziskus elbowed Steinhauer in the side. Steinhauer turned to interpose his breastplate between himself and the blow. Franziskus suffered the force of his own strike; lightning pain reached all the way up into the bones of his hand. Steinhauer pressed his advantage; Franziskus put up his left forearm, and got it badly cut.

Weiss loaded shot into the muzzle of his gun.

Angelika drove the dagger deep into Arzt's thigh. He jerked, freeing her. She seized him by the helmet straps and smashed his head down on the floor. Again, and again.

Steinhauer forced Franziskus backwards. He scraped his back on the battlements as he bobbed and twisted to duck or parry the older man's blows. He saw that Steinhauer's breaths were laboured.

'You're tiring,' he said.

Weiss sparked his tinder.

'Don't make me kill an old man,' Franziskus told Steinhauer.

Steinhauer's face went white with fury. He dived at Franziskus.

A mottled dove flapped above them.

Arzt shuddered and went limp. Angelika stopped pummelling his head.

Weiss lit his fuse.

Franziskus braced for Steinhauer's charge and smashed him in the jaw, visibly unmooring it from its hinges.

Angelika stood up.

Weiss aimed at her.

Steinhauer crumpled.

Weiss pulled his trigger.

At the head of the stairs, Gelfrat appeared, breastplate wet with blood.

The mechanism of Weiss's matchlock drove the fuse into the firing pan, lighting the powder. It sent a ball of shot cutting through the air.

Angelika ducked.

The shot hit Gelfrat.

It fell, flattened, from a dent in the big man's breastplate.

Weiss gulped.

'Bastard!' Gelfrat screamed. 'You shot me!'

Weiss stammered out a denial.

Gelfrat ran at him.

Weiss pulled his useless trigger.

'You shot me!' Gelfrat said.

He closed the distance between them. Weiss quivered. Gelfrat seized him by the belt and collar. Groaning, he heaved the begging, burbling soldier over his head.

Angelika and Franziskus ran to Lukas.

'What's your name?' Gelfrat demanded of Weiss, but gave him no time to answer. 'I just killed one brother. This is his blood on me! I'm about to kill another! What makes you think you can shoot me, and not have me kill you, too?' Dried tears marked Gelfrat's cheeks, like snail's trails.

Angelika and Franziskus tried to get Lukas to his feet.

'Please!' Weiss pleaded.

Gelfrat dropped to one knee. He lowered Weiss onto it, pressing him down. He broke Weiss's back; vertebrae crunched and popped. Gelfrat lifted Weiss once more over his head. He threw the gunman off the parapet. He stepped up to watch him fall, waited for the thud of impact, and watched appreciatively as a red pool spread around Weiss's shattered body.

Lukas was upright, tottering at first, and then leaning on both Angelika and Franziskus.

Gelfrat wheeled.

They tried to turn Lukas around, but he tangled his legs in theirs. They grabbed him before he could pitch face-first onto the floor, but then Gelfrat was upon them. He tore Angelika off the boy, pulling her off her feet with one powerful arm. She landed on her side and rolled, ending up about ten feet from the fray.

Gelfrat punched at Franziskus's face. Franziskus ducked the blow, but caught the next, a jab to his kidneys, delivered by Gelfrat's free hand. He felt himself doubling over but exercised all the control he could muster to stay upright. He saw Arzt's prone form behind Gelfrat and pushed on him, hoping to trip him. Franziskus slid down the big man's gore-slicked breastplate.

Gelfrat smacked him in the ear, punched him in the stomach, kicked him in the head, and stomped on his back.

Lukas turned to run. He got halfway to the stairs. Gelfrat slung a choking arm under his chin, dragging him backwards.

'Lukas, I want you to think about something as I murder you,' he said.

Angelika crept to Arzt's body. She pulled the blade from his thigh. He was breathing, shallowly.

'You aren't a hundredth of the man Benno was,' wheezed Gelfrat, 'yet he gave his life for you.'

Angelika jumped on Gelfrat's back. She jammed the dagger between his shoulder blades. He swatted her off before she could drive it the rest of the way in. She landed on her tailbone. The blade waggled back and forth; it was stuck in about an inch. If it had gone in any less, it would have fallen out of its own accord; any more, and it might have done the kind of harm needed to bring him down.

Angelika rose. Her legs refused to cooperate. She sat.

'You, who aren't even good enough for the maggots you're about to feed,' Gelfrat continued. He reached around to his back, located the dagger in it, plucked it out, and tossed it down the stairs. He leaned down, heaved Lukas over his shoulder, and strolled over to the edge of the parapet's southward edge. It faced out onto the city and south, toward the Blackfire Pass. He'd thrown Weiss into the town, but had evidently decided that Lukas did not deserve even the shelter of Grenzstadt's walls. 'Can you speak, boy?' he asked, standing at the edge.

Lukas made a vaguely affirmative noise.

'So tell me what you think of all this.'

'I don't want to die.'

Gelfrat dropped him on his head. 'Is that your problem, you knock-kneed fop? That you think you're somehow *alone* in that?' He seized Lukas by the heels and lifted him up. 'Eh? Or do you think you're too high-born to answer questions from the lowly likes of me?' He dangled Lukas, upside down, over the battlement, at least a hundred feet between him and the ground.

'I'm sorry!' Lukas cried.

'I won't disagree with you there. Sorry you are, for certain.' He let go of one leg, then grabbed it again.

'Just get it over with,' Lukas said.

'Oh, that must be that blue blood of yours, making you think you can still command me.' With Lukas's ankles caught securely in his fists, he snapped the boy's body as he would a crab leg. Lukas's face hit the side of the tower. Gelfrat dangled him up and down. Lukas sobbed.

Angelika got up, reminding herself that what she felt now was nothing compared to the pain she'd suffered back in the pit. Franziskus saw her, and struggled up, too. They advanced slowly on Gelfrat. Angelika went to pick up an abandoned long sword.

Gelfrat saw them from the corner of his eye. 'You're not stupid. You know he dies if you jump me now. It's too late for him already. I suggest you run, like the curs you are.'

'Lukas had no part in this rescue attempt,' Angelika said, hands up, slowly advancing on him. 'He didn't ask us to come. He's done nothing to warrant this.'

'He violated the oath of our company,' said Gelfrat, banging him once again into the tower wall. 'While he breathes, my honour is stained with filth. As is my father's honour, and that of all my comrades.' He shook his captive like he was a sifter full of floor. 'Isn't that right, Lukas?'

'Yes,' Lukas said.

'Gelfrat,' said Angelika. 'You may have hated your brother, but he was right in one thing: it will cost Jurgen more than he knows if Lukas is killed, either by his own hand, or by any who serve him. The entire bloodline will pay the price, if you don't pull him up and leave him be. Or do you want to inherit nothing?'

'You talk of politics,' Gelfrat said. He blew droplets of blood from his lip. 'My father and I, we speak the language of honour.'

'Honour is for some other world, my brother. Not this one.' Benno stood at the top of the steps. He trudged up onto the tower deck. He glistened with blood. It coated his face and matted his hair. He dragged his sabre in his hand; it made a rhythmic bumping noise as it moved from one stone tile to the next. The fingers of Benno's right hand had all been broken, and jutted out at various wrong angles. He limped. His left eye was swollen shut; his right was a mere slit. Blood dripped from both of his arms, and flowed down the length of his blade. He left a trail of it as he stumbled forwards. Angelika could not tell where the blood was coming from. It would have to be from several places.

Gelfrat tightened his grip on Lukas's left ankle, then his right. He turned his head sideways, to see Benno. 'I killed you already,' he said, annoyed. 'You've Chaos blood in you, haven't you?'

Benno smiled; a mixture of blood and saliva beaded on the yellow enamel of his teeth. 'Idiot.' A laugh, or maybe just a cough, escaped his lips. 'Those calloused hands of yours never could find a pulse, Gelfrat.'

'I'll drop him over and then complete my task with you,' Gelfrat threatened.

Angelika signalled to Franziskus. While Gelfrat concerned himself with Benno, she stole along the battlement, to the big man's right. Franziskus, scratching idly at his cheekbone, edged over on its other side, to the left of him.

'You keep saying you'll drop him, yet you haven't. You know what that says to me, half-brother?'

'What?'

'That a part of even your dim brain knows not to do this. Is it pride that prevents you from backing down?'

Angelika tried to catch Benno's eye, to shake her head in warning. He was taking the wrong tack by antagonising the big man. Yet he'd captured Gelfrat's attention, in a way she had not. She decided to keep her mind on a single objective: getting closer to Gelfrat, before he noticed her.

'I'll let you explain that remark,' Gelfrat said, 'because your arrogance always gives me a right fat laugh.'

'It took me some time to get up those stairs,' Benno said. He'd dragged himself within fifteen feet of his brother. He halted. 'I've had time to hear you talk. A moment ago, you were happily killing me. Now you're blaming this poor thing for forcing you into it. Care to reflect on the contradiction?'

Gelfrat gave Lukas another smack into the wall. Lukas cried out – something about taking mercy on him.

'Could it be that you hate and envy whoever you happen to be looking at, at any given moment?'

'Go choke yourself.'

'How much time have you devoted to wondering which of us is the better man? Always justifying yourself. Never being satisfied with the answers you dream up. You despise me, Gelfrat, but I feel pity for you.'

Gelfrat opened his left hand. But with his right, he drew scrawny Lukas higher, so that his face, upside-down, made ruddy by blood rushing to his head, could be seen between two merlons. 'I'll drop him. You know I'll drop him.'

Benno raised his sabre, his head lolling to one side. 'Yes, you're right; you must.'

Gelfrat saw how close Angelika and Franziskus were to him. He whipped his head from side to side, showing them he knew. They edged back. 'This is trickery. I'll drop him, and then where will your beloved politics be?'

'Here's a new story. Tell me if you like it,' Benno said. Now that he was nearer, Angelika could see at least one source of blood: a wide fold of exposed muscle below his neck, from which red fluid slowly pulsed. He continued, heedless of the life leaking out of him: 'Tonight, sadly, the lost son who was so recently reunited with his illustrious father was cruelly slain. Thrown off a tower, by his jealous half-brother, Gelfrat. Gelfrat was then himself slain by another of the Kopf sons, Benno, who suffered grievously in the battle. But survived. When he recovers from his wounds, brave Benno will surely be legitimised. Elevated to the place of True Son, to take Claus's position as field commander. So throw the boy off, you fat, swaggering chunk of gutter spew, and let's have at it.'

Gelfrat gave Lukas one dangle, brushing him against the parapet, then opened his hands. Angelika leapt for the falling boy as Gelfrat turned to draw his weapon. She grabbed Lukas by the belt, her left hand finding purchase mere moments after the right. The force of the sudden weight drove her into the battlement, the edge caught her in the stomach, and knocked the air from her lungs. Her legs flew up. Before she could flip over the battlement to fall alongside Lukas, Franziskus seized her belt. His feet were braced against the battlement. In concert, Angelika and Franziskus groaned. Lukas dangled down into empty air. His dead bulk tore at Angelika's fingers. She gritted her teeth and shifted. She felt Franziskus tighten his hold on her, hugging her, pulling downwards, lending her the solidity of his weight. The strain moved from her hands to her shoulders. The bones of her arms fought to remain in their sockets.

Thick red tears squeezed themselves from Benno's damaged eye.

Gelfrat rumbled out a laugh. 'You're not exactly fit to take me on,' he said.

'Fit enough,' Benno choked. 'You're poisoned.'

'What?'

'The blades I gave them.' He meant Angelika and Franziskus. 'Poisoned, all. And I saw both of them hit you.'

'No!'

Angelika willed strength into her arms. Her bones were made of iron, she told herself. She pulled. She got Lukas pulled up a foot. Her muscles juddered with the effort. She couldn't maintain it. She let him lower slightly, so she wouldn't entirely lose her grip on him. She asked herself if it was possible to switch positions with Franziskus, letting him do the lifting. But no, a switch could never work. She had no choice but to keep on, and succeed.

'Yes,' Benno said to Gelfrat. 'Even now, black bile consumes your blood.'

Angelika called softly down to Lukas, instructing him to place his hands on the tower wall. Push against them. Do anything he could to support his own weight.

'The poison courses through your veins and arteries. It burns like acid. It's hot like fire.'

She tried again to pull Lukas up; this time, she had his assistance. He walked his hands up the wall. She got him up a decent foot.

'Already it slows your reflexes, distorts your vision. Soon it will travel to your heart, pool there, and cook it like a steak.

Until then, all I need do is avoid your weakened, ill-aimed blows.'

Gelfrat wailed and dived at Benno with a swinging sword.

Benno easily sidestepped the reckless charge, bringing his sabre down on Gelfrat's neck as he surged his way by. An artery opened. Blood spouted out, pulsing, jetting. Gelfrat pivoted back to face Benno. He clapped his left hand to his neck. The hand diverted the flow into three tighter streams of shooting gore.

'You bastard,' he said.

'The same, and proud,' said Benno, both eyes closed, a leg giving way beneath him. On bended knee, he looked like a supplicant. 'And you?'

Angelika got Lukas far enough up, and well enough braced, so that it was safe for Franziskus to let go of her. He stood up and grabbed onto the boy. They both pulled him up and over the battlements. He landed on top of them; they crawled out, disentangling themselves. He sank into a sitting position, panting.

Gelfrat wobbled over to a lantern pole and steadied himself against it. Benno fell over.

'You poisoned me, you two!' Gelfrat shouted, at Angelika and Franziskus.

'He lied. There was no poison,' Angelika told him.

'No?' He slid down the pole.

'No.' She could say it with authority. If you wanted to go sorting through piles of dead soldiers, you had to be able to sniff out the various types of blade venom. If the blades had really been coated in poison, she would have known the instant he handed them over. In truth, no poison that did any good on a blade was half as swift or lethal as Benno had said. He'd given a good speech, though. She'd have believed it, if she hadn't known better.

'He tricked me,' Gelfrat said. 'Into...' He convulsed and went slack.

Benno wasn't moving, either. When she'd recovered her strength sufficiently, Angelika got up and examined him. He was gone, too.

Bells rang. Angelika looked to the opposite tower. There were men stationed there, too. They were the ones sounding the alarm.

CHAPTER THIRTEEN

'How long have they been ringing?' Angelika asked, referring to the alarm bells.

'I don't know,' Franziskus said.

'A long time,' Lukas said.

Angelika muttered a choice epithet. 'Then get up and run, curse your hide!'

Lukas placed his palms on the floor and tried to push himself up. He collapsed, sobbing, dryly. Franziskus put an arm on his elbow and pulled him. Angelika wanted to kick the pathetic creature, but knew that wouldn't accomplish the desired end. Her desire to help the boy was always stronger when she did not have to suffer his direct presence.

With Franziskus's help, she jerked Lukas to his feet. She tugged on his arm, wrenching it, to make him run. He dropped like a sack of flour, throwing his arms around her ankles.

'Please, please, I can't... Just leave me be.'

She crouched beside him. She could hear footsteps and exclamations from the square below. 'Find the strength, Lukas, or you're dead.'

'Talk to my father. Convince him. You're persuasive.'

'This will be his excuse to execute you. If you truly want to die, tell us now, so we can escape without you.'

He sank lower, laying his face on the floor. 'Do that. Save yourselves.'

Then she did kick him, before hauling him up. With a child's reluctance, he let her bring him to his feet. She slapped him. He bristled, gathering up his slim, porcelain fist. She smiled inwardly.

'You're right,' she said, 'You're not worth it. You're just what they all say you are.'

'Stop caring about me!' he shouted, and bolted for the steps. They followed, catching up with him long before they reached the street. Angelika stayed behind him, fighting her natural urge to run, swatting him lightly between the shoulderblades whenever his pace flagged. They quickly covered the short flight of wooden steps, and made short work of the tower staircase. They ran past the cell, where they detected no trace of Nino or Renald. Angelika skipped a step so as not to slip on a pool of blood. She did not bother to guess who it belonged to.

They left the tower and hit the second stone staircase, which would take them from the top of the town wall to the cobbled square below. Soldiers had gathered. Armed townsfolk swarmed among them; they were, Angelika realised, angling for the reward on her head. There were perhaps two of them for every soldier.

She seized Lukas by the collar and pulled him away from the steps. The crowd boiled towards them. She turned to run along the wall, to the staircase on the other side. Franziskus initially missed the change in direction but finally reversed course and caught up speedily. He had his rapier out. Men were already rushing up the other stairway, but there were fewer of them. Igniting gunpowder crackled and flashed down in the square. Angelika flinched. As far as she could tell, the bullet hadn't come anywhere near them.

A man in mendicant's robes was the first to reach them as they rushed down the steps. Angelika pulled his hood over his face, spun him around, and tripped him, sending him crashing into the rush of pursuers behind him. They fell like dominoes, forming a great heap of flattened bodies on the stairs. With Lukas's hand tightly in hers, Angelika kept to the stairwell's extreme outward edge: it was clear of fallen men. A punch grazed her chin, but it was the feeblest hit she'd suffered all evening, and it did not slow her. Behind her, she heard the clash of steel on steel. Eyes fixed resolutely ahead, she concluded that Franziskus had found some blows to parry. She did not break stride to check. She and Lukas had reached the bottom. A soldier rushed at her with ready rapier-point. She sidestepped, letting him crash into one of his mates, who'd been positioning himself to leap on Lukas's back.

'You fools!' she shouted. 'This is Jurgen's son!' Only the men nearest her heard this, but it gave them pause long enough for her to elbow her way through them. Franziskus, pressed passed bladesmen, and leapt backwards from the stairs, landing cat-like in front of the gate. He stopped for an instant to marvel at the brilliance of his ten-foot-drop, then he dashed for the gate, which was closing. Angelika and Lukas were hard on his heels.

Angelika heard loosened chains spinning through a pulley. She pulled Lukas back and shouted to Franziskus. He jumped her way just as the gate's inner portcullis, a mass of spikes and wrought iron, rattled down, its arrow-shaped teeth falling flush into slots in the cobblestones. Lukas gaped; it would have split them down the middle.

A rock lobbed in at them; it hit Franziskus on the thigh. He exclaimed more in offence than pain. Lukas bent, straightened, and hurled the stone back into the mob. Angelika felt a pang of admiration – maybe there was hope for the boy, after all.

The soldiers and townsfolk had gathered in a rough crescent-shape, as they slowly crept up on the cornered fugitives. With the chase at a close, they were suddenly hesitant. It was the nature of a mob, Angelika reckoned; now no one wanted to be the first to act. Those who took the initiative would be rewarded by Angelika's dagger and Franziskus's sword. Only after their sacrifice would a second wave attempt to overwhelm them. Angelika steeled herself to seize their moment of hesitation. Holding up her hands, she took a step forward.

'You don't recognise him, because his head is shaven, but this is the von Kopf boy, delivered just this morning to your leader,' she said. Her words yielded a satisfying harvest of turned heads and questioning murmurs. 'Your master is the object of a plot by his enemies. Stand back, lest you make yourselves unwitting accomplices.'

The men didn't stand back exactly, but at least they remained at bay. She hoped the lie that was about to come out of her mouth would contain at least the vague appearance of plausibility. 'The plot is by some of Jurgen's jealous bastard sons. They wanted Lukas gone, so they could take his place. They switched him for a condemned man, thinking he'd be hanged before anyone knew the difference. You can see how they cut his locks, to further the deception!' She hoped for a chorus of affirmative replies, but got only puzzled looks. She was no orator. She felt ridiculous, using this rousing language.

'There's a reward out for you!' someone shouted.

'Also part of the plot – because we knew...'

A portly, puffy-faced man in a sergeant's uniform parted the crowd and spoke in a *basso* voice. 'Then we'll take the three of you to Jurgen, and let him work it out.'

Angelika attempted to look pleased by this announcement. It was preferable to being beaten to death on the spot, and might lead to a better chance for escape, later. She set the last of Benno's daggers on the stonework, and kicked it over to the sergeant. Franziskus placed his rapier down, hilt pointing politely outwards.

The sergeant shouted orders, and soldiers hemmed them in. Each of them was flanked by a pair of men, who seized them by the shoulders. The crowd, disappointed by the anticlimax of their peaceful capture, refused to separate to let them through. The sergeant removed his glove to clout at the faces of unyielding civilians. Particularly recalcitrant onlookers received sharp kicks to the shins. Eventually the soldiers threaded them through the crowd's other side. Flanked by lantern-bearing regulars, the sergeant led the way to a carriage across the square. He left the prisoners and their guards to stand fifty paces away, and marched up to speak with its coachman.

'I recognise what you have done for me,' Lukas said. 'Both of you.'

'I am sure all will be justly resolved,' she said, conscious of the soldiers all around them.

A gasp issued from the crowd; Angelika turned to see bodies on stretchers borne down the steps from the tower. Linen sheets had been draped over the corpses, but blood had already soaked through – especially on the lead stretcher, which she presumed to be Benno's. The sight of the dead seemed to arouse something within the mob: a grim murmuring spread among them. Angelika watched as young boys were placed on the shoulders of their fathers and uncles: for a better view of the slain.

The coachman waved angry arms at the sergeant. He repeatedly cited the name of Somebody von Something-or-Other. Finally he hopped off his perch, still gesticulating furiously. The sergeant took his place and whistled for his men. They opened the carriage doors and pushed the captives inside. Three soldiers cramped in with them, ordering the seating so that two of them flanked Lukas, and Angelika and Franziskus sat on either side of the third.

Angelika worked out that their best chance would be to get out of the carriage before it reached von Kopf's estate. Their guardians had made a stupid mistake: they had put her and Franziskus next to the doors. They were thinking only that Lukas was their most important prisoner. Any shrewd guard trains his attention on those most likely or able to escape.

To get Lukas out with them, though, they'd have to do more than leap out. Force would be called for. She glanced unobtrusively over at the soldier next to her, seeing that he had a knife sheathed at his hip. Her luck was turning; this would prove most convenient.

The coach lurched into motion.

She would seize the knife, backhand it across its owner's throat, then leap onto the guard opposite her. Franziskus would take this cue, and leap as well...

The sounds of the crowd were too loud, too close. She leaned back to look through the window without touching the curtain. She saw lamps and lanterns held aloft. The stupid fools were following the carriage! The throng swarmed all around it, slowing its progress to a snail's pace. Angelika heard laughter, as if it was a carnival.

'What's going on?' the youngest of the soldiers, at Claus's left, asked. He had a high forehead, a bulbous nose, and a sharp, deep voice.

'They think they've found themselves a little excitement,' drawled the sleepy-eyed soldier on Claus's right. 'Maybe they think it'll be like the witch burning we had last solstice.'

The young soldier smiled as understanding dawned. 'Ah, yes. You know, that's when me and this barmaid—'

'Stuff it,' ordered the soldier next to Angelika, expecting obedience.

Stuff it indeed, thought Angelika. The crowd had made escape impossible.

The carriage trundled on for what felt like hours. From the noise around them, Angelika could tell that the crowd was swelling. Through the window, she saw pre-dawn light. It surprised her that it had been so long since they'd set out. The young soldier yawned. She was grateful for the afternoon sleep she and Franziskus had had; it might give them an advantage, when everyone around them needed rest.

Maybe there would be a chance, as they were taken from the carriage, when they could dash for it, then blend into the crowd. Though *blending* was possibly an optimistic term, considering that the crowd was enthusiastically hoping to witness their summary executions...

The door wrenched open. Jurgen stood there. His face was two feet from her own. He was clad only in a white linen under-tunic, which stretched to his knees. It was wrinkled and slept in. Anger drew his features taut. He propelled himself up onto the runner, then reached in to seize Lukas's tunic in both hands. He lifted the boy from his seat and tore him from the carriage, throwing him onto the stones below. The crowd was silenced. Angelika leaned out to leap from the coach, but the soldier opposite her slammed into her, pinning her down. The one beside her seized a handful of her hair. She ceased her resistance.

'Were you born to bedevil me?' Jurgen demanded of his son, who had gone limp on the ground. 'Were you?' Lukas did not answer; sobs wracked him.

Jurgen bent down to haul Lukas upright. His feet were bare. His hair, a moppy mess. 'Answer your father!' he commanded. Lukas stammered. Jurgen slapped him in the face, spinning Lukas off his heels. Jurgen caught him, pulling the boy into his chest. 'Answer!' he repeated, slightly lessening his previous ferocity.

From the carriage, Angelika could see only a few dozen faces. Most had lost their jovial anticipation of violence; this was not the victim they'd come to see.

'Sword!' Jurgen called. He turned back and seemed to take note of the crowd for the first time. 'Get back!' he ordered them. 'What are you doing here? Get back to your homes!' The spectators at the front tried to move back, but Jurgen's courtyard was too tightly packed for them to have much success. Jurgen scanned the crowd for a retainer. 'Sword!' he called.

An odd note sounded, in the distance – a bugler testing his instrument. Annoyed by the intrusion of this irrelevance, Angelika hunched forward, to see better.

A scraping servant pushed his way through the crowd, and handed a sheathed sabre to Jurgen. The prow-faced general took it from him without acknowledging his presence. He tore the scabbard from the sword, tossing it at his feet. Confused, unhappy sounds issued forth from the crowd.

With naked toes, Jurgen pressed his foot down on Lukas's ankle, pinning his scrabbling form to the ground.

Angelika pushed forward, to get at Jurgen. Her guards bashed her head into the side of the carriage until she let up.

Jurgen raised his sabre above his head. Onlookers moaned their protest. He hesitated, turning his head to them, but they would not be silent. Some brave soul lobbed a clod of unidentifiable trash; it barely missed the general's white, exposed calves. He rounded on the crowd, sword upraised. 'Listen, my people!' They roared back at him, displeased. 'Listen!' he said. 'Listen!'

He waited until they made themselves quiet. 'You must understand!' he demanded of them. 'Yes, this is my son, and yes, he must die! He has broken our family oath. You all know this!'

A chorus of murmurs said that the mob did not know, or begin to understand, this.

'It is our oath! The boy's very existence is a crime, one I have every right to end! No Black Sabre may walk away from a defeat. For us, it is victory or death!'

Angelika shook her head in disgust. It was happening exactly as Benno had feared it would. Suddenly, she knew why. It was also clear what was about to transpire. What the bugle note meant. She took a breath. The tension fell from her body.

'Your safety depends on my family!' Jurgen spat.

Lukas crawled away, but the sergeant, having hopped from the carriage, saw him, and blocked his way. Lukas quivered.

'When my company has been strong, Grenzstadt's walls have gone untested by the greenskin horde! When we have been weak, your ancestors have all paid the price! Our honour is your survival!'

A few onlookers nodded their heads, as if this were a reasonable proposition. But most kept their eyes trained on poor, whimpering Lukas. One wizened woman, clad in well-worn velvet, took the liberty of dismissively pawing the air.

Jurgen lunged at her. 'How dare you even question my rights, in this private affair?' He widened his gaze to take in the entire mob. 'How dare any of you?'

Angelika saw the first of them: a raised fist, safely back in the crowd. Another, closer, joined it. Somewhere – just out of her field of view, Angelika guessed – a hand would now be going up. A signal given.

'Pah!' Jurgen said, giving the collected busy bodies of Grenzstadt his back. He nodded to the sergeant, who threw Lukas at his feet. He lifted up his sabre.

The bugles now cried out, with trumpets, and drums. It was hard to tell, with the echoes that came off the armoury buildings, but Angelika judged that they were back on the street. Heads turned. Jurgen stopped.

'What is it?' asked the bulb-nosed soldier.

'Shut it,' replied the one beside Angelika.

'What's going on?' asked the bulb-nosed soldier. He opened the carriage door.

'Get back.'

'Something's going on,' he said, hopping down.

'Get back here!'

Recognition wrote itself on the young soldier's face. 'Gods and daemons!' he exclaimed. The mob mirrored his expression.

'It's the count,' Angelika mouthed, to Franziskus.

'It's the count!' gasped the soldier, and the crowd.

'Shallya's teats!' the senior soldier swore.

Angelika tore the curtains from their rod and switched sides for a better view of the procession. Townspeople crushed into one another, forced forward. Angelika could not yet see what pushed them, but she felt well prepared to guess. Elbows and curses flew. Finally the crowd parted, revealing the procession Angelika expected.

Flanked by willowy, boyish lantern-bearers, who wore fancy Araby turbans and robes of silk, came a troop of fresh warriors in Averlandish livery. They held shields aloft; from each of these shields grimaced the solar emblem of Count Marius Leitdorf. Then came a cantering, coal-coloured charger, on which the count himself perched. A fan of monstrous plumes jutted up from his floppy cap of silk. Embossed sun emblems glowed from his massive plates of shoulder armour. A heavy gold medallion, of the same design, dangled from his neck. It glowed, as if imbued by magic – which it doubtless was. Chained to his ankle with mighty links was an enormous greatsword, an ornament of painted flames flaring above its hilt and onto the base of its blade. He held it up for the crowd to gawk at: some, hushed and reverent, couldn't help but say its famous name: 'Runefang!'

Jurgen looked for the sheath to his quite ordinary sabre. Some gawpers were standing on it. He crossed his arms, sword still in hand. He faced away from Angelika, toward his count, so she couldn't tell if he now, finally, wore a look of comprehension.

Riding behind Marius, on a nondescript nag, wearing a moleskin robe and a drab-feathered felt chapeau, came his counsellor, Anton Brucke.

The columns of attendants stopped, with smooth precision; even the pretty, purse-lipped boys in the turbans proved themselves expert horsemen. Marius clopped his magnificent horse onward until its front hooves stood no more than seven feet from Jurgen's feet. With chiselled, craggy features, he surveyed the vast crowd. He reached into a brocade bag that swung at his hip on a golden rope. Scrupulously, he untied its top. From it he withdrew a cloisonné box, oval-shaped and a few inches long. He plucked its lid off, pinched a ball of snuff between his gloved fingers, and inserted it daintily into his nostril. He inhaled it noisily, blew out his cheeks, and loosed a plaintive sigh. 'What occurs here, my good Kopf?' His horse pointed its head and red-rimmed eyes down at Lukas, its expression carnivorous.

Jurgen looked down at the nightshirt he wore. 'You find me at an awkward moment, your excellency.'

Marius tittered. He licked his lips. 'Apparently.'

'Let's retire into my receiving chamber, your excellency, and we can–'

'Oh,' Marius said, drawing the word out. He wanted to show both his profound disappointment, and pity for Jurgen, as the cause of it. 'The disarray I see before me sharpens my curiosity to fever pitch. I must know all.' He executed a half-turn on his horse, to look into the crowd. He raised his voice. 'Don't we all deserve to know what is happening here?' he asked his subjects. They murmured in an inarticulate affirmative, and stepped back from him. He turned back to Jurgen. 'So explain, before my impatience curdles into... some other thing.'

Jurgen finally repositioned himself so that Angelika could see his face and, yes, he already wore the knowledge of his undoing. He closed his eyes. 'It is a family matter, your excellency. The oath of the Black Sabres–'

'A colourful custom,' Marius interrupted.

'Yes, your excellency, as you know, a Sabre vows never to flee from a battle–'

'A quaint barbarism, I think you might call it.'

'This is my son, Lukas, your excellency–'

Marius peered over his horse's neck. 'Stand up, boy. Let me have a look at you.'

Lukas meekly obeyed.

'I see,' said the count. 'Your father has sentenced you to death for sporting such an appalling haircut?'

Marius waited, but no one dared respond to this witticism. 'But surely,' he said, playing to the crowd, 'that would be no more absurd than the thought that a noble of the Empire, a scion of Averland, would actually be slain by his own father, for failing to uphold such an antiquated decree? A rule which, I hasten to add, is not any kind of law that I have set down, not a law of the land, but a mere family vow?'

'It is a family vow, your excellency,' Jurgen said.

'Does it not seem,' Marius pondered, 'that a vow is an individual matter, for a person to break, or not to break, as his conscience dictates? That neither state, nor familial patriarch, may enforce its terms on persons unwilling to uphold it?'

'Honour is inflexible, your excellency, even when it conflicts with state prerogatives, or our personal wishes.'

'The pronunciation is *pre*rogatives, Jurgen. You know I hate that.'

As Jurgen's face fell, Angelika felt a sickly thrill pass through her. She no longer had any sense of where her sympathies should lie. Her pulse raced hard around her ears. Jurgen's chagrin was plain on his face: *of course he knew the proper pronunciation of the word. Any person can make a simple error in speech.*

'Surely, Jurgen,' the count continued, 'this whole – this whole...' He waved his hand indistinctly about. 'This whole *matter* is but a theatrical, a ritual gesture. You meant, did you not, to pull up at the last moment, to spare your son the penalty of death?'

Resolve and resignation seemed to settle on Jurgen in equal measure. He took a step forward. 'No, your excellency, I did not. Because that would be immoral.'

Marius lowered his voice. 'Jurgen,' he began. The closest onlookers edged in to hear him better. 'Do not deprive me of my battlefield genius. Tell us that you did not mean it.'

'He must die,' Jurgen said. 'No matter what the consequences.'

'Then you leave me no choice.' Marius made his horse rear up. It bellowed a high note of protest, sharpening the mob's attention. Marius projected his voice, so that all of his gathered subjects could hear. 'I cannot bear it! My valiant servitor stands revealed, by his own admission, of barbaric and criminal intent! Can we allow such a man to carry forth the banner of our homeland?'

The crowd rumbled its confusion.

'Even though he has served us well, we cannot permit him to continue. Without the favour of our battle god, Sigmar, all is lost. History shows that, when we are wicked and apostate, we lose our wars, and die in droves before the heathen greenskin! Only when we act righteously does Sigmar reward us with his crucial favour.

'You have seen it here tonight – we have given our Jurgen every chance to repent of his folly, yet he cleaves ever more tightly to it. O woe, this day is a day of sorrow!' He turned back to von Kopf. 'Jurgen von Kopf, you are hereby removed from all duties as field general of Averland. All of your *pre*rogatives and authorities are now revoked! You are stripped utterly of all military rank. You may command no soldier, issue no order, receive no deference! Until further notice, all your duties, including leadership of the Sabres, now devolve to me.'

Jurgen hung his head. He let his sabre fall from his hand.

'My people,' boomed Marius, 'I shall personally lead you into the coming fray!' The throng responded with tepid cheers. Marius brandished his sword. 'Runefang shall smite the foe!' The sight of the legendary weapon brought a measure of enthusiasm to the crowd's shouting. 'Victory shall be ours!' The third cheer was almost ardent.

'The boy is spared, Jurgen,' Marius commanded. 'Should any harm come to him, by your hand, or by the actions of your loyalists or dogsbodies, I shall consider it an affront to my authority. And that, naturally, would force me to adopt remedies of the gravest and most permanent kind.'

Jurgen maintained stony-featured.

'Make some acknowledgement that you have heard me, Jurgen.'

'I have heard you, your excellency.'

Marius's eyes rolled up suddenly. 'Ah. Then. That is it, I believe.'

Behind him, with exquisite delicacy, Brucke coughed.

'Ah yes,' Marius said, in a conversational voice, 'those two in the carriage. They are to be spared, also.'

The soldiers inside the coach looked at one another for guidance. The commander leaned over to open the door nearest to Marius and Jurgen. Angelika opened the door on the opposite side, waited for Franziskus to exit through it, and then followed him out. They heard Marius's procession turn and ride. Angelika leaned against the coach until it seemed they had gone.

Franziskus held himself at a remove, examining her mood with what he hoped was a casual air. 'We were not serving Prince Davio at all, were we?' he asked.

'No, we were not.'

Lukas popped his head around, and moved skittishly toward them. 'What's to become of me?' he asked Angelika.

Angelika found some dirt under a fingernail. She slid the nail along her bottom incisors, then spat. 'Didn't you hear? You're absolutely free. Your father can't lay a hand on you.'

'But what do I do?'

'Do?'

'Where do I go?'

She appraised his grimy, bloodied state. 'To an inn, I'd recommend. For a bath and some decent food. After that... You'll have to think of something, won't you?'

He fixed her in his most imploring look.

'Oh no,' she said. 'You won't be going with me. One displaced blueblood is enough to be stuck with. Maybe the two of you should head off together. Do whatever it is that people like you ought to be doing.'

Lukas moved his beggar's gaze from Angelika to Franziskus.

Franziskus put up his hands. 'I'm sorry, Lukas, but I've made a vow...'

'I'll be at the Hat and Pony,' Lukas said. Then he ran out of the courtyard.

'Go ahead,' said Angelika, as Franziskus watched him go. 'Go with him. I can tell you want to.'

'You're mistaken.'

The coach pulled away, exposing them to the rapidly thinning crowd. They moved into it, receiving little attention from the people of Grenzstadt. They listened in as the consequences of Marius' appearance were debated:

'Death and woe will be the result of this, I tell you.'

'–seemed right in the head, comparatively–'

'–won't miss him one inch–'

'–didn't seem happy to do it, did he?'

'–won't have the strategy we did with Jurgen, but Runefang will make up for it.'

'So you hope.'

They broke from the crowd at Jurgen's gate. 'And what of us?' Franziskus asked. 'What do we do? Where do we go?'

'Our business here is not quite concluded,' Angelika said, making her way north, toward the estates of the wealthy. Franziskus followed, thinking of the quick glimpse he'd had of the count's face. There was a scar on it, old, and well-healed, but noticeable nonetheless. It was a white diagonal line that stretched from the hairline, over the bridge of his straight and sloping nose, all the way to his jawbone. Something about the scar's position on the elector's face tugged at Franziskus's memory, and he was sure that if he could just kept thinking about it, its significance would spring eventually to mind.

THE TWO OF them found Brucke's carriage, identifying it by its Leitdorf colours. It was in the manor lane, not far from where they'd been when they passed it in the carriage. The manor, a thin, dark building, had seen prouder days; greenish stains ran down its walls from its roof troughs. Scorch marks marred the wooden posts of its lopsided porch. As for the grounds, crickets croaked from thorny patches of untended vegetation. Neglect freed topiary trees from their obligations; new shoots and leaves struggled to shrug off their old forms. Soon they would not look at all like blocks, or domes, or spires; they would just be yews again. Old stone statues, faces worn into complacency by centuries of rain, regarded them with satisfied complicity.

The pair hopped – Angelika first, then Franziskus – over the low stone walls and onto its mossy lawn. Franziskus crept low. Angelika told him to stop looking like a thief or night-skulker. She straightened her posture, and strode boldly up the laneway. They saw no signs of life or movement, not through the shuttered windows, or on the narrow porch.

Angelika walked past the porch to the side of the house. She found a wooden cellar door, secured with a rusted padlock. With the flat of her dagger, she easily pried it open. She lifted the door and slipped in.

Franziskus landed behind her, touching down on a moist earthen floor. They stood among bundles of carrots and parsnips. Franziskus had left the door open, giving them sufficient light to see a set of well-worn steps leading up to an unpainted door. Angelika tested the third step with the toe of her boot, wincing when it creaked. She stepped delicately up onto the steps, moving with slow fastidiousness, minimising the noise they made. She got to the top, tried the handle, and found it unlocked. She teased the doorknob from its mechanism. When opened, the door revealed a small pantry, which adjoined a larger kitchen, hung with pots and cooking implements. A black-bellied stove sat cold in a cobwebbed corner. She beckoned for Franziskus to remain below, and vanished from his sight.

A few exhausting minutes later, Franziskus heard a crash directly above his head. He bounded up the steps, through the kitchen, and into a drawing room filled with furniture that smelled faintly of mildew.

'You should have stayed in the cellar,' Angelika told him. 'I was about to bring her down to you.'

She held her knife to Petrine Guillame's throat. Petrine sat on a low couch, upholstered in dusty green. Her flaxen hair, perched up on her head, in an elaborate coiffure, was held in place by jade-tipped pins. She wore a gown of blue brocade, much finer than her previous garb. Her delicate hands lay on her knees with relaxed composure. A complex aroma of spice and persimmons wafted from the back of her neck to Franziskus's nose.

'Have a seat, Franziskus,' Petrine said, patting the cushion beside her. Now she spoke with only the slightest whisper of a Bretonnian accent. Though she'd replaced feminine breathiness with a piercing clarity, Franziskus could not say that he found the new voice entirely unseductive.

'Go ahead,' Angelika told him. But he knew better, and looked towards an open archway that led to a set of narrow stairs.

'Is anyone else here?'

'Unfortunately, no,' answered Petrine, 'though you're welcome to look. The count maintains his own local manor, near the north gate. Anton has his staff over there, helping to reopen it. It's been neglected for many years, I'm afraid...' Franziskus saw that she was slowly feeding a long, needle-like device from the sleeve of her gown.

'Drop it or die,' Angelika told her.

It tinkled to the floor. A small quantity of green tincture had been applied to its sharp end. Angelika sniffed the air. 'Erasmal's Wort?'

'A new hybrid, unique to my herbarium.'

'Dangerous, if it pricks you.'

'I've rendered myself immune, through consumption of antidote.'

Angelika kicked the needle under the couch.

'You would lose respect for me if I didn't try anything,' Petrine explained, shrugging slimly.

Franziskus saw a variety of strange metal parts laid out on a side-table, and walked over to examine them. He picked up gears, wheels, belts, and an ornamented casing that looked as if it were meant to be placed on the head. Dark grease smeared his fingers. He rubbed them clean on the lacy edge of a doily.

'One of the count's inventions,' Petrine told him. 'I'm not sure what it's meant to do. Cure his moods, perhaps. He tinkered away at it as he waited to make his grand entrance.'

'How long has he been here?' Angelika asked.

'He arrived a few days before you.'

'And it's him you answer to, through Brucke. Prince Davio has nothing to do with this.'

Petrine curtly nodded. 'We required a scapegoat if things went awry. Jurgen's campaign against the border princes made Davio the obvious candidate.' She suppressed a feline smile.

'You feel no shame for your base deceit?' Franziskus blurted. Both women's faces turned to him; his cheeks bloomed red.

'If it is any consolation, *mon cher*, there would surely be no man happier than Davio to see Jurgen stripped of all rank.' She shifted her attention back to Angelika. 'Obviously, the count's stratagem fails if his hand is seen in it. Will his hand be seen in it?'

'That remains subject to negotiation,' Angelika said, pulling up a chair to sit opposite Petrine. She kept the dagger pointed at her fine Bretonnian breastbone. 'First, you tell me if I have it all correct. The count enjoys few things more than leading his troops into battle, but every so often he goes embarrassingly mad. Until recently, he's been in a lunatic phase, and during that time, his man, Jurgen, became a little too popular for his own good.'

'It has happened before in Averland's history – tension between the elector and the head of the Sabres.'

'The count wants to get rid of him, without looking ungrateful and petulant.'

'When lucid, Leitdorf suffers from a curious need to be loved by his rabble. Some might call this a greater madness.'

'Or maybe he's clever,' Franziskus interjected, 'and knows he stands a better chance of winning the war if the soldiers stand behind him.'

'Perhaps,' Petrine allowed.

'So the count gets word that one of von Kopfs has possibly fled from battle, and gets word to the Brucke, who gets word to you, and you hire Goatfield and his cronies. All to get Lukas here, to Grenzstadt, to engineer the scene we saw this morning. Marius knew of the Sabre vow, and of Jurgen's inflexible cast of mind. So he showed Jurgen up in public, as the heartless, arrogant fanatic he is. In that way he could take up his command again without a hint of mutiny.'

'All went according to plan, then?'

'The soldiers are still doubtful – but for men who only yesterday considered Jurgen second in importance only to Sigmar himself, I'd say your count accomplished his objectives.'

'Then I am proven wrong. I was sure that Jurgen would become clever at the last moment. I never like a scheme that relies entirely on one man's stupidity.'

'Not stupidity – blindness. And blindness is extremely reliable.'

'I bow to your superior insight. You were present, I take it? Did you need sparing? I told Anton to make sure you were pardoned, if necessary.'

'You saved us the nuisance of escaping. Why the concern?'

She shrugged. 'You caused us some trouble, granted, but ultimately you served us well. You kept Jurgen distracted and angry, which is how we wanted him.'

'And that's why you sprang us from Jurgen's jail cell.'

'*Naturellement.*'

'Thank you for that, incidentally.'

'Not at all. Please put the knife down, so I needn't say this under duress.'

Angelika kept the knife steady.

'Very well.' Petrine sighed. 'I think you two might be of future use to us. You can't imagine how tiresome it is, trying to get the likes of Toby Goatfield to execute a delicate mission properly.'

'As a matter of fact, I can imagine that.'

'There's good pay in it. You won't need to soil yourself any more, rooting through wormy corpses. And Franziskus, you can still be of great service to the Empire. To a crucial part of it, at any rate.'

'What kind of pay?' Angelika demanded.

'It will depend on the nature of the work, but it will be much more than you earn now, I guarantee it.'

'And if I say no?'

Petrine looked at the knife. 'You have me at your mercy. But it is not me who will determine the ultimate outcome here, as you well suspect. If you leave without making a commitment, my benefactor may well feel uneasy. You know too much to be left to roam about, unfettered by loyalty. The count has taken a close interest in your story, Angelika.'

Angelika edged her chair nearer to Petrine. It scraped loudly. 'Even with the threat,' she said, 'my answer is no. My answer is: not for a second would I even dream of serving Marius Leitdorf in any way. Franziskus, what say you?'

'I do as you do,' he said, straightening his back.

'We will both regret this, Angelika,' said Petrine.

'You'll regret it sooner than I do,' replied Angelika. She stood up, seized Petrine by the nape of her neck, and pushed her velvety throat toward the point of her blade.

'Don't,' said Petrine. For the first time there was an edge in her voice.

'You had us nearly killed. Casually, when we were inconvenient to you, you sent us off to be beaten like dogs. By people who had nothing to do with anything, and who lost their home as a result. You used us all, like pawns to be swept off a chessboard. I don't have the words to describe the agony we lived through, in that pit. Did you think I wouldn't want to make you pay for that?'

'Remember the money,' Petrine said.

'There's a few things even I find more precious than gold.'

'Franziskus,' she choked, as Angelika pushed her closer to the blade-tip, 'stop her.'

He crossed his arms.

'Please!' Petrine shrieked.

Angelika seized her hair and pulled her, wailing, onto the floor, until she was on hands and knees. 'If it were you with the knife, and me helpless before you,' Angelika said, 'I'd already be dead. Be thankful I'm not as much like you as you thought.'

Thunder rolled overhead. Angelika turned to the shuttered windows, through which bright sunlight streamed. She opened them. The sky was blue and clear. The thunder continued, it grew louder; it was coming from the south.

'War drums,' she said. 'Orcs!' She hesitated. 'Lukas!' she said. She ran.

CHAPTER FOURTEEN

THEY STOOD ON the city walls, looking south to the mouth of the Blackfire Pass. Now she could see where its name came from. Billowing, inky plumes rose into the air above it. The orcs were burning the forests. They had decided that the trees in the foothills were their enemies. And orcs did only one thing with their enemies – they destroyed them. They would deprive their human foes of the cover Jurgen had used so well against them in previous battles.

The crashing of the drums continued, relentless, like waves on a stony shore. Angelika could not guess how many green-skinned drummers it would take to produce such a cacophony. And for every drummer there would be at least a hundred warriors, armed with heavy axes and massive swords. Angelika did not need to see them to imagine how they looked. She could still remember them as they had been when she rescued Franziskus from an orcish war wagon: their enormous frames, their blocky muscles. Their great, mask-hard faces, mottled with warts and scars. Mouths dripping slime. Nails sharp and fecund with disease. Gulping in good air and breathing out the stench of hell. But most of all, it was their eyes that jabbed through her recollections, to terrify her all over again: narrow, beady, and filled with malice and a craving for blood.

On the plain outside the town, Marius reared on his charger, spearing the sky with his well-polished sword, as his sergeants did the real work of assembling the Averlandish regiments into battle formation. The state of Marius's preparations was not Angelika's main interest, and she wasted little time counting columns or identifying war banners. Still, she saw nearly a thousand infantrymen, several units of cavalry, and a good scattering of scouts, militia, and mercenary irregulars, attracted to the battle scene by the promise of gold. Wide-eyed flagellants had gathered, in their hot and itchy robes, ready to throw themselves onto the blades of the foe, in fatal expiation of crimes real or imagined. There were cannoneers, who would be fairly useless in a rolling skirmish against advancing orcs. Off to one side, the full complement of Black Field Sabres uncertainly milled, as a commander Angelika did not recognise shouted down at them from horseback. He was gesticulating with wild vigour. This would be one of the other illegitimate Kopfs, Angelika surmised, raised up from the ranks of Benno and Gelfrat's unnamed rivals. He exhorted their obedience without detectable result.

She tore her eyes from the scene outside the town walls. She reminded herself why she'd come here – to look down on Grenzstadt's streets and laneways, in the hope of finding Lukas. With Marius gone to war, his protection would be absent, too.

'The Hat and Pony,' she prompted Franziskus. 'You're certain you have no idea where it is?' She was sure, at least, that this is where he said he was headed, when he'd run off.

'Just as certain as the last time you asked, and the time before that. It's just one tavern in this enormous town. And I certainly don't see a sign with a hat and a pony on it from here.'

'What's got into you? You're the one who likes the little snot. You spoke with him, on the trail. What did he tell you about his friends?'

'He didn't have any. Everyone shunned him, he said. He said he tried to recite his epic poetry, but the talentless scribes in town laughed at him.'

'So it will be near a bookseller's, perhaps...'

'But why don't we just ask someone where it is?'

Angelika shook her head in exasperation. 'Because we're wanted by–' She stopped herself short. A crimson flush rose up to colour her chalky face. 'No, we've been pardoned. So there's no good reason why we couldn't just ask someone.' She worked her lower lip beneath her teeth. 'So you could have told me this earlier,' she recriminated, spinning on her heel and rushing for the nearest set of stairs.

THE FIRST GRENZSTADTER they found was a red-hatted old man with only a few teeth left. He claimed to know the Hat and Pony well, and happily provided elaborate and incomprehensible directions. They ran through the lanes and alleys of Grenzstadt, Franziskus puffing to keep up with Angelika. They ducked under planks carried by scurrying townsfolk, who were rushing home to board up their doors and windows. They careened through a brawl of beggars, fighting over squatting rights to an abandoned basement. They shrank back against a wall to evade the charge of a loose and maddened horse, its reins flying out behind it. They found the bookseller's, its shutters already nailed together, its ironshod door securely locked.

Angelika turned her head to listen for laughter and the clattering of flagons against tables. Even in a town under threat of invasion, the last places to close were always the taverns.

'There!' she pointed. Across the lane and four doors down, a painted sign protruded out over the street on a wrought-iron bracket. A swelling wind creaked it from side to side. On the sign, a grinning pony wore a ridiculous hat. Angelika sprinted for the door beneath it.

The smell of boiling chicken made siege on her nostrils. A sleepy-eyed man with a well-fattened face stood before an iron cauldron, wearing only a leather apron and a pair of worn trousers speckled with paint and gravy. He stirred the soup with a wooden paddle. With his free hand, he wiped sweat from his balding pate. Angelika leapt over the threshold.

'Have you seen–' she asked him. She turned and saw Lukas, sitting amid a knot of drunken, red-faced men. Lukas did not have a cup in front of him, but he did have a bowl of soup, filled to the brim. The men wore ragged finery; their fashions, on average, two decades out of date. Years of methodical drinking had brought twisting veins to the surfaces of their cheeks and noses. Pot bellies bulged above their belts.

'Poets,' said Angelika, grimly.

One of them, the oldest but with hints of handsomeness still clinging to his ruined face, had been in the middle of a rude stanza when Angelika had burst in. It was the old one about the charwoman from Altdorf. The man stood with open mouth and flagon frozen stupidly up beside his head. Angelika sneaked a dagger from her belt and held it in his general direction. 'Clear out,' she told them.

The poet spluttered. 'Who are you, you distaff brigand, to–'

Angelika crooked her elbow, ready to throw the blade at his throat. He turned white and backed away from the table. The others stood and held their hands up, placatingly. At least one of them whimpered.

'Nidungus,' the lead poet demanded of the pot-stirrer. 'Do you mean to allow this outrage in your very own tavern?'

Nidungus spat disinterestedly, scarcely turning from the pot. The poets scattered, rushing chaotically for the exit. Lukas remained in his seat, staring down into his watery soup.

'I think I'll have that ale after all, Nidungus,' he said. 'Hand me down my stein.'

'The lot of them just left without paying,' Nidungus told him. 'Finish their leftovers.' He dug into an armpit, homing in on a nit.

Angelika walked over to the boy's table. 'We've got to get moving, Lukas.'

He kept his eyes down. 'I'm not going anywhere any more. Certainly not with you.'

'All of Marius's men are departing for war. That leaves no one to protect you from your father. Grenzstadt has become unsafe for you, again.'

'I intend to stay here and die, along with everyone else.'

'That won't happen.'

'Only my father could have led the troops to victory. Marius will lose. It's my fault. My weakness will destroy the town. The least I can do is stay here and meet the same fate as those whose dooms I've sealed.'

She grabbed him by the ear. 'You morose little – useless – If you propose to do something useful to help someone, then very well, I'll let you do it. But I haven't suffered and scraped just to let you sit here like a sluggard and wait for the orcs to stomp in and take your head! Get up!'

'Ow!' he complained, rising.

Behind her, Franziskus softly called her name. She turned.

Henty Redpot stood in the tavern doorway. He exposed a smile full of yellow teeth. He had his big axe already out.

Without taking her eyes off him, Angelika pivoted. She had heard the creak of stairs behind her. Elennath, diagonal scar blazing, moved lithely down them. Toby Goatfield crunched carelessly down after his elven partner.

'Well, well, well,' he said. Toby leaned over the stairway railing and dropped a leather purse into the taverner's hand. Nidungus rattled the coins inside the purse and departed through the front door. Henty swooshed theatrically aside to let him pass.

'Ah,' said Toby, expansively lifting up his arms. 'The Hat and Pony. You shouldn't have spent so much of your time babbling away to us, boy.' He winked at Lukas. 'You described it so poetically that it was easy to find.' He reached the bottom of the stairs and bounced onto the springy floorboards. 'And wherever you were, boy, we'd find these two. If we waited long enough. What they see in you, I don't know.'

Angelika opened her mouth and covered it with her hand, in a mocking, artificial yawn. 'While there's nothing I enjoy so much as listening to a good gloat, maybe you should just tell us what you want from us.'

Goatfield laughed. Elennath sneered. Henty chortled.

'You've done your job,' said Angelika, wondering which of them to go for first. 'You got paid.'

'Paid in money, perhaps,' said the elf. 'But not in blood. Not for this.' He pointed to his ruined face.

'Don't be so narrow-minded,' she said. 'The scar gives you character.'

'Before,' cried Elennath, 'I was perfect-looking!'

'And you two halflings,' she said, 'you care so much about his porcelain features?'

'No,' said Henty, behind her. 'We just enjoy killing people we don't like.'

'If you murder the boy, you'll ruin your employer's plans. It will spoil their story if the henchmen who so generously delivered him turn around and gut him, for no apparent reason.'

'Our employment has come to an end, girlie,' Toby said. 'Apparently the Bretonnian bitch finds us bloodthirsty, uncouth and uncontrollable. How she could come to that conclusion I can't possibly reckon.'

'We're not here to murder the boy,' Elennath told her. 'Just the two of you.'

Goatfield cracked his knuckles. 'Oh, I think I'd like to kill the boy, too. What say you, Henty?'

'Indeed,' Henty said, investing the second syllable with lusty fervour.

'Well then,' said Angelika. She hurled herself at Elennath, knife outstretched.

Franziskus ducked Henty's axe. It splintered the doorframe.

Elennath twisted to dodge Angelika's blow. Her dagger tore open his left side, skating up his ribcage. The elf screeched.

Henty directed a second, lower, blow at Franziskus. He jumped aside. The axe stuck in the frame, causing the wall to shed flakes of stucco.

Goatfield kicked out at Angelika's legs, trying to trip her. She grabbed Elennath and spun him into the leering halfling. The elf fell into Toby's dagger; parting the muscles of his lower back. His eyes widened as he became aware of agony. Goatfield pushed him off his blade. He stumbled onto his knees. Goatfield regarded the thick elfin blood on his dagger with bemused detachment. With a swinging, backhanded blow, Angelika sliced open Elennath's throat, just below the jaw. Voice box destroyed, he gargled angrily. Only when words refused to form did he seem to comprehend what had happened. He touched fingers to his throat. They came back coated in red. He gargled some other threat or insult. Blood drenched him. It pooled on the floor, seeking the deep cracks between floorboards. He fell face-first.

'I never truly cared for him,' Goatfield eulogised, rushing at Angelika.

Henty's axe was stuck again in the shattered frame of the tavern doorway. Franziskus drew his rapier and warily advanced. The monolithic halfling took quick sideways glances as Franziskus searched for an advantageous position.

Henty kept working at the axe. Franziskus decided to use his height advantage, slashing down at the halfling's neck. Faster than he should have been, Henty edged away from the blow. He elbowed Franziskus in the gut. Franziskus wheeled back. He thought he might fall over, but he didn't.

Still facing Goatfield, Angelika jumped onto the stairs. He came at her. She kicked him in the face. A loose nail on the heel of her boot tore into it, ripping a white gash up the side of his right cheek. The gash filled and turned red. She kicked at his throat. He grabbed her leg and pulled her down. The back of her head smacked against one of the steps. Then another. He dragged her like a mop through Elennath's blood.

Henty freed his axe. He surged at Franziskus. Franziskus feinted left, then dodged right. Henty crashed into a table. Franziskus smashed his hilt-pommel into the base of Henty's skull. Henty made a woofing noise. He swung at Franziskus with the axe. Franziskus danced back toward the stairs. He hit the spreading patch of elfin gore and his feet flew out from under him. His fall saved him from Henty's sweeping axe, which otherwise might have detached his head and sent it flying across the tavern.

Franziskus found himself at Goatfield's feet. Goatfield let go of Angelika to send a stomping boot down on the Stirlander's face. Franziskus met it with the palm of his hand, which he then wrenched sideways with all his might. Goatfield toppled off balance.

Angelika took stock. She was face to face with Henty. He drooled at her. She threw her knife at his eye. He moved and it hit his forehead instead. It bounced off, and not so much as a red mark appeared on his skin. He brought his axe down. She leapfrogged over him, pushing on his back on the way over. He struggled to keep his footing. She turned, spun, and tried to topple him with a kick to his blocky posterior.

Though well placed, it failed to budge him. He whirled and crashed his axe down, splintering floorboards all around him.

Franziskus poked the tip of his rapier into Toby's side. The halfling was still flat on his back and struggling to right himself, but his feet were skidding in sticky gore. He grabbed Franziskus's blade, wrinkling his eyes up as it cut into the soft flesh of his hand. He grunted and bent the rapier to a right angle. He released it, rolled onto his stomach, and used Elennath's blood as lubricant to slide himself quickly across the floor to Franziskus, whose ankles he seized with gnarled hands. He bit Franziskus's ankle, then yanked forward, bringing the Stirlander down on his buttocks. Franziskus kicked him in the face, widening the narrow, riverine wound Angelika had inflicted there.

Angelika took hold of a flimsy wooden chair, to use as a shield against Henty's axe. Henty smashed it to bits. She picked up a second chair. He smashed, too, leaving her holding a broken spindle from the chair's back. Its end had sheared through crosswise, leaving it sharpened like a stake. She drove it into the side of Henty's neck. He staggered back, goggled his eyes in pain, but then recovered to swing his axe furiously at her. She leapt up onto the table. He hammered the axe down on it, breaking it in two. As it fell, she leapt backwards onto the table behind it. To get at her, he parted the wreckage of the first table.

Toby grunted and scrabbled forward, hauling himself up onto Franziskus's body, and clambering along his legs. He bit down on Franziskus's crotch. He growled and spat out a tooth. Franziskus silently thanked his sister for giving him a codpiece as an enlistment gift, and himself for remembering to put it on, under his trousers. Then he stuck his thumbs in Toby's eye sockets and started gouging. Toby reared back, snapped at his fingers like a turtle, then got to his knees, driving an elbow down onto Franziskus's sternum. Franziskus groaned.

Angelika alighted from the table before Henty could smash this one too. She reached for a beer stein. It was made of pewter and weighed at least ten pounds. She hurled it at Henty's head. It hit the bridge of his nose. His eyes glazed. A viscous dribble of blood emerged shyly from his left nostril. Redpot blinked and cracked his neck. He advanced on her.

A shape appeared behind him. It was Lukas. He held a heavy club of wood, its end still coaled in white and yellow embers, from the taverner's firepit. He crashed it across the back of Henty's skull.

Henty teetered forward, then back. He elbowed Lukas in the chest, dropping him. Embers clung to his head and shoulders. They burned through his tunic. Strands of his hair singed, curling up. He raised his axe.

Toby seized Franziskus by the back of his neck, hauling him to his feet. He pressed the Stirlander's face into a table. Franziskus groped its surface. His searching fingers found a paring knife. He slashed it backwards, prompting Toby to release him. Franziskus whirled to face the halfling. He jabbed the knife at Goatfield's ear. Toby grabbed his wrist and twisted. The knife fell. Franziskus kneed him in the stomach. He doubled over.

Henty swung his axe. Angelika dodged.

Franziskus took a step back and then hit Toby with his shoulder, catching him full in the face. Toby skidded back, his right arm making contact with the soup cauldron. He squawked in pain and drew back from it. His arm, from the elbow down, had gone pink; it bubbled with blisters. Franziskus tried another shoulder slam; Toby adjusted his stance to forestall another slide into the cauldron. The impact nonetheless drove him back; he turned his ankle and fell to one knee. Franziskus knelt, grabbed each of the halfling's stubby legs, and pulled, upturning him. Goatfield flailed his arms as Franziskus held him upside down. Shaking from muscle strain, the young deserter staggered over to the pot. Toby worked to clamp his legs around his neck, but Franziskus resisted. He leaned ahead, letting the halfling's weight carry him forward, and dropped Toby headfirst into the pot of boiling soup.

In the soup, Toby's legs thrashed. The cauldron rocked on its metal bracket. It dropped off, into the fire, and overturned. Franziskus sidestepped the ensuing splash. Toby rose screaming from inside the pot, bone exposed, eye sockets empty. Small bits of chopped leek dotted his cooked flesh. He teetered to the side and fell to the floorboards, where he twitched and expired, barely two feet from Elennath's dead and staring face.

Franziskus checked to see how Angelika fared. Plainly, she was tiring: each dodge of Henty's axe-blows was slower than the last. The murderous halfling had manoeuvred her to the front of the tavern. She was pressed against a wall, where an old bronze shield hung. She ducked as he swung; he hit it, folding it in two.

Franziskus cast about for a weapon. He found only Toby's dropped dagger, a pathetic implement against so unrelenting a foe. He required something that had reach.

He kept searching, but saw nothing long enough. Puny dagger in hand, he ran at Henty.

The halfling backed Angelika into an alcove, framed with oaken beams. He swung. The axe caught in the timber. Franziskus leapt onto Henty's back, pulling him off his weapon.

Angelika grabbed the sharpened chunk of chair-back she'd plunged into Henty earlier. She strained to yank it out. It wouldn't go. She leapt up on it, pushing down on it, driving it further into him.

'Doxy!' he yelled at her.

Franziskus put a leg between Henty's and tripped him. Henty crashed headlong into the wall. He recovered. Franziskus stepped beside Angelika. Now both of them blocked the muscle-bound mercenary's path back to his great axe.

'Your friends are dead,' Angelika told him. 'Time to cut your losses.'

He laughed and hurled himself at Franziskus. He picked up the skinny Stirlander and threw him into a pile of chairs. Franziskus stayed down. Henty, arms open, lunged at Angelika, hoping to wrap her in a crushing hug. She slipped aside, picked up a chair, and brought it splintering down on his back. One of its legs broke. She hit him with it again. It fell to bits. He smashed her in the temple with a closed fist. Dazed, she toddled sideways. She reached the door, steadying herself on its shattered frame. Henty jumped up, grabbed her shoulders, and pulled her down. He kicked her. She inched backwards.

He turned and sprinted for his axe. She took this brief reprieve to lie back and breathe. She closed her eyes and searched herself for hidden reserves of strength. She panted.

Henty was back. He had his axe over his head. Tongue waggling wormishly in his mouth, he sniggered. 'I told you I'd get you,' he said.

Jurgen von Kopf stepped from the street into the tavern doorway, both hands wrapped around the hilt of a mammoth greatsword. He chopped it down on the haft of Henty's axe, cutting through the halfling's wrist. The axe thunked to the tavern floor. Henty's hand dangled from a skein of cartilage and skin. Jurgen brought his greatsword down on the mercenary again, making a wedge through the side of his head, cutting away his ear and cheek. Blood spouted from the wrist-stump and then pulsed up through the head wound. Still Henty did not fall. Jurgen kicked him over.

'I've come for my son,' he told Angelika.

Angelika made it to her feet. The room was spinning. Jurgen's face went in and out of focus. 'You've come to your senses, then?' she said. She did not believe this, but hoped to shame him.

He hardened his features. 'Where is he?'

Lukas came up from behind a shattered table. He met his father's sharp blue gaze. He spoke steadily. 'I am here, father.'

'You have shamed me, Lukas. You've brought disgrace and ruin crashing down on our family.'

'Am I the one who's done that, father?'

Jurgen ground his teeth together. He tightened his grip on his greatsword. 'It is beyond question that you have. From the cradle, you knew our rules. Come here. At least allow the chronicles to say that, in the end, you took the chance to atone for your crimes against our blood.'

Lukas straightened his shoulders. 'If you intend to kill me, you'll succeed. But I won't help you butcher me. I reject your nonsense of honour and crimes against the blood. I am Lukas von Kopf. I have done what I have done.'

Jurgen took a step. 'Then I will come to you.'

Franziskus clutched Toby's dagger. Lukas saw this. 'What do you intend to do with them?' he asked.

'Yesterday I hankered for comeuppance.' Jurgen regarded Angelika and the Stirlander. 'Now I see them again, and they mean nothing. They may go.'

Lukas addressed Franziskus. 'Go, please. Please.' He turned to Angelika. 'You, too. Thank you for what you've done. I don't see how I deserved it.'

'Swear not to harm him,' Angelika said to Jurgen, 'and we'll happily leave.'

'I've sworn the contrary,' Jurgen said.

'There is not a part of you that feels doubt, is there?'

'No,' said Jurgen. His demeanour had changed. Though he still held himself upright, and spoke with clear, ringing tones, the old imperious manner was gone. He no longer dripped haughty contempt. She did not know, at first, what sentiment to attribute to this new demeanour. For a moment, she dared to hope that it was sympathy, or regret. Those feelings she could make use of. Then it came to her: Jurgen was in mourning. In the old man's mind, his boy was already killed.

'No matter what the situation,' stalled Angelika, 'you always know what to do next.'

'Yes,' said Jurgen.

'You don't remember the last time you hesitated.' She saw that she was backing up, and giving him ground. She forced herself to hold her position. 'Or were torn between two choices.'

'That is correct.'

'Jurgen, that's a madness as great as Marius's.'

He cocked his head as if considering the point. 'Fine, then. I've given you a chance to insult me. Now begone, and vex me and mine no more.'

'Go, both of you,' Lukas said, to Franziskus and Angelika.

'But I've made a stupid vow of my own,' said Angelika. She kept her eyes on Jurgen's sword. 'So here we find ourselves.'

'Then that is how it is,' Jurgen said. He distractedly pawed the floor with the toe of his boot, scraping grit between sole and floorboard.

'Does honour allow you to fight with that enormous sword, when we are all but disarmed?' Angelika asked him.

He laid the sword carefully on a table. He clenched and unclenched the fists of both hands.

Franziskus sniffed; his nose had started running.

Jurgen pushed past Angelika. She dived at him, knocking him off course. He stumbled into a wall. She charged him. He clamped hands on her shoulders and tossed her aside. She fell into Franziskus, blocking his charge at Jurgen.

Lukas stood, waiting. His father strode at him. Angelika leapt on Jurgen's back. He bucked her off. She landed on a table. He flipped the table away from him, rolling her off it and onto the floor. Franziskus dropped Toby's knife and thumped both fists against Jurgen's back. Jurgen whirled, head-butted Franziskus, sent him wobbling. Angelika crawled up, throwing her arms over the upended tabletop, hauling herself to her feet. Jurgen kicked the table, sending it sliding into its neighbour, and pinning Angelika between them. She fell back, trapped, head lolling.

Franziskus ran at him. He turned. He grabbed Franziskus by the collar and the belt. He threw him over past Angelika.

He approached Lukas. 'You think I want to do this,' he said. 'I do not. It is because I love you, my son, that I must.'

'She's right – you're not merely stubborn. You're crazed,' Lukas said, his newfound composure cracking. He backed away. He bounded over a broken table. Jurgen leapt after him. He turned and punched his father in the jaw. His finger bones crackled like leaves in a fire. Face drained, he nursed his hand. He turned to run. Jurgen tackled him. He fell.

From Angelika's vantage point, the two momentarily disappeared behind wrecked furniture. She'd wiggled herself out from between the tables pinning her. Father and son came up again, Jurgen clasping the boy from behind, lifting him up, mighty arms around the boy's neck and chest. 'I love my son,' Jurgen choked, 'so I give you your honour back.' His eyes were wet.

In both hands, Angelika held a spindle from one of the broken chair backs.

Jurgen constricted his grip on Lukas's neck.

A snapping sound rang through the tavern. Lukas went slack. Jurgen turned him around, held him. He pulled open one of Lukas's eyelids. He made a noise midway between an ordinary sob and the neigh of a horse. Gently he laid Lukas's body on the tavern floor, taking care to keep him clear of the various patches of blood that adorned it. Tears flooding, he turned a hate-frozen visage on Angelika and Franziskus.

'You made it happen this way,' he said.

'No,' said Angelika.

'I was not supposed to be the one to do it,' he said.

'Maybe that should have told you something.' Her hand wandered from the snapped chair spindle to the dagger dropped first by Toby, then by Franziskus.

'He was supposed to do it himself. You put ideas in his head. You're to blame for this.'

He stepped on heavy feet toward her. She coiled up, sprang, hurling herself through the air. She planted the dagger in the side of his neck.

She crashed into a cart laden with stoneware. Plates and mugs fell all around her. He tottered at her. Red liquid erupted from the wound. 'I thought we were fighting unarmed,' he said. 'Is that honourable?'

'I don't believe in honour,' Angelika told him.

'Ah,' he nodded. 'I thank you regardless, for the favour you've done me. A father should not outlive... Pardon my...' He reached for an overturned chair, righted it, sat down, blinked, and died. His head slumped to his chest.

Angelika waited. 'It's safe now,' she said, after it was clear that Jurgen was finished.

Lukas sat up. He spoke to Angelika, but his eyes were on his slain father.

'Did we plan that?' he asked.

'Plan what?'

'When he had my neck, and you made that snapping noise – what was that?'

'A piece of chair.'

'When you made the noise, I knew what to do – to play dead, as if we planned it. Did we plan that?' He spoke as if mesmerised.

'We didn't plan it. It's just that, when the moment came, you understood.'

'It's as if we planned it,' he said. With movements slow and stunned, he went over to his father. He knelt beside the chair and pulled Jurgen down into his arms, cradling the man's head in his shoulder. 'I'm so sorry,' he told his father. His face contorted. 'I wasn't what you wanted. I wish I was.' He bawled the words; they were hard to make out. Angelika wished she couldn't hear them at all.

Franziskus surveyed the carnage and thought it remarkable that he felt no great urge to vomit. He told himself that he was getting used to such sights, and, for this freshly-acquired hardness, begged forgiveness of the mercy goddess, Shallya.

Angelika found an undisturbed chair and eased herself into it. She assured herself that she would soon find the energy to search the mercenaries' corpses for saleable items. She would not try it with Jurgen's body, so as not to upset the boy. 'I just want to sit here for a time,' she heard her voice saying. She looked at her arms and counted the cuts, looking for injuries serious enough to warrant bandaging. She looked over to Franziskus, who was likewise covered with welts and bruises. A nasty, rattling sound assailed her and she looked about to see what it might be. After some blurry thought, she isolated it as the issue of her own tortured lungs. Franziskus's breath was even more laboured than her own.

Bells rang out, outside in the street. There were shouts. Franziskus hauled himself to the door. The cries grew louder. Now that she was again ready to pay heed to the world outside the tavern, Angelika realised that the orcish war drums had increased in volume. They were very close now. Maybe just a few miles away.

Franziskus appeared in the doorway, panting. 'Evacuate – we've got to evacuate! Marius has pulled his forces back, north of the city. He's going to let the town fall!'

CHAPTER FIFTEEN

GRENZSTADT BURNED.

The three of them – Angelika, Franziskus, Lukas – huddled on the far side of a low, uneven stone wall that separated one stretch of grassy, bumpy sheep pasture from another. They were a mile or so from town. On the other side of the wall, a runtish orc, scarcely bigger than a goblin, prowled and snuffled. They kept their heads down and waited for it to go. It trundled up to an abandoned farmhouse and disappeared through an open door. They calmly sat as it banged around inside. Angelika popped her head up to see it wander back toward town, where its fellows would still be rampaging. When it was far enough away, she stood to watch smoke clouds drift up from the ruins. Making out details of the destruction was difficult from their present position. Large gaps had been pounded in the walls. One of the south towers had somehow been rocked on its foundations – perhaps by some primitive war machine, or enormous battering ram – and had fallen into the town. It was the tower where Benno and Gelfrat had died.

Angelika tried to remember her south Averlandish geography. If she recalled correctly, there was a river a dozen miles up, a tributary from the Upper Reik. Marius's forces, which had bypassed the city in a heedless rout, would most likely retrench there, to meet the orcs when they grew bored with smashing empty buildings and were ready to continue their push up into the Empire's belly. Messengers, she reckoned, would already be on their way to the courts of Wissenland, Stirland, and the halflings' Moot. Reinforcements would come from Averheim and from Nuln. Despite Marius's folly in plotting against his own general on the eve of battle, the orcs would, in the end, be repulsed. She declined to speculate on the precise cost in lives. The toll would be paid mostly in the blood and flesh of peasants, townsfolk, and common soldiers; it was always they who took the brunt when games of power played out.

Lukas asked her what would happen, and she told him about the river, and the reinforcements, and how orcs fought badly in water. Typically, they rushed in with lunatic abandon, obliging their enemies by drowning in great numbers.

Lukas nodded. 'An encouraging thought.'

'In war, the less stupid side eventually wins.'

'Thank you for saving my life,' he said.

'You're welcome.'

'Do either of you have a weapon I can borrow?'

Neither did. Franziskus's rapier had been wrecked back in the tavern; Angelika had left her last knife in Jurgen. 'Why?' asked Angelika.

'I've made a decision,' Lukas said. 'I'm going north. I'll find the troops. I'll locate the Sabres. It's me who should lead them now. I am the heir; it is my blood. So say the ancient laws of my lineage. If anyone attempts to stop me, I'll fight them. Then I'll lead my company against the greenskins, when they come.' He waited for a reaction.

'Why?' Angelika asked, after a pause.

'It is what you said. I should do something useful for someone.'

'When did I say that?'

'The Empire must be defended. What else could be more useful?'

Franziskus cleared his throat. 'But, Lukas. You're no trained warrior.'

The boy held his look of determination. 'Battle will test me. I've seen the two of you. Henty and the others, they were stronger than you. You fought them and won. My father, he outmatched you, too. Yet you didn't flee, even when you could have, to be free and clear. All that you've done for me – what will it matter if I wasn't worth saving in the first place?'

Angelika gazed away in the opposite direction. A rain of fine ashes fell. She brushed them from her arms. 'Don't look to us as exemplars of anything. A corpse robber and a... a...'

Franziskus completed the sentence for her. 'And a deserter,' he said.

'I know what I saw. What I will do now, I do to honour you.'

She shoved him into the wall. She grabbed him by the ears. 'Do nothing for honour!' she cried. 'Or for us! Are you doing this to impress us? Is that it?'

He writhed away from her, stepping back over the low wall. He sucked in a breath, marshalling steely calm. 'I do it because it must be done.'

'And who do you do it *for*?' she demanded.

He thought for a moment. 'Myself. I do it for myself.'

She turned from him. 'Good. That's the answer I'll accept.'

Lukas stood there.

Franziskus leapt the wall. He clapped a hand on the young man's shoulder. 'Farewell,' he said. The two junior nobles embraced; Angelika huffed disapproval. Franziskus broke the embrace and studied Lukas's dirtied, resolute features. 'What you do now – you are braver than me.'

Lukas gently smiled. 'I'll try not to be too brave. So one day we can meet again.' He moved toward Angelika. He said her name.

She held him off with a warning hand. 'If you think this is your chance to grope me, you haven't been paying attention.' Lukas forced a comradely laugh. 'Go,' she said. 'Get going. And if you get your head removed, don't come whining to either of us about it. We're off to find new idiots to rescue.'

'Even if you won't admit it,' Lukas said, 'I owe you everything.'

'Oh, sod off.'

She started walking south. Lukas waved and said goodbye and she did not turn back. Franziskus returned the gesture for her, and then hurried to catch up, leaving Lukas to watch them depart.

They walked back toward the mouth of the pass, seeking cover whenever they heard the hissings and growlings of straying orcs. They passed overturned carts, half-eaten livestock, stripped bodies and smouldering cottages.

They travelled without speaking. In his mind, Franziskus turned over various ways in which to broach the subject of Marius and Elennath, and their almost identical scars. A matter of interest lay therein. But, seeing the black mood that had descended on her, he could not conceive of a way to ask.

At dusk, they reached the pass. The mountains looked different, with so many of their trees burnt, and the brush gone. The forests would regrow, Franziskus thought. The occasional fire kept them strong.

'Which one,' asked Angelika, 'do you feel sorry for – Benno or Gelfrat?'

Franziskus thought for a while, as they walked. 'I don't think either of them,' he finally said. 'What about you?'

'I'm not certain.'

They kept going.

In a gully, they came upon the corpses of cavalrymen, twisted in amongst the long limbs and muscular bodies of their dead stallions. Angelika waded into their midst. She bent down to unbuckle the belt of a rider skewered to his horse's haunch by a long, crude lance. His sabre had never cleared its sheath. She pulled it out now and admired it; it was a display piece, with a hilt of filigreed brass.

'Now this is the sort of battle that profits a looter,' Angelika said.

ABOUT THE AUTHOR

Robin D Laws is an acclaimed designer of games, perhaps best known for the roleplaying games *Feng Shui*, *Dying Earth* and *Rune*. He has also worked on computer and collectible card games and is currently a columnist for *Dragon* magazine.
Just recently, Robin began working as a writer for Marvel Comics, including an *Iron Man* story arc and the upcoming miniseries *Hulk: Nightmerica*.
Honour of the Grave is Robin's third fantasy novel.

More Warhammer from the Black Library

RIDERS OF THE DEAD
By Dan Abnett

GERLACH DREW HIS sabre and spurred Saksen forward, blade and standard raised as high as he could lift them, steering his trotting horse with his knees.

'For the company! For the company! For the Emperor!' he yelled.

Two Northers came for him, riding hard, standing in their saddles, heads and swords low. Gerlach turned Saksen in time to slash one across the back, and then reeled as a sword-edge smashed into his right arm's plating.

The company standard tumbled from his hand and stuck base-first in the ground, tilted at an angle. Cursing, Gerlach wheeled his gelding around and exchanged sword strikes with the Norther. Steel on iron, a furious ring.

FAR TO THE NORTH of the Empire lies the dreaded Chaos Wastes, a dark landscape permeated by the corrupting magic of Chaos. Standing between this gateway to hell and the civilised world lies the frozen land of Kislev, bastion against the rising tide of evil.
Two Empire soldiers get their first taste of battle as they join the campaign to repel the savage Northern tribes. As the winter draws in, the last major battle sees their destinies thrown into turmoil as circumstances tear them apart and throw them onto opposite sides.

More Warhammer from the Black Library

The Gotrek & Felix novels by William King

THE DWARF TROLLSLAYER Gotrek Gurnisson and his long-suffering human companion Felix Jaeger are arguably the most infamous heroes of the Warhammer World. Follow their exploits in these novels from the Black Library.

TROLLSLAYER

TROLLSLAYER IS THE first part of the death saga of Gotrek Gurnisson, as retold by his travelling companion Felix Jaeger. Set in the darkly gothic world of Warhammer, *Trollslayer* is an episodic novel featuring some of the most extraordinary adventures of this deadly pair of heroes. Monsters, daemons, sorcerers, mutants, orcs, beastmen and worse are to be found as Gotrek strives to achieve a noble death in battle. Felix, of course, only has to survive to tell the tale.

SKAVENSLAYER

SEEKING TO UNDERMINE the very fabric of the Empire with their arcane warp-sorcery, the skaven, twisted Chaos rat-men, are at large in the reeking sewers beneath the ancient Empire city of Nuln. Led by Grey Seer Thanquol, the servants of the Horned Rat are determined to overthrow this bastion of humanity. Against such forces, what possible threat can just two hard-bitten adventurers pose?

DAEMONSLAYER

GOTREK AND FELIX join an expedition northwards in search of the long-lost dwarf hall of Karag Dum. Setting forth for the hideous Realms of Chaos in an experimental dwarf airship, Gotrek and Felix are sworn to succeed or die in the attempt. But greater and more sinister energies are coming into play, as a daemonic power is awoken to fulfil its ancient, deadly promise.

DRAGONSLAYER

IN THE FOURTH instalment in the saga of Gotrek and Felix, the fearless duo find themselves pursued by the insidious and ruthless skaven-lord, Grey Seer Thanquol. *Dragonslayer* sees the fearless Slayer and his sworn companion back aboard an dwarf airship in a search for a golden hoard – and its deadly guardian.

BEASTSLAYER

STORM CLOUDS LOOM over the icy city of Praag as the foul hordes of Chaos lay ruinous siege to northern lands of Kislev. Will the presence of Gotrek and Felix be enough to prevent this ancient city from being overwhelmed by the massed forces of Chaos and their fearsome leader, Arek Daemonclaw?

VAMPIRESLAYER

AS THE FORCES of Chaos gather in the north to threaten the Old World, the Slayer Gotrek and his companion Felix are beset by a new, terrible foe. An evil is forming in darkest Sylvania which threatens to reach out and tear the heart from our band of intrepid heroes. The gripping saga of Gotrek & Felix continues in this epic tale of deadly battle and soul-rending tragedy.

GIANTSLAYER

A DARKNESS IS gathering over the storm-wracked isle of Albion. Foul creatures stalk the land and the omens foretell the coming of a great evil. With the aid of the mighty high elf mage Teclis, Gotrek and Felix are compelled to fight the evil of Chaos before it can grow to threaten the whole world.

INFERNO!™

INFERNO! is the indispensable guide to the worlds of Warhammer and Warhammer 40,000 and the cornerstone of the Black Library. Every issue is crammed full of action packed stories, comic strips and artwork from a growing network of awesome writers and artists including:

- William King
- Brian Craig
- Gav Thorpe
- Dan Abnett
- Graham McNeill
- Gordon Rennie

and many more

Presented every two months, Inferno! magazine brings the Warhammer worlds to life in ways you never thought possible.

For subscription details ring:
US: 1-800-394-GAME   UK: (0115) 91 40000

For more information see our website:
www.blacklibrary.co.uk/inferno